Philip Phillips

Standard Gems - a Beautiful Present

comprising the Singing pilgrim, Musical leaves, and New standard singer

Philip Phillips

Standard Gems - a Beautiful Present
comprising the Singing pilgrim, Musical leaves, and New standard singer

ISBN/EAN: 9783337291617

Printed in Europe, USA, Canada, Australia, Japan

Cover: Foto ©Andreas Hilbeck / pixelio.de

More available books at **www.hansebooks.com**

STANDARD GEMS,

A BEAUTIFUL PRESENT:

COMPRISING THE

Singing Pilgrim, Musical Leaves,

AND

New Standard Singer.

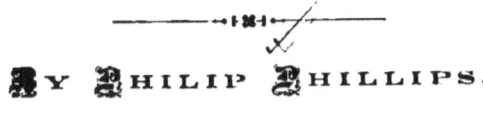

By Philip Phillips.

PHILIP PHILLIPS & CO.:
NEW YORK.

HITCHCOCK & WALDEN:
CINCINNATI, CHICAGO, AND ST. LOUIS.

THE

Singing Pilgrim:

OR,

Pilgrim's Progress Illustrated in Song:

FOR THE SABBATH SCHOOL, CHURCH, AND FAMILY.

"Thy Statutes habe been my Songs

In the House of my Pilgrimage."

BEULAH

BY PHILIP PHILLIPS.

With CONDENSED NOTES by REV. I. W. WILEY, D. D.

PHILIP PHILLIPS, Author and Publisher,
805 BROADWAY, NEW YORK.

HITCHCOCK & WALDEN, Cincinnati, Chicago, and St. Louis.

PREFACE.

QUESTION. What is the chief object of Sunday school music?

ANSWER. To aid in worship and to make more impressive and enduring the lessons which are taught in the school.

Q. What kind of songs or hymns should be used?

A. Such as will be attractive, interesting, and profitable to children, and which will, at the same time, instruct, elevate, and make better.

Q. Should we ever in our Sunday schools use music that serves only for pastime, recreation, or amusement?

A. Never. The Sunday school is no place for music of a mere pleasure-inspiring nature; and we should have a higher and holier mission for our music—"All must be earnest in a world like ours."

Q. How can we best interest our Sunday schools in our hymns and tunes?

A. By giving them FIRST a clear understanding of what they are about to sing.

Q. How can we best do this, so as "to sing with the spirit and with the understanding also?"

A. By a practical and spiritual exposition of the hymn, either verbal or written.

Q. How can we make our singing profitable as well as interesting?

A. By making it a regular part of the exercises, and during the time allotted to this, laying every thing else aside, and every soul in the house heartily engaging in singing the hymns, or in reading them if they can not sing.

Q. How much time should be devoted to singing in the Sabbath school?

A. This must depend on circumstances and the wise judgment of the officers of the school. IT SHOULD NOT TAKE THE PLACE OF THE LESSONS, NOR SHOULD IT EVER BECOME A SUNDAY SCHOOL HOBBY.

Q. How shall we from time to time select the proper music for the occasion?

A. By considering carefully the circumstances of the occasion, and the spiritual condition of the school, as far as possible. A happy adaptation of the right song in the right place often itself proves a great blessing to the school.

Q. How can we make our Sunday school music a power for good?

A. By observing carefully the above suggestions, and holding a meeting every week for the purpose of learning new pieces and improvement generally in music. It is at these meetings, rather than in the Sunday school, that new pieces and new music ought to be learned.

It is for the public to examine and judge for themselves whether the Singing Pilgrim is in accordance with the above suggestions.

EXPLANATION.

The Singing Pilgrim consists of three parts: First. The Singing Pilgrim proper, in which the design has not been to paraphrase the famous Pilgrim's Progress, or to change it into poetry, but to furnish hymns illustrative of the same features of Christian experience as are illustrated by the allegories of Bunyan. Each page contains a hymn, an appropriate passage of Scripture, and a condensed note from Bunyan, each illustrating the same phase of Christian experience. In this way is provided a solid, substantial hymn on each shade of Christian experience from the awakening of the sinners to the arrival of the Christian in the celestial city. In using this part of the book the passage of Scripture and the note should ALWAYS be read before singing the hymn. The second part consists of a large and NEW collection of Sunday school hymns and music, on subjects adapted for all religious occasions. The third part is a choice collection of our best and most substantial hymns for various purposes of Christian worship. A complete classified index of subjects will be found in the book, which will facilitate the finding of an appropriate hymn for any occasion. There is also a large variety of opening exercises which may be used at the discretion of the Superintendent. The hymns and music are believed to be of the very best and most substantial kind, such as will aid in elevating the standard of Sunday school music, and will not minister to a false and transient taste.

PHILIP PHILLIPS.

THE SINGING PILGRIM.

Children's Praises.   Sing for Jesus.   Home Devotions.

Introductory or Preface Hymn.

L. M.

Joyous, with simplicity.

1. A sing-ing pil-grim, glad and free, As yon-der bird that wings the air; My pu-rest earth-ly joy shall be, To sing for Je-sus ev'-ry-where, To sing for Je-sus ev'-ry-where.

2. A sing-ing pil-grim— O, how sweet To teach the young those songs of praise, That win them to a Sav-ior's feet In hap-py childhood's sun-ny days, In hap-py childhood's sun-ny days.

3. If we our Sab-bath-schools de-sign The nurse-ries of our ten-der youth, The sim-plest les-son must com-bine A pre-cept of e-ter-nal truth, A pre-cept of e-ter-nal truth.

PERCHANCE my pilgrim songs may lead
A wanderer to the fold above;
In pastures green a soul may feed,
By fountains of immortal love.

GLORIOUS hope, transporting bliss!
A pilgrim in a world of care;
I ask no higher joy than this,
To sing for Jesus every-where.

Awakened Sinner.

"What shall I do to be saved?"

1. What shall I do to be saved? Weeping and trembling with fear: Roused by conviction I wake, Si-nai's loud thun-der I hear. Now on the brink of despair, Death and destruc-tion I see; What shall I do to be saved? Is there redemption for me?

CHORUS. *Faster.*

What shall I do, What shall I do, What shall I do to be saved?

HAVE rejected with scorn
Blessings I might have received;
Often the spirit of grace
Wounded, insulted, and grieved.
Broken the law of my God,
Nailed him again to the tree;
Can I forgiveness implore?
Is there salvation for me?
What shall I do, etc.

TO my Father will go,
Now, like the prodigal son;
Down at his feet I will fall,
Tell him the wrong I have done.
There if I perish, I'll pray,
This my petition shall be:
Lord, I repent and believe;
Jesus, have mercy on me.
This will I do, etc.

"I DREAMED, and behold I saw a Man clothed with Rags, standing in a certain place, with his face from his own house, a Book in his hand, and a great Burden upon his back; and as he read, he wept and trembled. And I saw again, when he was walking in the fields, that he was, as he was wont, reading in his Book, and greatly distressed in his mind; and as he read, he burst out, as he had often done before, crying, *What shall I do to be saved?*

I saw also that he looked this way and that way, as if he would run; yet he stood still, because as I perceived, he could not tell which way to go. I looked then, and saw a man named *Evangelist*, coming to him, and asked, *Wherefore dost thou cry?* He answered, Sir, I perceive by the Book in my hand, that I am condemned to die, and after that to come to judgment, and I find that I am not willing to do the first, nor able to do the second."

NOTE.—Superintendent always read the Note and Scripture before singing the Hymn.

Flee from Wrath.

"Flee from the wrath to come."

5th P. M.

1. Make no tar - ry frightened soul, Lo! pur - su - ing bil - lows roll;
2. Hap - ly yet thy strength may last Till the dangerous way be passed;

Fraught with hor - ror and with scorn, Haste thee from the wrath to come.
Fas - ter speed thee from the gloom, Haste thee from the wrath to come.

LOOK not back when clouds of wrath
Roll and gather in thy path,
And the fires of hell consume,
Haste thee from the wrath to come.

BY the life that gleams before,
When the struggle shall be o'er,
By the hopes in Christ that bloom,
Haste thee from the wrath to come.

The Voice of Jesus.

5th P. M.

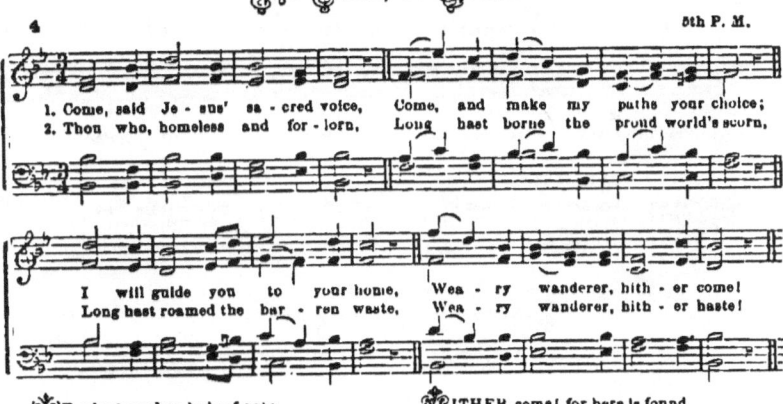

1. Come, said Je - sus' sa - cred voice, Come, and make my paths your choice;
2. Thou who, homeless and for - lorn, Long hast borne the proud world's scorn,

I will guide you to your home, Wea - ry wanderer, hith - er come!
Long hast roamed the bar - ren waste, Wea - ry wanderer, hith - er haste!

YE who tossed on beds of pain,
Seek for ease, but seek in vain;
Ye, by fiercer anguish torn,
In remorse for guilt who mourn,

HITHER come! for here is found
Balm that flows for every wound;
Peace that ever shall endure,
Rest eternal, sacred, sure.

"THEN said *Evangelist*, Why not willing to die, since this life is attended with so many evils? The Man said, Because I fear that this Burden that is upon my back will sink me lower than the Grave, and I shall fall into *Tophet*. And, Sir, if I be not fit to go to Prison, I am not fit to go to Judg- ment, and from thence to Execution. Then said *Evangelist*, If this be thy condition, why standest thou still? He answered, Because I know not whither to go. Then he gave him a *Parchment-roll*, and there was written within, *Fly from the wrath to come!*"

Eternal Life, My Cry.

"Fight the good fight of faith; lay hold on eternal life."

5   L. M.

SOLO.

EVANGELIST. Wouldst thou be saved? no time to lose, A-rise, and run the heavenly road;
PILGRIM. O, 'ell me how! O, tell me where! The way I long have sought to know;

Wouldst thou be blest? then, pil-grim, haste To leave destruction's dread a-bode.
But fear the guilt and sin I bear Will sink me in the depths of woe.

CHORUS. *Very soft.* *pp*

O, come! O, come! the Sav-ior calls, I am the way, the

truth, the life; Come, hith-er, bur-dened soul, to me.

NOTE.—The Chorus should be sung from another room, or gallery, as an echo, only after Pilgrim's verse.

EVANGELIST.

GOD'S word will guide thee; dost thou see
   A light from yonder distant hill?
On, Pilgrim, on! it shines for thee,
   With steady course pursue it still.

PILGRIM.

GOD'S word shall guide me; yea, I see
   A light from yonder distant hill;
O, tell me, does it shine for me?
   Hail, glorious light! I will, I will!
     O, come, etc.

EVANGELIST AND PILGRIM.

FAREWELL, a long farewell to those
   Who seek to stay me as I fly;
My ears against their call I close,
   Life, life, eternal life! my cry.
     O, come, etc.

"THE Man, therefore, looking upon *Evangelist* very carefully, said, Whither must I fly? Then said *Evangelist,* pointing with his finger over a very wide field, Do you see yonder *Wicket-gate?* The Man said, No. Then said the other, Do you see yonder shining Light? He said, I think I do. Then said *Evangelist,* keep that Light in your eye, and go up directly thereto: so shalt thou see the Gate; at which when thou knockest, it shall be told thee what thou shalt do. So I saw in my Dream that the man began to run. Now he had not run far from his own door, but his Wife and Children, perceiving it, began to cry after him to return; but the man put his fingers in his ears, and ran on, crying, *Life! Life! Eternal Life!* So he looked not behind him, but fled towards the middle of the Plain. On the Plain he was joined by two companions, whose names were *Obstinate* and *Pliable,* but *Obstinate* soon grew tired of the way, and turned back."

Come, Crown and Throne.

"Having promise of the life that now is, and of that which is to come."

C. M.

1. These are the crowns that we shall wear When all thy saints are crowned; These
2. These are the robes, un-soiled and white, Which we shall then put on, When
3. That is the cit-y of the saints, Where we so soon shall stand, When

are the palms that we shall bear On yon-der ho-ly ground, On yonder ho-ly ground, On
foremost 'mong the sons of light, We sit on yon-der throne, We sit on yonder throne, We
we shall strike these desert-tents, And quit this desert-land, And quit this desert-land, And

yon-der ho-ly ground; These are the palms that we shall bear On yonder ho-ly ground.
sit on yonder throne; When, foremost 'mong the sons of light, We sit on yon-der throne.
quit this desert-land; When we shall strike these desert-tents, And quit this desert-land.

THEN welcome toil and care and pain!
  And welcome sorrow too!
All toil is rest, all grief is gain,
  With such a prize in view.

COME, crown and throne; come, robe and palm,
  Burst forth, glad stream of peace!
Come, holy city of the Lamb!
  Rise, Sun of Righteousness!

"NOW I saw in my Dream, that when *Obstinate* was gone back, *Christian* and *Pliable* went talking over the Plain to encourage themselves by the way with the good things that had been promised them. Then said *Pliable*, Tell me, Neighbor *Christian*, what the things are, and how to be enjoyed, whither we are going? I can better conceive of them with my Mind, said *Christian*, than speak of them with my Tongue: but yet, since you are desirous to know, I will read of them in my Book. There is an endless Kingdom to be inhabited, and everlasting Life to be given us, that we may inhabit that Kingdom forever. There are Crowns of Glory to be given us, and Garments that will make us shine like the Sun in the firmament of Heaven. There shall be no more crying, nor sorrow; for He that is owner of the place will wipe all tears from our eyes."

Trembling Expectation.

"Save me, O God! for the waters are come in unto my soul."

7   9th P. M.

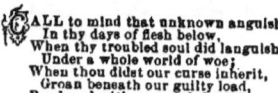

1. Full of trembling ex-pect-a-tion, Feel-ing much, and fear-ing more,

Might-y God of my sal-va-tion, I thy time-ly aid im-plore.

Suffering Son of man be near me, All my sufferings to sus-tain;

Ritard.

By thy sor-er griefs to cheer me, By thy more than mor-tal pain.

CALL to mind that unknown anguish
In thy days of flesh below,
When thy troubled soul did languish
Under a whole world of woe;
When thou didst our curse inherit,
Groan beneath our guilty load,
Burdened with a wounded spirit,
Bruised by all the wrath of God.

BY thy most severe temptation,
In that dark, satanic hour;
By thy last, mysterious passion,
Screen me from the adverse power.
By thy fainting in the garden,
By thy bloody sweat, I pray,
Write upon my heart the pardon,
Take my sins and fears away.

"Now I saw in my Dream, that just as they had ended this talk, they drew near to a very miry Slough that was in the midst of the plain; and they, being heedless, did both fall suddenly into the bog. The name of the Slough was *Dispond.* Here therefore they wallowed for a time, being grievously bedaubed with the dirt; and *Christian*, because of the Burden that was on his back, began to sink in the mire. But still he endeavored to struggle to that side of the Slough that was still further from his house, and next to the Wicket-gate; the which he did, but could not get out, because of the Burden that was upon his back. But I beheld in my Dream, that a man came to him, whose name was *Help*, and said, *Give me thy hand*; so he gave him his hand, and he drew him out, and set him upon sound ground, and bid him go on his way."

At Eve it Shall be Light.

"I will turn their mourning into joy, and will comfort them."

C. M. D.

1. We jour-ney through a vale of tears, By many a cloud o'er-cast;
And world-ly cares, and world-ly fears, Go with us to the last.
Not to the last! Thy word hath said, Could we but read a-right—
Poor pil-grim, lift in hope thy head; At eve it shall be light.

THOUGH earth-born shadows now may shroud
Thy thorny path awhile,
God's blessed word can part each cloud,
And bid the sunshine smile.
Only believe in living faith,
His love and power divine;
And ere thy sun shall set in death,
His light shall round thee shine.

WHEN tempest clouds are dark on high,
His bow of love and peace
Shines sweetly in the vaulted sky—
A pledge that storms shall cease,
Hold on thy way, with hope unchilled,
By faith and not by sight,
And thou shalt own his word fulfilled—
At eve it shall be light.

"AS I was in my sleep, I dreamed, and behold the Heavens grew exceeding black; also it thundered and lightened in most fearful wise, that it put me into an agony; so I looked up in my Dream, and saw the Clouds rack at an unusual rate, upon which I heard a great sound of a Trumpet, and saw also a Man sit upon a Cloud, attended with the thousands of Heaven; they were all in flaming fire, also the Heavens were in a burning flame. I heard then a Voice saying, *Arise ye Dead, and come to Judgment;* and with that the Rocks rent, the Graves opened, and the Dead that were therein came forth. Some of them were exceeding glad, and looked upward; and some sought to hide themselves under the Mountains. And I heard it proclaimed to them that attended on the Man that sat on the cloud, *Gather my wheat into the Garner.* And I saw many catched up and carried away into the clouds, to be forever with the Lord. Now when the morning was come *Christian* again took to his *journey*."

Where Do you Journey, my Brother?

"While they communed together and reasoned, Jesus himself drew near and went with them."

9

SOLO.

1, Where do you jour-ney, my broth-er,   O, where do you journey, I   pray?

Where do you jour-ney, my sis-ter?   For storm-y and dark is the   way.

DUET.

We're jour-ney-ing on-ward to   Ca-naan, Through suff'ring and tri-al and   care,

And when we get safe-ly to   glo-ry,   O say, shall we meet you all   there?

CHORUS.

O say shall we meet you all   there?   O say, shall we meet you all   there?

And when we get safe-ly to   glo-ry,   O say, shall we meet you all   there?

WHAT is your mission, my brother,
What is your mission below?
What is your mission, my sister,
As journeying onward you go?
Our mission is practicing mercy,
Sweet charity, patience, and love,
And following the footsteps of Jesus,
That lead to the mansions above.
O say, shall we meet, etc.

YES! you will meet us, my brother,
God helping our weakness and sin;
Bearing the cross, we, my sister,
The crown will endeavor to win.
We'll walk through the vale and the shadow,
Through suff'rings and trials and care,
And when you get safely to glory,
You'll meet, yes, you'll meet us all there!
O say, shall we meet, etc.

"THEN one asked him whence he was, and whither he was going. 'I am come from the City of Destruction,' said Christian, 'and am going to Mount Zion.' 'What is your name, Pilgrim?' 'My name is now Christian, but my name at the first was Graceless.' 'But what moved you at first to betake yourself to a Pilgrim's life?' 'I was driven out of my Native Country by a dreadful sound that was in mine ears, that unavoidable destruction did attend me, if I abode in that place where I was.' 'Do you not think sometimes of the country from whence you came?' 'Yes, but with shame and detestation; but now I desire a better country, that is an Heavenly.' 'And what is it that makes you so desirous to go to Mount Zion?' 'Why, there I hope to see Him alive that did hang dead on the Cross; there, they say, there is no death; and there I shall dwell with such Company as I like best. I love Him because I was redeemed by Him, and I am weary of my inward sickness; I would fain be where I shall die no more, and with the Company that shall continually cry, Holy, Holy, Holy!'"

Guide Us, Savior.

"He will guide you into all truth."

10   8th P. M.

1. God has said, "For - ev - er bless - ed Those who seek me in their youth;
2. Be our strength, for we are weakness; Be our wis - dom and our guide;

They shall find the path of wis - dom, And the nar - row way of truth."
May we walk in love and meek - ness, Near - er to our Sav - ior's side.

Guide us, Sav - ior, Guide us, Sav - ior, In the nar - row way of truth; Guide us,
Naught can harm us, Naught can harm us, While we thus in thee a - bide; Naught can

Repeat. ad lib., pp.

Sav - ior. Guide us, Sav - ior, In the nar - row way of truth.
harm us, Naught can harm us, While we thus in thee a - bide.

MAY thy watchful angels hover
  Round us, when there's evil near;
May we hide beneath the cover
  Of thy wings, in time of fear;
    And in sorrow,
    And in sorrow,
Comfort our sad hearts, and cheer.

AND when death at last o'ertakes us,
  And we sink beneath his night,
May that blessed morn awake us,
  Safe in yonder realms of light;
    There forever,
    There forever,
Chant thy praise with angels bright.

"THEN was *Christian* met by one *Worldly Wiseman*, who began sorely to tempt him to turn out of the way, saying, There is not a more dangerous and troublesome way in the world, than that unto which *Evangelist* has directed thee. Thou hast met with something (as I perceive) already; for I perceive the dirt of the Slough of *Dispond* is upon thee; but that Slough is only the beginning of sorrows that do attend those that go on in that way: Hear me I am older than thou; thou art like to meet with, in the way which thou goest, Wearisomeness, Painfulness, Hunger, Perils, Sword, Lions, Dragons, Darkness, and in a word, Death, and what not! These things are certainly true, having been confirmed by many testimonies. So *Christian* turned out of his way. But, behold, when he had got but a little way, he found the road so hard and so steep, that he stood still and wot not what to do, and did quake for fear. And with that he saw *Evangelist* coming to meet him."

The Gate and the Way.

"Strive to enter in at the strait gate, for many, I say unto you, will seek to enter in, and shall not be able."

1. Strive to en-ter at the gate, Following those who've gone be-fore;

Pil-grims, poor and des-o-late, Now their work is o'er.

Now they rest, no more to stray, Nev-er more to weep and wait;

See their tracks upon the way, Fol-low to the gate, O! fol-low to the gate.

STRIVE to enter at the gate,
Casting every burden down;
'Tis but changing poor estate
For a heavenly crown.
Few there be upon the way,
Not for friends or kindred wait;
While upon the waste they stray,
Christ may shut the gate.

STRIVE to enter in to-day;
Almost now we hear the voice
At the limit of the way
Bidding us rejoice.
Every step the anthem swells—
Can we falter, can we wait?
Yonder, where the Savior dwells,
Enter at the gate.

"AND *Evangelist* said, What doest thou here, *Christian?* Art not thou the man that I found crying without the walls of the City of Destruction? Did I not direct thee the way of the little Wicket-gate? How is it thou art so quickly turned aside? for thou art now out of the way. Thy sin is very great, for by it thou hast committed two evils: thou hast forsaken the way that is good, to tread in forbidden paths. Yet will the man at the gate receive thee, for he has good-will for men; only, said he, take heed that thou turn not aside again,

lest thou perish from the way, when his wrath is kindled but a little. For the Lord says, *Strive to enter in at the strait gate, the gate to which I sent thee; for strait is the gate that leadeth unto life, and few there be that find it.* From this little Wicket-gate, and from the way thereto, hath this wicked *Worldly Wiseman* turned thee, to the bringing of thee almost to destruction; hate therefore his turning thee out of the way, and abhor thyself for hearkening unto him."

Jesus Alone Can Save.

"Being justified by faith, we have peace with God through our Lord Jesus Christ."

12   S. M.

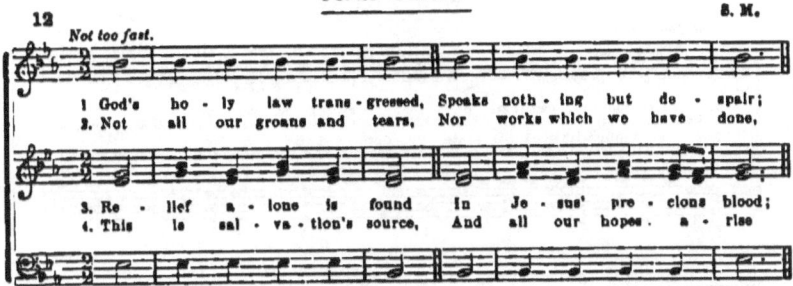

1 God's ho - ly law trans - gressed, Speaks noth - ing but de - spair;
2. Not all our groans and tears, Nor works which we have done,

3. Re - lief a - lone is found in Je - sus' pre - cious blood;
4. This is sal - va - tion's source, And all our hopes a - rise

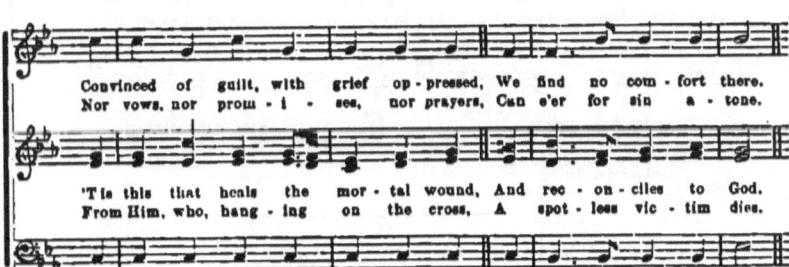

Convinced of guilt, with grief op - pressed, We find no com - fort there.
Nor vows, nor prom - i - ses, nor prayers, Can e'er for sin a - tone.

'Tis this that heals the mor - tal wound, And rec - on - ciles to God.
From Him, who, hang - ing on the cross, A spot - less vic - tim dies.

---

13 Diligence and Watchfulness.

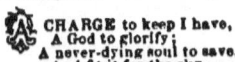 CHARGE to keep I have,
A God to glorify;
A never-dying soul to save,
And fit it for the sky.

2 To serve the present age,
My calling to fulfill—
O may it all my powers engage,
To do my Master's will.

3 Arm me with jealous care,
As in thy sight to live;
And O, thy servant, Lord, prepare
A strict account to give.

4 Help me to watch and pray,
And on thyself rely;
Assured, if I my trust betray,
I shall forever die.

14 Horrors of the Second Death.

WHERE shall rest be found—
Rest for the weary soul?
'T were vain the ocean's depths to sound,
Or pierce to either pole.

2 The world can never give
The bliss for which we sigh;
'Tis not the whole of life to live,
Nor all of death to die.

3 Beyond this vale of tears
There is a life above,
Unmeasured by the flight of years,
And all that life is love.

4 There is a death, whose pang
Outlasts the fleeting breath;
O what eternal horrors hang
Around the second death!

5 Thou God of truth and grace,
Teach us that death to shun;
Lest we be banished from thy face,
For evermore undone.

"THIS *Worldly Wiseman* bid me with speed get rid of my Burden; and I told him 't was ease that I sought. And, said I, I am therefore going to yonder Gate, to receive further direction how I may get to the place of deliverance. So he said that he would show me a better way, and short, not so attended with difficulties as the way that you set before me; which way, said he, will direct thee to a Gentleman's house that hath skill to take off these Burdens; So I believed him, and turned out of the way, if haply I might be soon eased of my Burden. But when I came to this place, and beheld things as they are, I stopped for fear of danger. Then said *Evangelist*, Believe me, there is nothing in all this noise, that thou hast heard of this sottish man, but a design to beguile thee of thy Salvation, by turning thee from the way in which I had set thee."

Plea for Mercy.

15   Thy mercy, O Lord, held me up.   5th P. M.

1. Depth of mer-cy, can there be, Mer-cy still re-served for me?}
   Can my God his wrath for-bear, Me, the chief of sinners spare? } God is love, I

2. I have long withstood his grace, Long provoked him to his face;}
   Would not hearken to his calls; Grieved him by a thousand falls. } God is love, I

know, I feel; Jesus weeps and loves me still; Je-sus weeps, He weeps and loves me still.

NOW incline me to repent;
Let me now my sins lament!
Now my foul revolt deplore,
Weep, believe, and sin no more.
God is love, etc.

THERE for me the Savior stands;
Shows his wounds, and spreads his hands;
God is love, I know, I feel;
Jesus weeps, and loves me still.
God is love, etc.

Jesus Waits for Thee.

"Ye would not come to me that ye might have life."

16   Tenderly.   5, 6, 5, 6.

1. Come, come to Jesus! He waits to welcome thee, O Wand'rer! eagerly; Come, come to Jesus!
2. Come, come to Jesus! He waits to ransom thee, O Slave! e-ter-nal-ly; Come, come to Jesus!
3. Come, come to Jesus! He waits to lighten thee, O Burdened! graciously; Come, come to Jesus!

4. Come, come to Jesus! He waits to give to thee, O Blind! a vision free; Come, come to Jesus!
5. Come, come to Jesus! He waits to shelter thee, O Weary! bless-ed-ly; Come, come to Jesus!
6. Come, come to Jesus! He waits to carry thee, O Lamb! so loving-ly; Come, come to Jesus!

THEN said *Evangelist*, Stand still a little, that I may show thee the words of God. So he stood trembling. Then said *Evangelist*, See that ye refuse not him that speaketh; for if they escaped not who refused him that spake on Earth, much more shall not we escape, if we turn away from him that speaketh from Heaven. He said moreover, Now the just shall live by faith: but if any man draws back my soul shall have no pleasure in him. He also did thus apply them: Thou art the man that art running into this misery; thou hast begun to reject the counsel of the Most High, and to draw back thy foot from the way of peace, even almost to the hazarding of thy perdition. Then *Christian* fell down at his feet as dead, crying, *Lord, be merciful to me a sinner.* Woe is me, *for I am undone.* At the sight of which, *Evangelist* caught him by the right hand, saying, All manner of sin and blasphemies shall be forgiven unto men; be not faithless, but believing. Now *Christian* was walking solitary by himself, and in process of time met *Evangelist* again."

Cross and Crown.

"They that trust in the Lord shall be as Mount Zion, which can not be removed, but abideth forever."

17   L. M.

1. While pilgrims on our journey here, We oft may faint and wea-ry be;
But soon our long-ing, waiting eyes, The cit-y that we seek shall see.

Unison.

And man-sions bright are wait-ing, where We all shall rest when

Refrain.

we get there; When we get there, when we get there, We

Ritard.

all shall rest when we get there, We all shall rest when we get there.

A DESERT wide before us lies,
  But when its barren sands are passed,
Beyond the Jordan we shall see
  The Canaan that we love, at last.
Its fields of fadeless green, its flowers,
  If faithful, shall at last be ours;
When we get there, when we get there,
How sweet our rest when we get there.

HERE we must bear the cross, and in
  The path our Master trod pursue,
And 'mid reproach and shame still keep
  His bright example in our view.
When we get there we shall lay down
  The cross and wear a glorious crown;
When we get there, when we get there,
How bright our crown when we get there.

"RIGHT glad am I, said *Evangelist*, not that you have met with trials, but that you have been victors: and for that you have continued in the way to this very day. I say, right glad am I of this thing, and that for mine own sake and yours: I have sowed and you have reaped; and the day is coming when both he that sowed and they that reaped shall rejoice together; that is, if you hold out; for in due time you shall reap, if you faint not. The Crown is before you, and it is an incorruptible one; so run that you may obtain it. Some there be that set out for this Crown, and after they have gone far for it, another comes in and takes it from them; hold fast therefore that you have, let no man take your Crown. Let the Kingdom be always before you, and believe steadfastly concerning things that are invisible. Set your faces like flint: you have all power in Heaven and Earth on your side."

Our Savior's Command.

"Knock and it shall be opened unto you."

18

1. O'er the portals of mer-cy these words are inscribed, And written in let-ters of gold;
2. O, ye wea-ry, draw nigh, 'tis the place of re-pose; Ye footsore your journeyings cease;
3. All ye mourners, be-liev-ing, in con-fi-dance come; Ye des-o-late, haste to look up;

The way-far-ing man may be-hold them a-far, And knock at the hea-ven-ly fold.
Ye tollworn with la-bor, new vig-or put on, And knock at the port-als of peace.
Ye troubled in heart be resigned to his word, And knock at the port-als of hope.

CHORUS.

Knock, knock, knock, 'tis the Savior's command, Knock at the port-als a-bove;

Knock, knock, knock, 'tis the Savior's command, En-ter in-to the mansion of love.

AND ye sinners, O come! there's a palace for you,
  Prepared by the Builder above;
Approach with your burden, in meekness sub-
    mit,
  And knock at the portals of love.
Knock, knock, knock, 'tis the Savior's com-
    mand,
  Knock at the portals above, etc.

THEY'RE all waiting within, and the feast is
  prepared,
  What folly to tarry and wait!
Let every one come in obedient haste,
  And knock at the heavenly gate.
Knock, knock, knock, 'tis the Savior's com-
    mand,
  Knock at the heavenly gate, etc.

 "THEN said *Evangelist*, pointing with his finger over a very wide field, Do you see yonder *Wicket-gate?* The Man said, No. Then said the other, Do you see yonder Shining Light? He said, I think I do. Then said *Evangelist*, Keep that Light in your eye, and go up directly thereto; so shalt thou see the Gate; at which, when thou knockest, it shall be told thee what thou shalt do. So in process of time *Christian* got up to the Gate. Now over the Gate there was written, *Knock and it shall*  *be opened unto you.* He knocked therefore more than once or twice, saying, Here is a poor burdened Sinner. I came from the City of *Destruction,* but am going to Mount *Zion,* that I may be delivered from the wrath to come. I would therefore, Sir, since I am informed that by this Gate is the way thither, know if you are willing to let me in. Then said he that kept the Gate, I am willing with all my heart; and with that he opened the Gate.

Do not Stray.

"There is a way that seemeth right unto a man, but the end thereof are the ways of death."

19

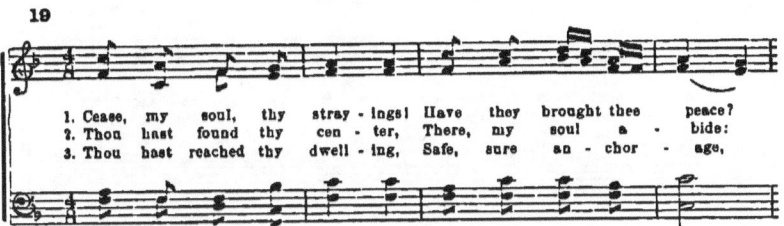

```
1. Cease, my soul, thy stray-ings! Have they brought thee peace?
2. Thou hast found thy cen-ter, There, my soul a - bide:
3. Thou hast reached thy dwell-ing, Safe, sure an - chor - age,
```

```
Come, no more de - lay - ings, Cease thy wand' - rings, cease.
Nev - er more ad - ven - ture Now to swerve a - side.
From the peril - ous swell-ing Of the tem - pest's rage.
```

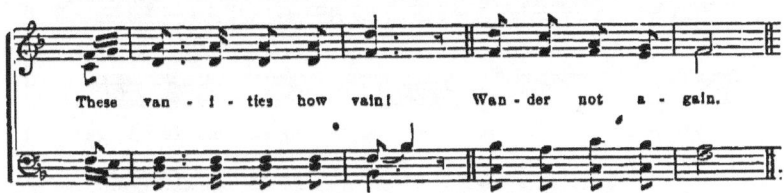

```
These van - i - ties how vain! Wan - der not a - gain.
```

RANQUIL hours now greet thee
In thy calm abode;
Gracious looks now meet thee
From thy loving God.
These vanities how vain!
Wander not again.

IERCE these mists that blind thee;
Press to yonder prize;
Break the bonds that bind thee:
Rise, my soul, arise!
These vanities how vain!
Wander not again.

"YOU are welcome here, *Christian*, though you have wandered from the right way. We make no objections against any; notwithstanding all that they have done before they come hither, they in no wise are cast out; and therefore, good *Christian*, come a little way with me, and I will teach thee about the way thou must go. Look before thee: dost thou see this narrow way? That is the way thou must go; it was cast up by the Patriarchs, Prophets, Christ and his Apostles; and it is as straight as a rule can make it. This is the way thou must go. But said *Christian*, are there no turnings nor windings, by which a stranger may lose the way? Yes, there are many ways bear down upon and lead away from it, and they are crooked and wide. But thou mayest easily distinguish the right from the wrong, the right only being straight and narrow. *Walk thou in the right.*"

Help, or I Perish.

"God is our refuge and strength, a very present help in trouble."

20

6th P. M.

1. By thy birth, and by thy tears; By thy hu-man griefs and fears;
2. By the ten-der-ness that wept O'er the grave where Laz'rus slept;

. By thy con-flict in the hour Of the sub-tle tempter's power—
By the bit-ter tears that flowed O-ver Sa-lem's lost a-bode—

Sav-ior, look with pity-ing eye; Sav-ior, help me, or I die.

Sav-ior, help me, Sav-ior, help me, Sav-ior, help me, or I die.

By thy lonely hour of prayer;
By the fearful conflict there;
By thy cross and dying cries;
By thy one great sacrifice—
Savior, look with pitying eye;
Savior, help me, or I die.
Savior, help me, etc.

By thy triumph o'er the grave;
By thy power the lost to save;
By thy high, majestic throne;
By the empire all thine own—
Savior, look with pitying eye;
Savior, help me, or I die.
Savior, help me, etc.

"NOW I saw as he went by the way, that he was, as he was wont, reading in his Book, and greatly distressed in his mind; and as he read, he burst out, as he had done before, crying, *What shall I do to be saved?* An I I saw in my Dream, that the highway up which *Christian* was to go was fenced on either side with a Wall and that Wall is called *Salvation*. Up this way therefore did burdened *Christian* run, but not without great difficulty, because of the load on his back. He ran thus till he came to a place somewhat ascending, and upon that place stood a Cross, and a little below in the bottom, a Sepulcher. So I saw in my Dream, that just as *Christian* came up with the *Cross*, his Burden loosed from off his shoulders, and fell from off his back, and began to tumble, and so continued to do, till it came to the mouth of the Sepulcher, where it fell in and I saw it no more."

I've Found Abiding Rest.

"I write unto you, little children, because your sins are forgiven you for his name's sake."

21

1. I now have found a-bid-ing rest For which I long was sigh-ing,
Now, on my Sav-ior's faith-ful breast My wea-ry head is ly-ing;
D. C. I now am safe, by Je-sus' power, From all that else would harm me.

2. He whis-pers me—"I'm whol-ly thine, And thou art mine for-ev-er;
Henceforth all fear and doubt re-sign, Con-fid-ing in my fa-vor!
D. C, I'll fill thy spir-it with my joy, The pledge of end-less pleas-ures."

This is the place where sin no more, And death and hell a-larm me;

Thy ev'-ry want shall find sup-ply From my ex-haust-less treas-ures;

FROM Jesus and his love, who now,
By terrors to divide me,
My great and many sins would show!
His wounds from vengeance hide me:
My sins are great—I'll not despair,
Though conscience, too, arraigns me,
Nor doubt my Savior's watchful care—
His arms of love sustains me.

THANK thee, God's beloved Son,
Thy boundless grace adoring,
Which brought thee from thy glorious throne,
Our peace with God restoring:
O make my heart a shrine, where peace
Shall keep her constant dwelling!
Where grateful praise shall never cease,
Abroad thy glories telling.

"THEN was Christian glad and lightsome, and said with a merry heart, He hath given me rest by his sorrow, and life by his death. Then I stood still awhile to look and wonder; for it was very surprising to him that the sight of the Cross should thus ease him of his Burden. He looked, therefore, and looked again, even till the springs that were in his head sent the waters down his cheeks. Now as he stood looking and weeping, behold three Shining Ones came to him and saluted him with Peace be to thee; so the first said to him, Thy sins be forgiven: the second stript him of his Rags, and clothed him with Change of Raiment: the third also set a mark in his forehead, and gave him a Roll with a Seal upon it, which he bid him look on as he ran, and that he should give it in at the Celestial Gate. So he went on his way."

O God, Keep Me.

"Be sober, be vigilant, because your adversary, the devil, as a roaring
lion, walketh about, seeking whom he may devour."

Slowly.

1. O, Lamb of God, still keep me Near to thy wound-ed side;

'T is on - ly then in safe-ty And peace I can a - bide.

What foes and snares sur - round me! What doubts and fears with - in!

The grace that sought and found me, A - lone can keep me clean.

'T IS only in thee hiding
    I feel my life secure—
Only in thee abiding
    The conflict can endure.
Thine arm the victory gaineth
    O'er every hateful foe;
Thy love my heart sustaineth
    In all its cares and woe.

SOON shall my eyes behold thee,
    With rapture, face to face;
One half hath not been told me
    Of all thy power and grace.
Thy beauty, Lord, and glory,
    The wonders of thy love,
Shall be the endless story
    Of all thy saints above.

"Now before he had gone far, he entered
into a very narrow passage, which was
about a furlong off of the Porter's lodge,
and which led to the Palace called *Beautiful;* and looking very narrowly as he went,
he espied two Lions in the way. The Lions
were chained, but he saw not the chains.
Then he was afraid, and thought to go
back, for he thought nothing but death
was before him; But the Porter at the
lodge, whose name is *Watchful,* perceiving
that *Christian* made a halt as if he would
go back, cried unto him, saying, Is thy
strength so small? Fear not the Lions,
for they are chained, and are placed there
for the trial of faith where it is, and for
the discovery of those that have none.
Keep in the midst of the Path, and no
hurt shall come unto thee. Then I saw
that he went on, trembling for fear of the
Lions, but taking good heed to the direc-
tions of the Porter; he heard them roar,
but they did him no harm."

Buckle on the Armor.

"And take the helmet of salvation, and the sword of the spirit, which is the word of God."

23   S. M. D.

1. Sol - diers of Christ, a - rise, And put your ar - mor on, Strong in the strength which God sup - plies Through his e - ter - nal Son. Strong in the Lord of Hosts, And in his might - y power, Who in the strength of Je - sus trusts, Is more than con - quer - or.

Strong in the Lord of Hosts, And in his might - y power, Who in the strength, etc.

STAND then in his great might,
  With all his strength endued;
But take, to arm you for the fight,
  The panoply of God:
That having all things done,
  And all your conflicts past,
Ye may o'ercome, through Christ alone,
  And stand entire at last.

LEAVE no unguarded place—
  No weakness of the soul;
Take every virtue, every grace,
  And fortify the whole:
Indissolubly joined,
  To battle all proceed;
But arm yourselves with all the mind
  That was in Christ your Head.

"THEN the Interpreter took him and led him up toward the door of the Palace; and behold, at the door stood a great company of men, as desirous to go in, but durst not. In the doorway stood also many men in armor to keep it, being resolved to do the men that would enter what hurt and mischief they could. At last, when every man started back for fear of the armed men, *Christian* saw a man of a very stout countenance come up to the man that sat there to write, saying, *Set down my name, Sir;* the which when he had done, he saw the man draw his Sword, and put an Helmet upon his head, and rush toward the door upon the armed men, who laid upon him with deadly force. So after he had received and given many wounds to those that attempted to keep him out, he cut his way through them all, and pressed forward into the Palace. And those that were within said, *Come in, Come in! Eternal Glory thou shalt win.*"

The Morning Star.

"We are troubled on every side, yet not distressed: we are perplexed,
but not in despair."

24

C. M. D.

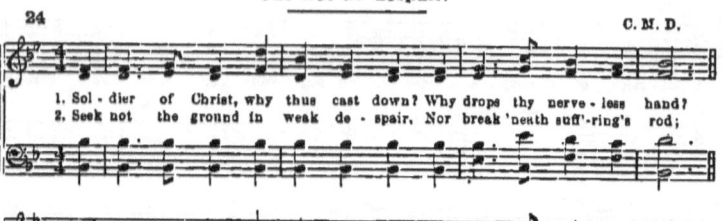

1. Sol - dier of Christ, why thus cast down? Why drops thy nerve - less hand?
2. Seek not the ground in weak de - spair, Nor break 'neath suff'-ring's rod;

Have faith and hope and cour - age gone? Fear'st thou the a - lien band?
The fight thou wag - est, is the care Of the all - lov - ing God.

Take heart, 't will not be al - ways night: Thro' riv - en clouds a - far Gleams
Joy comes through sor-row; death brings life; Peace rides on bat - tle's car; And

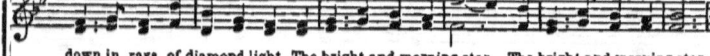

down in rays of diamond light, The bright and morning star, The bright and morning star.
beams, on darkest night of strife, The bright and morning star, The bright and morning star.

PRESS on the foe! God rules the years,
  Wrong shall not triumph long;
Expectant Faith already hears
  Truth's glad, victorious song.
The nations soon shall own their King,
  The wise from near and far,
Once more to him their offerings bring—
  The bright and morning star!

THEN fear not, Christian, for the right!
  Nor falter 'mid the fray;
For truth is victor: error's night
  Flies from the coming day.
Thine eye, through dust and tears, may see
  On heaven's broad scroll afar,
The promise sure: "I'll give to thee
  The bright and morning star!"

"THEN was *Christian* led into a very dark room, where there sat a Man in an Iron Cage. Now the Man, to look on, seemed very sad; he sat with his eyes looking down to the ground, his hands folded together; and he sighed as if he would break his heart. Then said *Christian, What means this?* The Man said, I am what I was not once. I was once a fair and flourishing professor, both in mine own eyes, and also in the eyes of others; I once was, as I thought, fair for the Celestial City, and had then even joy at the thoughts that I should get thither. I am now a man of *Despair*, and am shut up in it, as in this Iron Cage. I can not get out; O *now* I can not. I left off to watch and be sober; I laid the reins on the neck of my lusts; I sinned against the light of the Word and the goodness of God; I have grieved the Spirit, and he is gone; I have provoked God to anger, and he has left me. Then said the *Interpreter* to *Christian,* Let this man's misery be remembered by thee, and be an everlasting caution to thee."

My Beautiful Home Above.

"God hath set the land before thee, go up and possess it."

25

1. O, how my spir-it longs for thee, Beauti-ful home a-bove! Where I may rest from sorrow free, Beautiful home a-bove! Within the golden gates of light, Arrayed in garments pure and white, I'll walk with angels fair and bright, In my home above.

CHORUS.

Beautiful home a-bove, Beautiful home above—O, come and take me, Savior come; I love my beautiful home.

O reach thee safe I daily pray,
Beautiful home above!
And travel in the toilsome way,
Beautiful home above!
My weary feet are bruised and sore,
But Jesus' feet were bruised before,
To bring me to the open door
Of my home above.
Beautiful home, etc.

THY shining walls by faith I see,
Beautiful home above!
The mansions fair prepared for me,
Beautiful home above!
O let me keep my longing eyes,
Intently fixed upon the prize,
Till angels bear me to the skies,
In my home above.
Beautiful home, etc.

"THEN I saw in my Dream, that on the morrow, when the morning was up, they had him to the top of the House, and bid him look South; so he did; and behold at a great distance he saw a most pleasant Mountainous Country, beautified with Woods, Vineyards, Fruits of all sorts, Flowers also, with Springs and Fountains, very delectable to behold. Then he asked the name of the Country: They said it was *Immanuel's Land*; and it is as common, said they, as this *Hill* is, to and for all the Pilgrims. And when thou comest there, from thence, said they, thou mayest see to the gate of the Celestial City, as the Shepherds that live there will make appear."

I am Redeemed.

"Who is a God like unto thee, who pardoneth iniquity."

26

1. My doubts are gone, my fears are passed, A new-born soul at Je-sus feet;}
By grace renewed, I feel at last, A pardon sure, a joy complete.}
A ho-ly

ardor warms my breast; O, let my God, my Savior reign, Who, in his sor-row gives me

CHORUS.

rest, And in his death I live a-gain. I live again, I live again; O, let my

God, my Savior reign, Who in his sor-row gives me rest, And in his death I live a-gain.

A CHILD of God, an heir of heaven,
Though highest hopes my bosom swell,
The rapture of a soul forgiven,
No tongue can sing, nor language tell.
A sacred love inspires my breast;
O, let my God, my Savior reign,
Who in his sorrow gives me rest,
And in his death I live again.
I live again, etc.

I'LL sing the glory of his name,
Who bids the storm of trouble cease,
Who doth my wandering feet reclaim,
And keeps my soul in perfect peace.
Transporting thought, divinely blest,
With him to rise, with him to reign,
Who in his sorrow gives me rest,
And in his death I live again.
I live again, etc.

"THEN in the evening they talked together, and *Christian* told them whence he had come and whither he was going, and he said, As I went but a little farther, I saw one, as I thought in my mind, hang bleeding upon the Tree; and the very sight of him made my burden fall off my back, (for I groaned under a very heavy burden,) but then it fell down from off me. 'Twas a strange thing to me, for I never saw such a thing before; yea, and while I stood looking up (for then I could not forbear looking) three Shining Ones came to me. One of them testified that my sins were forgiven me; another stript me of my Rags, and gave me this broidered Coat; and the third set the Mark which you see in my forehead, and gave me this sealed Roll; and with that he plucked it out of his bosom."

Battling for the Lord.

"I must work the works of him that sent me, while it is day; the night cometh, when no man can work."

27

SOLO.   CHORUS.   SOLO.

1. We've list-ed in a ho-ly war, Battling for the Lord! E - ter - nal life, e-
2. Un - der our Captain, Je-sus Christ, Battling for the Lord! We've list-ed for this
3. We'll fight a-gainst the powers of sin, Battling for the Lord! In fa - vor of our

CHORUS.   FULL CHORUS.

ter - nal joy, Battling for the Lord! We'll work till Je-sus comes, We'll
mor - tal life, Battling for the Lord! We'll work, etc.
heavenly King, Battling for the Lord! We'll work, etc.

work till Je-sus comes, We'll work till Je-sus comes, And then we'll rest at home.

CODA FOR THE LAST VERSE.

Home, home, sweet, sweet home! Pre-pare me, dear Savior, for glo-ry, my home.

AND when our warfare here is o'er
  Battling for the Lord!
This strife we'll leave, and war no more,
  Battling for the Lord!
    We'll work, etc.

OUR friends and kindred there we'll meet,
  On the heavenly shore!
And ground our arms at Jesus' feet,
  On the heavenly shore!
    We'll work, etc.

"Now *Christian* bethought himself of setting forward, and they were willing he should: but first, said they, let us go into the Armory: for you have heard in the words of the truth of the Gospel, that you must through many tribulations enter into the Kingdom of Heaven. And again, that in every City bonds and afflictions abide you; and therefore you can not expect that you should go long on your Pilgrimage without them, in some sort or other. You have found something of the truth of these testimonies upon you already, and more will follow. So they went into the Armory; and when they came there, they harnessed him from head to foot with what was of proof, lest perhaps he should meet with assaults in the way. He being therefore thus accoutered, walketh out with his friends to the Gate."

The Living Well.

"Whosoever drinketh of the water that I shall give him, shall never thirst."

28

9th P. M.

Cheerful.

1. On the cross where Christ hung bleeding, Streams of love for - ev - er flow;

Fine.

Through the Sav - ior's in - ter - ced - ing, We that bless - ed stream may know.
D. S. Je - sus speaks so gent - ly, sweet - ly, List - en to his love - ly voice.

Ritard.

O, my heart, be filled com - plete - ly, And in grate - ful love re - joice!

Repeat the last strain to the words, "Drink of the water of life," *very softly.*

CHORUS.   *Ritard.*

Drink, and you 'll be thirsty nev-er, } Drink, O drink! Drink, O drink! Drink, O drink!
Drink, and you shall live for - ev-er; } Drink of the water of life.

THOUGH our way is often dreary,
  And in gloom the sky is clad;
Though the steps grow faint and weary,
  And the heart is sick and sad;
There 's a well of living pleasure,
Every night and morning too,
Flowing in exhaustless measure,
  Ever blessing, ever new.
    Drink, and you 'll, etc.

WE may ever have that fountain,
  Welling with exhaustless flow,
In the valley, on the mountain,
  Wheresoe'er our steps may go.
As we drink, a holy beauty
Fills our souls, so washed and blest,
And our hands grow strong for duty,
  And our weary hearts find rest.
    Drink, and you 'll, etc.

"I BEHELD then, that they all went on till they came to the foot of the Hill *Difficulty*, at the bottom of which was a Spring which is called the Well of Living Water. There was also in the same place two other ways besides that which came straight from the Gate; one turned to the left hand, and the other to the right at the bottom of the Hill; but the narrow way lay right up the Hill, and the name of the one going up

the side of the Hill is called *Difficulty*. *Christian* now went to the Spring, and drank thereof to refresh himself, and then began to go up the Hill. Now about the midway to the top of the Hill was a pleasant *Arbor*, made by the Lord of the Hill for the refreshing of weary travelers; thither therefore *Christian* got, where also he sat down to rest him."

Climbing up Zion's Hill.

"They shall mount up with wings as eagles, and they shall walk and not faint."

29

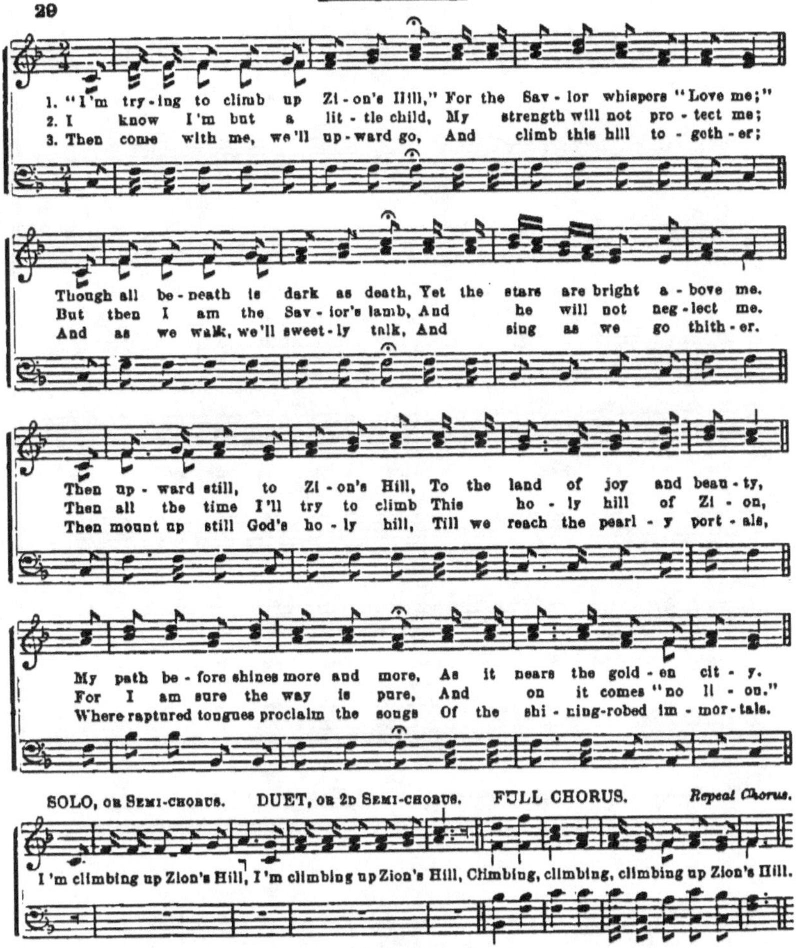

1. "I'm try-ing to climb up Zi-on's Hill," For the Sav-ior whispers "Love me;"
2. I know I'm but a lit-tle child, My strength will not pro-tect me;
3. Then come with me, we'll up-ward go, And climb this hill to-geth-er;

Though all be-neath is dark as death, Yet the stars are bright a-bove me.
But then I am the Sav-ior's lamb, And he will not neg-lect me.
And as we walk, we'll sweet-ly talk, And sing as we go thith-er.

Then up-ward still, to Zi-on's Hill, To the land of joy and beau-ty,
Then all the time I'll try to climb This ho-ly hill of Zi-on,
Then mount up still God's ho-ly hill, Till we reach the pearl-y port-als,

My path be-fore shines more and more, As it nears the gold-en cit-y.
For I am sure the way is pure, And on it comes "no li-on."
Where raptured tongues proclaim the songs Of the shi-ning-robed im-mor-tals.

SOLO, OR SEMI-CHORUS. DUET, OR 2D SEMI-CHORUS. FULL CHORUS. *Repeat Chorus.*

I'm climbing up Zion's Hill, I'm climbing up Zion's Hill, Climbing, climbing, climbing up Zion's Hill.

"I LOOKED then after *Christian* to see him go up the Hill, where I perceived he fell from running to going, and from going to clambering upon his hands and knees, be-cause of the steepness of the place. Now when he was got up to the top of the Hill, there came two men running against him amain; to whom *Christian* said, Sirs, what's the matter you run the wrong way? *Tim-orous* answered that they were going to the City of Zion, and had got up that difficult place, but, said he, the farther we go, the more danger we meet with. Yes, said *Mis-*

trust, for just before us lie a couple of Lions in the way, (whether sleeping or waking we know not,) and we could not think, if we came in reach, but they would presently pull us in pieces. Then said *Christian*, If I go back to mine own country, *that is pre-*pared for Fire and Brimstone. If I can get to the Celestial City I am sure to be in safety there. I must venture: To go back is nothing but death; to go forward is fear of death, but life everlasting beyond it. I will yet go forward."

Valley of Humiliation.

"And he shall save the humble person."

30   27th P. M.

1. While here in the val-ley of con-flict I stay, O, give me sub-
mis-sion and strength es my day; In all my af-flic-tions to
thee would I come, Re-joic-ing in hope of my glo-ri-ous
home, Re-joi-cing in hope of my glo-ri-ous home.

WHATE'ER thou deniest, O, give me thy grace,
The Spirit's sure witness, and smiles of thy
    face;
Endue me with patience to wait at thy throne,
And find, even now, a sweet foretaste of home.

LONG, dearest Lord, in thy beauties to shine;
No more as an exile in sorrow to pine;
And in thy dear image arise from the tomb,
With glorified millions to praise thee at home.

"THEN *Christian* began to go forward;
but *Discretion, Piety, Charity,* and *Prudence*
would accompany him down to the foot of
the Hill. So they went on together, reiter-
ating their former discourses, till they
came to go down the Hill. Then said
Christian, As it was *difficult* coming up, so
it is *dangerous* going down. Yes, said *Prudence,* so it is, for it is a hard matter for a
man to go down into the Valley of *Humiliation,* as thou art now, and to catch no
slip by the way; therefore, said they, are

we come out to accompany thee down the
Hill. So he began to go down, but very
warily; yet he caught a slip or two. Then
I saw in my Dream that these good Companions, when *Christian* had gone down to
the bottom of the Hill, and was weak and
sorrowful in the depth of the Valley, gave
him a loaf of Bread, a bottle of Wine, and
a cluster of Raisins; and then he went on
his way, but having many sore conflicts in
this Valley of *Humiliation.*"

I'm Walking in the Shadow.

"Yea, though I walk through the valley of the Shadow of Death, I will fear no evil."

31

1. I'm walking in the shadow, How lone-ly is my way; The night has gathered o'er me,
2. I'm walking in the shadow, But whither does it lead? My Father, deign to help me,

Nor left one cheering ray. No guiding star to light me A-long this dreary vale;
Thy gen-tle hand I need. I dare not ven-ture onward, Nor would I turn a-side;

Refrain, very softly.

My steps are weak and trembling, I feel my courage fail. I'm walking in the shadow,
Thou only canst direct me, My Shepherd and my Guide. I'm walking, etc.

Of darkness, gloom, and woe; Be with me, O my Savior, And show me where to go.

'M walking in the shadow,
But hark! methinks I hear
The voice of one before me,
That tells a friend is near.
A Pilgrim in the valley,
And yet he fears no ill,
For God the Lord is with him,
His staff a comfort still.
I'm walking, etc.

'M walking in the shadow,
But lo! the morning breaks,
And with its glad returning,
My hope renewed awakes.
The Lord from every danger
Has cleared my tangled way;
He brought deep things from darkness,
And turned my night to day.
I'm walking, etc.

"WHEN *Christian* had traveled in this disconsolate condition some considerable time, he thought he heard the voice of man, as going before him, saying, *Though I walk through the Valley of the Shadow of Death, I will fear no ill, for thou art with me.* Then was he glad, because he gathered from thence that some who feared God were in this Valley as well as himself, and because he perceived that God was with them, though in that dark and dismal state. So he went on, and called to him that was before; but he knew what to answer, for that he also thought himself to be alone. And by and by the day broke; then said *Christian, He hath turned the Shadow of Death into morning.* So he saw by the light of the day what hazards he had gone through in the dark; the Ditch that was on the one hand, and the Quag that was on the other. These things were discovered to him according to that which is written, *He discovereth deep things out of darkness, and bringeth out to light the Shadow of Death.*"

The Guiding Hand.

"Cast thy burden on the Lord."

32

With simplicity.   *Response.*

1. Is this the way, my Fath - er?   'T is, my child;

Response.

2. But en - e - mies are round;   Yes, child, I know,
3. My Fa - ther, it is dark;   Child, take my hand,

Response.

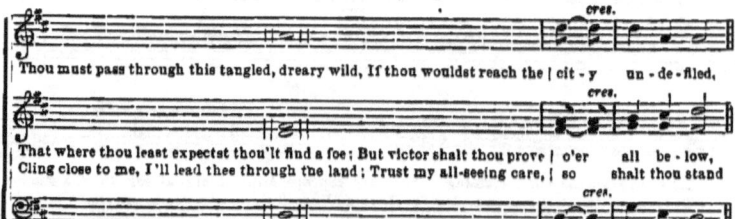

cres.

Thou must pass through this tangled, dreary wild, If thou wouldst reach the | cit - y un - de - filed,

cres.

That where thou least expectst thou'lt find a foe; But victor shalt thou prove | o'er all be - low,
Cling close to me, I 'll lead thee through the land; Trust my all-seeing care, | so shalt thou stand

cres.

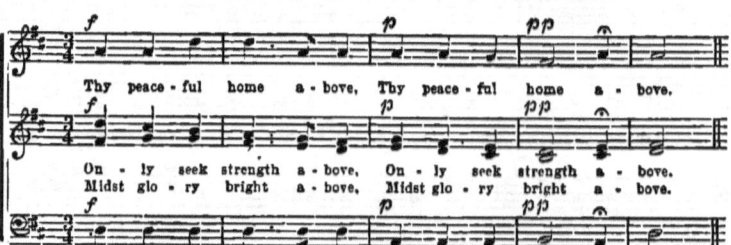

f   *p*   *pp*

Thy peace - ful home a - bove, Thy peace - ful home a - bove.

On - ly seek strength a - bove, On - ly seek strength a - bove.
Midst glo - ry bright a - bove, Midst glo - ry bright a - bove.

MY footsteps seem to slide.
  Response—Child, only raise
{ Thine eyes to me, then in these slippery ways
   I will hold up thy goings;
And thou shalt praise
   Me for each step above,
   Me for each step above.

FATHER, I am weary!
  Response—Child, lean thine head
{ Upon my breast; it was my love that spread
   Thy rugged path; hope on,
Till I have said:
   Rest, rest, forever rest,
   Rest, rest, forever rest.

N. B.—The *response* and *chant* should be sung as an *echo*, or from another room or gallery, just so as to be distinctly heard.

"I SAW then in my dream, that the pathway here was exceeding narrow, and therefore good Christian was the more put to it; for when he sought in the dark to shun the ditch on the one hand, he was ready to slip into the mire on the other. Thus he went on, and I heard him here sigh bitterly; for besides the dangers mentioned above, the pathway was here so dark, that ofttimes when he lift up his foot to set forward, he knew not where, or upon what he should set it next. So he cried in my hearing—'O Lord, I beseech thee, deliver my soul!'"

God of Mercy.

"Out of the depths have I cried unto thee, O Lord."

33   9th P. M.

Andante.

1 From the depths, O, God of mer - cy! Up to
2 Through the aw - ful shade of dark - ness, Cir - cling

thee I sent my cry; Thou didst bend thine
round thy match - less form, Thou didst make the

ear in pit - y, Thou didst hear me from on
wind to guide me, Thou didst ride up - on the

high, Thou didst hear me from on high.
storm, Thou didst ride up - on the storm.

FROM the depths thy hand hath brought me
To a bright and living way;
Crowned my head with richest blessing,
Turned my darkness into day.

SAFELY on the "Rock of Ages,"
Still to thee my voice I'll raise;
Thou didst give me joy for sadness,
And for mourning songs of praise.

"NOW morning being come, he looked back, not out of desire to return, but to see, by the light of the day, what hazards he had gone through in the dark. So he saw more perfectly the Ditch that was on the one hand, and the Quag that was on the other; also how narrow the way was which led betwixt them both; also now he saw the Hobgoblins, and Satyrs, and Dragons of the Pit, but all afar off; for after break of day they came not nigh; yet they were discovered unto him, according to that which is written, *He discovereth deep things out of darkness, and bringeth out to light the Shadow of Death.* Now was *Christian* much affected with his deliverance from all the dangers of his solitary way, and he said, *His candle shineth on my head, and by his light I go through darkness.*"

O, Christian, Awake!

"Stand, therefore, having your loins girt about with truth, and having the breastplate of righteousness."

34   27th P. M.

1. O, Christian, a - wake! for the strife is at hand, With hel - met and
2. What - ev - er thy danger, take heed and be - ware, And turn not thy

shield, and a sword in thy hand; To meet the bold tempt - er, go,
back, for no ar - mor is there; The le - gions of dark - ness, if

fear - less - ly go! And stand like the brave with thy face to the foe.
thou wouldst o'erthrow, Then stand like the brave with thy face to the foe.

SOLO.   SEMI-CHORUS.   FULL CHORUS.

Stand like the brave, Stand like the brave, Stand like the brave with thy face to the foe.

THE cause of thy Master, with vigor defend,
Be watchful, be zealous, and fight to the end;
Wherever he leads thee, go, valiantly go.
And stand like the brave with thy face to the foe.
Stand like the brave, etc.

PRESS on, never doubting, thy Captain is near,
With grace to supply, and with comfort to cheer;
His love, like a stream, in the desert will flow.
Then stand like the brave with thy face to the foe.
Stand like the brave, etc.

"BUT now in this Valley of *Humiliation,* poor *Christian* was hard put to it; for he had gone but a little way, before he espied a foul *Fiend* coming over the field to meet him; his name is *Apollyon.* Then did *Christian* begin to be afraid, and to cast in his mind whether to go back or to stand his ground: But he considered again that he had no Armor for his back, and therefore thought that to turn the back to him might give him the greater advantage with ease to pierce him with his darts. There- fore he resolved to venture and stand his ground: For, thought he, had I no more in mine eye than the saving of my life, 't would be the best way to stand. So he stood *having on the whole armor of God.*"

Do the Right.

"No man, having put his hand to the plow, and looking back, is fit for the kingdom of God."

9th P. M.

35

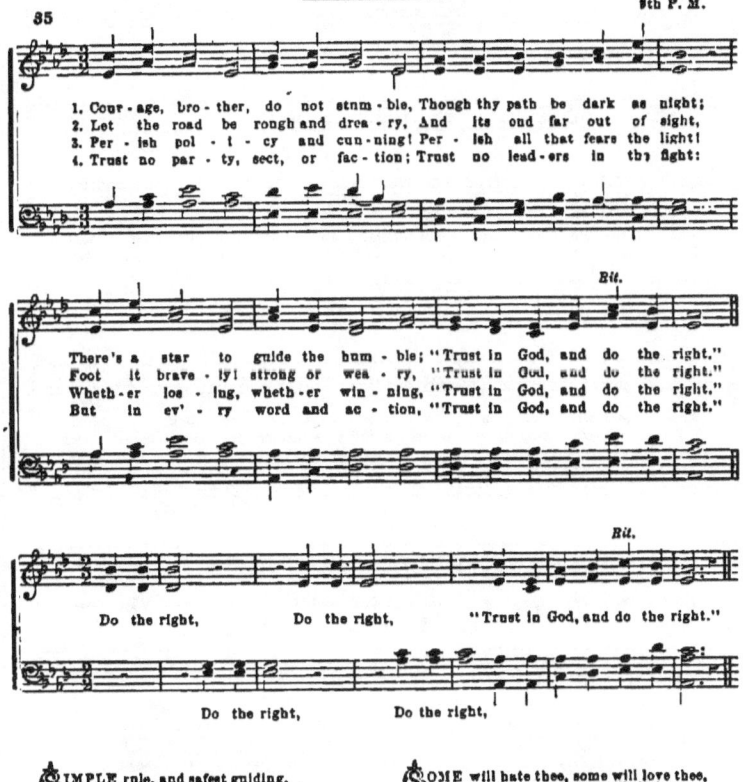

1. Cour - age, bro - ther, do not stum - ble, Though thy path be dark as night;
2. Let the road be rough and drea - ry, And its end far out of sight,
3. Per - ish pol - i - cy and cun - ning! Per - ish all that fears the light!
4. Trust no par - ty, sect, or fac - tion; Trust no lead - ers in the fight:

Rit.

There's a star to guide the hum - ble; "Trust in God, and do the right."
Foot it brave - ly! strong or wea - ry, "Trust in God, and do the right."
Wheth - er los - ing, wheth - er win - ning, "Trust in God, and do the right."
But in ev' - ry word and ac - tion, "Trust in God, and do the right."

Rit.

Do the right, Do the right, "Trust in God, and do the right."

Do the right, Do the right,

SIMPLE rule, and safest guiding,
  Inward peace, and inward might,
Star upon our path abiding,
  "Trust in God, and do the right."
  Do the right, etc.

COME will hate thee, some will love thee,
  Some will flatter, some will slight;
Cease from man, and look above thee,
  "Trust in God, and do the right."
  Do the right, etc.

"THEN said *Apollyon*, Thou knowest for the most part, the Servants of Prince Emanuel come to an ill end, because they are transgressors against me and my ways; and besides, thou countest his service better than mine, whereas he never came yet from the place where he is to deliver any that served him out of our hands; but as for me, how many times, as all the World knows, have I delivered those that have faithfully served me, from him and his, though taken by them. But *Christian* answered, His forbearing at present to deliver them is on purpose to try their love, whether they will cleave to him to the end; and as for the ill end thou sayest they come to, that is most glorious in their account; for, for present deliverance, they do not much expect it, for they stay for their Glory, and then they shall have it, when their Prince comes in his and the Glory of the Angels."

Stand Up for Jesus.

"**Stand, therefore, having your loins girt about.**"

36   *Firmly.*

1. Stand up! stand up for Je - sus! Ye sol - diers of the cross;
2. Stand up! stand up for Je - sus! The trum - pet call o - bey,

Lift high his roy - al ban - ner, Ye must not suf - fer loss.
Forth to the might - y con - flict, In this his glo - rious day.

From vic - t'ry un - to vic - t'ry His ar - my shall he lead,
"Ye that are men now serve him," A - gainst un - num - bered foes;

Till ev' - ry foe is van - quished, And Christ is Lord in - deed.
Your cour - age rise with dan - ger, And strength to strength op - pose.

STAND up! stand up for Jesus!
    Stand in his strength alone;
The arm of flesh will fail you,
    Ye dare not trust your own.
Put on the Gospel armor,
    And, watching unto prayer,
Where duty calls or danger,
    Be never wanting there.

STAND up, stand up for Jesus
    The strife will not be long;
This day the noise of battle,
    The next the victor's song
To him that overcometh,
    A crown of life shall be;
He with the King of glory
    Shall reign eternally.

"THEN *Christian* stood face to face with *Apollyon.* And *Apollyon* broke out into a grievous rage, saying, I am an enemy to this Prince; I hate his Person, his Laws, and People; I am come out on purpose to withstand thee. Beware what you do, *Apollyon,* said *Christian,* for I am in the King's Highway, the way of Holiness, therefore take heed to yourself. Then *Apollyon* straddled quite over the whole breadth of the way, and threw a flaming dart at his breast, but *Christian* had a shield in his hand, with which he caught it, and so prevented the danger of that. Then did *Christian* draw his sword, for he saw it was time to bestir him; and *Apollyon* as fast made at him, throwing darts as thick as hail. But *Christian* at last gave him a deadly thrust, saying, *In all these things we are more than Conquerors, through him that loved us.* And with that *Apollyon* spread forth his Dragon's wings, and sped him away."

He Delivered Me.

"Many are the afflictions of the righteous, but the Lord delivereth him out of them all."

37   9th P. M.

1. When we pass through yon-der riv - er, When we reach the far - ther shore,
2. Af - ter war - fare, rest is pleas - ant; O how sweet the pros - pect' is!
3. When we gain the heavenly re - gions, When we touch the heavenly shore—
4. O, that hope, how bright, how glo - rious! 'Tis his peo - ple's blest re - ward;

There's an end of war for - ev - er, We shall see our foes no more:
Though we toil and strive at pres - ent, Let us not re - pine at this;
Bless - ed thought, no hos - tile le - gions Can a - larm or trou - ble more:
In the Sav - ior's strength vic - to - rious, They at length be - hold their Lord:

All our con - flicts then shall cease, Fol - lowed by e - ter - nal peace.
Toil and pain and con - flict past, All en - dear re - pose at last.
Far be - yond the reach of foes, We shall dwell in sweet re - pose.
In his king - dom they shall rest, In his love be ful - ly blest.

DISMISSION.

"MY PEACE I LEAVE WITH YOU."

LORD, dismiss us with thy blessing,
  Fill our hearts with joy and peace;
Let us each thy love possessing,
  Triumph in redeeming grace.
    O refresh us, O refresh us,
    Traveling through this wilderness.

2 Thanks we give and adoration,
  For thy Gospel's joyful sound;
May the fruits of thy salvation

In our hearts and lives abound;
    May thy presence, may thy presence
With us evermore be found.

3 So, whene'er the signal's given,
  Us from earth to draw away,
Borne on angels' wings to heaven,
  Glad the summons to obey—
    May we, ready, may we, ready,
    Rise and reign in endless day.

"So when the Battle was over, *Christian* said, I will here give thanks to him that hath delivered me out of the mouth of the Lion, to him that did help me against *Apollyon*. And so he did, saying, Great *Beelzebub*, the Captain of this Fiend designed my ruin; therefore to this end he sent him against me. But the strong one helped me and I did prevail. Therefore to him let me give lasting praise, and always thank and bless his name. Then there  came to him a hand, with some of the leaves of the tree of Life, the which *Christian* took, and applied to the wounds that he had received in the battle, and was healed immediately. He also sat down in that place to eat bread, and to drink of the Bottle that was given him a little before; so being refreshed, he addressed himself to his journey with his sword drawn in his hand."

Watch with Me.

"And that, knowing the time, that now it is high time to awake out of sleep."

38 　　　　　　　　　　　　　　　　　　　　　　　S. M.

1. Bid me of men be - ware, And to my ways take heed;
2. O, may I calm - ly wait Thy suc - cors from a - bove;

Dis - cern their ev' - ry se - cret snare, And cir - cum - spect - ly tread.
And stand a - gainst their o - pen hate, And well - dis - sem - bled love.

MY spirit, Lord, alarm,
　　When men and devils join;
'Gainst all the powers of Satan arm,
　　In panoply divine.

HANG on thy arm alone,
　　With self-distrusting care,
And deeply in the Spirit groan
　　The never-ceasing prayer.

Watch and Wait.

39

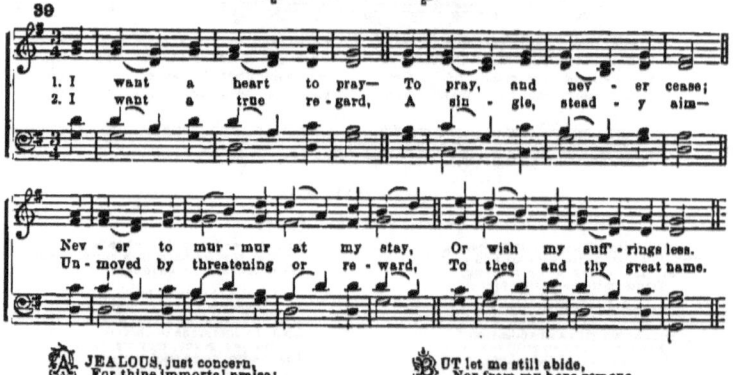

1. I want a heart to pray— To pray, and nev - er cease;
2. I want a true re - gard, A sin - gle, stead - y aim—

Nev - er to mur - mur at my stay, Or wish my suff - rings less.
Un - moved by threatening or re - ward, To thee and thy great name.

A JEALOUS, just concern,
　　For thine immortal praise;
A pure desire that all may learn,
　　And glorify thy grace.

BUT let me still abide,
　　Nor from my hope remove,
Till thou my patient spirit guide
　　Into thy perfect love.

NOW when he was out of this Valley he came upon a pleasant Hill on which was an Arbor, and in it he sat down and soon fell asleep; but when he woke he started on his journey, but his Roll had fallen from his bosom and he knew it not. When *Christian* found his Roll was gone he was sore perplexed, and turned back with sorrow seeking it as he went. Now by this time he was come to the *Arbor* again, where for awhile he sat down and wept; but at last, looking sorrowfully down under the settle, there he espied his Roll; the which he with trembling and haste catched up, and put it into his bosom. But who can tell how joyful this man was when he had gotten his Roll again! for this Roll was the assurance of his life and acceptance at the desired Haven. Therefore he laid it up in his bosom, gave thanks to God for directing his eye to the place where it lay, and with joy and tears he took himself again to his journey. But oh how nimbly now did he go up the rest of the Hill."

I Shall See Him.

"We know that when he shall appear, we shall be like him, for we shall see him as he is."

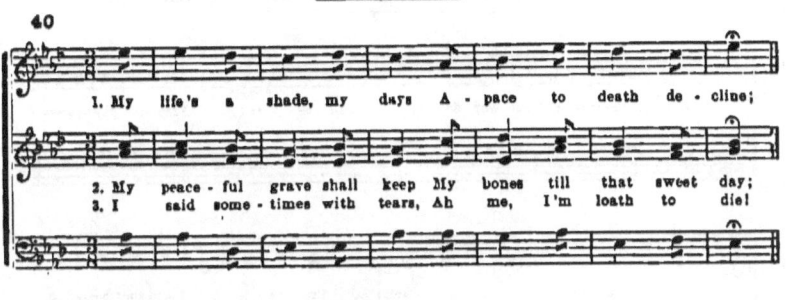

1. My life's a shade, my days Apace to death decline;
2. My peaceful grave shall keep My bones till that sweet day;
3. I said sometimes with tears, Ah me, I'm loath to die!

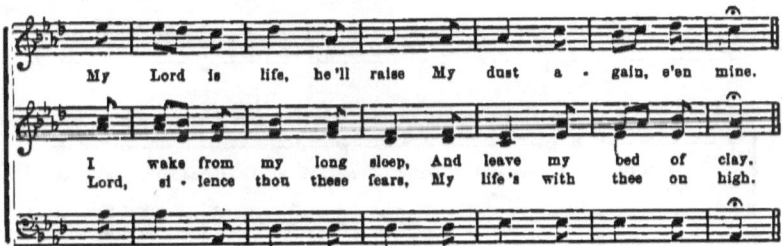

My Lord is life, he'll raise My dust again, e'en mine.
I wake from my long sleep, And leave my bed of clay.
Lord, silence thou these fears, My life's with thee on high.

CHORUS.

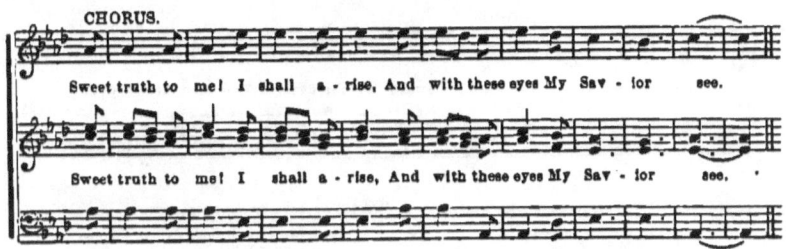

Sweet truth to me! I shall arise, And with these eyes My Savior see.

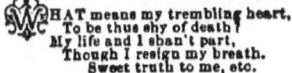HAT means my trembling heart,
To be thus shy of death?
My life and I shan't part,
Though I resign my breath.
Sweet truth to me, etc.

THEN welcome, harmless grave:
By thee to heaven I'll go;
My Lord his death shall save
Me from the flames below.
Sweet truth to me, etc.

"THEN some began to wonder at the Coat that was on *Christian's* back, which was so different from theirs. Then *Christian* said, As for this Coat that is on my back, it was given me by the Lord of the place whither I go, to cover my nakedness with, in order that I might appear before him without shame. And I take it as a token of kindness to me, for I had nothing but rags before. And besides, thus I comfort myself as I go: Surely, think I, when I come to the gate of the City, the Lord thereof will know me for good, since I have his Coat on my back; a coat that he gave me freely in the day that he stript me of my rags. I will tell you moreover, that I had then given me a Roll sealed, to comfort me by reading as I go in the way; I was also bid to give it in at the Celestial Gate, in token of my certain going in after it; for in this Roll I read that *I shall behold his face in righteousness*. Now *Christian*, being thus encouraged, went on his journey, and saw again *Evangelist* coming to him."

I Shall be Satisfied.

"I shall be satisfied when I awake with thy likeness."

41

1. Through the love of God, our Savior, All will be well; Free and changeless

is his fa - vor, All, all is well! Precious is the blood that healed us,

Per - fect is the grace that sealed us, Strong the hand stretched out to shield us;

CHORUS.

All must be well. Yes, when I awake in thy likeness, Then all must be well.

THOUGH we pass through tribulation,
  All will be well;
Ours is such a full salvation,
  All, all is well!
Happy, still in God confiding,
Fruitful, if in Christ abiding,
Holy, through the Spirit's guiding,
  All must be well.
    Yes, when I, etc.

WE expect a bright to-morrow,
  All will be well;
Faith can sing through days of sorrow,
  All, all is well!
On our Father's love relying,
Jesus every need supplying,
Or in living, or in dying,
  All must be well.
    Yes, when I, etc.

"THEN said Evangelist, Right glad am I that you have continued in the way to this very day. I have sowed and you have reaped; and the day is coming when both he that sowed and they that reaped shall rejoice together; for in due time you shall reap, if you faint not. The Crown is before you, and it is an incorruptible one; so run that you may obtain it. Some there be that set out for this Crown, and after they have gone far for it, another comes in and takes it from them; hold fast therefore that you have, let no man take your Crown. You have not yet resisted unto blood striving against sin; let the Kingdom be always before you, and believe steadfastly concerning things that are invisible. In this world ye shall have tribulation; but you have all power in Heaven and Earth on your side, and in the other world ye shall have rest for evermore. So Christian, more cheerful than ever, went on his journey."

We'll Journey Together to Zion.

"Iron sharpeneth iron, so a man sharpeneth the countenance of his friend."

42

1. We'll journey together to Zion, That beautiful city of light; Whose sky is unclouded forever,

Nor vailed by a shadow of night. We'll stay not to drink of the water, Nor rest in the valley below;

CHORUS.

But cheered by the cross and its banner, We'll sing and be glad as we go. We'll journey together to Zion,

Rit.

The beautiful, beautiful Zion; We'll journey together to Zi-on, The beautiful city of God.

WE'LL journey together to Zion,
Where all who are faithful may share
A place in the mansion of glory
Our Savior has gone to prepare.
His flock he will feed like a Shepherd,
And guard them by night and by day;
We'll talk of his goodness and mercy,
And tell of his love by the way.
We'll journey, etc.

WE'LL journey together to Zion,
With rapture we soon shall behold
The saints who have reached it before us,
The prophets and martyrs of old.
We'll learn the new song of redemption,
Which only the ransomed can sing;
Ascribing all honor and glory
To Jesus our Savior and King.
We'll journey, etc.

"Now as *Christian* went on his way, he came to a little ascent, which was cast up on purpose that Pilgrims might see before them. Up there, therefore, *Christian* went, and looking forward he saw *Faithful* before him upon his journey, and he cried, Stay, Stay, good Pilgrim, whence hast thou come? and whither dost thou journey? At that *Faithful* looked behind him, and said, I am come from the City of Destruction, and I journey to the City of the Great King. To whom *Christian* cried again, Stay, stay, till I come up to you. But *Faithful* answered, No, I am upon my life, and the Avenger of Blood is behind me. At this *Christian* was somewhat moved, and putting to all his strength he quickly got up with *Faithful*. Then I saw in my Dream they went very lovingly on together, and had sweet discourse of all things that had happened to them in their Pilgrimage."

The World will Mock the Backslider.

"Wherefore let him that thinketh he standeth take heed lest he fall."

43

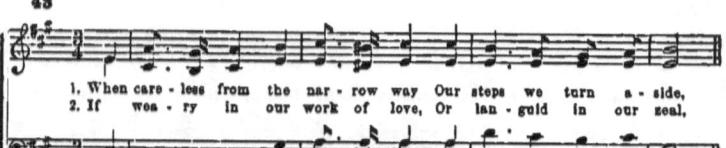

1. When care - less from the nar - row way Our steps we turn a - side,
2. If wea - ry in our work of love, Or lan - guid in our zeal,

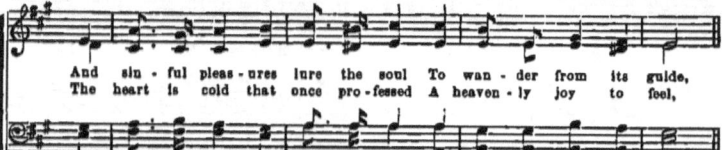

And sin - ful pleas - ures lure the soul To wan - der from its guide,
The heart is cold that once pro - fessed A heaven - ly joy to feel,

CHORUS.

The world will sure - ly mock us then, And cru - ci - fy our

Lord a - gain, And cru - ci - fy our Lord a - gain.

IF seldom found where once we met
To ask refreshing grace,
And seek, with humble Christian faith,
A Father's smiling face,
The world will surely mock us then,
And crucify our Lord again.

LET us guard our every thought,
And pray for strength divine,
That like a city on a hill,
Our light may ever shine,
Then may we boast, while thus we live,
A joy the world can never give.

"THEN said *Christian*, Did you hear no talk of Neighbor *Pliable?* Yes, *Christian*, said *Faithful*, I heard that he followed you till he came at the Slough of Dispond, where, as some said, he fell in. He hath since his going back been had greatly in derision, and that among all sorts of people; some do mock and despise him; and scarce will any set him on work. He is now seven times worse than if he had never gone out of the City. They say he is a Turncoat, he was not true to his profession: I think God has stirred even his enemies to hiss at him, and make him a Proverb, because he hath forsaken the way. I met him once in the Streets, but he leered away on the other side, as one ashamed of what he had done; so I spake not to him."

Be not Ashamed to be a Christian.

"Whosoever, therefore, shall confess me before men, him will I confess also before my Father which is in heaven."

44   26th P. M.

Ashamed to be a Chris-tian, A-fraid the world should know

I'm on my way to Zi-on, Where joys e-ter-nal flow!

For-bid it, O, my Sav-ior, That I should ev-er be

A-fraid to wear thy col-or, Or blush to fol-low thee.

ASHAMED to be a Christian,
To love my God and King!
The fire of zeal is burning,
My soul is on the wing.
I want a faith made perfect,
That all the world may see,
I stand a living witness
Of mercy, rich and free.

ASHAMED to be a Christian!
My guilty fear depart;
I will not heed the tempter
That whispers to my heart.
Dear Savior, though unworthy,
Yet this my only plea,
Thy all-atoning merit,
For thou hast died for me.

"THEN there came unto *Christian* one whose name was *Shame*, and he spoke great swelling words even against Religion itself; he said it was a pitiful, low, sneaking business for a man to mind Religion, that a tender conscience was an unmanly thing; he objected also that but few of the Mighty, Rich, or Wise were ever of this opinion, and objected to the base and low estate and condition of those that were chiefly the Pilgrims of the times in which they lived. But *Christian* boldly withstood him and said, What God says is best, though all the men in the world are against it. Seeing then that God prefers his Religion, seeing God prefers a tender conscience, *Shame* depart, thou art an enemy to my Salvation: shall I entertain thee against my Sovereign Lord? How then shall I look him in the face at his coming?"

The Lord will Provide.

"Persecuted, but not forsaken; cast down, but not destroyed."

45   13th P. M.

1. Though trou-bles as - sail, and dan - gers af-fright; Though friends should all
2. The birds, with - out barn or store-house are fed; From them let us
3. When Sa - tan ap - pears to stop up our path, And fills us with
4. He tells us we're weak, our hope is in vain; The good that we

fail, and foes all u - nite, Yet one thing se - cures us, what-
learn to trust for our bread; His saints what is fit - ting, shall
fears, we tri-umph by faith; He can not take from us (though
seek we ne'er shall ob - tain; But when such sug - ges - tions our

ev - er be - tide, The prom - ise as - sures us— The Lord will pro - vide.
ne'er be de - nied, So long as 't is writ - ten— The Lord will pro - vide.
oft he has tried), The heart-cheer - ing prom - ise— The Lord will pro - vide.
gra - ces have tried, This an-swers all ques-tions— The Lord will pro - vide.

NO strength of our own, nor goodness we claim; Our trust is all thrown on Jesus' name; In this our strong tower for safety we hide; The Lord is our power—The Lord will pro-vide.

WHEN life sinks apace, and death is in view, The word of his grace shall comfort us through; Not fearing or doubting, with Christ on our side, We hope to die shouting—The Lord will provide.

"MY Sons, said Evangelist, you have heard, in the words of the truth of the Gospel, that you must through many tribulations enter into the Kingdom of Heaven. And again, that in every City bonds and afflictions abide you; and therefore you can not expect that you should go long on your Pilgrimage without them, in some sort or other. You have found something of the truth of these testimonies upon you already, and more will immediately follow; for now, as you see, you are almost out of the Wilderness; but you will soon come into a Town that you will by and by see before you; and in that Town you will be hardly beset with enemies, who will strain hard but they will not kill you, But be you faithful unto death, and the King will give you a Crown of life. Quit yourselves therefore like men, and commit the keeping of your souls to your God in well-doing, as unto a faithful Creator.

Our Trials.

"In the world ye shall have tribulation; but be of good cheer, I have overcome the world."

16   3d P. M.

1. Through trib - u - la - tions deep, The way to glo - ry is;
2. Some - times tempt - a - tions blow A dread - ful hur - ri - cane,
3. The Bi - ble is my chart, By it the seas I know;
4. When through the voyage I get, Though rough, it is but short;

This storm - y course I keep, O'er these tem - pes - tuous seas.
And high the wa - ters flow, And o'er the sides break in,
I can not with it part, It rocks and sands doth show,
The pi - lot an - gels meet, To bring me in - to port;

By waves and wind I'm tossed and driven, Yet full of hope, and bound for heaven.
But still my lit - tle ship out-braves The blustering winds and surg-ing waves.
It is a chart and com-pass too, Whose needle points for - ev - er true.
And when I land on that blest shore, I shall be safe for - ev - er - more.

SEEKING RESTORATION.

"MAKE HASTE, O GOD, TO DELIVER ME."

WHERE is the Savior now,
   Whose smiles I once possessed?
Till he return, I bow,
   By heavy guilt oppressed:
My days of happiness are gone,
And I am left to weep alone.

2 Where can the mourner go,
   And tell his tale of grief?
Ah, who can soothe his woe?

Ah, who can give relief?
Earth can not heal the wounded breast,
Or give the troubled conscience rest.

3 Jesus, thy smiles impart;
   My gracious Lord, return;
Bind up my broken heart,
   And bid me cease to mourn:
Then shall this night of sorrow flee,
And peace and heaven be found in thee.

"THEN I saw in my Dream, that when they were got out of the Wilderness, they presently saw a Town before them, and the name of the Town is *Vanity*; and at the Town there is a Fair kept, called *Vanity Fair*; it is kept all the year long; it beareth the name of *Vanity Fair*, because the Town where it is kept is *lighter than Vanity*; and also because all that is there sold, or that come thither, is *Vanity*. Now, the way to the Celestial City lies just through this Town where this lusty Fair is kept; and he that will go to the City and yet not go through this Town, *must needs go out of the world*. The Prince of Princes himself, when here, went through this Town to his own Country. Many poor Pilgrims are sorely beset in this Town to this day—some are seduced to the beholding of vanities; and others because they will not turn aside have been scourged and buffeted, and some have been stoned with Stones, and some have been burned to ashes at the Stake."

Love not the World.

"For what is a man profited if he shall gain the whole world, and lose his own soul."

47

1. Why should we covet the joy of a day, Things that will fade in a moment a-way;

Toiling for wealth and its honors to gain, Why are we liv-ing for trifles so vain.

CHORUS.

Trust not the world in its beau-ty ar-rayed, Though at our feet all its treasures be laid;

What would it profit its wealth to con-trol? What can we give in exchange for the soul?

WE have no promise that fame will endure;
Splendor will never our pardon secure;
Gold can not brighten the gloom of the grave;
Only the merits of Jesus can save.
   Trust not the world, etc.

BLESSED are they who are lowly in heart;
They, who like Mary, have chosen their part;
Learning of Jesus, their Master above,
Lessons of patience, of meekness, and love.
   Trust not the world, etc.

"THEN *Christian* and his new companion *Hopeful* went on together till they came to a delicate Plain, called *Ease*, where they went with much content; but that Plain was but narrow, so they quickly got over it. Now at the farther side of that Plain was a little Hill, called *Lucre*, and in that Hill a *Silver-mine*, which some of them that had formerly gone that way, because of the rarity of it, had turned aside to see; but going too near the brink of the pit, the ground being deceitful under them, broke, and they were slain; some also had been maimed there, and could not to their dying day be their own men again. And I saw in my Dream, that a little off the road, over against the *Silver-mine*, stood *Demas* to call to Passengers to come and see. But *Christian* said, Not I: I have heard of this place before now, and how many have there been slain; and besides, that Treasure is a snare to those that seek it, and hindereth them in their Pilgrimage."

The River of Life.

"And he showed me a pure river of water of life, clear as crystal, proceeding out of the throne of God and of the Lamb."

77th P. M.

48

1. O! there is a river whose fresh waters flow O'er earth's broadest surface, a cure for all woe;

Its streams are all healing, there's life in each wave, O, try it, and prove it, 't is mighty to save!

DRINK of this river, its full crystal flood
Refreshes and lightens of sin's weary load;
Its ripples ne'er mix with the billows of strife,
This is the "Pure River of Water of Life."

THIS beautiful river our boast well may be,
'Tis fresh, overflowing, and better, 't is free;
The sin-sick rejoice in this "peace-speaking" tide,
This river is Jesus, the "once crucified."

Healing Stream.

L. M.

49

Slow and soft.

1. There is a stream, whose gentle flow Sup-plies the cit-y of our God;
2. That sacred stream, thy ho-ly word, Sup-ports our faith, our fear con-trols;

Life, love, and joy still gli-ding through, And watering our di-vine a-bode.
Sweet peace thy prom-is-es af-ford, And give new strength to faint-ing souls.

"I saw then that as they went on their way, and were weary by reason of the roughness of the way, and their feet were tender by reason of their travels, they arrived at a pleasant River, which David, the King, called the *River of God*, but *John*, the *River of the Water of Life.* Now their way lay just upon the bank of the River; here therefore *Christian* and his Companion walked with great delight; they drank also of the water of the River, which was pleasant and enlivening to their weary

spirits; besides, on the banks of this River on either side were green Trees, that bore all manner of fruit; and the Leaves of the Trees were good for Medicine; with the Fruit of these Trees they were also much delighted; and the Leaves they ate to prevent Surfeits, and other Diseases that are incident to those that heat their blood by travels. So they ate of the Fruits and drank of the Water and were filled with gladness."

The Good Shepherd.

"He leadeth me beside the still waters."

50   L. M.

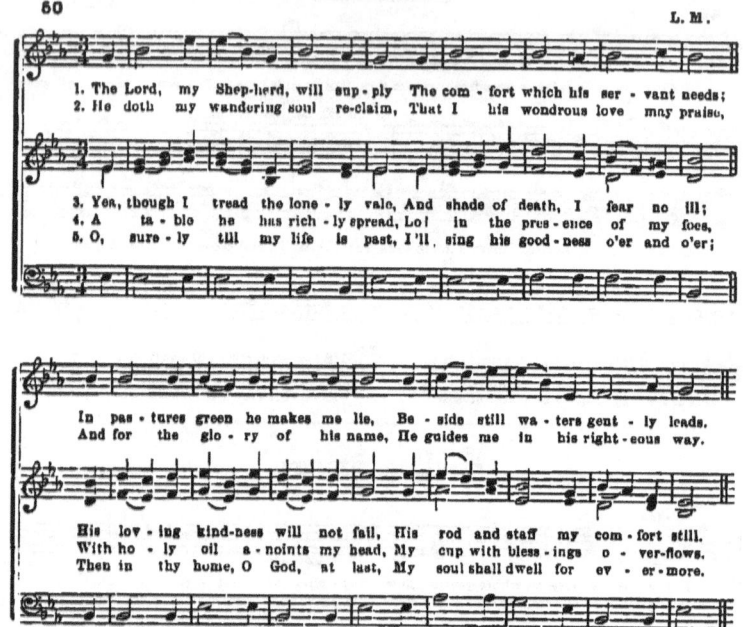

1. The Lord, my Shep-herd, will sup-ply The com-fort which his ser-vant needs;
2. He doth my wandering soul re-claim, That I his wondrous love may praise,

3. Yea, though I tread the lone-ly vale, And shade of death, I fear no ill;
4. A ta-ble he has rich-ly spread, Lo! in the pres-ence of my foes,
5. O, sure-ly till my life is past, I'll sing his good-ness o'er and o'er;

In pas-tures green he makes me lie, Be-side still wa-ters gent-ly leads.
And for the glo-ry of his name, He guides me in his right-eous way.

His lov-ing kind-ness will not fail, His rod and staff my com-fort still.
With ho-ly oil a-noints my head, My cup with bless-ings o-ver-flows.
Then in thy home, O God, at last, My soul shall dwell for ev-er-more.

WAITING SAVIOR.

51   "BEHOLD I STAND AT THE DOOR AND KNOCK."

BEHOLD! a stranger's at the door!
He gently knocks, has knocked before;
Has waited long, is waiting still;
You treat no other friend so ill.

2 But will he prove a friend indeed?
He will! the very friend you need!
The Man of Nazareth! 't is he,
With garments dyed at Calvary.

3 O, lovely attitude! he stands
With melting heart, and laden hands!
O, matchless kindness! and he shows
This matchless kindness to his foes.

4 Admit him, ere his anger burn—
His feet departed ne'er return,
Admit him, or the hour 's at hand
When at his door denied you 'll stand!

BY this River there were Cotes and Folds for Sheep, an House built for the nourishing and bringing up those Lambs, the Babes of those Women that go on Pilgrimage. Also there was here one that was entrusted with them, who would have Compassion, and that could gather these Lambs with his Arm, and carry them in his bosom. Here they will never want Meat and Drink and Clothing; and here were delicate Waters, pleasant Paths, dainty Flowers, variety of Trees, and such as bear wholesome Fruit. On either side of the River was also a Meadow, curiously beautified with Lilies; and it was green all the year long. In this Meadow the Pilgrims lay down and slept, for here they might lie down safely. When they awoke, they gathered again of the Fruit of the Trees, and drank again of the Water of the River, and then lay down again to sleep."

Doubting Castle.

"Lord, I believe! help thou mine unbelief."

52   9th P. M.

1. Chris - tian, why should earthly tri - al Make us lose our trust in God?
    Can we doubt a Father's good-ness, Though we feel his chastening rod?

2. If we lack a firm re - li - ance On his ev - er pres - ent aid,
    He may leave us in the darkness Which our un - be - lief has made.

3. Have we proved his sa - cred promise: If ye ask, ye shall re - ceive?
    Have we found his grace suf - fi - cient? Be not faithless, but be - lieve.

He has said, and will per - form it; He has spo - ken, it shall stand;
Gold - en mo-ments, rich in mer - cy, We are wast-ing day by day;
God will ne'er for - sake his peo - ple; They shall o - ver-come at last,

I will com - fort, help, and guide you By my own al - might - y hand.
How we wrong our bless - ed Sav - ior, When we doubt, and fear to pray.
If they trust him for the fu - ture, If they praise him for the past.

53   *QUICKENING INFLUENCES.*

COME, thou everlasting Spirit,
   Bring to every thankful mind
All the Savior's dying merit,
   All his sufferings for mankind.
True recorder of his passion,
   Now the living faith impart;
Now reveal his great salvation
   Unto every faithful heart.

COME, thou Witness of his dying;
   Come, Remembrancer divine;
Let us feel thy power applying
   Christ to every soul, and mine.
Let us groan thine inward groaning;
   Look on Him we pierced, and grieve;
All partake the grace atoning—
   All the sprinkled blood receive.

"NOW there was not far from the place where they lay, a Castle, called *Doubting* Castle, the owner whereof was Giant *Despair*, and it was in his grounds they now were sleeping: wherefore he, getting up in the morning early, and walking up and down in his fields, caught *Christian* and *Hopeful* asleep in his grounds. The Giant therefore drove them before him, and put them into his Castle, into a very dark Dungeon. Here then they lay from *Wednesday* morning till *Saturday* night, without one bit of bread, or drink of water, or light, or any to ask how they did; they were therefore here in evil case, and were far from friends and acquaintance. Then Giant *Despair* fell upon them and beat them fearfully, in such sort that they were not able to help themselves, or to turn them upon the floor. On *Saturday*, about midnight, they began to *pray*, and continued in *prayer* till almost break of day."

Pilgrims of the Cross.

"My flesh trembleth for fear of thee, and I am afraid of thy judgments."

54

1. Dear comrade pil - grims of the cross, Al - though the way be drea - ry,
2. Though sore be - set, not o - ver - come; Cast down, but not de - spair - ing;

Yet faint not, fail not, on - ward press, Though wounded, worn, and wea - ry.
We're trav'ling t'ward a heavenly home, Our Mas - ter's stand - ard bear - ing.

Toil on - ward still Through ev' - ry ill, Con - fid - ing in the Sav - ior;

The jour - ney done, And glo - ry won, We'll sing his praise for - ev - er.

WE'LL one another's burdens bear,
The toilsome journey cheering;
Our joys and all our sorrows share,
Each day our home we 're nearing.
Toil onward still, etc.

OUR Lord is God; his promise sure,
His help shall fail us never;
And they who to the end endure
Shall reign with him forever.
Toil onward still, etc.

"NOW a little before it was day, good *Christian*, as one half amazed, cried out, I have a Key in my bosom called *Promise*, that will, I am persuaded, open any lock in *Doubting* Castle. Then he pulled it out of his bosom and began to try at the Dungeon door, whose bolt, as he turned the key, gave back, and the door flew open with ease, and *Christian* and *Hopeful* both came out. Then he went to the outer door that leads into the Castle-yard, and with his key opened that door also. After he went to the iron Gate, for that must be opened too, but that Lock went exceedingly hard, yet the key did open it. Then they went out and came to the King's Highway again, and so were safe, because they were out of the power of Giant *Despair*. So they went on their way rejoicing, and talking of the things that belong to the Kingdom."

The Future Rest.

"Fear not, little flock, for it is your Father's good pleasure to give you the kingdom."

55

1st ending. 2d ending.

1. We shall meet no more to sever, By-and-by, by-and-by;
And the darkness will be over, (Omit.) - - - - - By-and-by, by-and-by.

2. Done with all the earth's delusion, By-and-by, by-and-by;
War and strife and sin's confusion, (Omit.) - - - - - By-and-by, by-and-by.

With the toll-some jour-ney done, And the glo-rious bat-tle won, We shall shine forth
We shall rest our pil-grim feet On the shores where loved ones meet, There to dwell in,

CHORUS.

as the sun, By - and - by, by - and - by. We shall meet no more to sev-er,
bliss com-plete, By - and - by, by - and - by. We shall meet, etc.

By-and-by, by-and-by; And the darkness will be over, By-and-by, by-and-by.

WE shall see and be like Jesus,
By-and-by, by-and-by;
He a crown of life will give us,
By-and-by, by-and-by.
And the angels who fulfill
All the mandates of his will,
Shall attend and love us still,
By-and-by, by-and-by.
We shall meet, etc.

THEN with robes of snowy whiteness,
By-and-by, by-and-by;
And with crowns of dazzling brightness,
By-and-by, by-and-by.
There our storms and perils passed,
And with glory ours at last,
We'll possess the kingdom vast,
By-and-by, by-and-by.
We shall meet, etc.

"COME, Neighbor *Christian*, tell me now further what the things are, and how to be enjoyed, whither we are going? Then said *Christian*, I can better conceive of them with my Mind, than speak of them with my Tongue: There is an endless Kingdom to be inhabited, and everlasting Life to be given us, that we may inhabit that Kingdom forever. There are Crowns of glory to be given us, and Garments that will make us shine like the Sun in the firmament of Heaven. There shall be no more crying, nor sorrow; for He that is owner of the place will wipe all tears from our eyes. There we shall be with *Seraphims* and *Cherubims*, creatures that will dazzle your eyes to look on them: There also you shall meet with thousands and ten thousands that have gone before us to that place; none of them are hurtful, but loving and holy; every one walking in the sight of God, and standing in his presence with acceptance forever."

4

Nearer my Home

"For now we see through a glass darkly; but then face to face."

56

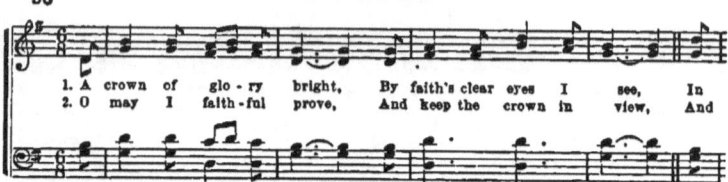

1. A crown of glo - ry bright, By faith's clear eyes I see, In
2. O may I faith - ful prove, And keep the crown in view, And

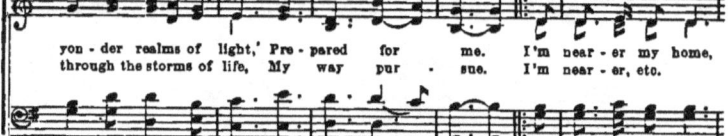

yon - der realms of light, Pre - pared for me. I'm near - er my home,
through the storms of life, My way pur - sue. I'm near - er, etc.

CHORUS.

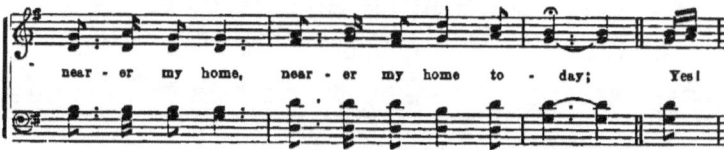

near - er my home, near - er my home to - day; Yes!

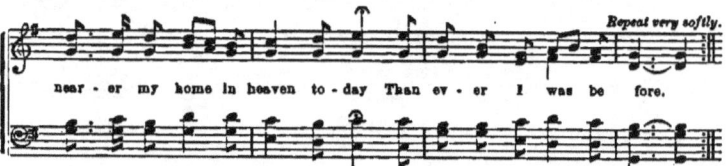

near - er my home in heaven to - day Than ev - er I was be - fore.

Repeat very softly.

JESUS, be thou my guide,
My daily steps attend;
O, keep me near thy side,
Be thou my friend.
I'm nearer, etc.

BE thou my shield and sun,
My Savior and my guard;
And when my work is done,
My great reward,
I'm nearer, etc.

"THEN they arrived at the delectable mountains, where the air was pure and every thing green and beautiful, and they could see far away in the distance; here they tarried, and the good Shepherds led them about and showed them all the wonders of the place. By this time the Pilgrims had a desire to go forward, and the Shepherds a desire they should: so they walked together towards the end of the Mountains. Then said the Shepherds one to another, Let us here show to the Pilgrims the Gates of the Celestial City, if they have skill to look through our Perspective-Glass. The Pilgrims then lovingly accepted the motion; so they had them to the top of a high Hill, called *Clear*, and gave them their Glass to look. Then they essayed to look, but by means of an impediment they could not look steadily through the Glass; yet they thought they saw something like the Gate, and also some of the Glory of the place. Then they went away and sang a song."

Pilgrim, Watch and Pray.

"Therefore let us not sleep as do others, but let us watch and be sober."

57

Earnestly.

1. Soft - ly on the breath of ev'-ning Comes the ten - der sigh of day;
2. Pearl - y dews, like tears, are fall - ing Gent - ly on the sleep - ing flowers;

Lone - ly heart, by sor - row la - den, 'Tis the time to pray.
Stars, like an - gel eyes, are beam - ing From ce - les - tial bowers.

CHORUS.

Wea - ry pil - grim, cease thy mourning; Wea - ry pil - grim,

Repeat Chorus.

cease thy mourn - ing; Rest be - yond for - ev - er.

3. 'TIS the hour where hallowed feelings
Chase our doubts and fears away;
'Tis the hour for calm devotion,
Pilgrim, watch and pray.
Weary pilgrim, etc.

4. THOUGH temptations dark oppress thee,
Jesus guides thee on thy way;
He will hear thy lightest whisper,
Pilgrim, watch and pray.
Weary pilgrim, etc.

"I saw then in my Dream, that they went till they came into a certain Country, whose air naturally tended to make one drowsy, if he came a stranger into it. And here *Hopeful* began to be very dull and heavy of sleep; wherefore he said unto *Christian*, I do now begin to grow so drowsy that I can scarcely hold up mine eyes, let us lie down here and take one nap. By no means, said the other, lest sleeping we never awake more. Do you not remember that one of the Shepherds bid us beware of the Enchanted Ground? He meant by that, that we should beware of sleeping; wherefore let us not sleep as do others, but let us watch and be sober. Now then, said *Christian*, to prevent drowsiness in this place, let us watch and pray, and fall into good discourse. With all my heart, said the other, and let us begin where God began with us."

Fear God.

"The fear of the Lord is the beginning of wisdom."

58   C. M.

1. Cre - a - tor, Sov' - reign Lord of all, In earth and sea and skies,
2. Teach us to know thy per - fect law, Whose judgments truth un - fold,

The source of wis - dom is thy fear, O! make us tru - ly wise.
More sweet than hon - ey in the comb, More pre - cious far than gold.

O! wisdom crieth at the gate,
And spreads her hands abroad;
O, hear the voice, ye sons of men,
And learn the fear of God.

CREATOR, Sovereign Lord of all,
In earth and sea and skies,
The source of wisdom is thy love,
O, make us truly wise.

Father, Take my Hand.

59   C. M.

1. Fa - ther, I stretch my hand to thee, No oth - er help I know;
2. Au - thor of faith! to thee I lift My wea - ry, long - ing eyes;

If thou with-draw thy - self from me, Ah! whither shall I go?
O let me now re - ceive that gift— My soul with-out it dies.

SURELY thou canst not let me die;
O speak, and I shall live;
And here I will unwearied lie,
Till thou thy Spirit give.

NOW would my fainting soul rejoice,
Could I but see thy face;
Now let me hear thy quick'ning voice,
And taste thy pard'ning grace.

THEN said *Hopeful*, I do believe, as you say, that fear tends much to men's good, and to make them right at their beginning to go on a Pilgrimage. Without doubt, said *Christian*, for so says the Word: *The fear of the Lord is the beginning of Wisdom.* True or right fear is discovered by three things: 1. By its rise; it is caused by saving conviction for sin. 2. It driveth the soul to lay fast hold of Christ for salvation. 3. It begetteth and continueth in the soul a great reverence of God, his Word, and Ways, keeping it tender, and making it afraid to turn from them, to the right hand or to the left, to any thing that may dishonor God, break its peace, grieve the Spirit, or cause the enemy to speak reproachfully. Now the ignorant know not that such convictions as tend to put them in fear are for their good, and therefore they seek to stifle them."

The Mourning Wanderer.

"The backslider in heart shall be filled with his own ways."

60 C. M.

Moderato.

1. O, could I feel and know a - gain The joy of sins for-
2. My bur - dened heart to Je - sus, then, Could tell its ev' - ry

given; That liv - ing faith that works by love, And points the
care; Could lean con - fid - ing on his breast, And find a

CHORUS. *Fast.*

soul to heaven. I will a - rise, no more de - lay, I'll seek a
bless - ing there. I will a - rise, etc.

Fa - ther's face; My sins con - fess, His par - don ask, And

fly to his em - brace, And fly to his em - brace.

WHY did I lose the guiding star
That cheered me on my way?
Why did I heed the tempter's voice,
And cease to watch and pray?
I will arise, etc.

DEAR Father, take the wanderer back,
Thy erring child forgive;
Restore me to thy love once more,
And teach me how to live.
I will arise, etc.

"NOW, *Christian*, I have shewed the reasons why some go back, do you shew me the manner thereof. So I will, willingly, said *Christian*. They draw off their thoughts, all that they may, from the remembrance of God, Death, and Judgment to come. Then they cast off by degrees private Duties, as Closet-prayer, Curbing their Lusts, Watching, Sorrow for sin, and the like. Then they shun the company of lively and warm Christians. After that they grow cold to public Duty. Then they begin to pick holes, as we say, in the Coats of some of the Godly; and that devilishly, that they may have a seeming color to throw Religion behind their backs. Then they begin to adhere to and associate themselves with carnal, loose, and wanton men. After this they begin to play with little sins openly. And then, being hardened, they shew themselves as they are, and unless a miracle of grace prevent it, they overlastingly perish."

Land of Beulah.

"But thou shalt be called Hephzibah, and thy land Beulah, for the Lord delighteth in thee."

61   C. M.

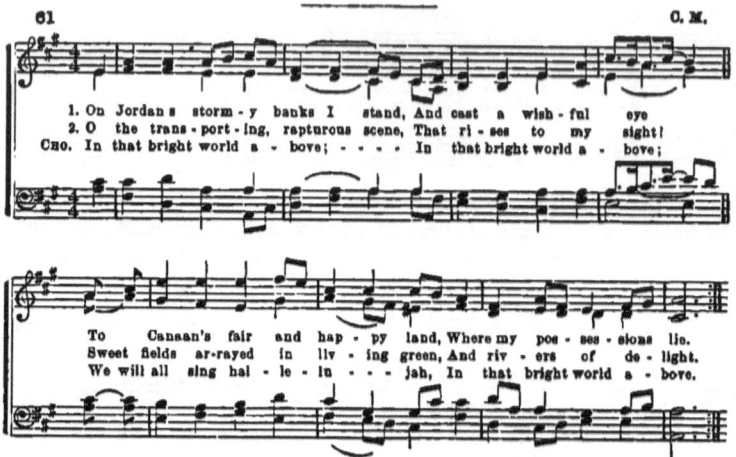

1. On Jordan's storm-y banks I stand, And cast a wish-ful eye
2. O the trans-port-ing, rapturous scene, That ri-ses to my sight!
Cho. In that bright world a-bove; - - - - In that bright world a-bove;

To Canaan's fair and hap-py land, Where my pos-ses-sions lie.
Sweet fields ar-rayed in liv-ing green, And riv-ers of de-light.
We will all sing hal-le-lu- - -jah, In that bright world a-bove.

THERE generous fruits that never fail,
On trees immortal grow;
There rock and hill and brook and vale,
With milk and honey flow.
In that bright, etc.

4 O'er all those wide-extended plains
Shines one eternal day;
There God the Son forever reigns,
And scatters night away.
In that bright, etc.

5 No chilling winds, or poisonous breath
Can reach that healthful shore;
Sickness and sorrow, pain and death
Are felt and feared no more.
In that bright, etc.

6 When shall I reach that happy place,
And be forever blest;
When shall I see my Father's face,
And in his bosom rest?
In that bright, etc.

7 Filled with delight, my raptured soul
Would here no longer stay;
Though Jordan's waves around me roll,
Fearless I'd launch away.
In that bright, etc.

62   *Heavenly Jerusalem.*

JERUSALEM, my happy home,
Name ever dear to me,
When shall my labors have an end,
In joy and peace and thee?

CHORUS.
In that bright world above;
In that bright world above;
We will all sing hallelujah,
In that bright world above.

2 There happier bowers than Eden's bloom,
Nor sin nor sorrow know;
Blest seats, through rude and stormy scenes,
I onward press to you.
In that bright, etc.

3 Why should I shrink at pain and woe,
Or feel at death dismay?
I've Canaan's goodly land in view,
And realms of endless day.
In that bright, etc.

4 Jerusalem, my happy home,
My soul still pants for thee;
Then shall my labors have an end,
When I thy joys shall see.
In that bright, etc.

"NOW I saw in my Dream, that by this time the Pilgrims were got over the Enchanted Ground, and entering into the Country of *Beulah*, whose air was very sweet and pleasant, the way lying directly through it, they solaced themselves there for a season. Yea, here they heard continually the singing of Birds, and saw every day the Flowers appear in the earth, and heard the voice of the Turtle in the land. In this country the Sun shineth night and day; wherefore this was beyond the Valley of the *Shadow of Death*, and also out of the reach of Giant *Despair*, neither could they from this place so much as see *Doubting* Castle. Here they were in sight of the City they were going to, also here met them some of the inhabitants thereof; for in this land the Shining Ones commonly walked, because it was upon the borders of Heaven. Here also they heard voices out of the City, loud voices, saying, *Behold thy salvation cometh, behold his reward is with him.*"

River of Death.

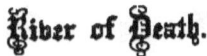

"When thou passeth through the waters, I will be with thee."

63

1. Riv - er of death, thy stream I see Be - tween the bright cit - y of
2. Why should I fear to stem the tide, With him who has loved me as

rest and me; Fearless thy sa - ble surge I'll brave, For sweet is the prospect be-
guard and guide; Wisdom and power con - trol thy flood, While faith says my passage was

CHORUS.

yond the grave. Waft me, O waft me safe - ly o'er, And land me, dear Sav-ior, on
paid with blood. Waft me, etc.

Ca - naan's shore, And land me, dear Sav - ior, on Ca - naan's shore.

WHAT is it gilds thy darksome foam?
'T is light shining forth from my happy home;
Music that thrills my soul to hear,
Seems floating me over thy surface drear.
Waft me, etc.

HELP me, I feel the waters rise,
Yet visions of glory still glad my eyes:
Savior, I come, I soon shall be
Among the saints ransomed by Calvary.
Waft me, etc.

"Now I further saw that betwixt them and the Gate was a River, but there was no Bridge to go over, and the River was very deep: at the sight therefore of this River the Pilgrims were much stunned; but the men that went with them said, You must go through or you can not come at the Gate. They then addressed to the Water; and entering, *Christian* began to sink, and crying out to his good friend *Hopeful*, he said, I sink in deep Waters; the Billows go over my head, all his Waves go over me. Then said the other, Be of good cheer, my Brother, I feel the bottom, and it is good. *Christian* therefore presently found ground to stand upon, and so it followed that the rest of the River was but shallow. And thus they got over."

The Shining Way.

"Then shall the righteous shine forth as the sun in the kingdom of their Father."

64   C. M. D.

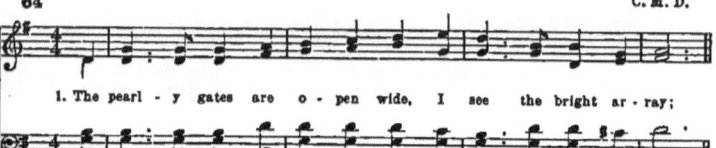

1. The pearl - y gates are o - pen wide, I see the bright ar - ray;

On ei - ther side The an - gels glide, To keep the shi - ning way.

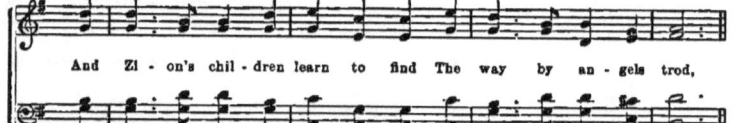

And Zi - on's chil - dren learn to find The way by an - gels trod,

Where Christ's redeemed in un - ion walk The shi - ning way of God.

WHEN storms arise, and darkness clouds
  The faithful pilgrim's way,
      The angels glide
      On either side,
  To drive the clouds away,
And brighter gleams the morning light
  Behind the gentle rod;
For Christ's redeemed more clearly see
  The shining way of Go,

AND soon they walk the golden streets,
  Not slighted and alone,
      On either side
      The angels glide,
  To lead them to the throne.
And there they wear a starry crown,
  While mortals tire and plod;
For Christ's redeemed are kings who praise
  The shining way of God.

"THEN I saw in my Dream that *Christian* was as in a muse awhile. To whom also *Hopeful* said, *Be of good cheer, Jesus Christ maketh thee whole.* Brother, I see the Gate and men standing by to receive us. And with that *Christian* brake out with a loud voice, Oh I see him again, and he tells me, *When thou passest through the Waters, I will be with thee; and through the Rivers, they shall not overflow thee.* Now upon the bank of the River, on the other side, they saw the two shining men again, who there waited for them; wherefore being come out of the River, they saluted them, saying, *We are ministering Spirits, sent forth to minister for those that shall be heirs of salvation.*"

Angels are Waiting.

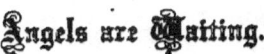

"**Are they not all ministering spirits, sent forth to minister for them who shall be heirs of salvation.**"

65

DUET. *Moderato.*

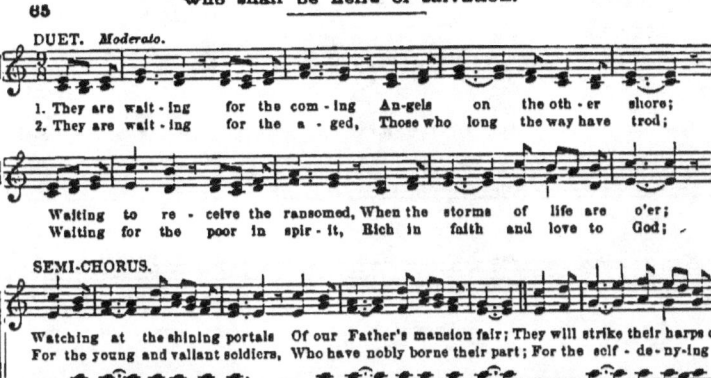

1. They are wait-ing for the com-ing An-gels on the oth-er shore;
2. They are wait-ing for the a-ged, Those who long the way have trod;

Waiting to re-ceive the ransomed, When the storms of life are o'er;
Waiting for the poor in spir-it, Rich in faith and love to God;

SEMI-CHORUS.

Watching at the shining portals Of our Father's mansion fair; They will strike their harps of
For the young and valiant soldiers, Who have nobly borne their part; For the self-de-ny-ing

FULL CHORUS.

glo-ry, They will bid us welcome there. They are wait-ing, waiting, waiting, Angels
Christian, For the meek, the pure in heart. They are wait-ing, etc.

on the other shore; Waiting to receive the ransomed, When the storms of life are o'er.

THEY are waiting for the heralds,
  Who in distant lands proclaim
Life eternal, free salvation,
  Through a dying Savior's name;
Waiting for the silent mourner,
  For the weary and oppressed,
Who have borne their cross with patience,
  And are going home to rest.
    They are waiting, etc.

IN the sunny vales of Eden,
  By the river, clear and bright,
Where the tree of life is planted,
  And our faith is lost in sight;
We shall join the "church triumphant,"
  Free from sorrow, toil, and care:
Every tie again united,
  There will be no parting there.
    They are waiting, etc.

"Now upon the bank of the River on the other side, they saw the two shining men again, who there waited for them. Now you must note that the City stood upon a mighty Hill, but the Pilgrims went up that Hill with ease, because they had these two men to lead them up by the arms; also they had left their *mortal garments* behind them in the River, for though they went in with them, they came out without them. They therefore went up here with much agility and speed, though the foundation upon which the City was framed was higher than the clouds. They therefore went up through the regions of the air, sweetly talking as they went, being comforted, because they safely got over the River, and had such glorious Companions to attend them."

The Heavenly Shore.

"Where the wicked cease from troubling, and the weary are at rest."

66

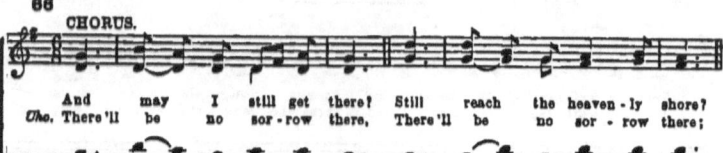

CHORUS.

And   may   I   still get   there? Still   reach   the heaven-ly shore?
Cho. There 'll   be   no   sor-row there, There 'll   be   no   sor-row there;

D. C.

The   land for-ev-er bright and   fair, Where   sor-row reigns no more?
In   heaven a-bove, where all   is   love, There 'll be   no   sor-row there.

THE HEAVENLY SHORE.

AND may I still get there?
   Still reach the heavenly shore?
The land forever bright and fair,
   Where sorrow reigns no more!

CHORUS.

There 'll be no sorrow there,
There 'll be no sorrow there;
   In heaven above, where all is love,
There 'll be no sorrow there.

2 Shall I, unworthy I,
   To fear and doubting given,
Mount up at last, and happy fly
   On angel's wings to heaven?

3 Hail, love divine and pure,
   Hail, mercy from the skies!
My hopes are bright, and now secure,
   Upborne by faith I rise.

4 I part with earth and sin,
   And shout the danger's past;
My Savior takes me fully in,
   And I am his at last.

67   HEAVENLY LAND.

SING to me of heaven,
   When I am called to die,
Sing songs of holy ecstasy,
   To waft my soul on high.

CHORUS.

There 'll be no sorrow there,
There 'll be no sorrow there;
   In heaven above, where all is love,
There 'll be no sorrow there.

2 When the last moment comes,
   O, watch my dying face,
To catch the bright seraphic gleam,
   Which o'er my features plays.

3 Then to my raptured soul,
   Let one sweet song be given,
Let music cheer me last on earth,
   And greet me first in heaven.

4 Then round my senseless clay,
   Assemble those I love,
And sing of heaven, delightful heaven,
   My glorious home above.

"THE talk they had with the Shining Ones was about the glory of the place, who told them that the beauty and the glory of it was inexpressible. There, said they, is the Mount *Sion*, the heavenly *Jerusalem*, the innumerable company of Angels, and the Spirits of just men made perfect. You are going now, said they, to the Paradise of God, wherein you shall see the Tree of Life, and eat of the never-fading fruits thereof; and when you come there you shall have white Robes given you, and your walk and talk shall be every day with the King, even all the days of Eternity. There you shall not see again such things as you saw when you were in the lower Region upon the earth, to-wit, sorrow, sickness, affliction, and death, *for the former things are passed away.* In that place you must wear Crowns of Gold, and enjoy the perpetual sight and vision of the Holy One, *for there you shall see him as he is.*"

Enter into Rest.

"Enter in through the gates into the city."

68

1. From this bleak hill of storms, En - ter thy rest; To you bright
2. From hun - ger and from thirst, En - ter thy rest; From toil and
3. From weak-ness and from pain, En - ter thy rest; From trem - bling

sun - ny heights, En - ter thy rest. Where love for - ev - er shines,
wea - ri - ness, En - ter thy rest. From shad - ows and from dreams,
and from strife, En - ter thy rest. From watch - ings and from fears,

RECITATIVE.   Rit.

En - ter in - to rest; En - ter in - to rest, The rest of God.
En - ter in - to rest; En - ter in - to rest, The rest of God.
En - ter in - to rest; En - ter in - to rest, The rest of God.

FROM vanity and lies,
  Enter thy rest;
From mocking and from snares,
  Enter thy rest.
From disappointed hopes,
  Enter into rest;
Enter into rest,
  The rest of God.

HERE thou art ever safe,
  Enter thy rest;
Pilgrim and child of God,
  Enter thy rest.
This is thy home at last,
  Enter into rest;
Enter into rest,
  The rest of God.

"Now while they were drawing towards the Gate, behold a company of the Heavenly Host came out to meet them; to whom it was said by the other two Shining Ones, These are the men that have loved our Lord when they were in the World, and that have left all for his holy Name, and he hath sent us to fetch them, and we have brought them thus far on their desired Journey, that they may go in and look their Redeemer in the face with joy. Then

the Heavenly Host gave a great shout, saying, *Blessed are they that are called to the Marriage Supper of the Lamb.* And thus they came up to the Gate. Now when they were come up to the Gate, there was written over it in letters of gold, *Blessed are they that do his commandments, that they may have right to the Tree of Life, and may enter in through the Gates into the City.*"

Lover of Jesus.

"Enter thou into the joy of thy Lord."

69

1. Lov-er of Je-sus, thy crown is be-fore thee, God was thy ref-uge, thy
2. Lov-er of Je-sus, the bat-tle is o-ver, Tri-als are end-ed, af-

cres.   *cres.*

comfort di-vine; Heir of sal-va-tion, his spir-it is with thee, Holding a bless-ed com-
flictions are past; Safe in the ha-ven of rest thou art welcomed, Glo-ry to God, thou hast

CHORUS.

mun-ion with thine.   Thou hast been faith-ful, and this thy re-ward,
conquered at last.   Thou hast been, etc.

| *Rit.*

"Enter thou in-to the joy of thy Lord," "Enter thou in-to the joy of thy Lord."

LOVER of Jesus, the life that awaits thee,
If, while a pilgrim, thy soul could have known,
Then thou hadst counted each trial a blessing,
Joy, like a river, had constantly flown.
Thou hast been, etc.

LOVER of Jesus, thy joy is unbounded,
Paradise opens its portals for thee;
Hear the sweet words from the lips of the Savior,
Dwell thou forever in glory with me.
Thou hast been, etc.

"NOW I saw in my Dream that these two men went in at the Gate; and lo, as they entered, they were transfigured, and they had Raiment put on that shone like Gold. There was also that met them with Harps and Crowns, and gave them to them, the Harps to praise withal, and the Crowns in token of honor. Then I heard in my Dream that all the Bells in the City rang again for joy, and that it was said unto them, *Enter ye into the joy of your Lord.* Now just as the Gates were opened to let in the men, I looked in after them, and behold, the City shone like the Sun; the Streets also were paved with Gold, and in them walked many men, with Crowns on their heads, Palms in their hands, and golden Harps to sing praises withal. After that they shut up the Gates. Which when I had seen, I wished myself among them."

Final Doxology.

"Praise ye the Lord."

CHORAL. *Loud and distinct.*

Allegro con Spirito.

ACCOMPANYING CHORUS.

ALTO.

SOPRANO.

BASS.

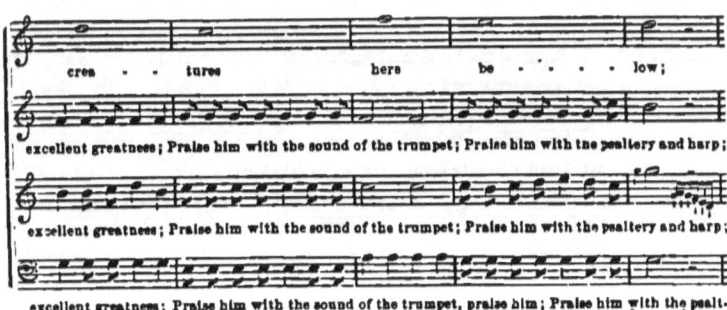

Final Doxology. Concluded.

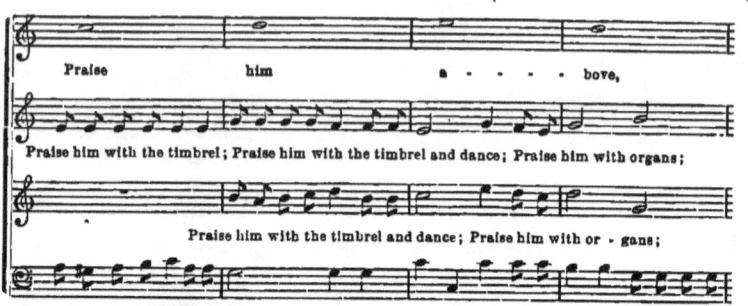

Praise him a - - - bove,

Praise him with the timbrel; Praise him with the timbrel and dance; Praise him with organs;

Praise him with the timbrel and dance; Praise him with or - gans;

Praise him with the timbrel and dance, with the timbrel; Praise him with stringed instruments and

ye heaven - - ly host; Praise

Praise him upon the loud cymbals, The high - sounding cym - bals. Let every

Praise him upon the loud cymbals, The high - sounding cym - bals. Let every

or - - gans, Praise him upon the loud cymbals, the high-sounding cymbals. Let every

Fath - - er, Son, and Ho - - ly Ghost

thing that hath breath praise the Lord; Praise ye the Lord, Praise ye the Lord

thing that hath breath praise the Lord; Praise ye the Lord, Praise ye the Lord.

thing that hath breath praise the Lord; Praise ye the Lord, Praise ye the Lord.

NOTE.—There should be voices enough upon the "Choral" to have it distinctly heard above all the other parts.

Standard Sabbath-School Hymns,

CAREFULLY SELECTED AND ADAPTED TO MUSIC,

GIVING THE FIRST STRAIN.

---

70   O, we are Volunteers.

mf O, we are volunteers in the army of the Lord,
Forming into line at our Captain's word;
We are under marching orders to take the bat-
tle-field,
And we 'll ne'er give o'er the fight till the foe
shall yield.

CHORUS.

mp Come and join the army, the army of the Lord,
f Jesus is our Captain, we rally at his word;
mf Sharp will be the conflict with the powers of
sin,
But with such a Leader, we are sure to win.

f 2 The glory of our flag is the emblem of the dove,
Gleaming are our swords from the forge of
love;
We go forth, but not to battle for earthly hon-
ors vain,
'Tis a bright immortal crown that we seek to
gain.

f 3 Our foes are in the field, pressing hard on every
side—
Envy, anger, hatred, with self and pride;
They are cruel, fierce, and strong, ever ready
to attack;
We must watch and fight and pray, if we'd
drive them back.

f 4 O, glorious is the struggle in which we draw
the sword,
Glorious in the kingdom of Christ, our Lord;
It shall spread from sea to sea, it shall reach
from shore to shore,
And His people shall be blessed for evermore.

---

71   Bonnie Doon. L. M.

f Jesus shall reign where'er the sun
Doth his successive journeys run;
His kingdom spread from shore to shore,
Till moon shall wax and wane no more.

f 2 From north to south the princes meet,
To pay their homage at his feet;
While western empires own their Lord,
And savage tribes attend his word.

f 3 To him shall endless prayer be made,
And endless praises crown his head;
His Name, like sweet perfume, shall rise
With every morning sacrifice.

f 4 People and realms of every tongue
Dwell on his love with sweetest song,
And infant voices shall proclaim
Their early blessings on his Name.

---

72   America. 6s & 4s.

f My country, 't is of thee,
Sweet land of liberty,
f Of thee I sing:
Land where my fathers died,
Land of the pilgrim's pride,
From every mountain side
Let freedom ring.

mp 2 My native country, thee—
Land of the noble, free—
Thy name I love;
f I love thy rocks and rills,
Thy woods and templed hills;
f My heart with rapture thrills
Like that above.

f 3 Let music swell the breeze,
And ring from all the trees
Sweet freedom's song;
f Let mortal tongues awake;
Let all that breathe partake;
Let rocks their silence break—
The sound prolong.

mp 4 Our fathers' God, to thee,
Author of liberty,
f To thee we sing:
f Long may our land be bright
With freedom's holy light;
mf Protect us by thy might,
Great God, our King.

---

73   Lenox. H. M.

mf Blow ye the trumpet, blow—
The gladly solemn sound!
Let all the nations know,
To earth's remotest bound,
f The year of jubilee is come;
f The year of jubilee is come;
Return, ye ransomed sinners, home.

m 2 Exalt the Lamb of God,
The sin-atoning Lamb;
Redemption by his blood
Through all the lands proclaim.
f The year of jubilee has come;
Return, ye ransomed sinners, home.

mf 3 The Gospel trumpet hear,
The news of pardoning grace
Ye happy souls draw near,
Behold your Savior's face.
f The year of jubilee is come;
Return, ye ransomed sinners, home.

m 4 Jesus, our great High Priest,
Has full atonement made;
Ye weary spirits, rest,
p Ye mournful souls be glad.
The year of jubilee is come;
f Return, ye ransomed sinners, home.

74   Balerma. C. M.

m   **When I can read my title clear,**
     To mansions in the skies,
mf   I bid farewell to every fear,
     And wipe my weeping eyes.

f   2 Should earth against my soul engage,
     And hellish darts be hurled,
mp   Then I can smile at Satan's rage,
f   And face a frowning world.

f   3 Let cares like a wild deluge come,
     And storms of sorrow fall;
p   May I but safely reach my home,
     My God, my Heaven, my All.

m   4 There I shall bathe my weary soul
     In seas of heavenly rest;
p   And not a wave of trouble roll
     Across my peaceful breast.

m   5 When I've been there ten thousand years,
     Bright shining as the sun,
     I've no less days to sing God's praise,
     Than when I first begun.

75   Arlington. C. M.

m   **Am I a soldier of the cross,**
     A follower of the Lamb?
     And shall I fear to own his cause,
     Or blush to speak his name?

m   2 Shall I be carried to the skies,
     On flowery beds of ease,
mf   While others fought to win the prize,
     And sailed through bloody seas?

mp   3 Are there no foes for me to face?
     Must I not stem the flood?
     Is this vain world a friend to grace,
     To help me on to God?

f   4 Sure I must fight, if I would reign;
     Increase my courage, Lord!
     I'll bear the toil, endure the pain,
     Supported by thy word.

     5 Thy saints in all this glorious war
mf   Shall conquer, though they die;
     They see the triumph from afar,
f   By faith they bring it nigh.

f   6 When that illustrious day shall rise,
     And all thy armies shine,
ff   In robes of victory through the skies
     The glory shall be thine.

76   Shepherd. 8s, 7s & 4s.

Slow and gentle.

m   **Savior, like a Shepherd lead us,**
     Much we need thy tenderest care;
     In thy pleasant pastures feed us,
     For our use thy folds prepare.
f   Blessed Jesus, blessed Jesus,
     Thou hast bought us, thine we are;
     Blessed Jesus, blessed Jesus,
     Thou hast bought us, thine we are.

m   2 We are thine, do thou befriend us,
     Be the Guardian of our way;
     Keep thy flock, from sin defend us,
     Seek us when we go astray.
f   Blessed Jesus, blessed Jesus,
     Hear young children when they pray.

m   3 Thou hast promised to receive us,
     Poor and sinful though we be;
p   Thou hast mercy to relieve us,
f   Grace to cleanse, and power to free.
     Blessed Jesus, blessed Jesus,
     Let us early turn to thee.

m   4 Early let us seek thy favor,
     Early let us do thy will;
     Blessed Lord and only Savior,
     With thy love our bosoms fill.
     Blessed Jesus, blessed Jesus,
     Thou hast loved us, love us still.

77   Courage.

f   **O, do not be discouraged,**
     For Jesus is your Friend!
     O, do not be discouraged,
     For Jesus is your Friend!
     He will give you grace to conquer,
     He will give you grace to conquer,
     And keep you to the end.

Chorus.

mf   I am glad I'm in this army,
     Yes, I'm glad I'm in this army,
     Yes, I'm glad I'm in this army,
     And I'll battle for the school.

f   2 Fight on, ye little soldiers,
     The battle you shall win;
     Fight on, ye little soldiers,
     The battle you shall win;
mf   For the Savior is your Captain,
     For the Savior is your Captain,
     And he has vanquished sin.
     I am glad, etc.

mp   3 And when the conflict's over,
     Before him you shall stand;
     And when the conflict's over,
     Before him you shall stand;
mf   You shall sing his praise forever,
     You shall sing his praise forever,
     In Canaan's happy land.
     I am glad, etc.

78   Woodworth. L. M.

m   **I know 'tis Jesus loves my soul,**
     And makes the wounded spirit whole;
     My nature is by sin defiled,
mp   Yet Jesus loves a little child.

p   2 How kind is Jesus, O, how good!
     'T was for my soul he shed his blood;
     For children's sake he was reviled,
     For Jesus loves a little child.

m   3 When I offend, by thought or tongue,
     Omit the right, or do the wrong;
     If I repent, he's reconciled,
     For Jesus loves a little child.

m   4 To me may Jesus now impart,
     Although so young, a gracious heart;
p   Alas! I'm oft by sin defiled,
     Yet Jesus loves a little child.

Doxology. C. M.

f   To Father, Son, and Holy Ghost,
     The God whom we adore,
     Be glory as it was, is now,
     And shall be evermore.

79 White Robes.

mp Who are these in bright array,
mf This exulting, happy throng,
m Round the altar night and day,
f Singing one triumphant song?

CHORUS.

f They have clean robes, white robes,
White robes are waiting for me!
Yes, clean robes, white robes,
cres Washed in the blood of the Lamb.

m 2 These through fiery trials trod,
These from great afflictions came;
Now before the throne of God,
Sealed with his almighty name.

mf 3 Clad in raiment pure and white,
Victor palms in every hand,
Through their great Redeemer's might,
f More than conquerors they stand.

mf 4 Joy and gladness banish sighs;
Perfect love dispels all fears;
And forever from their eyes
p God shall wipe away their tears.

80 My Immortal Home.

mp My latest sun is sinking fast,
My race is nearly run;
My strongest trials now are past,
mf My triumph is begun.

REFRAIN.

f O come, angel band, come and around me
stand,
O bear me away on your snowy wings,
cres To my immortal home!
O bear me away on your snowy wings,
f To my immortal home!

m 2 I know I'm nearing the holy ranks
Of friends and kindred dear,
For I brush the dews on Jordan's banks,
The crossing must be near.

mf 3 I've almost gained my heavenly home,
My spirit loudly sings;
The holy ones, behold, they come!
I hear the noise of wings.

mp 4 O, bear my longing heart to Him
Who bled and died for me;
p Whose blood now cleanses from all sin,
And gives me victory.

81 We are Pilgrims.

ff We are pilgrims on the earth,
Journeying onward from our birth,
m Every hour and every breath
Brings us nearer still to death.

CHORUS.

f Yes, we are pilgrims; yes, we are pilgrims;
Yes, we are pilgrims, on our journey home.

mf 2 But beyond this vale of tears,
Lies the land that knows no fears;
Where our steps no more may roam,
Pilgrims, we are going home!

f 3 Home to long-lost friends and dear,
Who are missed and mourned for here;
Home to endless peace and love,
In our Father's house above.

f 4 Let not trifles by the way,
Tempt our hearts or steps to stray
From that narrow path and strait,
Leading to the golden gate.

mf 5 No, our faith hath one in view
Who was once a pilgrim too;
From his track we will not roam,
For to Christ we're going home.

82 Land on High.

m There's a beautiful land on high,
To its glories I fain would fly,
f When by sorrows pressed down, I sing for my
crown,
In that beautiful land on high.

CHORUS.

cres In that beautiful land I'll be,
From earth and its cares set free;
mf My Jesus is there, he's gone to prepare
dim A place in that land for me.

m 2 There's a beautiful land on high,
I shall enter it by and by;
There, with friends, hand in hand, I shall walk
on the strand,
In that beautiful land on high.

m 3 There's a beautiful land on high,
p Then why should I fear to die;
When death is the way to the realms of day,
In that beautiful land on high?

m 4 There's a beautiful land on high,
And my kindred its bliss enjoy;
Methinks I now see how they're waiting for
me,
In that beautiful land on high.

m 5 There's a beautiful land on high,
And though here I oft weep and sigh,
My Jesus hath said that no tears shall be shed
In that beautiful land on high.

aff 6 There's a beautiful land on high,
Where we never shall say, "good-by!"
When over the river we're happy forever,
In that beautiful land on high.

83 Nettleton. 8s & 7s. Double.

aff Come, thou fount of every blessing,
Tune my heart to sing thy grace;
Streams of mercy, never ceasing,
Call for songs of loudest praise.
f Teach me some melodious sonnet,
Sung by flaming tongues above;
Praise the mount—I'm fixed upon it;
Mount of thy redeeming love!

m 2 Here I'll raise mine Ebenezer;
Hither by thy help I'm come;
And I hope, by thy good pleasure,
Safely to arrive at home.
Jesus sought me when a stranger,
Wand'ring from the fold of God;
He, to rescue me from danger,
Interposed his precious blood.

dol 3 O! to grace how great a debtor,
Daily I'm constrained to be!
Let thy goodness, like a fetter,
Bind my wand'ring heart to thee.
mf Prone to wander, Lord, I feel it—
Prone to leave the God I love;
Here's my heart, O take and seal it!
Seal it for thy courts above.

84   Communion.

mp   Sweet hour of prayer! sweet hour of prayer!
That calls me from a world of care,
And bids me at my Father's throne,
Make all my wants and wishes known;
In seasons of distress and grief,
My soul has often found relief,
And oft escaped the tempter's snare,
By thy return, sweet hour of prayer;
And oft escaped the tempter's snare,
By thy return, sweet hour of prayer.

mf 2 Sweet hour of prayer! sweet hour of prayer!
Thy wings shall my petition bear,
To him whose truth and faithfulness,
Engage the waiting soul to bless;
And since he bids me seek his face,
Believe his word, and trust his grace,
I'll cast on him my every care,
And wait for thee, sweet hour of prayer.

m 3 Sweet hour of prayer! sweet hour of prayer!
f   May I thy consolation share,
Till from Mount Pisgah's lofty height,
I view my home, and take my flight;
ff This robe of flesh I'll drop, and rise
To seize the everlasting prize;
And shout, while passing through the air,
mp Farewell, farewell, sweet hour of prayer.

85   Coronation.   C. M.

f   All hail the power of Jesus' name!
Let angels prostrate fall;
ff Bring forth the royal diadem,
And crown him Lord of all.

m 2 Ye chosen seed of Israel's race,
Ye ransomed from the fall,
Hail him who saves you by his grace,
f And crown him Lord of all.

mp 3 Sinners, whose love can ne'er forget
p   The wormwood and the gall;
f Go, spread your trophies at his feet,
ff And crown him Lord of all.

f 4 Let every kindred, every tribe,
On this terrestrial ball,
To him all majesty ascribe,
ff And crown him Lord of all.

f 5 O that with yonder sacred throng
We at his feet may fall;
We'll join the everlasting song,
ff And crown him Lord of all.

86   Resolution.   C. M.

mp   Come, humble sinner, in whose breast
A thousand thoughts revolve,
Come, with your guilt and fear oppressed,
And make this last resolve;

mf 2 I'll go to Jesus, though my sin
Like mountains round me close;
I know his courts, I'll enter in,
Whatever may oppose.

p 3 Prostrate I'll lie before his throne,
And there my guilt confess;
I'll tell him, I'm a wretch undone
Without his sov'reign grace.

m 4 Perhaps he will admit my plea,
Perhaps will hear my prayer;
But, if I perish, I will pray,
And perish only there.

87   Beatitudes.

(music)

Come unto Jesus, ye that mourn,
Our blessed Savior said;
His promises how sure they are,
"Ye shall be comforted."

CHORUS.

This promise, on that *sacred mount*,
Was given by our Lord;
"Rejoice, and be exceeding glad,
For great is your reward."

2 Ye poor in spirit, unto you
How great the blessings given;
His choicest promises are yours,
"Yours is the kingdom—Heaven."

3 The meek, and they for Jesus' sake,
Who persecutions bear;
His promises a heavenly home,
A crown of glory theirs.

4 Be merciful, for unto such
He spares his chastening rod;
Be pure in heart, our Savior says,
The pure shall dwell with God.

88   Ortonville.   C. M.

m   Remember thy Creator now,
In these thy youthful days;
He will accept thy earliest vow,
And listen to thy praise.

mf 2 Remember thy Creator now,
And seek him while he's near;
For evil days will come, when thou
Shalt find no comfort near.

m 3 Remember thy Creator now;
His willing servant be;
Then, when thy head in death shall bow,
He will remember thee.

m 4 Almighty God! our hearts incline
Thy heavenly voice to hear;
Let all our future days be thine,
Devoted to thy fear.

89   Martyn.   7s.   Double.

(music)

m   Mary to the Savior's tomb
Hasted at the early dawn;
Spice she brought, and sweet perfume,
But the Lord she loved had gone:
p For awhile she lingering stood,
Filled with sorrow and surprise,
mp Trembling, while a crystal flood
Issued from her weeping eyes.

mf 2 But her sorrows quickly fled
f When she heard his welcome voice;
Christ had risen from the dead,
Now he bids her heart rejoice.
What a change his word can make,
Turning darkness into day!
Ye who weep for Jesus' sake,
He will wipe your tears away.

90 Bethany. 6s & 4s.

af Nearer, my God, to thee,
Nearer to thee!
E'en though it be a cross
That raiseth me,
Still all my song shall be,
Nearer, my God, to thee,
Nearer to thee!

mp 2 Though like a wanderer,
The sun gone down,
Darkness comes over me,
My rest a stone,
af Yet in my dreams I'd be
Nearer, my God, to thee,
Nearer to thee!

mf 3 There let my way appear
Steps unto heaven;
All that thou sendest me
In mercy given;
af Angels to beckon me
Nearer, my God, to thee,
Nearer to thee!

mf 4 Or, if on joyful wing,
Cleaving the sky,
ff Sun, moon, and stars forgot,
Upward I fly,
af Still all my song shall be,
Nearer, my God, to thee,
Nearer to thee!

91 Disconsolate.

af Come, ye disconsolate, where'er ye languish;
Come to the mercy-seat, fervently kneel;
Here bring your wounded hearts, here tell your anguish;
mf Earth has no sorrow that heaven can not heal.

mp 2 Joy of the desolate, light of the straying,
Hope of the penitent, fadeless and pure;
Here speaks the Comforter, tenderly saying,
mf Earth has no sorrow that heaven can not cure.

mp 3 Here see the bread of life; see waters flowing
Forth from the throne of God, pure from above;
mf Come to the feast of love; come, ever knowing,
f Earth has no sorrow but heaven can remove.

92 Pleyel's Hymn. 7s.

af Hasten, sinner, to be wise!
Stay not for the morrow's sun;
f Wisdom if you still despise,
Harder is it to be won.

af 2 Hasten, mercy to implore!
Stay not for the morrow's sun,
f Lest thy season should be o'er
Ere this evening's stage be run.

af 3 Hasten, sinner, to return!
Stay not for the morrow's sun,
f Lest thy lamp should fail to burn
Ere salvation's work is done.

af 4 Hasten, sinner, to be blest!
Stay not for the morrow's sun,
f Lest perdition thee arrest
Ere the morrow is begun.

93 Windham. L. M.

p Show pity, Lord; O, Lord, forgive!
f Let a repenting rebel live.
Are not thy mercies large and free?
May not a sinner trust in thee?

af 2 My crimes are great, but don't surpass
The power and glory of thy grace;
Great God, thy nature hath no bound—
So let thy pard'ning love be found.

af 3 O wash my soul from every sin,
And make my guilty conscience clean;
Here on my heart the burden lies,
And past offenses pain my eyes.

m 4 My lips with shame my sins confess,
Against thy law, against thy grace;
Lord, should thy judgments grow severe,
I am condemned, but thou art clear.

af 5 Yet save a trembling sinner, Lord,
Whose hope, still hov'ring round thy word,
Would light on some sweet promise there—
Some sure support against despair.

94 Suffering Savior. C. M.

p Alas! and did my Savior bleed?
And did my Sov'reign die?
Would he devote that sacred head
For such a worm as I?

m 2 Was it for crimes that I have done,
He groaned upon the tree?
Amazing pity! grace unknown!
And love beyond degree!

mp 3 Well might the sun in darkness hide,
And shut his glories in,
When Christ, the mighty Maker, died,
For man, the creature's sin.

m 4 Thus might I hide my blushing face
While his dear cross appears;
Dissolve my heart in thankfulness,
p And melt mine eyes to tears.

m 5 But drops of grief can ne'er repay
The debt of love I owe;
Here, Lord, I give myself away—
'Tis all that I can do.

95 Dennis. S. M.

m Blest be the tie that binds
Our hearts in Christian love;
The fellowship of kindred minds
Is like to that above.

m 2 Before our Father's throne,
p We pour our ardent prayers;
Our fears, our hopes, our aims are one—
Our comforts and our cares.

m 3 We share our mutual woes,
Our mutual burdens bear,
And often for each other flows
p The sympathizing tear.

p 4 When we asunder part,
It gives us inward pain;
mf But we shall still be joined in heart,
And hope to meet again.

96   Coronation. C. M.

f   **O for a thousand tongues to sing**
My great Redeemer's praise;
The glories of my God and King,
The triumphs of his grace.

m   2 My gracious Master, and my God,
Assist me to proclaim—
To spread, through all the earth abroad
The honors of thy Name.

mp 3 Jesus—the Name that charms our fears,
That bids our sorrows cease;
'T is music in the sinner's ears,
''   'T is life and health and peace.

mp 4 He breaks the power of canceled sin,
He sets the prisoner free;
His blood can make the foulest clean;
His blood availed for me.

mp 5 He speaks—and, list'ning to his voice,
New life the dead receive;
The mournful, broken hearts rejoice,
The humble poor believe.

mf 6 Hear him, ye deaf; his praise, ye dumb,
Your loosened tongues employ;
Ye blind, behold your Savior come;
And leap, ye lame, for joy.

97   Retreat. L. M.

mf **From every stormy wind that blows,**
From every swelling tide of woes,
There is a calm, a sure retreat;
'T is found beneath the mercy-seat.

m   2 There is a place where Jesus sheds
The oil of gladness on our heads;
A place than all besides more sweet—
It is the blood-bought mercy-seat.

m   3 There is a scene where spirits blend,
Where friend holds fellowship with friend;
Though sundered far, by faith they meet,
Around one common mercy-seat.

m   4 Ah! whither could we flee for aid,
p   When tempted, desolate, dismayed?
Or how the hosts of hell defeat,
Had suffering saints no mercy-seat?

f   5 There, there on eagles' wings we soar,
And sin and sense molest no more;
And heaven comes down our souls to greet,
While glory crowns the mercy-seat.

98   Cross. C. M.

mp **Must Jesus bear the cross alone,**
And all the world go free?
No: there 's a cross for every one,
And there 's a cross for me.

m   2 How happy are the saints above
Who once went sorrowing here;
But now they taste unmingled love,
And joy without a tear.

mf 3 The consecrated cross I 'll bear,
Till death shall set me free,
And then go home my crown to wear,
For there 's a crown for me.

99   Martyn. 7s. Double.

m   **Jesus, lover of my soul,**
Let me to thy bosom fly,
While the nearer waters roll,
While the tempest still is high.
mf   Hide me, O my Savior, hide,
Till the storm of life is past;
Safe into the haven guide,
af   O receive my soul at last.

m   2 Other refuge have I none;
p   Hangs my helpless soul on thee;
Leave, O leave me not alone;
f   Still support and comfort me.
All my trust on thee is stayed;
All my help from thee I bring;
Cover my defenseless head
With the shadow of thy wing.

mf 3 Thou, O Christ, art all I want;
More than all in thee I find;
Raise the fallen, cheer the faint,
Heal the sick, and lead the blind.
Just and holy is thy name;
I am all unrighteousness;
False, and full of sin I am;
Thou art full of truth and grace.

m   4 Plenteous grace with thee is found—
Grace to cover all my sin;
Let the healing streams abound;
Make and keep me pure within.
mf   Thou of life the fountain art;
Freely let me take of thee;
f   Spring thou up within my heart;
ff   Rise to all eternity.

100   Talmar. 8s & 7s.

p   **Jesus, while our hearts are bleeding**
O'er the spoils that death has won,
We would, at this solemn meeting,
pp   Calmly say—Thy will be done.

m   2 Though cast down, we 're not forsaken;
Though afflicted, not alone;
Thou didst give, and thou hast taken;
Blessed Lord—Thy will be done.

m   3 Though to-day we 're filled with mourning,
Mercy still is on the throne;
With thy smiles of love returning,
We can sing—Thy will be done.

mp 4 By thy hands the boon was given;
Thou hast taken but thine own;
Lord of earth, and God of heaven,
f   Evermore—Thy will be done.

101   Evening. C. M.

af   **In mercy, Lord, remember me,**
Through all the hours of night,
And grant to me most graciously
The safeguard of thy might.

m   2 With cheerful heart I close mine eyes,
Since thou wilt not remove;
mf   O, in the morning let me rise
f   Rejoicing in thy love.

p   3 Or, if this night should prove my last,
And end my transient days;
Lord, take me to thy promised rest,
f   Where I may sing thy praise.

102   Warwick.   C. M.

m   Lord, in the morning thou shalt hear
    My voice ascending high;
    To thee will I direct my prayer,
    To thee lift up mine eye:

m   1 Up to the hills where Christ is gone,
    To plead for all his saints;
    Presenting, at the Father's throne,
    Our songs and our complaints.

m   3 Thou art a God before whose sight
    The wicked shall not stand;
    Sinners shall ne'er be thy delight,
    Nor dwell at thy right hand.

f   4 Now to thy house will I resort,
    To taste thy mercies there;
    I will frequent thy holy court,
    And worship in thy fear.

mf 5 O may thy Spirit guide my feet
    In ways of righteousness;
    Make every path of duty straight,
    And plain before my face.

103   Webb.   7s & 6s.

m   When shall the voice of singing
    Flow joyfully along?
    When hill and valley, ringing
    With one triumphant song,
f   Proclaim the contest ended,
    And Him who once was slain,
    Again to earth descended,
    In righteousness to reign.

m   2 Then from the craggy mountains
f   The sacred shout shall fly,
    And shady vales and fountains
    Shall echo the reply.
    High tower and lowly dwelling
    Shall send the chorus round,
f   All hallelujahs swelling
    In one eternal sound.

104   Penitence.   P. M.

af   Jesus, let thy pitying eye
    Call back a wand'ring sheep;
    False to thee, like Peter, I
    Would fain like Peter weep.
    Let me be by grace restored;
    On me be all long-suff'ring shown;
f   Turn, and look upon me, Lord,
    And break my heart of stone.

m   2 Savior, Prince, enthroned above,
    Repentance to impart,
    Give me, through thy dying love,
    The humble, contrite heart.
    Give what I have long implored,
    A portion of thy grief unknown;
f   Turn, and look upon me, Lord,
    And break my heart of stone.

m   3 For thine own compassion's sake,
    The gracious wonder show;
    Cast my sins behind thy back,
    And wash me white as snow.
    If now I do myself bemoan,
    If now I do myself bemoan,
f   Turn, and look upon me, Lord,
    And break my heart of stone.

105   Amboy.   6s & 4s.

mf   To-day the Savior calls:
    Ye wanderers, come;
f   O, ye benighted souls,
    Why longer roam?

f   2 To-day the Savior calls:
    O, listen now!
    Within these sacred walls
    To Jesus bow.

p   3 To-day the Savior calls:
f   For refuge fly;
    The storm of justice falls,
p   And death is nigh.

p   4 The Spirit calls to-day:
    Yield to his power;
af   O, grieve him not away!
    'T is mercy's hour.

106   Toplady.   8s, 7s & 4s.

m   Rock of ages, cleft for me,
    Let me hide myself in thee;
p   Let the water and the blood,
    From thy wounded side which flowed,
f   Be of sin the double cure,
    Save from wrath, and make me pure.

m   2 Could my tears forever flow,
    Could my zeal no languor know,
    These for sin could not atone;
    Thou must save, and thou alone:
p   In my hand no price I bring;
f   Simply to the cross I cling.

f   3 While I draw this fleeting breath,
p   When my eyes shall close in death,
    When I rise to worlds unknown,
    And behold thee on thy throne—
mf   Rock of ages, cleft for me,
    Let me hide myself in thee.

107   Old Hundred.   L. M.

f   Great God of nations, now to thee
    Our hymn of gratitude we raise;
    With humble heart, and bending knee,
    We offer thee our song of praise.

f   2 Thy Name we bless, Almighty God,
    For all the kindness thou hast shown
    To this fair land the pilgrims trod,
    This land we fondly call our own.

f   3 Here freedom spreads her banner wide,
    And casts her soft and hallowed ray;
    Here thou our fathers' steps didst guide
    In safety through their dang'rous way.

f   4 We praise thee that the Gospel's light
    Through all our land its radiance sheds;
    Dispels the shades of error's night,
    And heavenly blessings round us spreads.

f   5 Great God, preserve us in thy fear;
    In danger still our guardian be;
f   O, spread thy truth's bright precepts here;
    Let all the people worship thee.

108   Hamburg. L. M.

m   How blest the sacred tie that binds
In sweet communion kindred minds;
How swift the heavenly course they run,
Whose heart, whose faith, whose hopes are one!

m 2 To each the soul of each bow dear;
What tender love, what holy fear;
How does the generous flame within
Refine from earth, and cleanse from sin!

mp 3 Their streaming eyes together flow
For human guilt and human woe;
Their ardent prayers together rise,
Like mingling flames in sacrifice.

m 4 Nor shall the glowing flame expire,
When dimly burns frail nature's fire;
Then shall they meet in realms above—
A heaven of joy—a heaven of love.

109   Missionary Hymn. 7s & 6s.

m   From Greenland's icy mountains,
From India's coral strand;
Where Afric's sunny fountains
Roll down their golden sand;
f   From many an ancient river,
From many a palmy plain,
They call us to deliver
Their land from error's chain.

p 2 What though the spicy breezes
Blow soft o'er Ceylon's isle;
Though every prospect pleases,
And only man is vile:
f   In vain with lavish kindness
The gifts of God are strewn;
mp   The heathen in his blindness
Bows down to wood and stone.

f 3 Shall we, whose souls are lighted
With wisdom from on high,
Shall we to men benighted
The lamp of life deny?
ff   Salvation—O salvation!
The joyful sound proclaim,
Till earth's remotest nation,
Has learned Messiah's name.

mf 4 Waft, waft, ye winds, his story,
And you, ye waters, roll,
Till, like a sea of glory,
f   It spreads from pole to pole:
Till o'er our ransomed nature
The Lamb for sinners slain,
f   Redeemer, King, Creator,
In bliss returns to reign.

110   America. 6s & 4s.

m   God bless our native land!
Firm may she ever stand,
Through storm and night;
mf   When the wild tempests rave,
Ruler of winds and wave,
Do thou our country save
By thy great might.

mp 2 For her our prayer shall rise
To God, above the skies;
On him we wait:
m   Thou who art ever nigh,
Guarding with watchful eye,
To thee aloud we cry,
God save the State!

111   Boylston. S. M.

m   Sow in the morn thy seed;
At eve hold not thy hand;
To doubt and fear give thou no heed—
Broadcast it o'er the land.

m 2 Thou know'st not which shall thrive—
Tho late or early sown;
Grace keeps the precious germ alive,
When and wherever strewn.

mf 3 And duly shall appear,
In verdure, beauty, strength,
p   The tender blade, the stalk, the ear,
And the full corn at length.

m 4 Thou canst not toil in vain;
Cold, heat, and moist, and dry,
Shall foster and mature the grain
For garners in the sky.

112   St. Thomas. S. M.

m   I love thy kingdom, Lord—
The house of thine abode—
The Church our blest Redeemer saved
With his own precious blood.

m 2 I love thy Church, O God!
Her walls before thee stand,
Dear as the apple of thine eye,
And graven on thy hand.

m 3 For her my tears shall fall;
For her my prayers ascend;
To her my cares and toils be given,
Till toils and cares shall end.

m 4 Beyond my highest joy
I prize her heavenly ways;
Her sweet communion, solemn vows,
Her hymns of love and praise.

f 5 Sure as thy truth shall last,
To Zion shall be given
f   The brightest glories earth can yield,
And brighter bliss of heaven.

113   Talmar. 8s & 7s.

mf   Cast thy bread upon the waters,
Thinking not 't is thrown away;
God himself saith thou shalt gather
It again some future day.

2 Cast thy bread upon the waters;
Wildly though the billows roll,
They but aid thee as thou toilest
f   Truth to spread from pole to pole.

mf 3 As the seed, by billows floated,
To some distant island lone,
So to human souls benighted,
That thou flingest may be borne.

f 4 Cast thy bread upon the waters;
Why wilt thou still doubting stand?
Bounteous shall God send the harvest,
If thou sow'st with liberal hand.

f 5 Give then freely of thy substance—
O'er this cause the Lord doth reign:
Cast thy bread, and toil with patience,
Thou shalt labor not in vain.

114　　　The Dying Child.

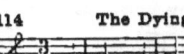

I 'll not be with you long, mother,
　I soon must say good-by;
But, mother, we shall meet again
　In God's bright home on high.
O, mother, do n't you know you said
　Sweet sisters 's living there,
And that she is an angel now,
　So beautiful and fair?

2 She 'll know me when I come, mother
　She 'll take me by the hand;
We 'll always be together there,
　In yonder peaceful land;
And, mother, I shall wear bright wings,
　I 'll be an angel, too,
And then before God's golden throne
　I 'll kneel and pray for you.

3 I like to feel your hand, mother,
　So soft upon my brow;
I always loved its gentle touch,
　'T is dearer to me now.
O, mother, do not weep for me,
　I 'm not afraid to die;
Your lip is trembling, and I see
　The tears are in your eye.

4 Lean closer down your ear, mother
　My voice is growing weak;
You 're weeping yet, I felt a tear
　Just fall upon my cheek.
My eyes grow dim, and O, I hear
　Sweet music from the sky;
It is for me, I 'm going now,
　O mother, dear mother, "good-by!"

115　　　Shirland.　S. M.

m　Blest are the sons of peace,
　　Whose hearts and hopes are one;
　Whose kind designs to serve and please,
　　Through all their actions run.

mf 2 Blest is the pious house
　　Where zeal and friendship meet;
　Their songs of praise, their mingled vows,
　　Make their communion sweet.

m　3 Thus on the heavenly hills
　　The saints are blest above,
　Where joy like morning dew distills,
　　And all the air is love.

116　　　Laban.　S. M.

mf　My soul, be on thy guard;
　　Ten thousand foes arise;
　The hosts of sin are pressing hard
　　To draw thee from the skies.

''　2 O watch and fight and pray;
　　The battle ne'er give o'er;
f　Renew it boldly every day,
　　And help divine implore.

m　3 Ne'er think the victory won,
　　Nor lay thine armor down;
　The work of faith will not be done,
　　Till thou obtain the crown.

f　4 Then persevere till death
　　Shall bring thee to thy God;
　He 'll take thee, at thy parting breath,
　　To his divine abode.

117　　　Balerma.　C. M.

af　O for a closer walk with God—
　　A calm and heavenly frame;
　A light to shine upon the road
　　That leads me to the Lamb.

m　2 Where is the blessedness I knew,
　　When first I saw the Lord?
　Where is the soul-refreshing view
　　Of Jesus and his word?

p　3 What peaceful hours I once enjoyed!
　　How sweet their memory still!
　But they have left an aching void
　　The world can never fill.

af 4 Return, O holy Dove, return!
　　Sweet messenger of rest;
　I hate the sins that made thee mourn,
　　And drove thee from my breast.

118　　　Arlington.　C. M.

m　There is a land of pure delight,
　　Where saints immortal reign;
　Infinite day excludes the night,
　　And pleasures banish pain.

mf 2 There everlasting spring abides,
　　And never-with'ring flowers;
　Death, like a narrow sea, divides
　　This heavenly land from ours.

mp 3 Sweet fields beyond the swelling flood
　　Stand dressed in living green;
　So to the Jews old Canaan stood,
　　While Jordan rolled between.

m　4 Could we but climb where Moses stood,
　　And view the landscape o'er,
　Not Jordan's stream, nor death's cold flood
f　Should fright us from the shore.

119　　　Zion.　8s, 7s & 4s.

m　Yes, my native land, I love thee;
　　All thy scenes, I love them well;
　Friends, connections, happy country!
　　Can I bid you all farewell?
　　　Can I leave you,
　Far in heathen lands to dwell?

< 2 Yes, I hasten from you gladly,
　　From the scenes I loved so well;
　Far away, ye billows, bear me;
　　Lovely native land, farewell!
　　　Pleasant I leave thee,
　Far in heathen lands to dwell.

m　3 In the desert let me labor;
　　On the mountains let me tell
　How he died—the blessed Savior—
　　To redeem a world from hell!
　　　Let me hasten
　Far in heathen lands to dwell.

m　4 Bear me on, thou restless ocean;
　　Let the winds my canvas swell—
　Heaven my heart with warm emotion
　　While I go far hence to dwell.
　　　Glad I bid thee,
　Native land—farewell—farewell.

120   **Webb. 7s & 6s.**

mf   The morning light is breaking,
    The darkness disappears;
The sons of earth are waking
    To penitential tears.
f   Each breeze that sweeps the ocean
    Brings tidings from afar
Of nations in commotion,
    Prepared for Zion's war.

f   2 Rich dews of grace come o'er us
    In many a gentle shower,
And brighter scenes before us
    Are opening every hour.
Each cry, to heaven going,
    Abundant answers brings,
And heavenly gales are blowing,
    With peace upon their wings.

m   3 See heathen nations bending
    Before the God we love,
And thousand hearts ascending
    In gratitude above;
While sinners, now confessing,
    The Gospel call obey,
And seek the Savior's blessing—
    A nation in a day.

mf   4 Blest river of salvation,
    Pursue thy onward way;
Flow thou to every nation,
    Nor in thy richness stay.
Stay not till all the lowly
    Triumphant reach their home;
Stay not till all the holy
f   Proclaim—"The Lord is come!"

121   **America. 6s & 4s.**

mf   Come, thou Almighty King,
Help us thy name to sing,
    Help us to praise!
Father, all glorious,
O'er all victorious,
Come and reign over us,
    Ancient of days.

mf 2 God of the right, arise!
Scatter our enemies;
    Now make them fall!
Let thine almighty aid
Our sure defense be made,
Our souls on thee be stayed;
    Lord, hear our call!

f   3 Come, thou eternal Word,
Gird on thy mighty sword;
    Our prayer attend!
Come, and thy people bless;
Come, give thy word success;
Spirit of holiness
    On us descend!

122   **Talmar. 8s & 7s.**

m   Savior, breathe an evening blessing,
    Ere repose our spirits seal;
Sin and want we come confessing;
    Thou canst save and thou canst heal.

f   2 Though destruction walk around us,
    Though the arrows past us fly,
Angel guards from thee surround us;
p   We are safe, if thou art nigh.

mp 3 Though the night be dark and dreary,
    Darkness can not hide from thee;
Thou art he who, never weary,
    Watchest where thy people be.

m   4 Should swift death this night o'ertake us,
    And command us to the tomb,
May the morn in heaven awake us,
    Clad in bright, eternal bloom.

123   **Carmarthen. H. M.**

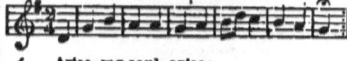

f   Arise, my soul, arise;
    Shake off thy guilty fears;
The bleeding sacrifice
    In my behalf appears;
Before the throne my surety stands,
My name is written on his hands.

f   2 He ever lives above
    For me to intercede
His all-redeeming love,
    His precious blood, to plead;
His blood atoned for all our race,
And sprinkles now the throne of grace.

p   3 Five bleeding wounds he bears,
    Received on Calvary;
They pour effectual prayers,
    They strongly plead for me:
Forgive him, O forgive, they cry,
Nor let that ransomed sinner die.

m   4 His Father hears him pray,
    His dear anointed One;
He can not turn away
    The presence of his Son;
His spirit answers to the blood,
And tells me I am born of God.

mf 5 My God is reconciled;
    His pard'ning voice I hear;
He owns me for his child;
    I can no longer fear:
With confidence I now draw nigh,
And Father, Abba, Father, cry.

124   **Frederick. 11s.**

m   I would not live alway; I ask not to stay
    Where storm after storm rises dark o'er the
      way;
The few lurid mornings that dawn on us here
Are enough for life's joys, full enough for its
    cheer.

m 2 I would not live alway; no—welcome the
      tomb!
Since Jesus hath lain there, I dread not its
    gloom;
f There sweet be my rest till he bid me arise,
To hail him in triumph descending the skies.

m 3 Who, who would live alway, away from his
      God—
mf Away from yon heaven, that blissful abode,
    Where rivers of pleasure flow bright o'er the
      plains,
And the noontide of glory eternally reigns?

m 4 There saints of all ages in harmony meet,
    Their Savior and brethren transported to
      greet;
f While anthems of rapture unceasingly roll,
    And the smile of the Lord is the feast of the
      soul.

125   Happy Zion.   8s, 7s & 4s.

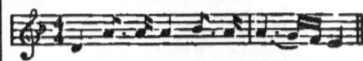

f   Zion stands with hills surrounded,
    Zion kept by power divine;
All her foes shall be confounded,
    Though the world in arms combine;
      Happy Zion!
   What a favored lot is thine!

mf 2 Every human tie may perish;
    Friend to friend unfaithful prove;
Mothers cease their own to cherish;
    Heaven and earth at last remove;
    But no change
   Can attend Jehovah's love.

mp 3 In the furnace God may prove thee,
    Thence to bring thee forth more bright,
But can never cease to love thee;
    Thou art precious in his sight;
      God is with thee—
f   God, thine everlasting light.

126   Oak.   6s & 4s.

m   I'm but a stranger here,
    Heaven is my home;
Earth is a desert drear,
    Heaven is my home.
Danger and sorrow stand
Round me on every hand;
Heaven is my fatherland,
    Heaven is my home.

m 2 What though the tempest rage,
    Heaven is my home;
Short is my pilgrimage,
    Heaven is my home.
Time's cold and wintry blast
Soon will be overpast;
I shall reach home at last,
    Heaven is my home.

mp 3 There at my Savior's side,
    Heaven is my home,
I shall be glorified,
    Heaven is my home.
f   There are the good and blest,
    Those I loved most and best,
There, too, I soon shall rest,
    Heaven is my home.

127   Weary.

m   In the Christian's home in glory,
mf   There remains a land of rest;
m   There the Savior's gone before me,
    To fulfil my soul's request.

CHORUS.

mf   There is rest for the weary,
    There is rest for the weary,
There is rest for the weary,
    There is rest for you.
On the other side of Jordan,
    In the sweet fields of Eden,
m   Where the tree of life is blooming,
    There is rest for you.

m 2 He is fitting up my mansion,
    Which eternally shall stand,
For my stay shall not be transient
    In that holy, happy land.

mp 3 Pain nor sickness ne'er shall enter,
    Grief nor woe my lot shall share;
But in that celestial center,
    I a crown of life shall wear.

m 4 Death itself shall then be vanquished,
    And his sting shall be withdrawn;
f   Shout for gladness, O, ye ransomed,
    Hail with joy the rising morn.

f 5 Sing, O, sing, ye heirs of glory;
    Shout your triumph as you go;
Zion's gate will open for you,
    You shall find an entrance through.

128   Flee, as a Bird.

  Flee, as a bird, to your mountain,
    Thou who art weary of sin;
Go to the clear flowing fountain
    Where you may wash and be clean;
Fly, for th' avenger is near thee;
Call, and the Savior will bear thee,
He on his bosom will bear thee,
    Thou who art weary of sin,
    O, thou, who art weary of sin.

2 He will protect thee forever,
    Wipe every falling tear;
He will forsake thee, O never,
    Sheltered so tenderly there.
Haste, then, the hours are flying,
Spend not the moments in sighing,
Cease from your sorrow and crying,
    The Savior will wipe every tear.
    The Savior will wipe every tear.

129   Kentucky.   S. M.

p   The Spirit, in our hearts,
    Is whispering, "Sinner, come;"
The bride, the Church of Christ, proclaims
    To all His children, "Come!"

mf 2 Let him that heareth, say
    To all about him, "Come;"
Let him that thirsts for righteousness,
    To Christ, the Fountain, come!

mf 3 Yes, whosoever will,
    O, let him freely come,
And freely drink the stream of life;
    'T is Jesus bids him come.

f 4 Lo! Jesus, who invites,
    Declares, "I quickly come;"
Lord, even so; we wait thine hour:
    O blest Redeemer, come!

130   China.   C. M.

p   I saw one hanging on a tree,
    In agony and blood;
Who fixed His languid eyes on me
    As near the cross I stood.

mf 2 Sure never, till my latest breath,
    Can I forget that look;
It seemed to charge me with His death,
    Though not a word He spoke.

p 3 Alas, I knew not what I did,
    But all my tears were vain;
Where could my trembling soul be hid?
    For I the Lord had slain.

pp 4 A second look He gave, that said,
    "I freely all forgive;
This blood is for thy ransom paid—
    I die that thou may'st live."

131   America. 6s & 4s.

m   Roll on, thou joyful day,
When tyranny's proud sway,
Stern as the grave,
f   Shall to the ground be buried,
And freedom's flag, unfurled,
Shall wave throughout the world
O'er every slave.

f   2 Trump of glad jubilee,
Echo o'er land and sea,
Freedom for all;
Let the glad tidings fly,
And every tribe reply,
f   Glory to God on high,
At slavery's fall.

f   3 Free, too, the captive mind,
By darkness long confined
In slavery's night;
The Savior's reign extend,
Virtue with freedom blend,
And full salvation send
With freedom's light.

132   He leadeth Me.

m   He leadeth me! O, blessed thought!
O! words with heavenly comfort fraught;
Whate'er I do, where'er I be,
Still 't is God's hand that leadeth me!

REFRAIN.

He leadeth me! he leadeth me!
By his own hand he leadeth me;
His faithful follower I would be,
For by his hand he leadeth me!

mp 2 Sometimes 'mid scenes of deepest gloom,
Sometimes where Eden's bowers bloom,
By waters still, o'er troubled sea—
Still 't is his hand that leadeth me!

m 3 Lord, I would clasp thy hand in mine,
Nor ever murmur nor repine—
Content, whatever lot I see,
Since 't is my God that leadeth me!

mf 4 And when my task on earth is done,
When, by thy grace, the victory's won;
E'er death's cold wave I will not flee,
Since God through Jordan leadeth me.

133   Balerma. C. M.

p   I heard the voice of Jesus say,
"Behold, I freely give
The living water! thirsty one,
Stoop down and drink and live."

m 2 I came to Jesus, and I drank
Of that life-giving stream;
My thirst was quenched, my soul revived
And now I live in him.

p 3 I heard the voice of Jesus say,
"I am this dark world's light:
f   Look unto me; thy morn shall rise,
And all thy day be bright."

mf 4 I looked to Jesus, and I found
In him my Star, my Sun;
And in that light of life I 'll walk
Till all my journey 's done.

134   Kindness. L. M.

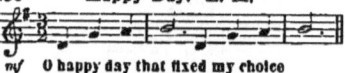

f   Awake, my soul, in joyful lays,
And sing thy great Redeemer's praise;
He justly claims a song from me,
His loving kindness, O, how free!
His loving kindness, loving kindness,
His loving kindness, O, how free!

mp 2 He saw me ruined by the fall,
Yet loved me, notwithstanding all;
He saved me from my lost estate,
His loving kindness, O, how great!

mf 3 Though numerous hosts of mighty foes,
Though earth and hell my way oppose,
He safely leads my soul along,
His loving kindness, O, how strong!

m 4 I often feel my sinful heart
Prone from my Savior to depart;
But though I oft have him forgot,
His loving kindness changes not.

f 5 Soon shall I pass the gloomy vale;
Soon all my mortal powers must fail;
O, may my last expiring breath
His loving kindness sing in death.

135   Happy Day. L. M.

mf   O happy day that fixed my choice
On thee, my Savior and my God!
Well may this glowing heart rejoice,
And tell its raptures all abroad.
f   Happy day, happy day,
When Jesus washed my sins away;
He taught me how to watch and pray,
And live rejoicing every day.
Happy day, happy day,
When Jesus washed my sins away.

m 2 O happy bond, that seals my vows
To Him, who merits all my love;
Let cheerful anthems fill his house,
While to that sacred shrine I move.

m 3 'T is done, the great transaction 's done,
I am my Lord's, and he is mine;
He drew me, and I followed on,
Charmed to confess the voice divine.

mp 4 Now rest, my long-divided heart;
Fixed on this blissful center, rest;
Nor ever from thy Lord depart:
With him of every good possessed.

136   Arlington. C. M.

mf   This precious truth his word declares,
And all his mercies prove;
While Christ, th' atoning Lamb, appears
To show that—God is love.

m 2 Behold, his loving kindness waits
For those who from him rove,
And calls for mercy reach their hearts,
To teach them—God is love.

mf 3 The work begun is carried on
By power from heaven above;
And every step, from first to last,
Proclaims that—God is love.

m 4 O! may we all, while here below,
This best of blessings prove;
Till warmer hearts, in brighter worlds,
f   Shall shout that—God is love.

137   Shining Shore.

m   **My days are gliding swiftly by,**
And I, a pilgrim stranger,
Would not detain them as they fly,
Those hours of toil and danger.

CHORUS.

f   For now we stand on Jordan's strand,
Our friends are passing over;
And just before the shining shore
We may almost discover.

m f 2   We'll gird our loins, my brethren dear,
Our heavenly home discerning;
Our absent Lord has left us word,
Let every lamp be burning.

m p 3   Should coming days be cold and dark,
We need not cease our singing;
That perfect rest naught can molest
Where golden harps are ringing.

m f 4   Let sorrows rudest tempest blow,
Each chord on earth to sever,
Our King says come, and there's our home,
Forever! O, forever!

138   Sweet Rest.

m f   **Come, brethren, don't grow weary,**
But let us journey on;
The moments will not tarry,
This life will soon be gone.
The passing scenes all tell us
That death will surely come;
These bodies soon will molder
In th' dark and weary tomb.

CHORUS.

m f   There is sweet rest in heaven,
There is sweet rest in heaven;
There is sweet rest, there is sweet rest,
There is sweet rest in heaven.

m p 2   Loved ones have gone before us,
They beckon us away,
O'er aerial plains they're soaring,
Blest in eternal day;
But we are in the army,
And dare not leave our post,
f   We'll fight until we conquer
The foe's most mighty host.

m 3   Our Captain's gone before us,
He kindly calls us home
To yonder world of glory,
And sweetly bids us come.
f   The world, the flesh, and Satan,
Will strive to hedge our way,
But we'll o'ercome these powers,
If we hourly watch and pray.

139   Azmon. C. M.

f   **Hark, how the angels sweetly sing!**
Their voices fill the sky;
They hail their great, victorious King,
And welcome him on high.

f 2   We'll catch the note of lofty praise:
Their joys, O, may we feel;
Our thankful song with them we'll raise,
And emulate their zeal.

m f 3   Come then, ye saints, and grateful sing
Of Christ, our risen Lord;
Of Christ, the everlasting King;
Of Christ, th' incarnate Word.

f 4   Hail, mighty Savior! thee we hail,
High on thy throne above;
Till heart and flesh together fail,
We'll sing thy matchless love.

140   Fountain. C. M.

m f   **I've found the Pearl of greatest price;**
My heart doth sing for joy;
And sing I must, for Christ is mine—
Christ shall my song employ.

m 2   Christ is my Prophet, Priest, and King;
My Prophet full of light;
My great High Priest before the throne;
My King of heavenly might.

m p 3   For he, indeed, is Lord of lords,
And he the King of kings;
He is the Sun of Righteousness,
With healing in his wings.

m 4   Christ is my Peace; he died for me
For me he gave his blood;
And, as my wondrous sacrifice,
Offered himself to God.

141   Windham. L. M.

m   **Broad is the road that leads to death,**
And thousands walk together there;
But wisdom shows a narrow path,
With here and there a traveler.

m 2   "Deny thyself, and take thy cross,"
Is the Redeemer's great command;
Nature must count her gold but dross,
If she would gain this heavenly land.

p 3   The fearful soul that tires and faints,
And walks the ways of God no more,
Is but esteemed almost a saint,
And makes his own destruction sure.

m f 4   Lord! let not all my hopes be vain;
Create my heart entirely new;
Which hypocrites could ne'er attain,
Which false apostates never knew.

142   St. Martyn's. C. M.

m f   **I know that my Redeemer lives;**
He lives who once was dead;
To me in grief he comfort gives;
With peace he crowns my head.

m 2   He lives triumphant o'er the grave,
At God's right hand on high,
My ransomed soul to keep and save,
To bless and glorify.

m 3   He lives to fill my breast with love,
With joy my heart to feed;
He lives to plead for me above,
To succor me in need.

m f 4   He lives that I may also live,
And now his grace proclaim;
He lives that I may honor give
To his most holy name.

143   Granville.   8s & 7s. Double.

m   In the cross of Christ I glory,
Towering o'er the wrecks of time;
All the lights of sacred story
Gathers round its head sublime.

mp 2 When the woes of life o'ertake me,
Hopes deceive, and fears annoy,
Never shall the cross forsake me:
Lo! it glows with peace and joy.

m 3 When the sun of bliss is beaming
Light and love upon my way,
From the cross, the radiance streaming,
Adds new luster to the day.

mf 4 Bane and blessing, pain and pleasure,
By the cross are sanctified;
Peace is there, that knows no measure,
Joys that through all time abide.

144   Happy Band.

mf   O, we're a band of brethren dear,
Who will join this happy band?
Who live as pilgrim strangers here,
Who will join this happy band?

CHORUS.

f   Hallelujah, hallelujah,
We will join this happy band;
Singing hallelujah, hallelujah,
We will join this happy band.

mf 2 The prophets and apostles, too,
Once belonged to this happy band,
And all God's children here below,
All have joined this happy band.

mf 3 Let no contention e'er divide
Members of this happy band;
But firm, united, side by side,
Through this life together stand.

mp 4 And when death comes, as come it must,
To divide this happy band,
The links will not return to dust,
f   They will shine at God's right hand.

145   Jesus Loves Me.

m   Jesus loves me! this I know,
For the Bible tells me so;
Little ones to him belong;
They are weak, but he is strong.

CHORUS.

f   Yes, Jesus loves me!
f   Yes, Jesus loves me!
Yes, Jesus loves me,
The Bible tells me so.

m 2 Jesus loves me! he who died,
Heaven's gate to open wide;
He will wash away my sin,
Let his little child come in.

m 3 Jesus loves me! loves me still,
Though I'm very weak and ill;
From his shining throne on high,
Comes to watch me where I lie.

m 4 Jesus loves me! he will stay
Close beside me all the way;
If I love him when I die,
He will take me home on high.

146   Peterboro.   C. M.

m   Holy and reverend is the name
Of our eternal King;
Thrice holy, Lord! the angels cry;
Thrice holy! let us sing.

mf 2 Holy is he in all his ways,
And truth is his delight;
But sinners and their wicked ways
Shall perish from his sight.

mp 3 The deepest reverence of the mind,
Pay, O my soul, to God!
Lift with thy hands, a holy heart
To his sublime abode.

m 4 With sacred awe pronounce his name,
Abhor the lips profane;
Let not thy tongue the Lord blaspheme,
Nor take his name in vain.

147   Bright Mansions.

mf   "I feel like singing all the time,"
My heart with joy is ringing;
Since Jesus hath my sins forgiven,
I'm happiest when I'm singing.

REFRAIN.

f   O happy they who reach that place
Where sorrow cometh never;
p   Who rest within his loving arms
Forever and forever.

mf 2 Since I have found a Savior's love,
To him my hopes are clinging;
I feel so happy all the time,
My heart is always singing.

f 3 A light I never knew before,
Around my path is breaking,
And cheerful songs of grateful praise,
My raptured soul is waking.

148   Even Me.

af   Lord, I hear of showers of blessings
Thou art scattering full and free;
Showers the thirsty land refreshing,
Let some droppings fall on me.
Even me, even me,
Let some droppings fall on me.

m 2 Pass me not, O God, my Father,
Sinful though my heart may be;
Thou might'st leave me, but the rather
Let thy mercy light on me.
Even me, even me,
Let thy mercy light on me.

m 3 Pass me not, O, gracious Savior,
Let me live and cling to thee;
Fain I'm longing for thy favor!
Whilst thou rt calling, call for me.
Even me, even me,
Whilst thou 'rt calling, call for me.

mf 4 Pass me not, thy lost one bringing;
Bind my heart, O Lord, to thee!
Whilst the streams of life are springing,
Blessing others, O, bless me!
Even me, even me,
Blessing others, O, bless me!

149   Boylston. S. M.

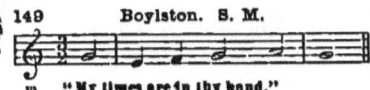

m   "My times are in thy hand,"
My God, I wish them there;
My life, my friends, my soul I leave
Entirely to thy care.

m 2 "My times are in thy hand,"
Whatever they may be:
Pleasing or painful, dark or bright,
As best may seem to thee.

m 3 "My times are in thy hand,"
Why should I doubt or fear?
My Father's hand will never cause
His child a needless tear.

m 4 "My times are in thy hand,"
I'll always trust in thee;
And after death, at thy right hand
f   I shall forever be.

150   Jesus Loves Me.

mf   Jesus, Savior, pity me,
Hear me when I cry to thee;
I've a very wicked heart,
Full of sin in every part.

CHORUS.

f   Dear Jesus, hear me;
Dear Jesus, hear me;
Dear Jesus, hear me,
O, listen to my prayer.

f 2 I can never make it good,
Wilt thou wash me in thy blood?
p   Jesus, Savior, pity me,
Hear me when I pray to thee.

m 3 When I try to do thy will,
Sin is in my bosom still,
And I soon do something bad;
Then my heart is dark and sad.

mf 4 Now I come to thee for aid,
All my hope on thee is stayed;
Thou hast bled and died for me,
I will give myself to thee.

151   Sabbath Song.

lar   Strains of music often greet me,
As I join the busy throng;
But there's nothing half so pleasant
As the holy Sabbath song.

CHORUS.

mf   No fear of ill, no fear of wrong,
While I can sing my Sabbath song;
My Sabbath song, my Sabbath song,
I love to sing my Sabbath song.

lar 2 'Tis a song of love and mercy,
Speaking peace to all mankind;
Telling sinners, poor and needy,
Where the Savior they may find.

mf 3 Angels sweetly sing in glory
Songs of praise to God, their King;
But the song of blest redemption
Man, redeemed, alone can sing.

mp 4 While I live, O, may I ever
Love the holy Sabbath song;
And when death shall call me homeward,
Join it with the blood-bought throng.

152   Royal Proclamation.

mf   Hear the royal proclamation,
The glad tidings of salvation,
Publishing to every creature,
To the ruined sons of nature:

CHORUS.

f   Jesus reigns, Jesus reigns, Jesus reigns;
Jesus reigns, he reigns victorious,
Over heaven and earth most glorious.
Jesus reigns, Jesus reigns, Jesus reigns,

mf 2 See the royal banner flying,
Hear the heralds loudly crying,
"Rebel sinners, royal favor
Now is offered by the Savior."

mp 3 "Here is wine and milk and honey;
Come, and purchase without money;
Mercy flowing from a fountain,
Streaming from the holy mountain."

f 4 Shout, ye tongues of every nation,
To the bounds of the creation;
f   Shout the praise of Judah's Lion,
The Almighty Prince of Zion.

f 5 Shout, ye saints, make joyful mention,
Christ hath purchased our redemption;
Angels, shout the pleasing story,
Through the brighter worlds of glory.

153   Downs. C. M.

m   How shall the young secure their hearts,
And guard their lives from sin?
Thy Word the choicest rules imparts,
To keep the conscience clean.

mp 2 'Tis, like the sun, a heavenly light,
That guides us all the day;
And, through the danger of the night,
A lamp to lead our way.

m 3 Thy precepts make me truly wise;
I hate the sinner's road;
I hate my own vain thoughts that rise,
But love thy law, my God.

mf 4 Thy Word is everlasting truth,
How pure is every page!
Thy holy book shall guide our youth,
And well support our age.

154   Olmuts. S. M.

mp   How gentle God's commands!
How kind his precepts are!
Come, cast your burdens on the Lord,
And trust his constant care.

m 2 His bounty will provide,
His saints securely dwell;
That hand which bears creation up,
Shall guard his children well.

m 3 Why should this anxious load
Press down your weary mind?
O, seek your heavenly Father's throne,
And peace and comfort find.

mf 4 His goodness stands approved,
Unchanged from day to day;
I'll drop my burden at his feet,
And bear a song away.

155   Dare to do Right.

mf   **Dare to do right! dare to be true!**
You have a work that no other can do;
Do it so bravely, so kindly, so well,
Angels will hasten the story to tell.

CHORUS.

f   Dare, dare, dare to do right!
Dare, dare, dare to be true!
Dare to be true! dare to be true!

mf 2 Dare to do right! dare to be true!
Other men's failures can never save you;
Stand by your conscience, your honor, your faith;
Stand like a hero, and battle till death.

mf 3 Dare to do right! dare to be true!
God, who created you, cares for you too;
Treasures the tears that his striving ones shed,
Counts and protects every hair of your head.

mf 4 Dare to do right! dare to be true!
Keep the great judgment-seat always in view;
Look at your works as you 'll look at it then—
Scanned by Jehovah and angels and men.

mf 5 Dare to do right! dare to be true!
Jesus, your Savior, will carry you through;
City and mansion and throne all in sight,
f   Can you not dare to be true and do right?

---

156   Precious Name.

mf   **There is no name so sweet on earth,**
No name so sweet in heaven,
The name, before his wondrous birth,
To Christ, the Savior given.

REFRAIN.

f   We love to sing around our King,
And hail him blessed Jesus:
For there 's no word ear ever heard,
So dear, so sweet as Jesus.

mp 2 His human name they did proclaim,
When Abram's son they sealed him,
The name that still, by God's good will,
Deliverer revealed him.

mp 3 And when he hung upon the tree,
They wrote this name above him,
That all might see the reason we
For evermore must love him.

mf 4 So now upon his Father's throne,
Almighty to release us
From sin and pains, he gladly reigns,
The Prince and Savior Jesus.

---

157   Jesus Loves Me.

m   **Jesus from his throne on high**
Came into this world to die—
That I might from sin be free,
p   Bled and died upon the tree.

CHORUS.

f   Yes, Jesus loves me;
f   Yes, Jesus loves me;
ff   Yes, Jesus loves me,
The Bible tells me so.

mf 2 I can see him even now,
With his pierced, thorn-clad brow,
Agonizing on the tree;
O, what love! and all for me!

m 3 Now I feel this heart of stone
Drawn to love God's holy Son,
p   "Lifted up" on Calvary,
Suffering shame and death for me.

aff 4 Jesus, take this heart of mine,
Make it pure and wholly thine;
Thou hast bled and died for me,
I will henceforth live for thee.

---

158   The Gospel Ship.

m   **The Gospel Ship is sailing,**
Sailing, sailing;
The Gospel Ship is sailing,
mf   Bound for Canaan's happy shore.
All who would ship for glory,
Glory, glory;
All who would ship for glory,
Come and welcome, rich and poor.

CHORUS.

f   Glory, hallelujah!
All on board are sweetly singing;
ff   Glory, hallelujah!
Hallelujah to the Lamb!

mf 2 She has landed many thousands,
Thousands, thousands;
She has landed many thousands
mp   On fair Canaan's happy shore.
And thousands now are sailing,
Sailing, sailing;
And thousands now are sailing,
Yet there 's room for thousands more.

mf 3 Sails filled with heavenly breezes,
Breezes, breezes;
Sails filled with heavenly breezes,
Swiftly glides the ship along.
Her company are singing,
Singing, singing;
mf   Her company are singing,
Glory, glory is their song.

m 4 Take passage now for glory,
Glory, glory;
Take passage now for glory,
Sailing o'er life's troubled sea.
With us you shall be happy,
Happy, happy;
mf   With us you shall be happy,
Happy through eternity.

---

159   Rest. L. M.

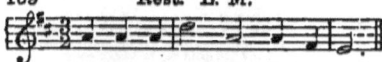

p   **Asleep in Jesus! blessed sleep!**
From which none ever wakes to weep;
A calm and undisturbed repose,
Unbroken by the last of foes.

mp 2 Asleep in Jesus! O how sweet
To be for such a slumber meet!
With holy confidence to sing
That death hath lost its venomed sting.

p 3 Asleep in Jesus! peaceful rest!
Whose waking is supremely blest;
No fear, no woe, shall dim that hour,
mf   Which manifests the Savior's power.

p 4 Asleep in Jesus! O, for me
May such a blissful refuge be!
Securely shall my ashes lie,
f   And wait the summons from on high.

160   Sabbath Call.

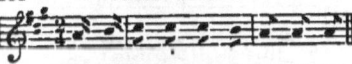

m   **Hark! the morning bells are ringing!**
     Children, haste without delay;
     Prayers of thousands now are winging
     Up to heaven their silent way.

       CHORUS.

f   Come, children, come! the bells are ringing,
     To the school with haste repair;
     Let us all unite in singing,
     All unite in solemn prayer.

mf 2 'Tis an hour of happy meeting,
     Children meet for praise and prayer;
     But the hour is short and fleeting,
     Let us then be early there.

m 3 Do not keep our teachers waiting,
     While you tarry by the way;
     Nor disturb the school reciting,
     'Tis the holy Sabbath day.

mf 4 Children, haste! the bells are ringing,
     And the morning's bright and fair;
     Thousands now unite in singing,
     Thousands, too, in solemn prayer.

161   Canaan's Land.

f   **We are bound for Canaan's happy land;**
     We are bound for Canaan's happy land;
     We are bound for Canaan's happy land;
     O, will you meet us there?

       CHORUS.

ff   Singing glory, hallelujah;
     Singing glory, hallelujah;
     Singing glory, hallelujah,
     We're bound for Canaan's land.

m 2 Say, comrades, will you go with us;
     Say, comrades, will you go with us;
     Say, comrades, will you go with us
     To Canaan's happy land?

mf 3 To our Sunday-school we'll all repair;
     To our Sunday-school we'll all repair,
     And we'll sing with one accord while there
     Of Canaan's happy land.

m 4 Our Savior he will lead us on;
     Our Savior he will lead us on;
     Our Savior he will lead us on
     To Canaan's happy land.

m 5 Let us meet dear parents in that land;
     Let us meet dear teachers in that land;
     Let us meet dear schoolmates in that land,
     On Canaan's happy shore.

162   ' Never be Afraid.

m f   **Never be afraid to speak for Jesus,**
     Think how much a word can do;
     Never be afraid to own your Savior,
     He who loves and cares for you.

       CHORUS.

f,   Never be afraid, never be afraid,
ff   Never, never, never;
     Jesus is your loving Savior,
     Therefore never be afraid.

mf 2 Never be afraid to work for Jesus,
     In his vineyard day by day;
     Labor with a kind and willing spirit
     He will all your toil repay.

mf 3 Never be afraid to bear for Jesus
     Keen reproaches when they fall;
     Patiently endure your every trial,
mp   Jesus meekly bore them all.

m 4 Never be afraid to live for Jesus;
     If you on his care depend,
mp   Safely shall you pass through every trial,
     He will bring you to the end.

p 5 Never be afraid to die for Jesus;
     He the life, the truth, the way,
     Gently in his arms of love will bear you
f   To the realms of endless day.

163   Hosanna.

mf   **Glory to God in the highest!**
     Glory to God, glory to God!
     Glory to God in the highest!
     Shall be our song to-day;
p   Another year's rich mercies prove
     His ceaseless care and boundless love;
     So let our loudest voices raise
     Our anniversary song of praise.

       CHORUS.

f   Glory to God in the highest!
     Glory to God in the highest!
     Glory, glory, glory, glory,
     Glory be to God on high!

mf 2 Glory to God in the highest!
     Shall be our song to-day;
     The song that woke the glorious morn
     When David's greater son was borne,
     Sung by an heavenly host, and we
     Would join th' angelic company.

f 3 Glory to God in the highest!
     Shall be our song to-day;
     And while we with the angels sing,
     Gifts, with the wise men, let us bring
     Unto the Babe of Bethlehem,
     And offer our young hearts to him.

f 4 Glory to God in the highest!
     Shall be our song to-day;
     O, may we, an unbroken band,
     Around the throne of Jesus stand,
     And there with angels and the throng
     Of his redeemed ones, sing the song.

164   Jesus Loves Me.

p   **Jesus on the cross I saw,**
     Bleeding, dying, all for me;
     I could almost hear him say,
     All thy sins are pardoned thee.

       CHORUS.

mf   I have seen Jesus;
     I have seen Jesus;
     I have seen Jesus,
     My Savior, on the cross.

m 2 First my heart could scarce believe,
     That my sins were all forgiven,
     But assurance I've received,
     And I hope to sing in heaven.

f 3 Now my soul is full of joy,
     "I love Jesus, yes, I do;"
     Singing is my chief employ,
     "Jesus smiles, and loves me too."

165　Cry from Macedonia.

m　There's a cry from Macedonia—Come and
help us;
　The light of the Gospel bring, O come!
Let us hear the joyful tidings of salvation,
　We thirst for the living spring.
O ye heralds of the cross be up and doing,
　Remember the great command, away!
Go ye forth and preach the word to every
creature,
　Proclaim it in every land.
f　They shall gather from the East,
　They shall gather from the West,
With the patriarchs of old,
　And the ransomed shall return
To the kingdoms of the blest
　With their harps and crowns of gold.

CHORUS.

f　There's a cry from Macedonia—Come and
help us;
　The light of the Gospel bring, O come!
Let us hear the joyful tidings of salvation,
　We thirst for the living spring.

mf 2 O how beautiful their feet upon the mount-
ains,
　The tidings of peace who bring, *Who bring*
To the nations of the earth who sit in dark-
ness,
　And tell them of Zion's king;
Then ye heralds of the cross be up and doing,
　Go work in your Master's field, away!
Sound the trumpet, sound the trumpet of sal-
vation,
　The Lord is your strength and shield.
Let the distant isles be glad,
　Let them hail the Savior's birth,
And the news of pardon free,
　Till the knowledge of the truth
Shall extend to all the earth,
　As the waters o'er the sea.

m 3 Ye have listed in the army of the faithful,
　Like heroes the battle fight, away!
There are foes on every hand that will assail
you,
　Then gird on your armor bright;
With the banner of the cross unfurled before
you,
　The sword of the spirit wield, away!
Ye shall conquer through his mercy who hath
loved you,
　The Lord is your strength and shield.
f　Ye are marching to the land
　Where the saints in glory stand,
And the just for joy shall sing;
　Ye by faith may bring it nigh,
Ye shall reach it by-and-by,
　And your shouts of triumph ring.

166　Gather them in.

m　Gather them in, gather them in,
　Gather the children in;
f　Gather them in from the broad highway,
　Gather them in, gather them in;
Gather them in in this Gospel day,
　Gather, gather them in.
Gather them in from the prairies vast.
　Gather them in, gather them in;
Gather them in of every cast,
　Gather, gather them in.

CHORUS.

m　Gather them in, let the house be full,
　Gather them in to the Sunday-school;
Gather them in, gather them in,
　Gather the children in.

m 2 Gather them in, gather them in,
　Gather the children in;
f　Gather them in from the street and lane,
　Gather them in, gather them in;
Gather them in, both the halt and lame,
　Gather, gather them in.
Gather the deaf and the poor and blind,
　Gather them in, gather them in;
Gather them in with a willing mind,
　Gather, gather them in.

m 3 Gather them in, gather them in,
　Gather the children in;
Gather them in that are seeking rest,
　Gather them in, gather them in;
Gather them in from the East and West,
　Gather, gather them in.
mf　Gather them in that are roaming about,
　Gather them in, gather them in;
Gather them in from the North and South,
　Gather, gather them in.

m 4 Gather them in, gather them in,
　Gather the children in;
Gather them in from all over the land,
　Gather them in, gather them in;
mf　Gather them in to our noble band,
　Gather, gather them in.
Gather them in with a Christian love,
　Gather them in, gather them in;
f　Gather them in for the Church above,
　Gather, gather them in.

167　Mear.　C. M.

mf　God moves in a mysterious way,
　His wonders to perform;
He plants his footsteps in the sea,
　And rides upon the storm.

m 2 Deep in unfathomable mines
　Of never-failing skill,
He treasures up his bright designs,
　And works his sovereign will.

mf 3 Ye fearful saints, fresh courage take:
　The clouds ye so much dread
Are big with mercy, and shall break
　In blessings on your head.

m 4 Judge not the Lord by feeble sense,
　But trust him for his grace;
Behind a frowning providence,
　He hides a smiling face.

168　Missionary Hymn.

f　From northern skies where quiver,
　Our lakes of silver light,
To many a southern river,
　Where blooms the orange bright;
From eastern shores to ocean,
　Where flames the setting sun,
ff　We've no divided portion,
　God made our country one.

f　Linked by our lofty mountains,
　Where golden treasures lie;
By noble streams, whose fountains
　Gush 'neath the northern sky;
No freer, prouder nation,
　The sun e'er shone upon,
ff　Talk not of separation,
　God made our country one.

f　One eagle o'er us towers
　Amid the stars of light;
One holy Bible ours,
　Our union is our might;
One kindred, and one destiny,
　Our brilliant race begun,
ff　Land of the fair, the brave, the free,
　Our country must be one.

169. No Tears in Heaven.

ad l. 1 I met a child, his feet were bare,
His weak frame shivered with the cold;
His youthful brow was knit with care,
His dashing eye his sorrow told.
Said I, "Poor boy, why weepest thou?"
"My parents both are dead," he said;
"I have not where to lay my head;
O, I am lone and friendless now!"
Not friendless, child; a Friend on high
For you his precious blood has given;
Cheer up, and bid each tear be dry,
"There are no tears, no tears in heaven."

2 I saw a man in life's gay noon,
Stand weeping o'er his young bride's bier;
"And must we part," he cried, "so soon!"
As down his cheek there rolled a tear.
"Heart-stricken one," said I, "weep not!"
"Weep not!" in accent wild, he cried;
"But yesterday my loved one died,
And shall she be so soon forgot?
Forgotten? No! I still let her love
Sustain thy heart, with anguish riven;
Strive thou to meet thy bride above,
And dry your tears, your tears in heaven."

3 I saw a gentle mother weep,
As to her throbbing heart she pressed
An infant, seemingly asleep
On its kind mother's sheltering breast.
"Fair one," said I, "pray weep no more."
Sobbed she, "The idol of my hope
I now am called to render up,
My babe has reached death's gloomy shore."
Young mother, yield no more to grief,
Nor be by passion's tempest driven,
But find in these sweet words relief,
"There are no tears, no tears in heaven."

4 Poor traveler o'er life's troubled wave,
Cast down by grief, o'erwhelmed by care,
There is an arm above can save,
Then yield not thou to fell despair.
Look upward, mourners, look above!
What though the thunders echo loud,
The sun shines bright beyond the cloud;
Then trust to thy Redeemer's love,
Where'er thy lot in life be cast,
Whate'er of toil or woe be given;
Be firm—remember to the last,
"There are no tears, no tears in heaven."

170. Happy New Year.

f Come, children, and join in our festival
song,
The New Year has come, and the old year has
gone;
We'll join our glad voices in one hymn of
praise,
To God, who has kept us and lengthened our
days.

CHORUS.

f Happy New Year to all! happy New Year to
all!
Happy New Year, happy New Year, happy New
Year to all!

f 2 Our Father in heaven, we lift up to thee
Our voice of thanksgiving, our glad jubilee;
O, bless us, and guide us, dear Savior, we pray,
That from thy blest precepts we never may
stray.

f 3 And if, ere this New Year has drawn to a
close,
Some loved one among us in death shall repose,
Grant, Lord, that the spirit in heaven may
dwell,
In the bosom of Jesus, where all shall be well.

171. Arlington. C. M.

p When languor and disease invade
This trembling house of clay,
'T is sweet to look beyond my pains,
And long to fly away;—

p 2 Sweet to look inward, and attend
The whispers of his love;
Sweet to look upward to the place
Where Jesus pleads above;—

m 3 Sweet to look back, and see my name
In life's fair book set down;
Sweet to look forward, and behold
Eternal joys my own;—

m 4 Sweet to reflect how grace divine
My sins on Jesus laid;
Sweet to remember that his blood
My debt of suffering paid;—

m 5 Sweet to rejoice in lively hope,
That, when my change shall come,
Angels shall hover round my bed,
And waft my spirit home.

mp 6 If such the sweetness of the stream,
What must the fountain be,
Where saints and angels draw their bliss
Directly, Lord, from thee.

172. Atonement. C. M.

m There is a fountain filled with blood,
Drawn from Immanuel's veins;
And sinners, plunged beneath that flood,
Lose all their guilty stains.

mp 2 The dying thief rejoiced to see
That fountain in his day;
And there may I, though vile as he,
Wash all my sins away.

p 3 Thou dying Lamb! thy precious blood
Shall never lose its power,
Till all the ransomed Church of God
Are saved, to sin no more.

mf 4 Then in a nobler, sweeter song,
I'll sing thy power to save,
When this poor lisping, stammering tongue
Lies silent in the grave.

173. St. Thomas. S. M.

mf And are we yet alive,
And see each other's face?
Glory and praise to Jesus give,
For his redeeming grace.

m 2 Preserved by power divine
To full salvation here,
Again in Jesus' praise we join,
And in his sight appear.

m 3 What troubles have we seen!
What conflicts have we past!
Fightings without, and fears within,
Since we assembled last!

mf 4 But out of all the Lord
Hath brought us by his love;
And still he doth his help afford,
And hides our life above.

mf 5 Then let us make our boast
Of his redeeming power,
Which saves us to the uttermost,
Till we can sin no more.

174   Brother, thou art gone to rest.

mf **Brother, thou art gone to rest,**
    We will not weep for thee;
    For thou art now where oft on earth
    Thy spirit longed to be.

m 2 Brother, thou art gone to rest;
    Thine is an earthly tomb;
    But Jesus summoned thee away,
    Thy Savior called thee home.

m 3 Brother, thou art gone to rest;
    Thy toils and cares are o'er;
    And sorrow, pain, and suff'ring, now,
    Shall ne'er distress thee more.

m 4 Brother, thou art gone to rest;
    Thy sins are all forgiven;
    And saints in light have welcomed thee,
    To share the joys of heaven.

m 5 Brother, thou art gone to rest;
    And this shall be our prayer,
    That, when we reach our journey's end,
    Thy glory we shall share.

175   Missionary Song.

p **If you can not be the watchman,**
    Standing high on Zion's wall,
    Pointing out the path to heaven,
    Offering life and peace to all;
pp With your prayers and with your bounties,
    You can do what heaven demands,
    You can be like faithful Aaron,
    Holding up the prophet's hands.

p 2 If for you the lines have fallen
    In this land of Gospel light,
    Can ye cast no ray of gladness
    Through the heathen's cheerless night?
pp Cast thy bread upon the waters,
    For the pledge of God is given,
    Thou shalt find it, surely find it,
    'Mid the shining hosts of heaven.

176   The Three Last Calls.

THIRD HOUR.

O slumberer, rouse thee! despise not the truth,
But give thy Creator the days of thy youth;
Why standeth there idle? the day breaketh, see!
The Lord of the vineyard is waiting for thee.

    Holy Spirit, by thy power,
    Grant me yet another hour;

Earthly pleasures I would prove,
Earthly joy and earthly love;
Scarcely yet has dawned the day,
Holy Spirit, wait I pray.

SIXTH AND NINTH HOURS.

O, loiterer, speed thee, the morn wears apace,
Then squander no longer the moments of grace;
But haste while there's time, to thy Master agree,
The Lord of the vineyard stands waiting for thee.

    Gentle Spirit, stay, O, stay!
    Brightly beams the early day;
    Let me linger in these bowers,
    God shall have my noontide hours;
    Chide me not for my delay,
    Gentle Spirit, wait I pray.

ELEVENTH HOUR.

O, sinner, arouse thee, thy morning is past,
Already the shadows are lengthening fast;
Escape for thy life, from the dark mountains flee,
The Lord of the vineyard yet waiteth for thee.

    Spirit, cease thy mournful lay,
    Leave me to myself, I pray;
    Earth hath flung her spell around me,
    Pleasure's silken chain hath bound me;
    When the sun his path hath trod,
    Spirit, then I'll turn to God.

[Interlude, imitating the tolling bell.]

Hark! borne on the wind is the bell's solemn toll,
'T is mournfully pealing the knell of a soul;
The Spirit's sweet pleadings and striving's are o'er,
The Lord of the vineyard stands waiting no more.

177   Temperance Mission.

Leagued with all the powers of darkness,
    Foe to every friend of truth;
    In our midst, behold the tempter
    Dealing poison to our youth.
    See him press with gentle whisper,
    To their lips the fatal bowl;
    While its maddening drops bewilder
    Every feeling of the soul.

2 Step by step he leads his victim
    To the verge of dread despair;
    Hurls him o'er the brink of ruin,
    Laughs and leaves him hopeless there.
    Widowed hearts and homes deserted,
    Helpless children orphans made;
    What a picture! God of mercy!
    Let this cruel tide be stayed.

3 Friends of temperance, Christian workers,
    Let your glorious standard wave;
    Up and arm yourselves for conflict,
    Fired with zeal and courage brave,
    Touch not, taste not, be your motto,
    And your watchword in the fight;
    God will give you strength to conquer,
    He'll protect you in the right.

Thanksgiving Chant.

"The Lord is good to all, and his tender mercies are over all his works."

178

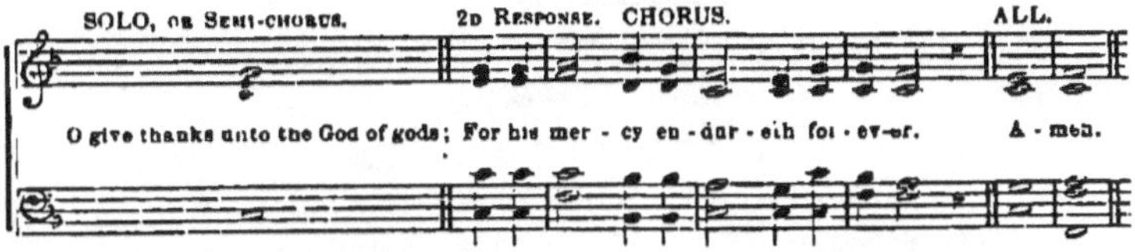

SOLO, or Semi-chorus.　　1st Response. CHORUS.

O give thanks unto the Lord, for he is good; For his mer - cy en - dur - eth for - ev - er.

SOLO, or Semi-chorus.　　2d Response. CHORUS.　　ALL.

O give thanks unto the God of gods; For his mer - cy en - dur - eth for - ev - er.　A - men.

GIVE thanks unto the Lord, for he is good;　　　1 *Cho.* For his mercy endureth forever.
O give thanks unto the God of gods;　　　　　2 *Cho.* For his mercy endureth forever.
2 O give thanks unto the Lord of lords;　　　　1 *Cho.* For his mercy endureth forever.
　To him who alone doeth great wonders;　　　　2 *Cho.* For his mercy endureth forever.
3 To him that by wisdom made the heavens;　　　1 *Cho.* For his mercy endureth forever.
　To him that stretched out the earth above the waters;　2 *Cho.* For his mercy endureth forever.
4 To him that made great lights;　　　　　　1 *Cho.* For his mercy endureth forever.
　The sun to rule by day; the moon and stars to rule by night; 2 *Cho.* For his mercy endureth forever.
5 Who remembered us in our low estate;　　　　1 *Cho.* For his mercy endureth forever.
　And hath redeemed us from our enemies;　　　2 *Cho.* For his mercy endureth forever.
6 Who giveth food to all flesh;　　　　　　1 *Cho.* For his mercy endureth forever.
　O give thanks unto the God of heaven;　　　　2 *Cho.* For his mercy endureth forever.
　　　　　　　　　　　　　　　　　　　　　　　Amen.

NOTE.—The Solo, or Semi-chorus should be sung by the Teachers, or Chorister.

Our Father, Who art in Heaven.

"After this manner, therefore, pray ye."

179

1. Our Father, who art in } Thy kingdom come; thy }
　heaven, hallowed } be thy | name; will be done on } earth, as it | is in | heaven.

2. Give us this day our | daily | bread; And forgive us our tres- } them that | trespass a- | gainst us.
　　　　　　　　　　　　passed, as we forgive }

3. And lead us not into temp- } For thine is the kingdom, }
　tation, but deliver } us from | evil; and the power, and the } glory, for | ever and | ever.
　　　　　　　　　　　　　　　　　　　　　　　　　　　　Amen.

Tis not for Man to Trifle.

"Ponder the path of thy feet, and let all thy ways be established."

180

Tis not for man to trifle! Life is brief and | sin is | here.
Our age is but the falling of a leaf—A | dropping | tear.
We have no time to sport a- | way the | hours,
All must be earnest in a world like ours.

2 Not many lives, but only one have we, one, | only | one!
How sacred should that one life ever be—That | narrow | span!
Day after day filled up with | blessed | toil,
Hour after hour still bringing in new spoil.

3 Our being is no shadow of thin air, no | vacant | dream,
No fable of the things that never were, but | only | seem.
'Tis full of meaning as of | myste- | ry,
Though strange and solemn may that meaning be.

4 Our sorrows are no phantom of the night, no | idle | tale;
No cloud that flits along the sky of light on | summer | gale.
They are the true reali- | ties of | earth,
Friends and companions even from our birth.

5 O life below! how brief, and poor, and sad! One | heavy | sigh.
O life above! how long, how fair and glad! One | endless | joy.
O! to be done with daily | dying | here!
O! to begin the living in yon sphere!

6 O day of time, how dark! O sky and earth, how | dull your | hue!
O day of Christ, how bright! O sky and earth, made | fair and | new!
Come, better Eden, with thy | fresher | green;
Come, brighter Salem, gladden all the scene.

Wilt Thou not Visit Me?

"Our soul waiteth for the Lord. He is our help and our shield."

181

from "Hallowed Songs."

Wilt thou not visit me?

Wilt thou not visit me?
The plant beside me feels thy | gentle | dew;
Each blade of grass I see,
From thy deep earth its quickening | moist- | ure | drew.
Wilt thou not visit me?

Wilt thou not visit me?
Thy morning calls on me with | cheering | tone;
And every hill and tree
Lend brr one voice, the voice of | thee a- | lone.
Wilt thou not visit me?

Wilt thou not visit me? I need thy love,
More than the flower, the dew, or | grass, the | rain,
Come, like thy holy dove,
And let me in thy sight rejoice to | live a- | gain.
Wilt thou not visit me?

Yes! thou wilt visit me;
Nor plant, nor tree, thine eye de- | lights so | well,
As when from sin set free, [dwell.
Man's spirit comes with thine in | peace to |
Yes, thou wilt visit me.

Singing for Jesus.

"And he ministered with singing."

182

Moderato.

1. Sing-ing for Je - sus, sing-ing for Je - sus, Try-ing to serve him wher-ev-er I go; Point-ing the lost to the way of sal - va - tion— This be my mis - sion, a pil - grim be - low. When in the strains of my coun-try I mingle, When to ex-alt her my voice I would raise; 'Tis for *his* glo - ry whose arm is her ref - uge, Him would I hon - or, his name would I praise, his name would I praise.

Rit.

His.

SINGING for Jesus glad hymns of devotion,
Lifting the soul on her pinions of love;
Dropping a word or a thought by the wayside,
Telling of rest in the mansions above.
Music may soften where language would fail us,
Feelings long buried 't will often restore,
Tones that were breathed from the lips of departed,
How we revere them when they are no more!

SINGING for Jesus, my blessed Redeemer,
God of the pilgrims, for thee I will sing;
When o'er the billows of time I am wafted,
Still with thy praise shall eternity ring.
Glory to God for the prospect before me,
Soon shall my spirit transported ascend;
Singing for Jesus, O blissful employment,
Loud hallelujahs that never will end.

"Inasmuch as ye have done it unto one of the least of these, my brethren, ye have done it unto me."

183   C. M.

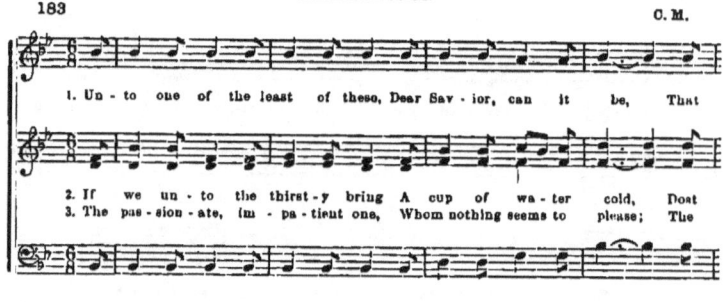

1. Un - to one of the least of these, Dear Sav - ior, can it be, That

2. If we un - to the thirst - y bring A cup of wa - ter cold, Dost
3. The pas - sion - ate, im - pa - tient one, Whom nothing seems to please; The

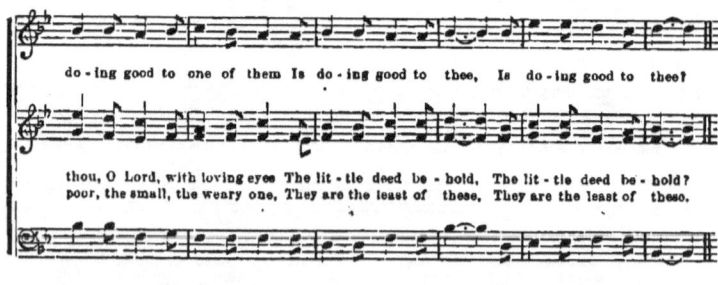

do - ing good to one of them Is do - ing good to thee, Is do - ing good to thee?

thou, O Lord, with loving eyes The lit - tle deed be - hold, The lit - tle deed be - hold?
poor, the small, the weary one, They are the least of these, They are the least of these.

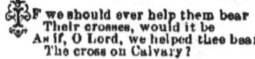F we should ever help them bear
Their crosses, would it be
As if, O Lord, we helped thee bear
The cross on Calvary?

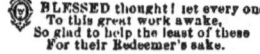BLESSED thought! let every one
To this great work awake,
So glad to help the least of these
For their Redeemer's sake.

The Little Pilgrim.

184

"Feed my lambs."

1. I'm a lit - tle pil - grim, And a stran - ger here; Though this world is
2. Mine's a bet - ter coun - try, Where there is no sin; Where the tones of
3. But a lit - tle pil - grim Must have garments clean, Ere he'd wear the

REFRAIN.

pleas - ant, Sin is al - ways near. Je - sus loves our pilgrim band; He will lead us
sor - row Nev - er en - ter In. Je - sus loves, etc.
white robe, And with Christ be seen. Je - sus loves, etc.

by the hand, Lead us to the bet - ter land, Hap - py home on high.

JESUS, hear and save me;
Teach me to obey;
Holy Spirit, guide me
In the heavenly way.

'M a little pilgrim,
And a stranger here,
But my home in heaven
Cometh ever near.

I Can, I Will, I Do Believe.

185

"Believe on the Lord Jesus Christ, and thou shalt be saved."

1. Just as I am, with - out one plea, But that thy blood was shed for me,
2. Just as I am, and wait - ing not To rid my soul of one dark blot,
3. Just as I am, though tossed about, With many a con - flict, many a doubt,
Cho.—I can, I will, I do be - lieve; I can, I will, I do be - lieve;

D. C.

And that thou bidd'st me come to thee, O, Lamb of God, I come!
To thee, whose blood can cleanse each spot, O, Lamb of God, I come!
With fears with - in, and wars with - out, O, Lamb of God, I come!
I can, I will, I do be - lieve That Je - sus died for me.

JUST as I am, poor, wretched, blind,
Sight, riches, healing of the mind,
Yea, all I need, in thee to find,
O, Lamb of God, I come!

JUST as I am, thy love unknown
Has broken every barrier down;
Now to be thine, yea, thine alone,
O, Lamb of God, I come!

Shall we Gather at the River?

"I will gather you from all nations."

186

1. Shall we gath·er at the riv·er Where bright an·gel feet have
2. On the mar·gin of the riv·er, Wash·ing up its sil·ver
3. Ere we reach the shin·ing riv·er, Lay we ev'·ry bur·den

trod; With its crys·tal tide for·ev·er Flow·ing
spray, We will walk and wor·ship ev·er, All the
down; Grace our spir·its will de·liv·er, And pro·

CHORUS.

by the throne of God? Yes, we'll gath·er at the
hap·py, gold·en day, Yes, we'll gath·er, etc.
vide a robe and crown. Yes, we'll gath·er, etc.

p

riv·er, The beau·ti·ful, the beau·ti·ful riv·er;

Gath·er with the saints at the riv·er That flows by the throne of God.

A T the smiling of the river,
Mirror of the Savior's face,
Saints whom death will never sever
Lift their songs of saving grace.
Yes, we'll gather, etc.

S OON we'll reach the silver river,
Soon our pilgrimage will cease;
Soon our happy hearts will quiver
With the melody of peace.
Yes, we'll gather, etc.

I will Sing for Jesus.

"Singing and making melody in your heart to the Lord."

187

1. I will sing for Je - sus, With his blood he bought me; And
2. Can there o - ver - take me An - y dark dis - as - ter,

3. I will sing for Je - sus! His name a - lone pre - vail - ing, Shall
4. Still I'll sing for Je - sus! O! how will I a - dore him, A-

all a - long my pil - grim way His lov - ing hand has brought me.
While I sing for Je - - - sus, My bless - ed, bless - ed Mas - ter?

be my sweet - est mu - - - sic, When heart and flesh are fall - ing,
mong the cloud of wit - ness - es, Who cast their crowns be - fore him.

CHORUS.

O! help me sing for Je - sus, Help me tell the sto - ry Of

O! help me sing for Je - sus, Help me tell the sto - ry Of

him who did re - deem us, The Lord of life and glo - ry.

him who did re - deem us, The Lord of life and glo - ry.

Come unto Me.

"Come unto me, all ye that labor and are heavy laden, and I will give you rest."

188　　　　　　　　　　　　　　　　　　　　　　　　　L. M.

With tear-ful eyes I look a-round, Life seems a dark and storm-y sea;

Yet, 'midst the gloom, I hear a sound, A heavenly whis-per, "Come to me."

SOLO.　　　　DUET.

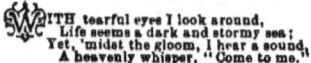

Come to me, Come to me, A heavenly whis-per, Come to me.

"COME UNTO ME."

"COME UNTO ME, ALL YE ENDS OF THE EARTH, AND BE YE SAVED."

WITH tearful eyes I look around,
　Life seems a dark and stormy sea;
Yet, 'midst the gloom, I hear a sound,
　A heavenly whisper, "Come to me."

2 It tells me of a place of rest—
　It tells me where my soul may flee;
O! to the weary, faint, oppressed,
　How sweet the bidding, "Come to me."

3 Come, for all else must fail and die,
　Earth is no resting-place for thee;
Heavenward direct thy weeping eye;
　I am thy portion, "Come to me."

4 O voice of mercy, voice of love!
　In conflict, grief, and agony,
Support me, cheer me from above!
　And gently whisper, "Come to me."

NEEDY SINNER, COME.

"IF ANY MAN THIRST, LET HIM COME UNTO ME."

189

JUST as thou art, without one trace
　Of love or joy or inward grace,
Or fitness for the heavenly place—
　O, guilty sinner, come! O come!

2 Burdened with guilt, wouldst thou be blest?
　Trust not the world, it gives no rest;
I bring relief to hearts oppressed;
　O, weary sinner, come! O come!

3 Come, leave thy burden at the cross;
　Count all thy gains but empty dross,
My grace repays all earthly loss—
　O, needy sinner, come! O come!

4 Come, hither bring thy boding fears,
　Thy aching heart, thy bursting tears;
'Tis mercy's voice salutes thine ears—
　O, trembling sinner, come! O come!

The Christian's Mission.

"Now will I sing of my beloved touching his vineyard."

180

1. Brother, you may work for Je - sus; God has giv - en you a place
2. Brother, you may pray for Je - sus, In your clos - et and at home,

In some por - tion of his vine - yard, And will give sus - tain - ing grace.
In the vil - lage, in the cit - y, Or wher - ev - er you may roam;

He has bid - den you "Go la - bor," And has promised a re - ward, Ev - en
Pray that God may send the spir - it In - to some dear sin - ner's heart, And that

Rit.

joy and life e - ter - nal In the kingdom of your Lord, In the kingdom of your Lord.
In his soul's sal - va - tion You may bear some humble part, You may bear some humble part.

BROTHER, you may "sing for Jesus,"
O how precious is his love!
Praise him for his boundless blessings
Ever coming from above.
Sing how Jesus died to save you,
How your sin and guilt he bore;
How his blood hath sealed your pardon:
"Sing for Jesus" evermore.

BROTHER, you may live for Jesus,
Him who died that you might live;
O then all your ransomed powers
Cheerful to his service give.
Thus for Jesus, you may labor,
And for Jesus sing and pray;
Consecrate your life to Jesus—
Love and serve him every day.

191

Moderato and affectuoso.

1. I will sing you a song of that beau-ti-ful land, The far a-way

2. O, that home of the soul in my vi-sions and dreams, Its bright jas-per
3. There the great trees of life in their beau-ty do grow, And the river of

home of the soul, Where no storms ev-er beat on the glit-tering strand, While the

walls I can see, Till I fan-cy but thin-ly the vale in-ter-venes Be-
life flow-eth by, For no death ev-er en-ters that cit-y you know, And

1st time. 2d. Fine.   Dal Seg.

years of e-ter-ni-ty roll, While the years of e-ter-ni-ty roll.

tween the fair cit-y and me, Be-tween the fair cit-y and me.
noth-ing that mak-eth a lie, And noth-ing that mak-eth a lie.

THAT unchangeable home is for you and for me,
Where Jesus of Nazareth stands;
The King of all kingdoms forever is he,
And he holdeth our crowns in his hands.

HOW sweet it will be in that beautiful land,
So free from all sorrow and pain!
With songs on our lips and with harps in our [hands,
To meet one another again.

Ten Commandments.

"And God spake these words, saying."

192

1. Down the a - ges, long de - part-ed, For a moment, look and wonder; Listen to the
2. See the clouds are round about him, And the aw - ful trumpet soundeth, While the Lord up-

ten commandments, Louder far than Sinai's thunder, Hear a voice which speaks to thee,
on the mountain, His unchanging law profoundeth. Jeal-ous is thy God, and thou

Thou shalt have no gods but me; Hear a voice which speaks to thee, Thou shalt have no gods but me.
To an idol shalt not bow; Jealous is thy God, and thou To an idol shalt not bow.

III.

O! he rides upon the tempest,
Death and hell themselves do fear him;
All the worlds he hath created,
When he speaketh, let us hear him.
Never shalt thou take the name
Of the Lord thy God in vain."

IV.

STANDING by the quaking mountain,
All the hosts of Israel tremble;
In the presence of the holy,
Who can trifle or dissemble.
Thou shalt mind the Sabbath day
Keep it holy, hear him say.

V.

KING of kings! Jehovah! Jireh!
Thou art God, there is no other;
From of old we hear thee saying,
Thou shalt honor Father, Mother,
That thy days full long may be
In the land God gives to thee.

VI.

AWFUL words from Sinai sounding,
Who shall question or gainsay them?
Graven deep on marble tables,
Who shall dare to disobey them?
There, Thou shalt not kill was writ,
Nor adultery commit.

VII.

O! he looks through all disguises;
Tears each flimsy vail asunder;
Like the lightning are his glances,
And his voice is like the thunder.
And to us he doth reveal,
This his will, Thou shalt not steal.

VIII.

NO false witness 'gainst thy neighbor
Shalt thou bear, and thou shalt never
Covet aught that he possesseth,
Saith thy God, who lives forever;
The great God, who from on high
Waits to judge thee by-and-by.

Christian Reunion.

"Let brotherly love continue."

193　　　　　　　　　　　　　　　　　　　9th P. M.

1. Sol - diers in the ranks of Je - sus, Work - ers in the field of grace,
2. Some are here whose locks be - tok - en Years of watch-ing, toil, and care;
3. Tell us, brethren, are you plant-ing Good - ly seed on fer - tile ground?
4. Do not think of earth - ly tri - als, With your crown of life in view;

Preachers of our bless - ed Gos - pel, Wel-come to this sa - cred place.
Oth - ers in the prime of man - hood, Just be - gin their cross to bear.
Is the glo - rious work pro - gress - ing, Does the fruit of joy a - bound?
Though af - flict - ed, bear it meek - ly, Je - sus bled and died for you.

CHORUS.

What an hour of ho - ly trans - port, God is in our midst to - day!

Praise the Lord this hap - py un - ion, How' it cheers us on our way.

THOUGH you sometimes feel discouraged,
　And your labor seems in vain,
Look to God, and seek his blessing,
　He will bring the promised reign.
　　What an hour, etc.

PATIENT, then, be persevering;
　Soon your mission will be o'er;
Through the glass of hope, though darkly,
　You can see the other shore.
　　What an hour, etc.

Jesus is Here.

"Behold I stand at the door and knock."

194

1. O, come to Je-sus now, Je-sus is here, Je-sus is here;
2. O, come this place with-in, Je-sus is here, Je-sus is here;
3. Come, then, to Je-sus now, Je-sus is here, Je-sus is here;
4. O, come to Je-sus now, Je-sus is here, Je-sus is here;

All low be-fore him bow, Je-sus is here, Je-sus is here.
He sees you full of sin, Je-sus is here, Je-sus is here.
All near him low-ly bow, Je-sus is here, Je-sus is here.
Old and young together bow, Je-sus is here, Je-sus is here.

Too man-y go a-way, Too man-y still de-lay, Though
He knows you when you come, Poor, wretch-ed, and un-done, Seeking
O, ye that feel your sin, And com-ing long have been, Now
O, what a glo-rious thing, Sin's wea-ry load to bring, And

Je-sus bids them stay; Je-sus is here, Je-sus is here.
Him and Him a-lone; Je-sus is here, Je-sus is here.
find your rest in him; Je-sus is here, Je-sus is here.
lose it while we sing; Je-sus is here, Je-sus is here.

195   *JESUS IS MINE.*

"AND THEY SHALL BE MINE IN THAT DAY WHEN I MAKE UP MY JEWELS."

FADE, fade each earthly joy,
    Jesus is mine!
Break every tender tie,
    Jesus is mine!
Dark is the wilderness,
Earth has no resting-place,
Jesus alone can bless,
    Jesus is mine!

2 Tempt not my soul away,
    Jesus is mine!
Here would I ever stay,
    Jesus is mine!

Perishing things of clay,
Born but for one brief day,
Pass from my heart away,
    Jesus is mine!

3 Farewell, mortality,
    Jesus is mine!
Welcome eternity,
    Jesus is mine!
Welcome, O loved and blest,
Welcome, sweet scenes of rest,
Welcome, my Saviour's breast,
    Jesus is mine!

Sow and Faint Not.

"Be not weary in well doing, for in due time ye shall reap, if ye faint not."

198

8th P. M.

Very earnest.

1. On - ward, fel - low - teach - ers, on - ward! Sow the seed with faith and prayer;

2. Cour - age, fel - low - teach - ers, cour - age! Though we now see no suc - cess;

None can wrest these weapons from us, Let us nev - er then de - spair.

Wait his time with faith and pa - tience, God will yet our la - bors bless.

CHORUS.

Sow and faint not, Sow and faint not, Till the seed a har - vest bear;

Look to Je - sus, Look to Je - sus, When dis - cour - age - ments dis - tress;

Sow and faint not, Sow and faint not, Till the seed a har - vest bear.

Look to Je - sus, Look to Je - sus, When dis - cour - age - ments dis - tress.

WRESTLE, fellow-teachers, wrestle!
With the God of Jacob plead;
Pray until you get the blessing.
Which your fainting spirits need.
Plead with Jesus;
For these little children plead.

HEAR us, O, our Savior, hear us!
While we supplicate thy throne!
Let us be successful pleaders,
Savior, make our cause thine own.
Let these children
All be saved and gathered home.

THE words of this truly beautiful song were written by Mrs. ELLEN H. GATES.
The music will be found on page 90, "Musical Leaves," as sung by PHILIP PHILLIPS at the great Anniversaries of the U. S. Christian Commission in New York, Philadelphia, Washington, Cincinnati, Chicago, St. Louis, and many other places.

When our lamented President LINCOLN heard Mr. PHILLIPS sing it at the Hall of Representatives in Washington, Feb. 29, 1865, he was overcome with emotion, and sent up the following written request (facsimile) to Hon. WM. H. SEWARD, Chairman, for its repetition:

"Near the close let us have "Your Mission" repeated by Mr Phillips. Dont say I called for it. A. Lincoln"

197

I.

IF you can not on the ocean
  Sail among the swiftest fleet,
Rocking on the highest billows,
  Laughing at the storms you meet,
You can stand among the sailors,
  Anchored yet within the bay;
You can lend a hand to help them,
  As they launch their boat away.

II.

IF you are too weak to journey
  Up the mountain, steep and high,
You can stand within the valley,
  While the multitudes go by;
You can chant in happy measure,
  As they slowly pass along;
Though they may forget the singer,
  They will not forget the song.

III.

IF you have not gold and silver
  Ever ready to command;
If you can not t'ward the needy
  Reach an ever open hand;
You can visit the afflicted,
  O'er the erring you can weep;
You can be a true disciple
  Sitting at the Savior's feet.

IV.

IF you can not in the harvest
  Garner up the richest sheaves,
Many a grain both ripe and golden
  Will the careless reapers leave;
Go and glean among the briers,
  Growing rank against the wall,
For it may be that their shadow
  Hides the heaviest wheat of all.

V.

IF you can not in the conflict
  Prove yourself a soldier true—
If, where fire and smoke are thickest,
  There 's no work for you to do;
When the battle-field is silent,
  You can go with careful tread,
You can bear away the wounded,
  You can cover up the dead.

VI.

DO not, then, stand idly waiting,
  For some greater work to do;
Fortune is a lazy goddess—
  She will never come to you.
Go and toil in any vineyard,
  Do not fear to do or dare;
If you want a field of labor,
  You can find it any where.

NOTE.—May be sung as a Chorus to opposite tune.

The New Birth.

"Verily, verily, I say unto you, except a man be born again, he can not see the kingdom of God."

193   C. M. D.

Moderato.

1. O, sin-ner, on the brink of death, Why plod thy toil-some
2. Where is thy trust be-yond the grave, And where thy hope of

way, A-long the slip-pery path of guilt, With-out one
heaven? Thou hast no par-doning voice with-in, To speak thy

cheer-ing ray? Shall love im-plore with tear-ful eye, Shall Je-sus
sins for-given. Boast not thy mer-its or thy works, For both a-

die in vain? Stop, sin-ner, in thy mad ca-reer, Thou
like are vain; If thou wouldst win e-ter-nal life. Thou

must be born a-gain, Ye must be born a-gain.
must be born a-gain, Ye must be born a-gain.

OLD things must pass, thy nature change,
  By sovereign grace renewed;
Thy temper, gentle as a child,
  Thy every thought subdued.
And in the temple of thy heart,
  The Lord of glory reign,
Whose law demands of every soul,
  Ye must be born again.

GIVE him thy heart, a simple act,
  He justly claims of thee;
Repent, believe, and thou shalt find
  A pardon, full and free.
Behold the bleeding Lamb of God,
  The Lamb for sinners slain,
Whose law demands of every soul,
  Ye must be born again.

Come to Jesus Just Now.

"Behold! now is the day of salvation."

Rev. EDWARD PAYSON HAMMOND says this was first sung in Scotland, when hundreds
199 were asking, "What shall we do to be saved?"

With feeling and earnestness.

Come to Je - sus, come to Je - sus, Come to Je - sus, just

Come to Je - sus, come to Je - sus, Come to Je - sus, just

now, just now; Come to Je - sus, come to Je - sus, just now.

now, just now; Come to Je - sus, come to Je - sus, just now.

SUPT.—"COME UNTO ME, all ye that labor and are heavy laden, and I will give you rest."—*Matt. xi: 28.*

1. *Come to Jesus, just now, etc.*

SUPT.—"Believe on the Lord Jesus Christ, and thou shalt be SAVED."—*Acts xvi: 31.*

2. *He will save you, just now, etc.*

SUPT.—"God so loved the world that he gave his only-begotten Son, that whosoever BELIEVETH in him should not perish, but have everlasting life."—*John iii: 16.*

3. *O, believe him, just now, etc.*

SUPT.—"He is ABLE to save them to the uttermost that come unto God by him, seeing he ever liveth to make intercession for us."—*Heb. vii: 25.*

4. *He is able, just now, etc.*

SUPT.—"The Lord is long-suffering to us-ward, not WILLING that any should perish, but that all should come to repentance.—*2 Pet. iii: 9.*

5. *He is willing, just now, etc.*

SUPT.—"Him that cometh to me, I WILL IN NO-WISE CAST OUT."—*John vi: 37.*

6. *He'll receive you, just now, etc.*

SUPT.—"FLEE from the wrath to come."—*Matt. iii: 7.*

7. *Flee to Jesus, just now, etc.*

SUPT.—"Whosoever shall CALL on the name of the Lord shall be saved."—*Acts ii: 21.*

8. *Call unto him, just now, etc.*

SUPT.—"And Jesus said unto him, Go thy way; THY FAITH HATH MADE THEE WHOLE."—*Mark x: 52.*

9. *He will hear you, just now, etc.*

SUPT.—"Jesus, thou son of David, have MERCY on me."—*Mark x: 47.*

10. *He'll have mercy, just now, etc.*

SUPT.—"If we confess our sins, he is faithful and just to FORGIVE US our sins.—1 John i: 9.

11. *He'll forgive you, just now, etc.*

SUPT.—"The blood of Jesus Christ, his Son, CLEANSETH US from all sin.—1 John i: 7.

12. *He will cleanse you, just now, etc.*

SUPT.—"Therefore, if any man be in Christ, he is a NEW CREATURE."—*2 Cor. v: 17.*

13. *He'll renew you, just now, etc.*

SUPT.—"He that overcometh, the same shall be CLOTHED in white raiment."—*Rev. iii: 5.*

14. *He will clothe you, just now, etc.*

SUPT.—"Greater LOVE hath no man than this, that a man should lay down his life for his friends."—*John xv: 13.*

15. *Jesus loves you, just now, etc.*

The Scripture, pertaining to each verse should be read or recited by the superintendent in a plain and impressive manner *before* singing the verse.

The Lord's Prayer.

"But in every thing by prayer and supplication let your requests be made known unto God."

200

TENOR.

1. If any be distressed, and fain would gather
   Some comfort, let him haste unto . . . } Our - - - - - Father,

ALTO.

2. Thou showest mercy, therefore for the same
   We praise Thee, Singing, ... } Hallowed be Thy name;

SOPRANO.

3. We mortal are, and ever changing from our
   birth; Thou constant art, ... } Thy will be done on earth,

BASS.

For we of hope and help are quite bereaven
Except thou succor us, ... } Who art in heaven,

Of all our miseries cast up the sum; Show us
thy joys, and let . . . . } Thy king - dom come;

Thou mad'st the earth, as well as the planets
seven; Thy name be blessed here, ... } As it is in heaven.

OTHING we have to use, or debts to pay,
Except thou give it us, ... } Give us this day
Wherewith to clothe us, wherewith to be fed,
For without thee we want . . . . . } Our dai - ly bread;

E want, we want forgiveness, for no day
passes But we sin . . . . } Forgive us our trespasses,
No man free from sinning ever did live;
Forgive us, Lord, our sins, ... } As we for - give

F we repent our faults, thou wilt bless us,
We pardon them . . . . } That trespass against us.
Forgive us that is past, a new path tread us;
Direct us always in thy way, ... } And lead - - - us

E thine own people, and thy chosen nation;
Guide us into all truth, but . . . . } Not into tempt - ation,
Then that of all good graces art the Giver,
Suffer us not to wander, ... } But de - - - liver

S from the fierce assaults of world and devil
And flesh, So shalt thou free us . . . } From - - all evil.
To these petitions let all on earth respond then
With one consent and heart and voice, say, } A - - - - - men.

My Home Above.

"In my Father's house are many mansions."

201

1 There's a beau - ti - ful home for thee, brother, A home, a home for thee;
2. There's a beau - ti - ful rest for thee, brother, A rest, a rest for thee;
3. There's a beau - ti - ful crown for thee, brother, A crown, a crown for thee;

In that land of bliss, where pleasure is, There, brother's a home for thee.
In those mansions a - bove, where all is love, There, brother's a rest for thee.
When the battle is done, and the victory won, Our Savior will give it to thee.

CHORUS.

A beau - ti - ful home for thee, brother, A beau - ti - ful home for thee;
A beau - ti - ful rest for thee, brother, A beau - ti - ful rest for thee;
A beau - ti - ful crown for thee, brother, A beau - ti - ful crown for thee;

In that land of bliss, where pleasure is, There, brother's a home for thee.
In those mansions a - bove, where all is love, There, brother's a rest for thee.
When the battle is done, and the victory won, Our Savior will give it to thee.

THERE'S a beautiful robe for thee, brother,
A robe, a robe for thee;
A robe of white, so pure and bright,
A glorious robe for thee,
A beautiful robe for thee, etc.

WILT seek that beautiful home, brother,
That home, that home above;
In that land of light, where all is bright,
That land where all is love?
A beautiful home for thee, etc.

Our Sabbath Home.

"How amiable are thy tabernacles, O Lord of Hosts! My soul panteth for Thee."

202

1. We love the sun-ny days of spring, With ear-ly buds and birds and flowers, But most we love when Sun-day brings Of Sab-bath-school the hap-py hours. Sweet Sun-day-school, our

2. We love to learn all through the week The things that make us good and wise, But most we love those truths to seek That light our path-way to the skies. Sweet Sun-day-school, etc.

3. We love the sto-ries of the brave, The no-ble men who earth have trod, But more to hear of *Him* who gave His life to bring us up to God. Sweet Sun-day-school, etc.

CHORUS. *Allegro.*

Rit. pp   *Allegretto*

Sab-bath home, Sab-bath home, "Home, sweet home;" Dear Sun-day-school, our "Home, sweet home," Our beau-ti-ful Sab-bath home.

WE may not climb fair Olivet,
Nor roam the pleasant Jordan near,
But he who there the children met
Will surely come to meet us here.
Sweet Sunday-school, etc.

CHILDREN, hither will you turn
With willing hearts your Lord to meet!
O, teachers, while of him you learn,
Like Mary, sit "at Jesus' feet."
Sweet Sunday-school, etc.

Remember the Poor.

"Blessed is he that considereth the poor."

203

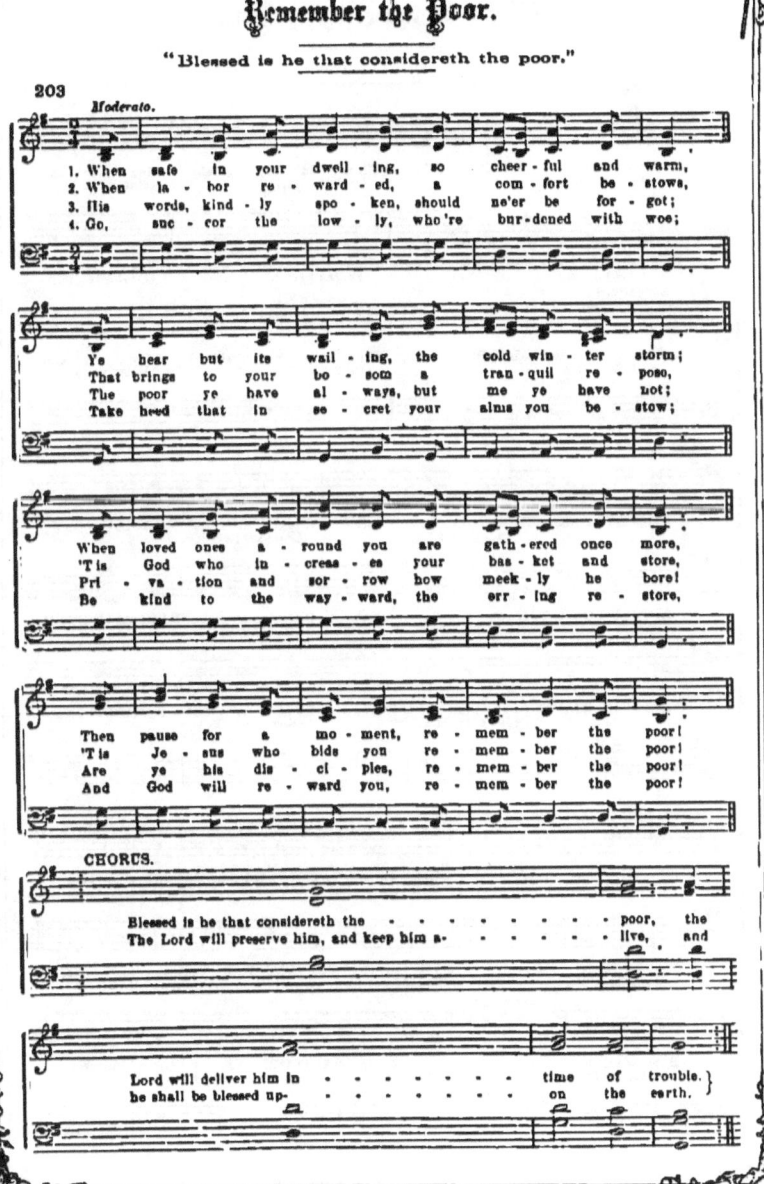

Moderato.

1. When safe in your dwell - ing, so cheer - ful and warm,
2. When la - bor re - ward - ed, a com - fort be - stows,
3. His words, kind - ly spo - ken, should ne'er be for - got;
4. Go, suc - cor the low - ly, who're bur-dened with woe;

Ye hear but its wail - ing, the cold win - ter storm;
That brings to your bo - som a tran - quil re - pose,
The poor ye have al - ways, but me ye have not;
Take heed that in se - cret your alms you be - stow;

When loved ones a - round you are gath - ered once more,
'T is God who in - creas - es your bas - ket and store,
Pri - va - tion and sor - row how meek - ly he bore!
Be kind to the way - ward, the err - ing re - store,

Then pause for a mo - ment, re - mem - ber the poor!
'T is Je - sus who bids you re - mem - ber the poor!
Are ye his dis - ci - ples, re - mem - ber the poor!
And God will re - ward you, re - mem - ber the poor!

CHORUS.

Blessed is he that considereth the . . . . poor, the
The Lord will preserve him, and keep him a- . . . . . live, and

Lord will deliver him in . . . . time of trouble. }
he shall be blessed up- . . . . on the earth. }

Cling to the Mighty One.

204   "But cleave unto the Lord your God."

Earnest and pleading.

TENOR.

1. Cling to the MIGHTY ONE, Cling in thy grief, Cling to the
(Ps. lxxxix: 19.)   (Heb. xii: 11.)   (Heb. i: 22.)

ALTO.

2. Cling to the LOVING ONE, Cling in thy woe, Cling to the
(Heb. vii: 25.   (Ps. lxxxvi: 7.)   (1 John iv: 16.)

SOPRANO.

3. Cling to the BLEEDING ONE, Cling to his side, Cling to the
(1 John i: 7.)   (John xx: 27.)   (Rom. vi: 9.)

BASS.

HO - LY ONE, He gives re - lief; Cling to the GRACIOUS ONE,
(Ps. cxvi: 8.)   (Ps. cxvi: 5.)

LIV - ING ONE, Through all be - low; Cling to the PARDONING ONE,
(Rom. viii: 38-39.)   (Is. iv: 7.)

RIS - EN ONE, In him a - bide; Cling to the COMING ONE,
(John xv: 4.)   (Rev. xxii: 20.)

Cling in thy pain, Cling to the FAITHFUL ONE, He will sus - tain.
(Ps. lv: 4.)   (1 Thess. v: 24.)   (Ps. lii: 5.)

He speaketh peace, Cling to the HEALING ONE, Anguish shall cease.
(John xiv: 27.)   (Exod. xv: 26.)   (Ps. cxviii: 3.)

Hope shall a - rise. Cling to the REIGNING ONE, Joy lights thine eyes.
(Titus ii: 13.)   (Ps. xcvii: 1.)   (Ps. xvi: 2.)

I'd tell Them to be True.

"Be ye steadfast, unmovable, always abounding in the work of the Lord."

205 SOLO. MELODY.

With great expression.

1. If I were a voice, a per - sua - sive voice, That could
2. If I were a voice, a con - sol - ing voice, I'd fly

trav - el the wide world through, I would fly on the beams of the
on the wings of the air; The homes of sor - row and

morn - ing light, And speak to men with a gen - tle might, And
guilt I'd seek, And calm and truth - ful words I'd speak To

tell them to be true. I would fly, I would fly o - ver
save them from de - spair. I would fly, I would fly o'er the

land and sea, Wher - ev - er a hu - man heart might be,
crowd - ed town, And drop like the hap - py sun - light down

Tell - ing a tale, or sing - ing a song, In praise of the right, in
In - to the hearts of suf - fer - ing men, And teach them to look

CHORUS. *Ad lib.*

blaze of the wrong. I would fly, ... I would fly, I would fly, ...
up a - gain. I would fly, ... I would fly, I would fly, ...

I would fly, I would fly o - ver land and sea.
I would fly, I would fly o'er the crowd - ed town.

If I were a voice, a convincing voice,
I'd travel with the wind;
And where'er I saw the Nation's torn
By warfare, jealousy, spite, or scorn,
Or hatred of their kind—
I would fly, I would fly on the thunder crash,
And into their blinded bosoms flash,
Then with the devil thoughts subdued,
I'd teach them Christian brotherhood.
I would fly, would fly, etc.,
I would fly o' the thunder crash.

If I were a voice, an immortal voice.
I would fly the earth around;
And wherever man to his idols bowed,
I'd publish in notes both long and loud,
The Gospel's joyful sound.
I would fly, I would fly on the wings of day,
Proclaiming peace on my world-wide way,
Bidding the maddened earth rejoice.
If I were a voice, an immortal voice.
I would fly, I would fly, etc.,
I would fly on the wings of day.

Our Call.

"Whatsoever thy hand findeth to do, do it with thy might."

208

MAY BE SUNG AS A SOLO.

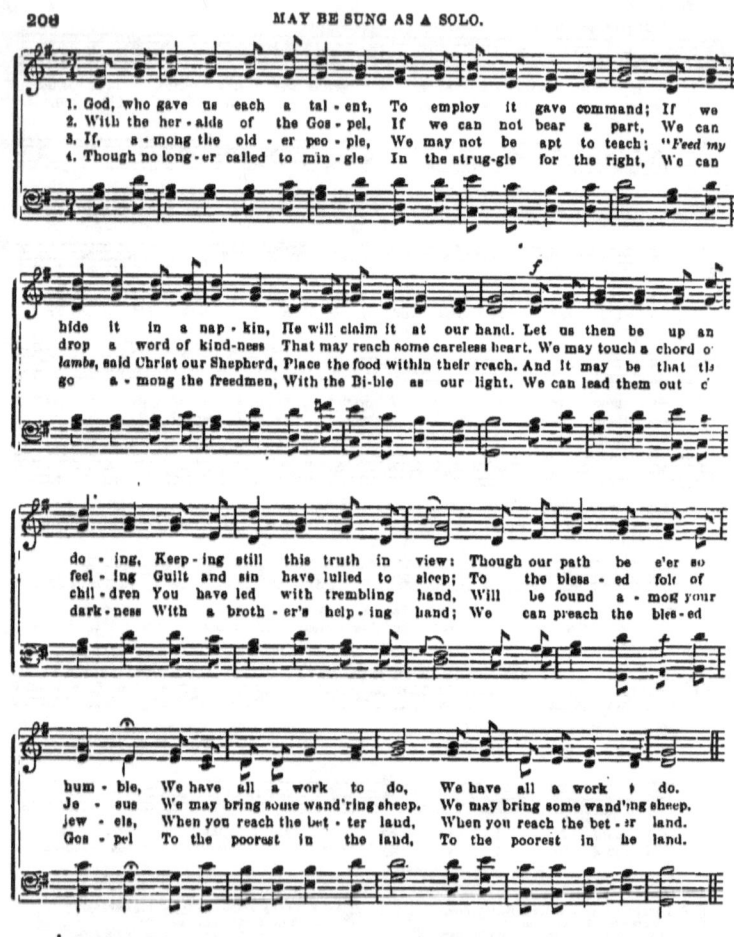

1. God, who gave us each a tal-ent, To employ it gave command; If we
2. With the her-alds of the Gos-pel, If we can not bear a part, We can
3. If, a-mong the old-er peo-ple, We may not be apt to teach; "Feed my
4. Though no long-er called to min-gle In the strug-gle for the right, We can

hide it in a nap-kin, He will claim it at our hand. Let us then be up an
drop a word of kind-ness That may reach some careless heart. We may touch a chord o'
lambs, said Christ our Shepherd, Place the food within their reach. And it may be that tha
go a-mong the freedmen, With the Bi-ble as our light. We can lead them out o'

do-ing, Keep-ing still this truth in view: Though our path be e'er so
feel-ing Guilt and sin have lulled to sleep; To the bless-ed folk of
chil-dren You have led with trembling hand, Will be found a-mong your
dark-ness With a broth-er's help-ing hand; We can preach the bles-ed

hum-ble, We have all a work to do, We have all a work ' do.
Je-sus We may bring some wand'ring sheep, We may bring some wand'ng sheep,
Jew-els, When you reach the bet-er land, When you reach the bet-er land,
Gos-pel To the poorest in the land, To the poorest in he land.

For our mission does not lead us
  O'er the deep to climes afar,
We perhaps may guide a seaman,
  By the Christian's Polar Star.
We can make the burden lighter,
  Which the weary long have borne;
We can smooth the dying pillow,
  We can comfort those who mourn.

These are precious, golden moments,
  Kindly lent us to improve;
Are we faithful to our calling,
  Earnest in our work of love—
Ever at our post of duty
  Wheresoe'er our call may be?
Let our lamp be trimmed and burning,
  And the world the glory see.

Death of a Christian.

"Thy sleep shall be sweet."

207

TO BE SUNG AT THE GRAVE.

DUET.

1. She sleeps in the val - ley   so   sweet,   A - bove her the green willows   wave;
2. How calmly she rest - ed   in   God: "To thy arms, my Savior, I   come;

We plant - ed the rose at her   feet,   To bloom and de - cay o'er her grave.
Come quickly, come quickly, O   Lord,   And welcome thy wan - der - er home!"

She sleeps in   the val - ley   so   sweet,   No sound e'er disturbs her   re - pose;
She sleeps in   the val - ley   so   sweet,   Her spir - it has tak - en   its flight;

So qui - et   in this calm re - treat,   She rests safe, se - cure from life's woes.
Her form is   but dust 'neath our   feet,   While she is   an an - gel of   light.

CHORUS.

She sleeps in the val - ley,   She sleeps in the val - ley,   She sleeps in the val - ley   so sweet;

She sleeps in the val - ley,   She sleeps in the val - ley,   She sleeps in the val - ley   so sweet;

She sleeps in the val - ley,   She sleeps in the val - ley,   She sleeps in the val - ley   so sweet;

pp

She sleeps in the val - ley,   She sleeps in the val - ley,   She sleeps in the val - ley   so sweet.

She sleeps in the val - ley,   She sleeps in the val - ley,   She sleeps in the val - ley   so sweet.

pp

She sleeps in the val - ley,   She sleeps in the val - ley,   She sleeps in the val - ley   so sweet.

They took my Savior's Name in Vain.

"But above all things swear not, but let your yea be yea, and your nay, nay."

208   L. M.

Moderato.

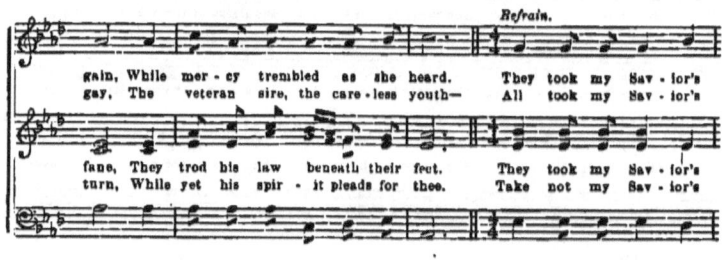

1. They took my Sav - ior's name in vain,   To
2. Where pleas - ure lured the soul a - way,   To
3. They took my Sav - ior's name in vain,   In
4. Poor, sin - ful man, why wilt thou spurn   Re -

thorn was in such cru - el word,   That pierced his sa - cred brow a -
leave the pleas - ant path of truth,   The cold, the heart - less, and the

fes - tive hall, in crowd - ed street;   With i - dle jest, and song pro -
deem - ing love, so pure and free?   A - wake, re - pent, be - lieve, re -

Refrain.

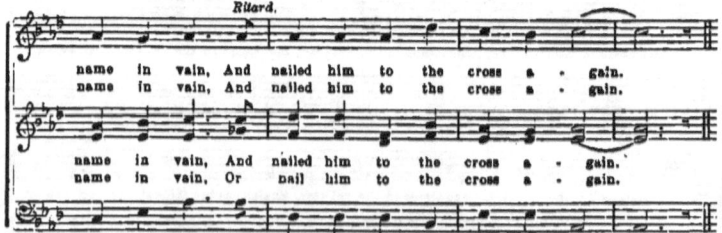

gain, While mer - cy trembled as she heard.   They took my Sav - ior's
gay, The veteran sire, the care - less youth—   All took my Sav - ior's

fane, They trod his law beneath their feet.   They took my Sav - ior's
turn, While yet his spir - it pleads for thee.   Take not my Sav - ior's

Ritard.

name in vain, And nailed him to the cross a - gain.
name in vain, And nailed him to the cross a - gain.

name in vain, And nailed him to the cross a - gain.
name in vain, Or nail him to the cross a - gain.

The World is my Parish.

'Lo! I am with you alway, even unto the end of the world.'

209

1. Dis - ci - ples of Je - sus, why stand ye here idle, Go work in his vineyard, he calls you to-day;
2. Our field is the world, and our work is before us, To each is ap - point-ed a message to bear;
3. Perhaps we are called from the highways and hedges, To gather the lowly, despised, and oppressed;

The night is approaching, when no man can labor, Our Master commands us, and shall we delay,
At home or abroad, in the cottage or palace, Wherev-er di - rect - ed, our mission is there.
If this be our duty, then why should we falter, We'll do it, and trust to our Savior the rest.

CHORUS.

The field is the world! The field is the world! Look up, for the har - vest is near;

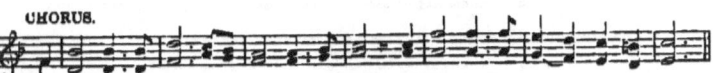

When the reapers from glo-ry Will shout as they come, And the Lord of the harvest ap - pear.

'ER islands that sleep in the wave-crested ocean,
We'll scatter the truth, and its fruit it shall bear;
O'er ice-covered regions, and rock-girded mountains,
The Lord will protect as his children are there.
Our field is the world, etc.

INSTEAD of the thorn shall the myrtle be planted;
The desert shall blossom and bloom as the rose;
The palm tree rejoicing shall spread forth her branches,
The lamb and the lion together repose,
Our field is the world, etc.

Worldling and Christian.

"Lay up for yourselves treasures in heaven."

210

WORLDLING.—If I had but the wealth of the world, Evangel, O, how hap-py a man I would be!
CHRISTIAN.— Have you thought of the riches of God, erring one? Of the city that's builded above?

I   would gath - er   all gems, I   would search through all   lore, I   would
Of   the gems and   the pearls and   the streets made of   gold,   Of   the

trav - el all lands, and return with my store, And how hap-py   a man   I would be!
beauties and glories whose wealth is untold, That are kept for the saints of his love?

WORLDLING.—I would build me a mansion of stone, Evangel,
　　　　　Out of gems, clear and polished like glass;
　　　　　I'd surround it with lawns and with trees and with flowers,
　　　　　With rich statues, pure streams, and with green rosy bowers,
　　　　　Such as nothing on earth could surpass.

CHRISTIAN.—Have you thought of the mansions of God, erring one,
　　　　　Which he builds for his children on high?
　　　　　Can you build as can he who hath made the great world?
　　　　　Or adorn as can he who the sky hath unfurled,
　　　　　And whose bounties all creatures supply?

WORLDLING.—I would fill it with pictures, and purchase rare wines;
　　　　　I'd surround me with children and friends;
　　　　　And with music and song. and with dance would be gay,
　　　　　And would fear for no want, and world dread no decay,
　　　　　And my pleasures would never have end.

CHRISTIAN.—Have you thought how earth's riches take wings, erring one—
　　　　　How our children and friends pass away?
　　　　　How the strong man grows weak, and how pleasures grow stale,
　　　　　Or how beauty soon fades, and our senses soon fail,
　　　　　As we haste to that infinite day?

WORLDLING.—I would seek the world's honors, and make me a name;
CHRISTIAN.—　But your honor and fame would soon die!
WORLDLING.—Can I claim nothing, then, Evangel, as my own?
CHRISTIAN.— If you had all the world, nothing's yours, erring one;
　　　　　All is his who doth reign in the sky.

WORLDLING.—Can I have, then, these riches of God, Evangel,
　　　　　That honor, those mansions above?
CHRISTIAN.— God hath made them for you and for me and for all.
BOTH.— Who before him in faith, love, and duty will fall,
　　　　　He will raise to the bliss of his love.

NOTE.—May be sung as a dialogue between the Teacher and School.

Dedication Anthem.

"My feet shall tread thy courts, O Zion."

211

Our earthly temple now complete, We come to worship at thy feet; O, Lord of Hosts, thou God of love,

Behold us from thy throne above. The Lord is in his holy temple, Unto him, unto him shall our

vows be paid; He will vis-it his children in mer - cy, And show us the light of his countenance.

DUET.   Repeat pp.

My feet shall tread thy courts, My feet shall tread thy courts, O Zion, O Zion; Hallelujah to the Lord!

Here will I go, Here will I go into the house of the Lord; My feet shall tread thy courts, My

feet shall tread thy courts, O Zion, O Zi-on; Halle - lu - jah, Halle-lu - jah, Halle - lu - jah to the Lord!

Christmas Anthem.

"Christ is born in Bethlehem."

212

1. Lo! descending, the heavens rending, Messen - gers from God to men; Angels winging,
2. Dearest Savior, grant thy favor, While in these thy courts we stay; Thy rich blessing

tidings bringing, Christ is born in Beth-le-hem; Come, with gladness, and ban - ish sadness,
on us resting, On this happy, festive day; Bells are ringing, and birds are singing,

Children, sweetly tune your voices,   Sing aloud while heaven rejoices: Hal-le - lu-jah!
Woods and fields their tribute bringing, Back the hills the echoes flinging; Let our voices

Hal - le - lu-jah! "Peace on earth, good will to men." Lift aloud a lofty strain, God is re-con-
swell the chorus In   a grateful song of praise. Joyful, come before him now, Humbly in his

Cres.

ciled to man; Glory to our Savior King, Heaven and earth with glory ring. Praise him, praise him, the
presence bow; Now to him our tribute bring, Lord of lords, and King of kings. Praise him, praise him, ye

FINE.

Lord Jehovah praise; Praise him, praise him, the Lord Jehovah praise. Hosanna! Hosan - na!
grateful children praise: Praise him, praise him, ye grateful children praise. Hosanna! Hosan - na!

Mercy's Free for You and Me.

"Without money and without price."

213

1. By faith I view my Sav-ior dy-ing, On the tree, on the tree;
2. Did Christ, when I was sin pur-su-ing, Pit-y me, pit-y me?

3. Je-sus, the might-y God hath spo-ken Peace to me, peace to me;
4. Je-sus my wea-ry soul re-fresh-es, Mer-cy's free, mer-cy's free;

To ev'-ry na-tion he is cry-ing, Look to me, look to me.
And did he snatch my soul from ru-in? Can it be, can it be?

Now all my chains of sin are bro-ken, I am free, I am free.
And ev'-ry mo-ment Christ is pre-cious Un-to me, un-to me.

He bids the guilt-y now draw near, Re-pent, be-lieve, dis-miss their fear;
O, yes! he did sal-va-tion bring, He is my Pro-phet, Priest, and King,

Soon as I in his name believed, The ho-ly spir-it I re-ceived,
None can de-scribe the bliss I prove, While through this wilder-ness I rove;

Hark! hark! what precious words I hear! Mer-cy's free, mer-cy's free.
And now my hap-py soul can sing, Mer-cy's free, mer-cy's free.

And Christ from death my soul re-trieved, Mer-cy's free, mer-cy's free.
All may en-joy the Sav-ior's love, Mer-cy's free, mer-cy's free.

8

'Tis Blessed to Give.

"God loveth the cheerful giver."

214

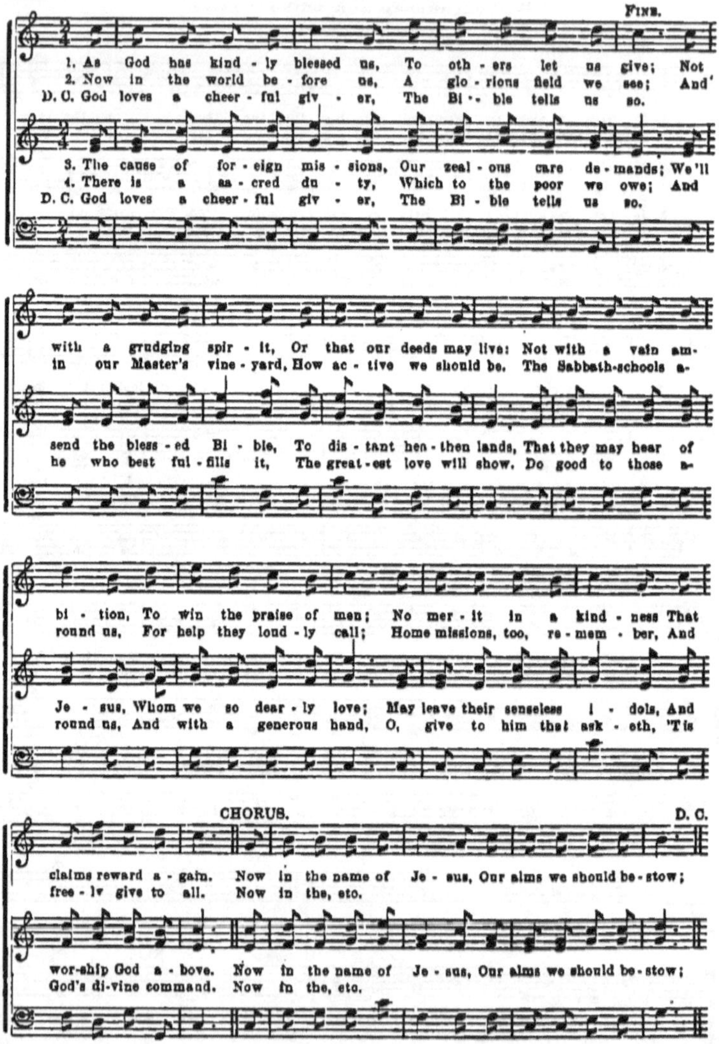

FINE.

1. As God has kind-ly blessed us, To oth-ers let us give; Not
2. Now in the world be-fore us, A glo-rious field we see; And
D. C. God loves a cheer-ful giv-er, The Bi-ble tells us so.

3. The cause of for-eign mis-sions, Our zeal-ous care de-mands; We'll
4. There is a sa-cred du-ty, Which to the poor we owe; And
D. C. God loves a cheer-ful giv-er, The Bi-ble tells us so.

with a grudging spir-it, Or that our deeds may live: Not with a vain am-
in our Master's vine-yard, How ac-tive we should be. The Sabbath-schools a-

send the bless-ed Bi-ble, To dis-tant hea-then lands, That they may hear of
he who best ful-fills it, The great-est love will show. Do good to those a-

bi-tion, To win the praise of men; No mer-it in a kind-ness That
round us, For help they loud-ly call; Home missions, too, re-mem-ber, And

Je-sus, Whom we so dear-ly love; May leave their senseless I-dols, And
round us, And with a generous hand, O, give to him that ask-eth, 'Tis

CHORUS.   D. C.

claims reward a-gain. Now in the name of Je-sus, Our alms we should be-stow;
free-ly give to all. Now in the, etc.

wor-ship God a-bove. Now in the name of Je-sus, Our alms we should be-stow;
God's di-vine command. Now in the, etc.

Three Steps of Intemperance.

215 (Descriptive.)

MELODY.

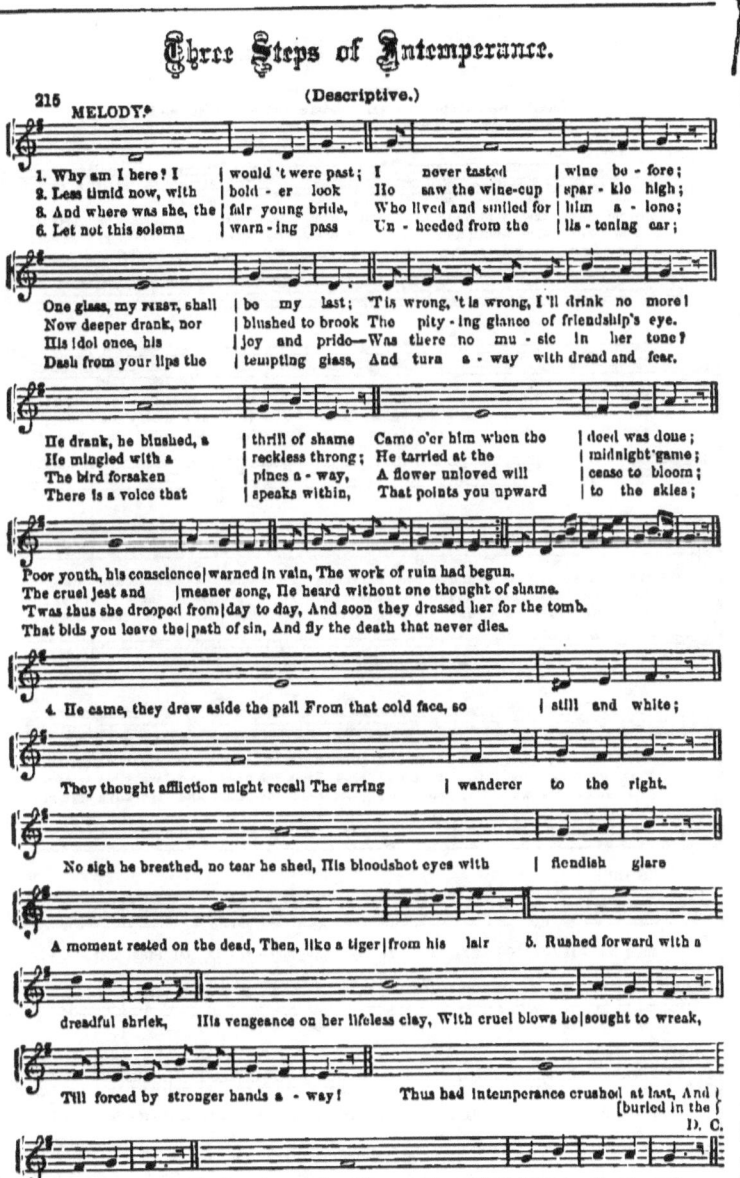

1. Why am I here? I | would 't were past; | I   never tasted | wine be - fore;
2. Less timid now, with | bold - er look | Ho   saw the wine-cup | spar - kle high;
3. And where was she, the | fair young bride, | Who lived and smiled for | him   a - lone;
6. Let not this solemn | warn-ing pass | Un - heeded from the | lis - tening ear;

One glass, my first, shall | be   my   last; | T is wrong, 't is wrong, I'll drink no more!
Now deeper drank, nor | blushed to brook The   pity - ing glance of friendship's eye.
His idol once, his | joy and pride—Was there no   mu - sic in her tone?
Dash from your lips the | tempting glass, And turn a - way with dread and fear.

He drank, he blushed, a | thrill of shame   Came o'er him when the | deed was done;
He mingled with a | reckless throng; He tarried at the | midnight-game;
The bird forsaken | pines a - way,   A flower unloved will | cease to bloom;
There is a voice that | speaks within, That points you upward | to   the skies;

Poor youth, his conscience | warned in vain, The work of ruin had begun.
The cruel jest and | meaner song, He heard without one thought of shame.
'Twas thus she drooped from | day to day, And soon they dressed her for the tomb.
That bids you leave the | path of sin, And fly the death that never dies.

4. He came, they drew aside the pall From that cold face, so | still and white;

They thought affliction might recall The erring | wanderer to   the   right.

No sigh he breathed, no tear he shed, His bloodshot eyes with | fiendish   glare

A moment rested on the dead, Then, like a tiger | from his lair   5. Rushed forward with a

dreadful shriek,   His vengeance on her lifeless clay, With cruel blows he | sought to wreak,

Till forced by stronger hands a - way!   Thus had intemperance crushed at last, And
                                          [buried in the
                                                     D. C.

fa - tal bowl, The dearest memories of the past, The noblest | feelings of the soul.

Clear Cold Water.

"Look not thou on the wine when it is red."

216

Lively.

1. Some sing the praise of ro - sy wine, Its sparkling col - or bright;
2. This will give health and joy and peace, Re - fresh-ing ev' - ry power;
3. Our sires drank from this liv - ing spring, Two hundred years a - go;

But in such songs with them to join We can not take de - light;
We want no bet - ter drink than this In tri - al's dark - est hour;
And from this fount - ain wa - ter clear Con - tin - ues still to flow;

We have a rich and no - ble theme, Fit for a prince and king,
To cheer the heart and quench the thirst, It is the ver - y thing;
Then we, on this our fes - tal day, Will of its vir - tues sing,

'Tis wa - ter pure and fresh and good, From the bright and sparkling spring.
Then give us wa - ter, pure and good, From the bright and sparkling spring.
And drink this wa - ter, pure and good, From the bright and sparkling spring.

CHORUS.

Sing mer - ri - ly, O! sing mer - ri - ly! Sing mer - ri - ly, O! Sing mer - ri - ly!

Sing mer - ri - ly, O! sing mer - ri - ly O! Sing mer - ri - ly, mer - ri - ly, O!

The Flag of the Free.

"And all nations shall flow unto it."

217

1. Na-tive land! na-tive land! with a chap-let of fame, We
2. O! Co-lum-bia, Co-lum-bia, how tran-quil and bright, Was the

hallow thy mem'ry, we hon-or thy name; Like a watch-fire ascend-ing, be-
morning that dawned on that per-il-ous night, When the an-gel of peace spread her

hold on the sea, Wav-ing proud-ly as ev-er, "The Flag of the Free."
wings o'er the sea, And she blessed the old standard, "The Flag of the Free."

CHORUS.

The Flag of our Un-ion; The Flag of our Un-ion;

The Flag of our Un-ion, The Flag of the Free.

NOW the day-star of hope in its glory appears,
Then awake from thy sorrow and banish thy
    fears;
For thy heroes have planted o'er land and o'er
    sea,
Waving proudly as ever, "The Flag of the
    Free."
The Flag of our Union, etc.

LET it wave, let it wave to the breezes unfurled,
'T is the pride of the vet'ran, the boast of the
    world;
Then hurra for the brave, and our motto shall
    be,
God protect the old standard, "The Flag of the
    Free."
The Flag of our Union, etc.

We are Rising as a People.

"A nation whose God is the Lord."

A NEW SOUL-STIRRING SONG AND CHORUS FOR THE TIMES.

218

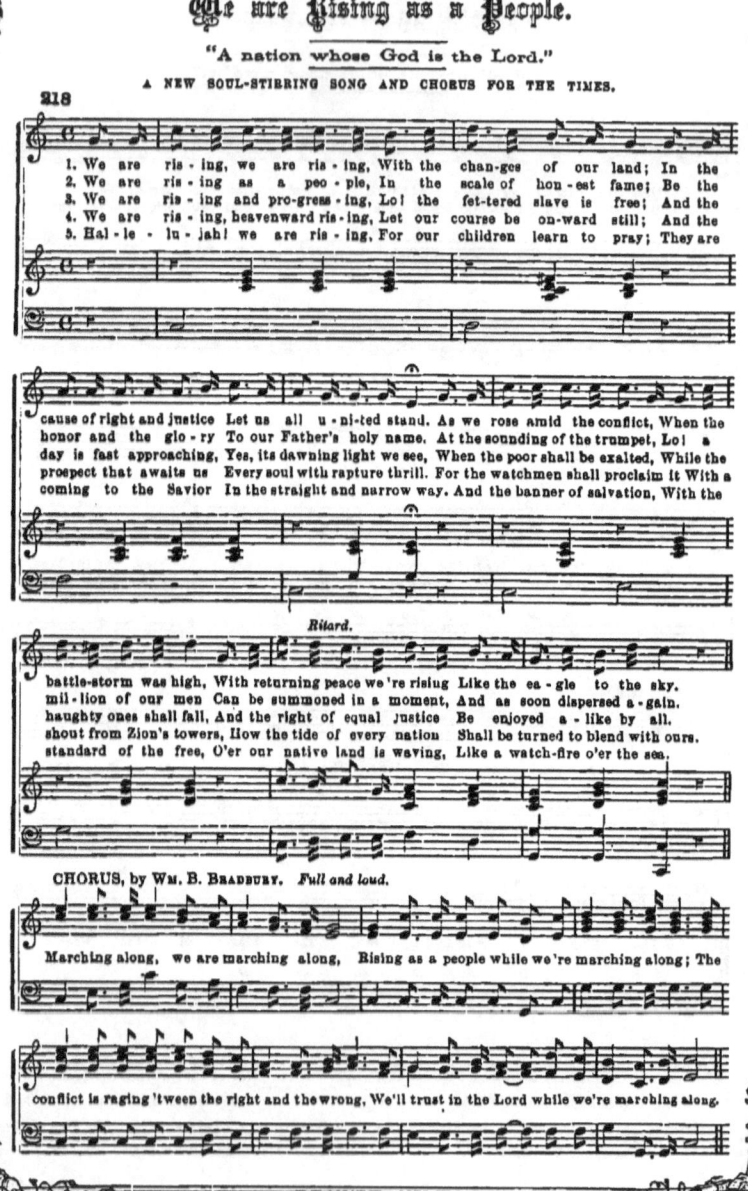

1. We are ris - ing, we are ris - ing, With the chan - ges of our land; In the
2. We are ris - ing as a peo - ple, In the scale of hon - est fame; Be the
3. We are ris - ing and pro-gress - ing, Lo! the fet-tered slave is free; And the
4. We are ris - ing, heavenward ris - ing, Let our course be on-ward still; And the
5. Hal - le - lu - jah! we are ris - ing, For our children learn to pray; They are

cause of right and justice Let us all u - ni-ted stand. As we rose amid the conflict, When the
honor and the glo - ry To our Father's holy name. At the sounding of the trumpet, Lo! a
day is fast approaching, Yes, its dawning light we see, When the poor shall be exalted, While the
prospect that awaits us Every soul with rapture thrill. For the watchmen shall proclaim it With a
coming to the Savior In the straight and narrow way. And the banner of salvation, With the

Ritard.

battle-storm was high, With returning peace we're rising Like the ea - gle to the sky.
mil - lion of our men Can be summoned in a moment, And as soon dispersed a - gain.
haughty ones shall fall, And the right of equal justice Be enjoyed a - like by all.
shout from Zion's towers, How the tide of every nation Shall be turned to blend with ours.
standard of the free, O'er our native land is waving, Like a watch-fire o'er the sea.

CHORUS, by WM. B. BRADBURY. *Full and loud.*

Marching along, we are marching along, Rising as a people while we're marching along; The

conflict is raging 'tween the right and the wrong, We'll trust in the Lord while we're marching along.

Opening and Closing Exercises.

ARRANGED BY REV. J. M. REID, D. D.

To be used at the discretion of the Superintendent.

The Ten Commandments.

Supt. And God spake all these words, saying:

Resp. Thou shalt have no other Gods before me.

Supt. We know that an idol is nothing in the world, and that there is none other God but one. 1 Cor. viii : 4.

Resp. Thou shalt not make unto thee any graven image, or any likeness of *anything* that *is* in heaven above, or that *is* in the earth beneath, or that *is* in the water under the earth: Thou shalt not bow down thyself to them, nor serve them; for I the Lord thy God am a jealous God, visiting the iniquity of the fathers upon the children unto the third and fourth *generation* of them that hate me; and shewing mercy unto thousands of them that love me and keep my commandments.

Supt. We ought not to think that the Godhead is like unto gold, or silver, or stone, graven by art and man's device. Acts xvii : 29.

Resp. Thou shalt not take the name of the Lord thy God in vain; for the Lord will not hold him guiltless that taketh his name in vain.

Supt. Let your yea, be yea; and your nay, nay; lest ye fall into condemnation. James v : 12.

Resp. Remember the sabbath day to keep it holy. Six days shalt thou labor, and do all thy work: But the seventh day *is* the sabbath of the Lord thy God; *in it* thou shalt not do any work, thou, nor thy son, nor thy daughter, thy manservant, nor thy maidservant, nor thy cattle, nor thy stranger that *is* within thy gates: For *in* six days the Lord made heaven and earth, the sea, and all that in them *is*, and rested the seventh day: wherefore the Lord blessed the sabbath day and hallowed it.

Supt. The sabbath was made for man, and not man for the sabbath. Mark ii : 27.

Resv. Honor thy father and thy mother: that thy days may be long upon the land which the Lord thy God giveth thee.

Supt. Children, obey your parents in all things: for this is well-pleasing unto the Lord. Col. iii : 20.

Resp. Thou shalt not kill.

Supt. Whosoever hateth his brother is a murderer: and ye know that no murderer hath eternal life abiding in him. I Jno. iii : 15.

Resp. Thou shalt not commit adultery.

Supt. Know ye not that ye are the temple of God? * * * If any man defile the temple of God, him shall God destroy. I Cor. iii : 16, 17.

Resp. Thou shalt not steal.

Supt. Nor thieves, nor covetous, nor drunkards, nor revilers, nor extortioners, shall inherit the kingdom of God. I Cor. vi : 10.

Resp. Thou shalt not bear false witness against thy neighbor.

Supt. Let no corrupt communication proceed out of your mouth. Eph. iv : 29.

Resp. Thou shalt not covet thy neighbor's house, thou shalt not covet thy neighbor's wife, nor his manservant, nor his maidservant, nor his ox, nor his ass, nor anything that *is* thy neighbor's.

Supt. How hard is it for them that trust in riches to enter into the kingdom of God ! Mark x : 24.

Reverence.

Supt. O come, let us worship and bow down: let us kneel before the Lord our maker. For he is our God; and we are the people of his pasture, and the sheep of his hand. Ps. xcv : 6, 7.

Resp. God is a spirit; and they that worship him, must worship him in spirit and in truth. Jno. iv : 24.

Supt. The sacrifice of the wicked is an abomination to the Lord : but the prayer of the upright is his delight. Prov. xv : 8.

Resp. If my people, which are called by my name, shall humble themselves, and pray, and seek my face, and turn from their wicked ways; then will I hear from heaven, and will forgive their sin, and will heal their land. II Chron. vii : 14.

Supt. Return, we beseech thee, O God of hosts: look down from heaven, and behold, and visit this vine. Ps. lxxx : 14.

Resp. For the same Lord over all, is rich unto all that call upon him. For whosoever shall call upon the name of the Lord shall be saved. Rom. x : 12, 13.

Supt. and Resp. Glory to God in the highest, and on earth peace, good will toward man. Luke ii : 14.

PRAYER.

HEAVENLY FATHER! Bow down thine ear, and hear me; hearken unto the voice of my supplication, for unto thee do I pray. I will lift up my voice in the morning, and meditate on thee in the night-watches, for thou art my Father and my God. I will pay thee my vows, for thou art my hope, my trust, and the God of my strength. Be pleased to hear me, O Lord; turn unto me, and pardon my iniquity. Cleanse thou me from secret faults; wash me and I shall be whiter than snow; reveal thyself unto me and show me thy ways; lead me in thy truth; teach me thy paths, for thou art the God of my salvation. Let the words of my mouth and the meditations of my heart be acceptable in thy sight, O Lord, my strength and my Redeemer, forever and ever. Amen.

Opening and Closing Exercises.

Golden Truths.

Supt. The rich and poor meet together: the Lord is the maker of them all. Prov. xxii: 2.

Resp. And he hath made of one blood all nations of men for to dwell on all the face of the earth. Acts xvii: 26.

Supt. Be not thou envious against evil men, neither desire to be with them. Prov. xxiv: 1.

Resp. Be not deceived: evil communications corrupt good manners. I Cor. xv: 33.

Supt. Divers weights are an abomination unto the Lord; and a false balance is not good. Prov. xx: 23.

Resp. That no man go beyond and defraud his brother in any matter; because that the Lord is the avenger of all such. I Thess. iv: 6.

Supt. Keep thee from the evil woman, from the flattery of the tongue of a strange woman. * * * Her house is the way to hell, going down to the chambers of death. Prov. vi: 24; and vii: 27.

Resp. Denying ungodliness and worldly lusts, we should live soberly, righteously, and godly, in this present world. Titus ii: 12.

Supt. Be not amongst wine-bibbers; among riotous eaters of flesh; For the drunkard and the glutton shall come to poverty: and drowsiness shall clothe a man with rags. Prov. xxiii: 20, 21.

Resp. Of the which I tell you before, as I have also told you in time past, that they which do such things shall not inherit the kingdom of God. Gal. v: 21.

Supt. Lying lips are abomination to the Lord: but they that deal truly are his delight. Prov. xii: 22.

Resp. There shall in no wise enter into it any thing that defileth, neither whatsoever worketh abomination, or maketh a lie. Rev. xxi: 27.

Supt. He that is slow to anger is better than the mighty; and he that ruleth his spirit, than he that taketh a city. Prov. xvi: 32.

Resp. Let all bitterness, and wrath, and anger, and clamor, and evil speaking be put away from you, with all malice. Eph. iv: 31.

Supt. The liberal soul shall be made fat; and he that watereth shall be watered also himself. Prov. xi: 25.

Resp. Every man according as he purposeth in his heart so let him give; not grudgingly or of necessity; for God loveth a cheerful giver. II Cor. ix: 7.

Supt. Every one that is proud in heart is an abomination to the Lord: though hand join in hand, he shall not be unpunished. Prov. xvi: 5.

Resp. Let nothing be done through strife or vain glory; but in lowliness of mind let each esteem other better than themselves. Phil. ii: 3.

Supt. and Resp. Godliness is profitable unto all things, having promise of the life that now is, and of that which is to come. I Tim. iv: 8.

Thanksgiving.

Supt. Praise ye the Lord. Sing unto the Lord a new song, and his praise in the congregation of saints. Ps. cxlix: 1.

Resp. Speaking to yourselves in psalms, and hymns, and spiritual songs, singing and making melody in your heart to the Lord. Eph. v: 19.

Supt. I will sing of mercy and judgment: unto thee, O Lord, will I sing. Ps. ci: 1.

Resp. Rejoice in the Lord alway: and again I say, rejoice. Phil. iv: 4.

Supt. Sing unto the Lord with the harp; with the harp, and the voice of a psalm. Ps. xcviii: 5.

Resp. And I heard the voice of the harpers harping with their harps; and they sung, as it were, a new song before the throne. Rev. xiv: 2, 3.

Supt. I will sing of the mercies of the Lord forever: with my mouth will I make known thy faithfulness to all generations. Ps. lxxxix: 1.

Supt. and Resp. Praise him with the psaltery and harp: Praise him with stringed instruments and organs. Let every thing that hath breath praise the Lord.

PRAYER.

IT is good for us to draw near to thee, O God, for thou art the strength of our hearts, and our portion forever. Unto thee, O God, do we give thanks: unto thee do we give thanks: for many are thy wonderful works which thou hast done, and thy thoughts which are toward us. Show us thy ways, O Lord; teach us thy paths. Lead us in thy truth and teach us, for thou art the God of our salvation. Have mercy upon us, O God, according to thy loving-kindness: according unto the multitude of thy tender mercies blot out our transgressions. Wash us thoroughly from our iniquities, and cleanse us from our sins. Create in us clean hearts, O God, and renew right spirits within us. Withhold not thou thy tender mercies from us; but let thy loving kindness and thy truth continually preserve us. Thy mercy, O Lord, is in the heavens, and thy faithfulness reacheth unto the clouds: therefore the children of men put their trust under the shadow of thy wings. O Lord our God, we will give thanks unto thee forever. *Amen.* "Our Father, who art in heaven," etc.

Opening and Closing Exercises.

What Jesus said.

Supt. Except a man be born again, he can not see the kingdom of God.

Resp. If a man have not the spirit of Christ, he is none of his.

Supt. God is a spirit, and they that worship him must worship him in spirit and in truth.

Resp. I am the way, the truth, and the life: no man cometh unto the Father but by me.

Supt. Look unto me, and be ye saved, all ye ends of the earth, for I am God, and there is none else.

Resp. Search the Scriptures, for they are they which testify of me.

Supt. Ye will not come unto me that ye might have life.

Resp. Behold I stand at the door, and knock: if any man hear my voice, and open the door, I will come in and sup with him, and he with me.

Supt. Come unto me all ye that labor and are heavy laden, and I will give you rest.

Resp. I came not to call the righteous, but sinners to repentance.

Supt. Him that cometh to me, I will in no wise cast out.

Resp. If any man thirst, let him come unto me and drink.

Supt. Whosoever will let him take of the water of life freely.

Resp. I am the door: by me, if any man enter in, he shall be saved.

Supt. Verily, verily, I say unto you, he that believeth on me hath everlasting life.

Resp. Except ye be converted and become as little children, ye can not enter into the kingdom of heaven.

Supt. and Resp. I am the good shepherd: the good shepherd giveth his life for the sheep: my sheep hear my voice and I know them, and they follow me.

Beatitudes.

Supt. Blessed are the poor in spirit:

Resp. For theirs is the kingdom of heaven.

Supt. Blessed are they that mourn:

Resp. For they shall be comforted.

Supt. Blessed are the meek:

Resp. For they shall inherit the earth.

Supt. Blessed are they which do hunger and thirst after righteousness:

Resp. For they shall be filled.

Supt. Blessed are the merciful:

Resp. For they shall obtain mercy.

Supt. Blessed are the pure in heart:

Resp. For they shall see God.

Supt. Blessed are the peacemakers:

Resp. For they shall be called the children of God.

Supt. Blessed are they which are persecuted for righteousness' sake:

Resp. For theirs is the kingdom of heaven.

Supt. Blessed are they that dwell in thy house:

Resp. They will be still praising thee.

Supt. Blessed is he that considereth the poor:

Resp. The Lord will deliver him in time of trouble.

Supt. Blessed is the man that endureth temptation:

Resp. For when he is tried he shall receive the crown of life.

Supt. and Resp. The blessing of the Lord it maketh rich, and he addeth no sorrow with it.

Consoling Promises of Christ.

Supt. Where two or three are gathered together in my name, there am I in the midst of them.

Resp. Whatsoever ye shall ask the father in my name, he will give it you: ask and ye shall receive, that your joy may be full.

Supt. He that endureth to the end shall be saved.

Resp. It is your father's good pleasure to give you the kingdom.

Supt. I go to prepare a place for you, that where I am ye may be also.

Resp. And I will give them eternal life, and they shall never perish, neither shall any man pluck them out of my hands.

Supt. Peace I leave with you: my peace I give unto you.

Resp. They that seek me early shall find me.

Supt. and Resp. Eye hath not seen, nor ear heard; neither have entered into the heart of man the things which God hath prepared for them that love him.

THE LORD'S PRAYER.

OUR FATHER, who art in heaven, hallowed be thy name; thy kingdom come, thy will be done on earth, as it is in heaven. Give us this day our daily bread; and forgive us our trespasses, as we forgive them that trespass against us. And lead us not into temptation, but deliver us from evil; for thine is the kingdom, and the power, and the glory, forever and ever. Amen.

Index of Tunes.

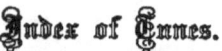

Index of Hymns.

Index of Hymns.

Classified Index of Subjects.

Classified Index of Subjects.

USICAL EAVES

FOR

SABBATH SCHOOLS,

COMPOSED OF

MUSICAL LEAVES Nos. 1, 2, 3, and 4,

WITH AN ADDITION OF

ONE HUNDRED POPULAR HYMNS.

BY

PHILIP PHILLIPS.

NEWLY REVISED EDITION, ENLARGED.

CINCINNATI:

PUBLISHED BY PHILIP PHILLIPS & CO.,

FOR SALE BY THE PUBLISHERS, AND THE
METHODIST BOOK CONCERN, CINCINNATI,
AND AT THE PRINCIPAL BOOKSTORES THROUGHOUT THE COUNTRY.

PREFACE.

THE *MUSICAL LEAVES were first issued periodically, in Numbers, with a view of making each number a complete Book of itself. When several numbers had been issued, sufficient to form a complete standard Sunday-School Singing Book, they were bound together, and in this form were widely sold throughout the country. Indeed so many have been printed that it has become necessary to make new plates, and rather than give the public the same old pieces, I have revised the book by taking out such songs as have become worn out or uninteresting, and put in their places choice gems. It will be seen that this revision makes it almost an entirely new Book.*

I have appended a special Department for Anniversaries and other occasions of interest in the Sunday-School work.

The book also contains a large collection of the most popular Sunday-School songs up to the present time.

I earnestly pray that these "Leaves," in the "revised" as in the original form, will gladden the hearts of many thousands in their journey to Zion.

Many thanks are due Messrs. T. C. O'Kane, S. J. Vail, Geo. F. Root, and Dr. Lowell Mason, and others for valuable and beautiful songs contributed.

PHILIP PHILLIPS.

MUSICAL LEAVES.

COME JOIN OUR BAND.

Hymn. No. 1.

T. C. O'KANE.

Lively.

1. We're marching to the promised land, A land all fair and bright;
2. The Sav - ior feeds his lit - tle flock, His grace is free - ly given;

Come join our hap - py youth-ful band, And seek the plains of light.
The liv - ing wa - ter from the rock, And dai - ly bread from heaven.

Chorus.

O! come and join our youth - ful band, Our songs and triumphs share;

We soon shall reach the promised land, And rest for - ev - er there.

3 In that bright land no sin is found,
  But all are happy there,
And happy, youthful voices join
  In the angelic choir.
    O! come and join, etc.

4 Our teachers kind point out the way,
  And guide our feet aright,
To the bright realms of endless day,
  Where Jesus is the light.
    O! come and join, etc.

4

WORK FOR THE NIGHT IS COMING.

From "Song Garden," by permission.

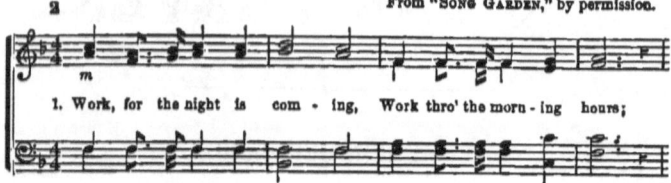

1. Work, for the night is com - ing, Work thro' the morn - ing hours;

Work, while the dew is spark - ling, Work 'mid spring - ing flowers;

Work when the day grows bright - er, Work in the glow - ing sun;

Work, for the night is com - ing, When man's work is done.

2. Work, for the night is coming;
   Work through the sunny noon;
   Fill brightest hours with labor;
   Rest comes sure and soon.
   Give every flying minute
   Something to keep in store;
   Work, for the night is coming,
   When man works no more.

3. Work, for the night is coming,
   Under the sunset skies;
   While their bright tints are glowing,
   Work, for daylight flies.
   Work till the last beam fadeth,
   Fadeth to shine no more;
   Work, while the night is darkening,
   When man's work is o'er.

"THE BIBLE SAYS I MAY."

"Out of the mouth of babes and sucklings thou hast perfected praise."

Music by PHILIP PHILLIPS.

1. I am a lit-tle sol-dier, And on-ly five years old;
I mean to fight for Je-sus, And wear a crown of gold;
I know he makes me hap-py, And loves me all the day,
I'll be his lit-tle sol-dier, "The Bi-ble says I may.

2. I love my Precious Saviour,
   Because he died for me,
   And if I did not serve him,
   How sinful I should be;
   He gives me every comfort,
   And hears me when I pray,
   I want to live for Jesus,
   "The Bible says I may."

3. I now can do but little,
   Yet, when I grow a man,
   I'll try and do for Jesus,
   The greatest good I can;
   God help and keep me faithful
   In all I do and say;
   I want to live a Christian,
   "The Bible says I may."

FATHER, TAKE MY HAND.

S. J. VAIL.

2. The day declines, my Father! | and the night
Is drawing darkly down. My faithless sight
Sees | ghostly | visions. | Fears of a spectral band
Encompass me. O Father, | take my | hand,
   And from the night lead up to light,
      Up to light, up to light,
   Lead up to light Thy child!

3. The way is long, my Father! | and my soul
Longs for the rest and quiet | of the | goal; |
While yet I journey through this weary land,
Keep me from wandering. Father, | take my | hand,
   And in the way to endless day,
      Endless day, endless day,
   Lead safely on Thy child!

4. The path is rough, my Father! | Many a thorn
Has pierced me; and my feet, all torn
And bleeding, | mark the | way. | Yet Thy command
Bids me press forward. Father, | take my | hand;
   Then safe and blest, O lead to rest,
      Lead to rest, lead to rest,
   O lead to rest Thy child!

5. The throng is great, my Father! | Many a doubt
And fear of danger compass me about;
And foes op- | press me | sore. | I cannot stand
Or go, alone. O Father! | take my | hand;
   And through the throng, lead safe along,
      Safe along, safe along,
   Lead safe along Thy child!

6. The cross is heavy, Father! | I have borne
It long, and | still do | bear it. | Let my worn
And fainting spirit rise to that bright land
Where crowns are given. Father, | take my | hand;
   And, reaching down, lead to the crown,
      To the crown, to the crown,
   Lead to the crown Thy child!

CHRISTMAS CAROL.

Words by MARIE MASON.   From "SONG-GARDEN," by permission.

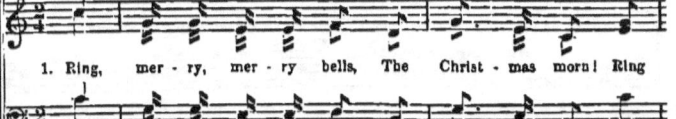

1. Ring, mer - ry, mer - ry bells, The Christ - mas morn! Ring

out a joy - ous peal! The Sav - iour comes, The

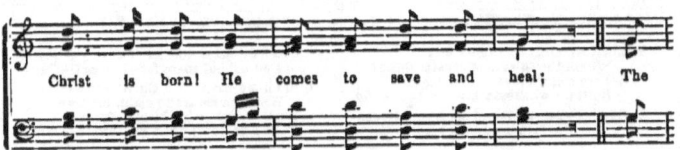

Christ is born! He comes to save and heal; The

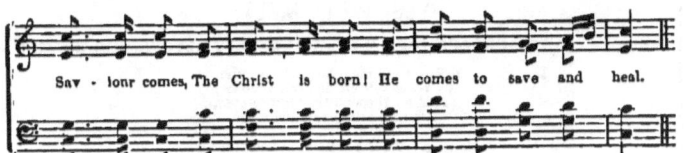

Sav - iour comes, The Christ is born! He comes to save and heal.

2. Ring, merry, merry bells,
   O'er all the land,
By hall and cottage fires—
   Let every home
   And household band
Hear music from your spires.

3. Ring, merry, merry bells!
   There cometh here
The wondrous Truth, at last,
   By ancient king
   And kingly seer,
So longed for, ages past!

4. Ring, merry, merry bells!
   Let hill and vale,
Through all the festal day—

In notes of joy
   Repeat the tale
Of Christ, the Living Way!

5. Ring, merry, merry bells!
   Our heavy load
We lay, rejoicing, down
   For by His cross
   We gain the road
To our eternal crown.

6. Ring, merry, merry bells!
   Your carols pour,—
Nor let your gladness cease:
   The Wonderful!
   The Counsellor!
The mighty Prince of Peace!

SHALL WE MEET BEYOND THE RIVER?

6 *Moderato.*

Music by PHILIP PHILLIPS.

1. Shall we meet beyond the riv-er, Where the surges cease to roll? Where, in all the

bright for-ev-er, Sor-row ne'er shall press the soul? Shall we meet? shall we meet?

CHORUS.

Shall we meet beyond the riv-er, Where the surg-es cease to roll?

2. Shall we meet in yonder city,
 Where the towers of crystal shine?
 Where the walls are all of jasper,
 Built by workmanship divine?—*Cho.*

3. Shall we meet with many a loved one,
 That was torn from our embrace?

Shall we listen to their voices,
 And behold them face to face?—*Cho.*

4. Shall we meet with Christ our Saviour,
 When he comes to claim his own?
 Shall we know his blessed favor,
 And sit down upon his throne?—*Cho.*

YES, WE'LL MEET.

ANSWER TO, OR CHORUS FOR, "SHALL WE MEET BEYOND THE RIVER?"

7

1 Yes, we'll meet beyond the river,
 When our conflicts all are o'er;
 And we'll spend the blest forever,
 On that bright celestial shore.

CHORUS.—We shall meet! we shall meet!
 We shall meet beyond the river,
 Where the surges cease to roll!

2 Yes, we'll meet in yonder mansions,
 Where our wand'rings all shall cease;
 There we'll meet our dear companions,
 And be crowned with perfect peace.—*Cho.*

3 Yes, we'll meet where bliss immortal,
 Sweeter far than rest can be;
 And before the throne eternal,
 All our earthly triumphs see.—*Cho.*

4 We shall meet, where all is onward,
 Every change new glories bring;
 And the host still moving forward,
 Glorify our heav'nly King.—*Cho.*

5 We shall meet, O weary brother,
 When the burden we lay down;
 We shall change our cross of anguish,
 For a bright unfading crown.—*Cho.*

"WHAT ARE YOU GOING TO DO, BROTHER."

8

Dedicated to the Young Men's National Christian Association. PHILIP PHILLIPS.

1. O what are you going to do, brother? Say, what are you going to do? You have
2. Will you honor His cause and kingdom, Wherever your path may be? And

thought of some useful labor, But what is the end in view? You are fresh from the home of your
stand as a bright example, That others your light may see? Are you willing to live for

boy-hood, And just in the bloom of youth! Have you tasted the sparkling water, That
Je - sus! And read-y the cross to bear? Are you willing to meet reproaches? The

CHORUS.

flows from the fount of truth? Is your heart in the Saviour's keeping? Remember he died for
frowns of the world to share? Your lot may perhaps be humble, But God has a work for

you! Then what are you going to do, brother? Say, what are you going to do?
you; Then what are you going to do, brother? Say, what are you going to do?

3. O what are you going to do, brother?
The morning of youth is past;
The vigor and strength of manhood,
My brother, are yours at last.
You are rising in worldly prospects,
And prospered in worldly things;—
A duty to those less favored
The smile of your fortune brings.
Cho.—Go, prove that your heart is grateful—
The Lord has a work for you;
Then what are you going to do, brother?
Say, what are you going to do?

4. O what are you going to do, brother?
Your sun at its noon is high;
It shines in meridian splendor,
And rides through a cloudless sky.
You are holding a high position
Of honor, of trust, and fame;—

Are you willing to give the glory
And praise to your Saviour's name?
Cho.—The regions that sit in darkness
Are stretching their hands to you;
Then what are you going to do, brother?
Say, what are you going to do?

5. O what are you going to do, brother?
The twilight approaches now;—
Already your locks are silvered,
And winter is on your brow.
Your talents, your time, your riches,
To Jesus, your Master, give;
Then ask if the world around you
Is better because you live.
Cho.—You are nearing the brink of Jordan,
But still there is work for you;
Then what are you going to do, brother?
Say, what are you going to do?

NEARER, MY GOD, TO THEE. Bethany. 6s & 4s.

From the "ASAPH," by permission of DR. LOWELL MASON.

1. Near - er, my God, to thee, Near - er to thee; E'en though it

be a cross, That rais - eth me, Still all my song shall be,

Near - er, my God, to thee, Near - er, my God, to thee, Near - er to thee.

2. Though like a wanderer,	4. Then with my waking thoughts,
Daylight all gone,	Bright with thy praise,
Darkness be over me,	Out of my stony griefs,
My rest a stone,	Bethel I'll raise;
Yet in my dreams I'd be	So by my woes to be
Nearer, my God, &c.	Nearer, my God, &c.
3. There let the way appear,	5. Or, if on joyful wing,
Steps up to heaven;	Cleaving the sky,
All that thou sendest me	Sun, moon, and stars forgot,
In mercy given,	Upward I fly,
Angels to beckon me,	Still, all my song shall be,
Nearer, my God, &c.	Nearer, my God, &c.

THE LORD'S PRAYER.*

MATT. VI : 9.

(PITCH E.) Our Father which art in heaven, Hallowed be thy name. Thy kingdom come. Thy will be done on earth, as it is in heaven. Give us this day our daily bread. And forgive us our trespasses, as we forgive those who trespass against us. And lead us not into temptation, but deliver us from evil. For thine is the kingdom, and the power, and the glory, for ever.

A - men.

* Let the words be deliberately, distinctly, and reverently pronounced to the given pitch (say E) either by a single voice, or in unison by all the voices, adding the Amen in harmony parts, as written.

THE STILL SMALL VOICE.

Words by S. H. Thayer, Esq.　　　　From "Happy Voices," by permission.

1. Oft as I rove, in thoughtless mood, A - long life's flow-ery, sun - ny
2. From day to day that voice I hear, And oft - enest when no friend is

road,...... Un - con - scious how the path may end,...... Un -
near—..... When, on some se - cret pur - pose bent,....:. Or

- heed - ing where my footsteps tend, I hear a voice which seems to
on some pleas-ure too in - tent— A still small voice, which seems to

pp

say, In a gen - tle whisper, "Come a - way, Come a - way!"
say, In a gen - tle whisper, &c.

pp

Soft - ly It whispers, "Come a - way, Come a - way, Come a - way!"

11

MY HEAVENLY HOME IS SURE.

Words by Mrs M. A. KIDDER.

PHILIP PHILLIPS.

| *Semi-chorus.* 1st time. | | *Semi-chorus.* 2d time.

1. Tho' clouds may fade before mine eyes, My heavenly home is sure;
Tho' stars should fall from out the skies, (Omit.) My heavenly home is sure.

If I but strive and watch and pray, And dai - ly cast my sins a - way, And

Ritard.

keep my conscience clean and pure, My heavenly home is sure, My heavenly home is sure.

2 Though loving friends should turn to foes,
  My heavenly home is sure;
Though every earthly blessing goes,
  My heavenly home is sure.
If I but seek Christ's pardoning grace,
And humbly bow before his face,
No matter what I may endure,
  My heavenly home is sure.

3 Though earthquakes rend the solid ground,
  My heavenly home is sure;
Though tempests roll destruction round,
  My heavenly home is sure.
If I but seek the better part,
And give to God my contrite heart,
In spite of sin and worldly lure,
  My heavenly home is sure.

12

JESUS BIDS US SHINE.

For the INFANT CLASS.

T. C. O'KANE.

1. Je - sus bids us shine With a pure, clear light, Like a lit - tle

can - dle, Burn - ing in the night. In a world of dark - ness, So

we must shine— You in your small cor - ner, And I in mine.

2 Jesus bids us shine,
    First of all for him;
  Well he sees and knows it,
    If our light grows dim.
  He looks down from heaven,
    To see us shine—
  You in your small corner,
    And I in mine.

3 Jesus bids us shine,
    Then for all around,
  Many kinds of darkness
    In the world abound.
  Sin and want and sorrow,
    So we must shine—
  You in your small corner,
    And I in mine.

THE MORNING LAND.

"So he bringeth them unto their desired haven."

13

T. C. O'KANE.

1. These many days 'mid storm and rain, We've sailed against the tide; But now the harbor
2. Wildly we've tossed upon the deep, Our hope a sin - gle ray; But see the star of

is in view, Where we may safe-ly ride. With anchor weighed, and canvas spread, A
morning beams, The harbin-ger of day. Soon we shall furl our tattered sail, And

weary, toiling 'band, We hail the breeze that speeds us on To the glorious morning land.
press the wished-for land; Our bark will moor beside thy shore, O! glorious morning land.

Chorus to each verse.

The morning land, bright morning land, O, glorious morning land!

Soon we shall rest on thy beau-ti - ful shore, O, glorious morning land!

3 A heavenly calm shall soothe the waves,
   And bid them hush to sleep;
Eternal sunbeams evermore
   Shall rest upon the deep.
Our bark no more by tempest tossed,
   Shall bear a weary band,
There's rest forever 'mid thy groves,
   O, glorious morning land.

4 Earth's pilgrims joyful walk thy streets
   In robes of shining white;
The city gates are built of pearl,
   And God is all the light.
We've looked from far upon thy shores;
   Our friends have reached the strand;
Soon we shall join the happy throng
   In the glorious morning land.

BE OF GOOD COURAGE.

14

Philip Phillips.

1. Faint not, droop not, wea - ry pil - grim! In the faith of Je - sus stand;
He will guard thee, and will guide thee Safe - ly to the promised land.
D. C. Love and joy and peace for - ev - er, In the sweet and promised land.

Chorus.

No more care and no more sor-row, But a bright, e - ter - nal mor-row;

2 What though storms beset thy pathway,
And the clouds are dark and drear,
Sing aloud the songs of Zion,
For the port of peace is near.—*Cho.*

3 Fear not, though the billows threaten,
God will send his angels down;
In their hands they'll bear thee upward,
To receive the shining crown.—*Cho.*

ALAS! AND DID MY SAVIOR BLEED?

15

S. J. Vail.

Fine.

1. A - las! and did my Sav - ior bleed? And did my Sovereign die?
D. C. Yes, Je - sus died for all man-kind, Bless God, sal - va - tion's free.

Would he de - vote that sa - cred head For such a worm as I?

Chorus.

D. C. *Chorus.*

Je - sus died for you; Je - sus died for me;

2 Was it for crimes that I had done,
He groaned upon the tree?
Amazing pity! grace unknown!
And love beyond degree.—*Cho.*

3 Well might the sun in darkness hide,
And shut his glories in,
When Christ, the mighty Maker, died,
For man, the creature's sin.—*Cho.*

4 Thus might I hide my blushing face
While his dear cross appears;
Dissolve my heart in thankfulness,
And melt mine eyes to tears.—*Cho.*

5 But drops of grief can ne'er repay
The debt of love I owe;
Here, Lord, I give myself away,
'Tis all that I can do.—*Cho.*

16

SPIRIT VOICES.

Words by Rev. L. HARTSOUGH.　　　　　　　　　Music by S. J. VAIL.

1. List-en to the promptings Of the Spir-it near, Call-ing to sal-va-tion, And from sin and fear; By them you may gath-er Light, and life, and power, Freedom from the lur-ings Of temp-ta-tion's hour.

CHORUS.

God is near thee night and day, God will hear thee, There-fore pray; God is near thee, Night and day, God will hear thee, There-fore pray.

2. Listen to the pleadings
Of the Saviour's love;
Calling thee from sinning,
To His home above.
He will save from sorrow,
And the night of death;
And the dread hereafter,
Where is felt his wrath.—*Cho.*

3. He is fitting mansions
For His followers true;
There is room now waiting,
Waiting just for you.

Will you taste the raptures
That His saints shall know?
Will you love the Saviour
And to glory go?—*Cho.*

4. Come, then, to the fountain,
Gushing from His side;
God and heaven invites you,
Plunge beneath the tide;
There is peace and pardon
For each sin-sick soul,
Hallelujah, glory!
Jesus died for all.—*Cho.*

SUNDAY-SCHOOL BAND.

P. Phillips.

ALTO.

1. Hark ! the Sab-bath-school bell ring - ing, Calls us from our homes a - way;
2. Come, O come, we dear - ly love you, Come and join our hap - py band;

TREBLE.

3. On our heads a crown of glo - ry, With a harp of sweetest tone,
4. Death no more can mar our pleasures, Nev-er take our friends a - way,

BASS.

Haste, or we shall miss the singing In the Sab - bath-school to-day.
You will nev - er once re - gret it, When a - round the throne we stand.

We will try and tell the story Of the Sav - ior's love a - lone.
But with them we 'll live for - ever, In the climes of end - less day.

2d Chorus. Come and join our happy band, Hap-py band, Hap-py band,

3d Chorus. Then we 'll be a happy band, Hap-py band, Hap-py band,

1st Chorus. For we are a hap - py band, Hap-py band, Hap-py band,

Repeat PP.

Come and join our hap - py band, In the Sab - bath - school.

Then we 'll be a hap - py land, When we all get home.

For we are a hap - py band, In the Sab - bath - school.

18

I WANT TO BE AN ANGEL.

Melody by E. L. WHITE.

1. I want to be an an - gel, And with the angels stand, A crown up-on my
2. I know I'm weak and sin-ful, But Je - sus will for-give, For man-y lit - tle
3. Oh, there I'll be an an - gel, And with the angels stand, A crown up-on my

fore - head, A harp with-in my hand; There, right be-fore my Sav - ior, So
child - ren Have gone to heaven to live; Dear Sav - ior, when I lan - guish, And
fore - head, A harp with-in my hand; And there, be - fore my Sav - ior, So

glorious and so bright, I'd wake the sweetest music, And praise him day and night.
lay me down to die, O! send a shining an-gel, And bear me to the skies.
glorious and s bright, I'll join the heavenly music, And praise him day and night.

19

DEATH OF A SCHOLAR. 8s & 7s.

Dr. L. MASON.

Andante.

1. Sis - ter, thou wast mild and love - ly, Gen - tle as the sum-mer breeze;
2. Peaceful be thy si - lent slum-ber, Peace-ful in the grave so low;
3. Dear-est sis - ter, thou hast left us, Here thy loss we deep - ly feel;
4. Yet a - gain we hope to meet thee, When the day of life is fled;

Pleasant as the air of ev'-ning, When it floats a - mong the trees.
Thou no more wilt join our number, Thou no . more our songs shalt know.
But 't is God that has be - reft us, He can still our sor - row heal.
Then, in heaven with joy to greet thee, Where no fare-well tear is shed.

NOTE.—Use brother, or sister, as the occasion may require.

2

CHILDREN'S ANTHEM.

S. J. VAIL.

Suf-fer the lit-tle children, Suf-fer the lit-tle children, Suf-fer the lit-tle chil-dren to come un-to me, and for-bid them not, and for-bid them not.

Suf-fer the lit-tle chil-dren, Suf-fer the lit-tle chil-dren, Suf-fer the lit-tle children to come un-to me, Suf-fer the lit-tle chil-dren to come un-to me, Suf-fer the lit-tle chil-dren to come un-to me,

SOLO or DUET.

for of such is the king-dom of heaven, for of such, of such, of such is the king-dom of

ad lib.

heaven, of such, of such is the king-dom of heaven. Suffer the lit-tle children,

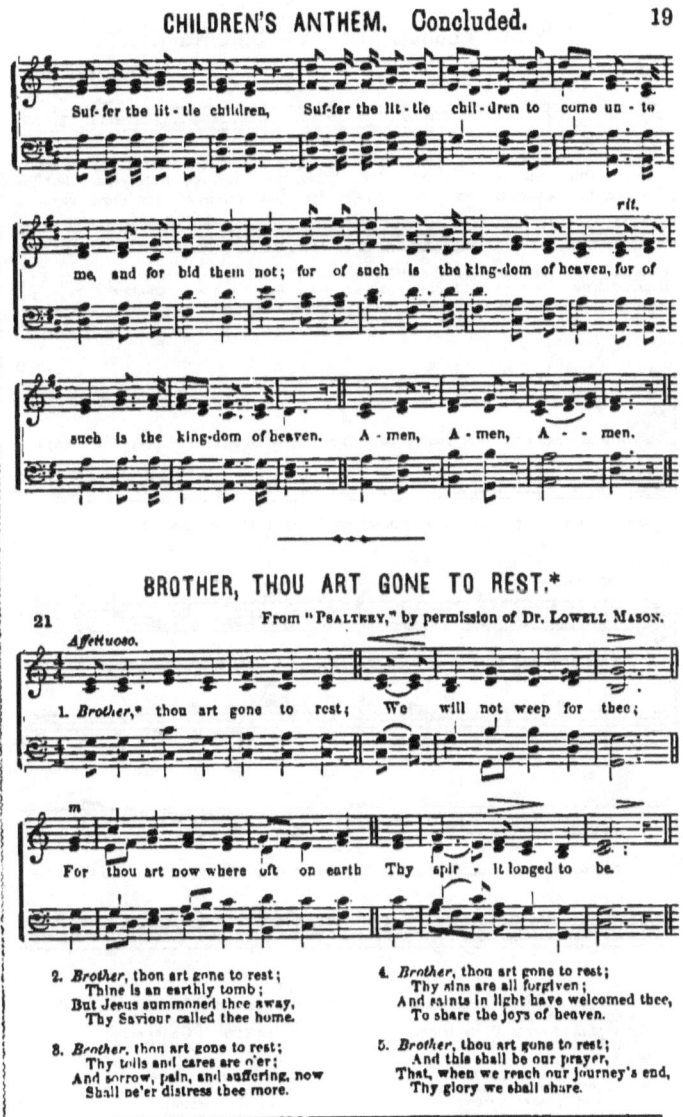

Suf-fer the lit-tle children, Suf-fer the lit-tle chil-dren to come un-to

me, and for bid them not; for of such is the king-dom of heaven, for of

such is the king-dom of heaven. A-men, A-men, A---men.

BROTHER, THOU ART GONE TO REST.*

21

From "PSALTERY," by permission of Dr. LOWELL MASON.

Affettuoso.

1. *Brother,* thou art gone to rest; We will not weep for thee;

For thou art now where oft on earth Thy spir - it longed to be.

2. Brother, thou art gone to rest;
    Thine is an earthly tomb;
    But Jesus summoned thee away,
    Thy Saviour called thee home.

3. Brother, thou art gone to rest;
    Thy toils and cares are o'er;
    And sorrow, pain, and suffering, now
    Shall ne'er distress thee more.

4. Brother, thou art gone to rest;
    Thy sins are all forgiven;
    And saints in light have welcomed thee,
    To share the joys of heaven.

5. Brother, thou art gone to rest;
    And this shall be our prayer,
    That, when we reach our journey's end,
    Thy glory we shall share.

* *Sister, Teacher,* or *Schoolmate* can be used in place of *Brother.*

"WHAT VESSEL ARE YOU SAILING IN?"

22

PHILLIPS AND DOANE.

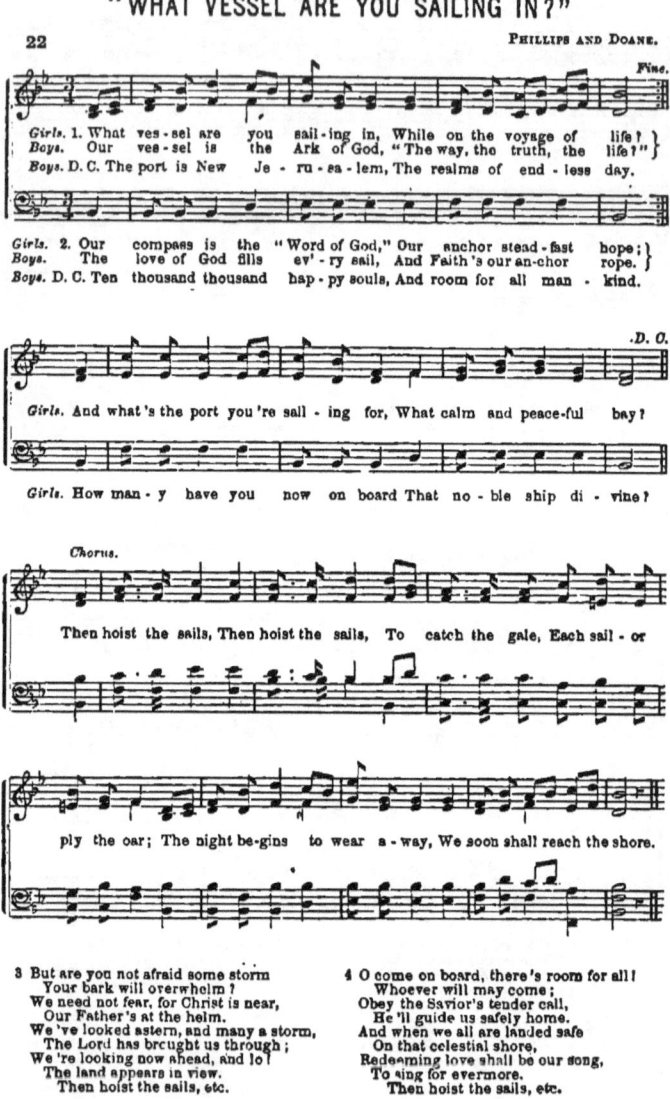

Girls. 1. What ves-sel are you sail-ing in, While on the voyage of life?
Boys. Our ves-sel is the Ark of God, "The way, the truth, the life?"
Boys. D. C. The port is New Je-ru-sa-lem, The realms of end-less day.

Girls. 2. Our compass is the "Word of God," Our anchor stead-fast hope;
Boys. The love of God fills ev'-ry sail, And Faith's our an-chor rope.
Boys. D. C. Ten thousand thousand hap-py souls, And room for all man-kind.

Girls. And what's the port you're sail-ing for, What calm and peace-ful bay?

Girls. How man-y have you now on board That no-ble ship di-vine?

Chorus.

Then hoist the sails, Then hoist the sails, To catch the gale, Each sail-or

ply the oar; The night be-gins to wear a-way, We soon shall reach the shore.

3 But are you not afraid some storm
　Your bark will overwhelm ?
We need not fear, for Christ is near,
　Our Father's at the helm.
We've looked astern, and many a storm,
　The Lord has brought us through ;
We're looking now ahead, and lo !
　The land appears in view.
　　Then hoist the sails, etc.

4 O come on board, there's room for all !
　Whoever will may come ;
Obey the Savior's tender call,
　He'll guide us safely home.
And when we all are landed safe
　On that celestial shore,
Redeeming love shall be our song,
　To sing for evermore.
　　Then hoist the sails, etc.

RECRUIT FOR THE ARMY ABOVE.

Words by A. W. Livingston.

Philip Phillips.

23

1. There's many a poor lit-tle boy, Whose fa-ther and moth-er are dead,
2. Go out in the hed-ges and find, (For Je-sus has giv-en the rule,)
3. Go, bear-ing the en-sign of love, Its glo-ries for-ev-er unfurled,

Whose heart is a stranger to joy, No home save a hov-el or shed.
The halt and the maimed and the blind, Go bring them all in-to the school.
Re-cruit for the ar-my a-bove, Your war-rant em-bra-ces the world.

Chorus, faster.

We care not how poor or rich he may be, Go bring him

2d Cho. We care not how poor or rich they may be, Go bring them

in, sal-va-tion is free; His soul is a jew-el, whose

in, sal-va-tion is free; Their souls are all jew-els, whose

light by-and-by, May shine in your crown, like a star in the sky.

light by-and-by, May shine in your crown, like the stars in the sky.

WHERE SHALL THE SOUL FIND REST?

PHILIP PHILLIPS.

1. { Tell me, ye wing- } { Do ye not know some }
   { ed winds, that } round my pathway roar, { spot where mortals } weep no more?

{ Some lone and pleasant } in the west, { Where, free from toil and } soul may rest?
{ dell, some valley...... } { pain, the weary....... }

{ Where, free from toil and pain, } soul may rest? { The loud wind dwin- } whisper low,
{ the weary.................. } { dled to a......... }

And sighed for pity, as it answered, "No! No! No! No!"

2. Tell me, thou mighty deep, whose | billows | round me | play,
Know'st thou some favored spot, some island | far a- | way,
Where weary man may find the bliss for | which he | sighs—
Where sorrow never lives, and friendship | never | dies?
Where sorrow never lives, and friendship | never | dies.
The loud waves, rolling in per- | petual | flow,
Stopped for awhile, and sighed to answer, | "No!"

3. And thou, serenest moon, that | with such | holy | face,
Dost look upon the earth asleep in | night's em- | brace,
Tell me, in all thy round, hast thou not | seen some | spot
Where miserable man might find a | happier | lot?
Where miserable man might find a | happier | lot?
Behind a cloud the moon with- | drew in | woe,
And a voice, sweet but sad, responded, | "No!"

4. Tell me, my secret soul—O | tell me, | Hope and | Faith,
Is there no resting-place from sorrow, | sin, and | death?
Is there no happy spot where mortals | may be | blest,
Where grief may find a balm, and weari- | ness a | rest?
Where grief may find a balm, and weari- | ness a | rest?
Faith, Hope, and Love—best boons to | mortals | given—
Waved their bright wings, and whispered, | "Yes! ▼ | yes, | in | heaven."

MISSIONARY HYMN. 26th P. M.

25

1. From Greenland's i - cy mount-ains, From In - dia's co - ral strand,

Where A - fric's sun - ny fount - ains Roll down their gold - en sand;

From many an an - cient riv - er, From many a palm - y plain,

They call us to de - liv - er Their land from er - ror's chain.

2. What though the spicy breezes
   Blow soft o'er Ceylon's isle ;
   Though every prospect pleases,
   And only man is vile :
   In vain with lavish kindness
   The gifts of God are strown ;
   The heathen in his blindness
   Bows down to wood and stone.

3. Shall we, whose souls are lighted
   With wisdom from on high,
   Shall we to men benighted
   The lamp of life deny ?

Salvation !—O salvation !
   The joyful sound proclaim,
   Till earth's remotest nation
   Has learn'd Messiah's name.

4. Waft, waft, ye winds, his story,
   And you, ye waters, roll,
   Till, like a sea of glory,
   It spreads from pole to pole :
   Till o'er our ransom'd nature
   The Lamb for sinners slain,
   Redeemer, King, Creator,
   In bliss returns to reign.

"CLIMBING UP ZION'S HILL."

26 Little Artie Bain, with tremulous voice and moistened eyes, uttered these words in the class-room.

Words by Rev. JOHN G. CHAFEE.　　　　Music by PHILIP PHILLIPS.

1. "I'm try-ing to climb up Zi - on's Hill," For the Sa-vior whispers "Love me;"
2. I know I'm but a lit - tle child, My strength will not protect me;
3. Then come with me, we'll up-ward go, And climb this hill to-geth-er;

Though all beneath is dark as death, Yet the stars are bright a - bove me.
But then I am the Sa-vior's lamb, And he will not neg-lect me.
And as we walk, we'll sweet-ly talk, And sing as we go thi - ther.

Then up - ward still, To Zi - on's Hill, To the land of joy and beau - ty,
Then all the time I'll try to climb This ho - ly hill of Zi - on,
Then mount up still God's ho - ly hill, Till we reach the pearl - y port - als,

My path be - fore Shines more and more, As it nears the gold - en cit - y.
For I am sure The way is pure, And on it comes "no li - on."
Where raptured tongues Proclaim the songs Of the shi - ning-robed im - mor-tals.

Solo, or Semi-chorus.　　　　*Duet, or 2d Semi-chorus.*

I'm climbing up Zi - on's Hill, I'm climbing up Zi - on's Hill.

Full Chorus.

Climb - ing, climb - ing, climb - ing up Zi - on's Hill.

GUIDE US, SAVIOR.

"He will guide you into all truth."

27

T. C. O'KANE.

Gently.

1. God has said, "For - ev - er bless - ed Those who seek me in their youth,
2. Be our strength, for we are weak-ness; Be our wis-dom and our guide;

They shall find the path of wisdom, And the nar-row way of truth."
May we walk in love and meekness, Near-er to our Sa-vior's side.

Guide us Sa - vior, Guide us Sa - vior, In the nar-row way of truth. Guide us
Naught can harm us, Naught can harm us, While we thus in thee abide, Naught can

Repeat, ad libitum, PP.

Sa - vior, Guide us Sa - vior, In the nar - row way of truth.
harm us, Naught can harm us, While we thus in thee a - bide.

3 Thus when evening shades shall gather,
   We may turn our tearless eye
To the dwelling of our Father,
To our home beyond the sky;
|: Gently passing :|
To the happy land on high.

2 May thy watchful angels hover
   Round us, when there's evil near;
May we hide beneath the cover
Of thy wings, in time of fear:
   And in sorrow,
   And in sorrow,
Comfort our sad hearts, and cheer.

28 Lend us Thy Favor.

BY MISS ANNIE E. HOWE.

1 Guide us! O thou blessed Savior;
Thoughtless little ones are we;
Lend us e'er thy loving favor,
May we strive to follow thee,
|: From temptation, :|
Bid our careless footsteps be.

4 And when death at last o'ertakes us,
   And we sink beneath his might,
May that blessed morn awake us,
Safe in yonder realms of light;
   There forever,
   There forever,
Chant thy praise with angels bright.

THE LION OF JUDAH.

Words and Theme by H. Q. Wilson.　　　　　　　　Composed by HENRY TUCKER.

DUET or SEMI-CHORUS.　　　　　　　　From "CHORAL HARP."

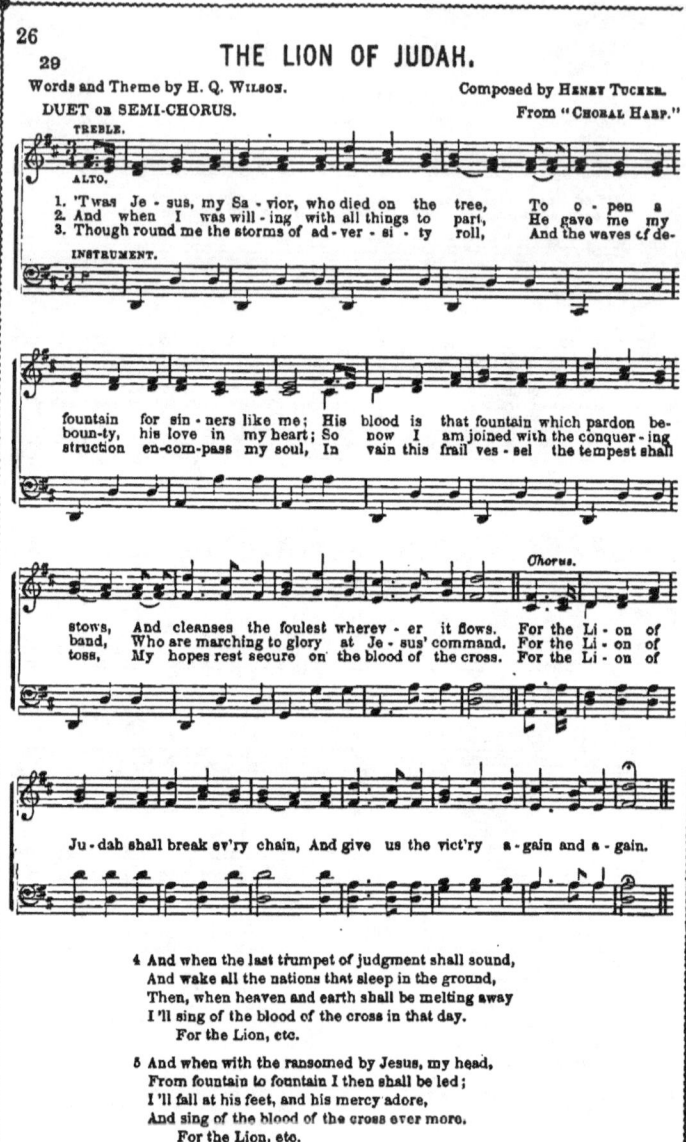

1. 'Twas Je - sus, my Sa - vior, who died on the tree, To o - pen a
2. And when I was will - ing with all things to part, He gave me my
3. Though round me the storms of ad - ver - si - ty roll, And the waves of de-

fountain for sin - ners like me; His blood is that fountain which pardon be-
boun-ty, his love in my heart; So now I am joined with the conquer - ing
struction en-com-pass my soul, In vain this frail ves - sel the tempest shall

stows, And cleanses the foulest wherev - er it flows. For the Li - on of
band, Who are marching to glory at Je - sus' command. For the Li - on of
toss, My hopes rest secure on the blood of the cross. For the Li - on of

Ju - dah shall break ev'ry chain, And give us the vict'ry a - gain and a - gain.

4 And when the last trumpet of judgment shall sound,
   And wake all the nations that sleep in the ground,
   Then, when heaven and earth shall be melting away
   I'll sing of the blood of the cross in that day.
   　　For the Lion, etc.

5 And when with the ransomed by Jesus, my head,
   From fountain to fountain I then shall be led;
   I'll fall at his feet, and his mercy adore,
   And sing of the blood of the cross ever more.
   　　For the Lion, etc.

JUST BEYOND.

Words and Music by T. C. O'KANE.

30 *First Voice.*

1. Hear you ev - er an - gels sing-ing, As a - round the throne they shine?
2. Hear you ev - er in your slumbers, Songs from those who 've gone before?

Second Voice.

Yes I oft - en hear them chanting, Chanting hymns of love di - vine.
O! how oft - en do I hear them, Sing-ing on the oth - er shore.

Chorus.

Heaven's plains are just be-fore us, Just be - yond the shores of Time;

Soon we 'll join the mighty cho - rus, In that bright - er, bet - ter clime.

3 Lo you ever feel like going
    To that land so bright and fair?
  O! how often would I gladly
    Go and join the loved ones there.
  Heaven's plains, etc.

4 Let us cherish, now and ever,
    Glowing hopes of joys to come,
  And when earthly ties we sever,
    Meet in heaven, our happy home.
  Heaven's plains, etc.

REMARK.—The 1st, 2d and 3d stanzas should be sung by *Solo* voices, as marked, and the 4th stanza as a *Duett*, by the two voices.

HITHERTO HATH THE LORD HELPED US.

28

1. Come thou fount of ev'-ry bless-ing, Tune my heart to sing thy grace;
Streams of mer-cy nev-er ceas-ing, Call for songs of loud-est praise.
D. C. Praise the mount, I'm fixed up-on it, Mount of thy re-deem-ing love.

D. C.

Teach me some me-lo-dious son-net, Sung by flaming tongues a-bove,

D. C.

2 Here I raise my Ebenezer,
  Hither by thy help I'm come,
And I hope, by thy good pleasure,
  Safely to arrive at home.
Jesus sought me when a stranger,
  Wand'ring from the fold of God,
He, to rescue me from danger,
  Interposed his precious blood.

3 O to grace how great a debtor,
  Daily I'm constrained to be!
Let thy goodness, like a fetter,
  Bind my wand'ring heart to thee.
Prone to wander, Lord, I feel it,
  Prone to leave the God I love,
Here's my heart, O take and seal it.
  Seal it for thy courts above.

THE BEAUTIFUL LAND.

32

From "SHINING STAR."

T. E. P.

1. A beau-ti-ful land by faith I see, A land of rest, from sorrow free, The home of the ransomed,
2. That beautiful land, the city of light, It ne'er has known the shades of night; The glory of God, the
3. The heavenly throng, arrayed in white, In rapture range the plains of light; And in one harmonious

Chorus.

bright and fair, And beautiful angels, too, are there. Will you go? Will you go? Go to that beautiful
light of day, Hath driven the darkness far away. Will you go? etc.
choir they praise Their glorious Savior's matchless grace. Will you go? etc.

Repeat Chorus p

land with me? Will you go? Will you go? Go to that beau-ti-ful land with me?

33

SUNDAY-SCHOOL BATTLE-SONG.

Published by the AMERICAN BAPTIST SOCIETY.   Words and Music by Rev. R. LOWRY.

1. Marching on! marching on! glad as birds on the wing, Come the bright ranks of
2. Press-ing on! press-ing on! to the din of the fray, With the firm tread of
3. Fight-ing on! fight-ing on! in the midst of the strife, At the call of our
4. Sing - ing on! sing - ing on! from the bat - tle we come, Ev' - ry flag bears a

children from near and from far; Hap - py hearts, full of song, 'neath our
faith to the bat - tle we go; 'Mid the cheer - ing of an - gels, our
Cap - tain, we draw ev' - ry sword; We are bat - tling for God, we are
wreath, ev'ry sol - dier renown; Heav'nly an - gels are wait - ing to

ban - ners we bring, Lit - tle sol - diers of Zi - on prepared for the war.
ranks march a-way, With our flags point-ing ev - er right on t'wards the foe.
struggling for life, Let us strike ev' - ry reb - el that fights 'gainst the Lord.
wel - come us home, And the Sa - vior will give us a robe and a crown.

Chorus.

Marching on! marching on! sound the bat - tle cry! sound the bat - tle cry!

For the Sa - vior is be - fore us, and for Him we draw the sword.

Marching on! marching on! shout the vic - to - ry! shout the vic - to - ry!

We will end the bat - tle sing - ing hal - le - lu - jahs to the Lord.

THE ANGELS IN THE AIR.

Contributed to "Musical Leaves." Rev. R. Lowry.

1. When life's la - bor-song is sung, And the e - bon arch is sprung, O'er the
2. Dark the shadows in the vale, Fierce the howling of the gale, But the
3. Flood the heart with parting tears, Frost the head with pass - ing years, Min-gle

sha - ded couch of death so still; Then the Lord will light the scene With the
shi - ning ones are near our door; With our robes as bright as they, We will
want and woe to - geth - er here; But the Lord will lift the cloud, That en-

an - gels' star - ry sheen, As they wel - come us to Zi - on's hill.
tread the star - ry way, With the sha - dow and the storm no more.
wraps the shi - ning crowd, And we'll nev - er know a sor - row there.

Chorus. Steady time.

We'll meet each oth - er there, Yes! we'll meet each oth - er there, With the

angels in the air, Yes! we'll meet each other there; We'll meet each other there, Yes! we'll

meet each oth - er there, With the an - gels, with the an - gels in the air.

35

CHRIST ON THE MOUNT.

Words by Dr. E. G. Sumner. (Matt. v.) Music by Philip Phillips.

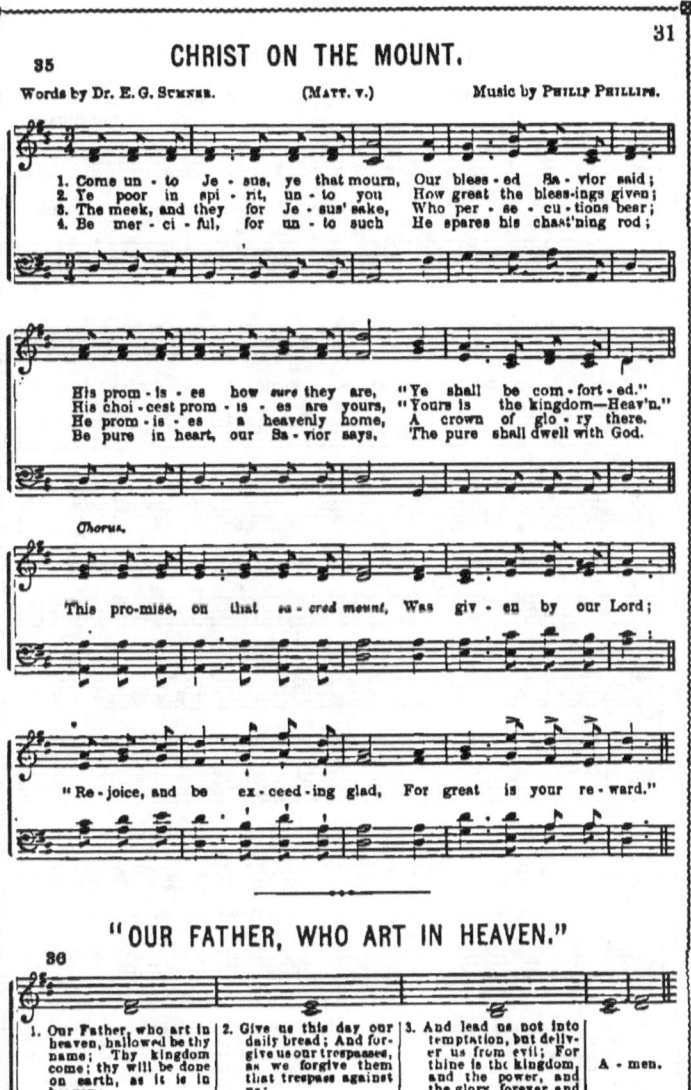

1. Come un-to Je-sus, ye that mourn, Our bless-ed Sa-vior said;
2. Ye poor in spi-rit, un-to you How great the bless-ings given;
3. The meek, and they for Je-sus' sake, Who per-se-cu-tions bear;
4. Be mer-ci-ful, for un-to such He spares his chast'ning rod;

His prom-is-es how sure they are, "Ye shall be com-fort-ed."
His choi-cest prom-is-es are yours, "Yours is the kingdom—Heav'n."
He prom-is-es a heavenly home, A crown of glo-ry there.
Be pure in heart, our Sa-vior says, The pure shall dwell with God.

Chorus.

This pro-mise, on that sa-cred mount, Was giv-en by our Lord;

"Re-joice, and be ex-ceed-ing glad, For great is your re-ward."

"OUR FATHER, WHO ART IN HEAVEN."

36

1. Our Father, who art in heaven, hallowed be thy name; Thy kingdom come; thy will be done on earth, as it is in heaven;

2. Give us this day our daily bread; And for-give us our trespasses, as we forgive them that trespass against us;

3. And lead us not into temptation, but deliv-er us from evil; For thine is the kingdom, and the power, and the glory, forever and ever.

A-men.

THERE, THERE IS REST.

"His rest shall be glorious."—Isaiah.

37

T. C. O'KANE.

Here o'er the earth as a stran-ger I roam, Here is no rest,

here is no rest; Here as a pil-grim I wan-der a-lone,

Yet I am blest, Yet I am blest, For I look for-ward to

that glo-rious day When sin and sor-row shall van-ish a-way;

My heart doth leap as I hear Je-sus say, There, there is rest, There, there is rest.

2 Here are afflictions and trials severe,
  Here is no rest, here is no rest;
Here I must part with the friends I hold dear,
  Yet I am blest, yet I am blest.
Sweet is the promise I read in his word,
Blessed are those who have died in the Lord,
They have been called to receive their reward,
  There, there is rest, There, there is rest.

3 This world of cares is a wilderness state,
  Here is no rest, here is no rest;
Here I must bear from the world all its hate,
  Yet I am blest, yet I am blest.
Soon shall I be from the wicked released,
Soon shall the weary forever be blest,
Soon shall I lean on my dear Savior's breast,
  There, there is rest, There, there is rest.

HEBRON. L. M.

38

Music by DR. L. MASON, by permission.

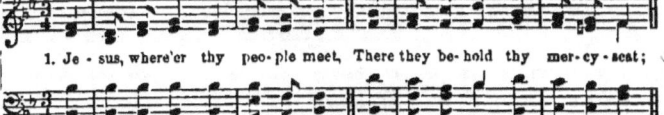

1. Je - sus, where'er thy peo - ple meet, There they be- hold thy mer - cy - seat;

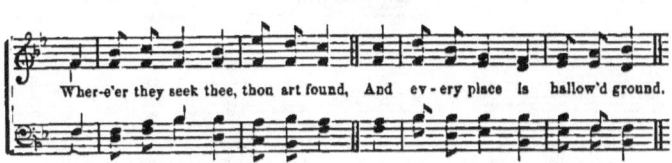

Wher-e'er they seek thee, thou art found, And ev - ery place is hallow'd ground.

2. For thou, within no walls confined,
Dost dwell with those of humble mind;
Such ever bring thee where they come,
And, going, take thee to their home.

3. Great Shepherd of thy chosen few,
Thy former mercies here renew;
Here, to our waiting hearts, proclaim
The sweetness of thy saving name.

BOYLSTON. S. M.

39

Words by NEWTON. Music by DR. L. MASON.

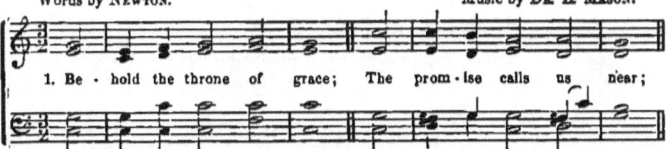

1. Be - hold the throne of grace; The prom - ise calls us near;

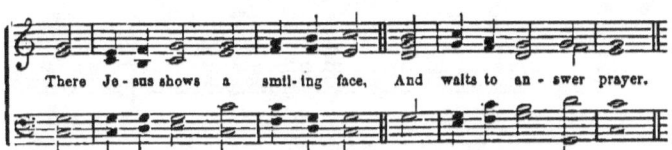

There Je - sus shows a smil- ing face, And waits to an - swer prayer.

2. Thine image, Lord, bestow,—
Thy presence and thy love,—
That we may serve thee here below,
And reign with thee above.

3. Teach us to live by faith,—
Conform our wills to thine

Let us victorious be in death,
And then in glory shine.

4. If thou these blessings give,
And thou our portion be,
All worldly joys we'll gladly leave,
To find our heaven in thee.

40

BATTLING FOR THE LORD.

Words by P. Phillips.　　　　　　　　　　　　　　　Music by T. E. Perkins.

Solo.

1. We've list - ed in a ho - ly war, Battling for the Lord!
2. Un - der our Cap-tain, Je - sus Christ, Battling for the Lord!
3. We'll fight a - gainst the powers of sin, Battling for the Lord!

Chorus.

E - ter - nal life, e - ter - nal joy, Battling for the Lord!
We've list - ed for this mortal life, Battling for the Lord!
In fa - vor of our heavenly King, Battling for the Lord!

Full Chorus.

We'll work till Je - sus comes, We'll work till Je - sus comes,

We'll work till Je - sus comes, And then we'll rest at home.

4 And when our warfare here is o'er,
　　Battling for the Lord!
This strife we'll leave, and war no more,
　　Battling for the Lord!
　　We'll work, etc.

5 Our friends and kindred there we'll meet,
　　On the heavenly shore!
And ground our arms at Jesus' feet,
　　On the heavenly shore!
　　We'll work, etc.

OUTSIDE THE GATE.

41

"Him that cometh unto me, I will in no wise cast out."

Words by JOSEPHINE POLLARD.

Music by PHILIP PHILLIPS

1. I stood out-side the gate, A poor, way-far-ing child; With-

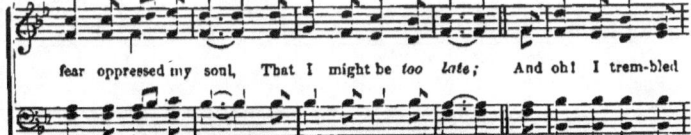

In my heart there beat A tem-pest, loud and wild. A

fear oppressed my soul, That I might be *too late;* And oh! I trem-bled

sore, And prayed, out-side the gate, And prayed, outside the gate.

2 "Mercy!" I loudly cried;
 "Oh, give me rest from sin!"
"I will," a voice replied;
 And Mercy let me in.
She bound my bleeding wounds,
 And carried all my sin;
She eased my burdened soul,
 Then Jesus took me in.

3 In Mercy's guise, I knew
 The Saviour long abused;
Who often sought my heart,
 And wept when I refused.
Oh! what a blest return
 For ignorance and sin!
I stood outside the gate,
 And Jesus let me in!

PILGRIM, WATCH AND PRAY.

Words by FANNY CROSBY.   T. E. P.

3 'T is the hour where hallowed feelings
  Chase our doubts and fears away;
  'T is the hour for calm devotion,
  Pilgrim, watch and pray.
  Weary pilgrim, etc.

4 Though temptations dark oppress thee,
  Jesus guides thee on thy way;
  He will hear thy lightest whisper,
  Pilgrim, watch and pray.
  Weary pilgrim, etc.

I DREAMED A DREAM OF HEAVEN.

43

Words by Mrs. M. A. KIDDER. Music by S. J. VAIL.

Solo.

1. I dreamed a dream of heaven So beautiful and bright, Where angels clad in spotless robes Walked
2. I dreamed a dream of heaven, A land beyond the tomb, Where tears are wiped from every eye, And

Duet.

forth in dazzling light; And from that vast and happy throng, Went up the soul-entrancing song,
flowers immortal bloom; My soul caught up with glad surprise, The glorious anthem of the skies,

Chorus.

Of glo - ry to God, Glo - ry to God, Glo - ry to God in the high - est; And

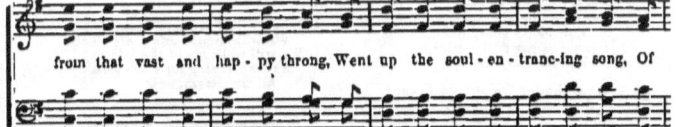

from that vast and hap - py throng, Went up the soul - en - tranc-ing song, Of

glo - ry to God, Glo - ry to God, Glo - ry to God in the high - est.

3. I dreamed a dream of heaven,
　　And bade adieu to woe,
　But, ah! my Saviour sent me back
　　To earthly scenes below;
　How then my weary soul did long
　　To hear again that heavenly song,
　　　Cho.—Of glory to God, &c.

4. Oh, may I reach that heaven,
　　When worldly cares are o'er,
　Yes, reach those sweet eternal scenes
　　On Canaan's happy shore;
　Then will I join the song above
　　Of saving grace and dying love,
　　　Cho.—Of glory to God, &c.

44

DENNIS.

From Nageli.

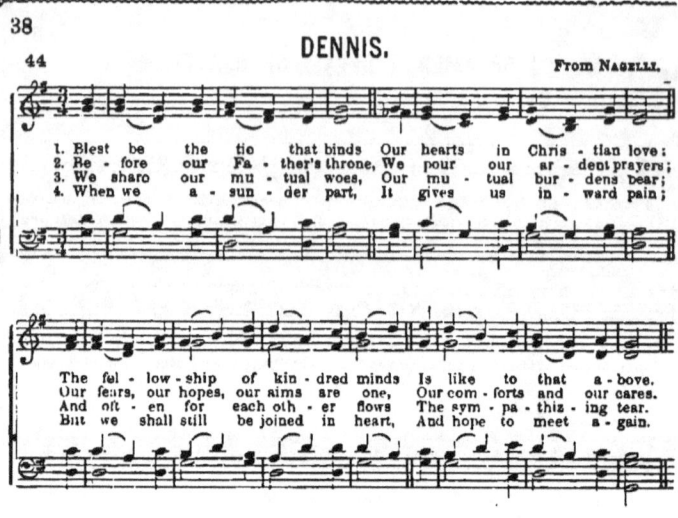

1. Blest be the tie that binds Our hearts in Chris - tian love;
2. Be - fore our Fa - ther's throne, We pour our ar - dent prayers;
3. We share our mu - tual woes, Our mu - tual bur - dens bear;
4. When we a - sun - der part, It gives us in - ward pain;

The fel - low - ship of kin - dred minds Is like to that a - bove.
Our fears, our hopes, our aims are one, Our com - forts and our cares.
And oft - en for each oth - er flows The sym - pa - thiz - ing tear.
But we shall still be joined in heart, And hope to meet a - gain.

---

45 **HEAVEN IS MY HOME.**

1 I 'm but a stranger here,
   Heaven is my home ;
   Earth is a desert drear,
   Heaven is my home ;
   Dangers and sorrows stand
   Round me on every hand,
   Heaven is my father-land,
   Heaven is my home.

2 What though the tempest rage?
   Heaven is my home ;
   Short is my pilgrimage,
   Heaven is my home.
   Time's cold and wint'ry blast
   Soon will be overpast,
   I shall reach home at last,
   Heaven is my home.

3 There at my Savior's side,
   Heaven is my home,
   I shall be glorified,
   Heaven is my home.
   There are the good and blest,
   Those I love most and best,
   There too I soon shall rest,
   Heaven is my home.

46
A HOME BEYOND THE TIDE.

1 We are out on the ocean sailing,
   Homeward bound, we sweetly glide;
   We are out on the ocean sailing
   To a home beyond the tide.
   All the storms will soon be over,
     Then we 'll anchor in the harbor;
   We are out on the ocean sailing,
   To a home beyond the tide ;
   We are out on the ocean sailing,
   To a home beyond the tide.

2 Come on board, O ! "ship" for glory,
   Be in haste—make up your mind !
   For our vessel 's weighing anchor,
   You will soon be left behind !
   All the storms, etc.

3 When we all are safely anchored,
   We will shout—our trials o'er !
   We will walk about the city,
   And we 'll sing for evermore.
   All the storms, etc.

47
MARCHING ALONG.

1 The children are gath'ring from near and
     from far,
   The trumpet is sounding the call for the war ;
   The conflict is raging, 't will be fearful and
     long,
   We 'll gird on our armor, and be marching
     along.
   Marching along, we are marching along,
   Gird on the armor, and be marching along.

2 We 've listed for life, and will camp on the
     field ;
   With Christ as our Captain, we never will
     yield ;
   The "sword of the Spirit," both trusty and
     strong,
   We 'll hold in our hands as we 're marching
     along. Marching along, etc.

3 Through conflicts and trials our crowns we
     must win,
   For here we contend 'gainst temptation and
     sin ;
   But one thing assures us, we can not go
     wrong,
   If trusting our Savior, while marching along.
   Marching along, etc.

COME TO JESUS!

48

Words by Dr. Geo. B. Peck, Clifton Springs, N. Y.   Hubert P. Main.

Tenderly.

1. Come, come to Je - sus! He waits to wel - come thee
2. Come, come to Je - sus! He waits to ran - som thee
3. Come, come to Je - sus! He waits to light - en thee.

4. Come, come to Je - sus! He waits to give to thee,
5. Come, come to Je - sus! He waits to shel - ter thee,
6. Come, come to Je - sus! He waits to car - ry thee.

O Wand'-rer! ea - ger - ly; Come, come to Je - sus!
O Slave! e - ter - nal - ly; Come, come to Je - sus!
O Burdened! gra - cious - ly; Come, come to Je - sus!

O Blind! a vi - sion free; Come, come to Je - sus!
O Wea - ry! bless - ed - ly; Come, come to Je - sus!
O Lamb! so lov - ing - ly; Come, come to Je - sus!

LORD, ABIDE WITH ME.

49

Words by a Blind Poetess.

1. Je - sus, Sav - ior! hear my call, Sin - ful though my heart may be;
2. Lone-ly in a stran - ger land, Cast me not a - way from thee;
3. Thou hast died the lost to save, Died to set the cap - tive free;

4. Fill me with thy love di-vine, Con - se - crate my life to thee;
5. When the shades of death prevail, Fa - ther, let me cling to thee;
6. Then, oh, then, my rap - tured soul Heaven's e - ter - nal rest shall see;

Thou, my life, my hope, my all, Lord, a - bide with me.
Lead me by thy gen - tle hand, Lord, a - bide with me.
Thou didst tri - umph o'er the grave, Lord, a - bide with me.

Bend my stub - born will to thine, Lord, a - bide with me.
When I pass the gloom - y vale, Lord, a - bide with me.
There, while end - less a - ges roll, Live and reign with thee.

GOD LOVETH THE CHEERFUL GIVER.

Written for the "Musical Leaves."   Music by Philip Phillips.

1. Give! give! give! Give of the fruits of thy
2. Give! give! give! Give to the pil - grim and
3. Give! give! give! Give to dis - trib - ute the

la - bor; Give of thy "bas - ket and store;"
stranger; Light - en their bur - den of care;
Bi - ble O - ver the isles of the sea;

Give to the cause of the need - y, Je - sus will give to thee more.
Give to the wid - ow and or - phan, Help them their sor - row to bear.
Na - tions now sit - ting in darkness Light from its pa - ges will see.

Chorus.

God lov - eth the cheer - ful giv - er, 'Tis

one of his sa - cred laws; He will bless your alms when

right - ly given, To the glo - ry of his cause.

CORONATION. C. M.

OLIVER HOLDEN.

51

1. O for a thousand tongues to sing My great Re-deem-er's praise;
2. My gra-cious Mas-ter and my God, As-sist me to pro-claim,

The glo-ries of my God and King, The triumphs of his grace!
To spread through all the earth a-broad, The hon-ors of thy name;

The glo-ries of my God and King, The tri-umphs of his grace!
To spread through all the earth a-broad, The hon-ors of thy name.

3 Jesus! the name that charms our fears,
That bids our sorrows cease;
'T is music in the sinner's ears,
'T is life and health and peace.

4 He breaks the power of canceled sin,
He sets the prisoner free;
His blood can make the foulest clean,
His blood availed for me.

GUIDE. 7s.

M. M. WELLS.

52

1. Ho-ly Spir-it, faith-ful Guide, Ev-er near the Christian's side;}
Gent-ly lead us by the hand, Pil-grims in a des-ert land.}
D. C. Whisp'ring soft-ly, wand'-rer come! Fol-low me, I 'll guide thee home.

D. C.

Wea-ry souls for-e'er re-joice, While they hear that sweet-est voice,

2 Ever present, truest friend,
Ever near, thine aid to lend,
Leave us not to doubt and fear,
Groping on in darkness drear;
When the storms are raging sore,
Hearts grow faint and hopes give o'er,
Whisper softly, wanderer come!
Follow me, I 'll guide thee home.

3 When our days of toil shall cease,
Waiting still for sweet release,
Nothing left but heaven and prayer,
Wondering if our names are there;
Wading deep the dismal flood,
Pleading naught but Jesus' blood;
Whisper softly, wanderer come!
Follow me, I 'll guide thee home.

RECRUIT FOR JESUS.

Words by MISS FANNY CROSBY.

Music by PHILIP PHILLIPS.

1. The ar - my of the Sun - day-school Is marching on its way;
2. Here let the orphan's cheek be dry, The wea - ry find a rest;
3. To Zi -' on we are marching home, Let all with us a - bide;
4. Fight on, young soldiers of the Cross, With courage true and brave;

Re - cruits, recruits, to fill our ranks, The bat - tle - cry to - day!
A Fa - ther stands with lov - ing arms, To fold you to his breast.
We need the eld - est of our band, The younger ones to guide.
Throw out your col - ors to the breeze, And let them bold - ly wave.

And though our numbers still in - crease, For vol - un - teers we call;
Come, you who tread life's hum - bler walks, Its hea - vy yoke who hear;
Let those whom God has prospered most, A grateful trib - ute bring;
Fight on; the conquest shall be yours, And when the bat - tle 's o'er,

Our doors are o - pen; chil - dren, come, For grace is free for all.
For when the Sav - ior dwelt on earth, You were his ten - der care.
And each un - hallowed feel - ing die, That in the heart would spring.
The ar - my of the Sun - day - school Shall sing on Canaan's shore.

Chorus.

Free grace, free grace for all, O, chil - dren hear the call! To

high and low its bless - ings flow, For Je - sus died for all.

LET IT PASS; Or, It is Better to be Wronged than Wrong.

54

S. J. VAIL, by permission.

1. Be not swift to take of - fense; Let it pass, Let it pass.
2. Strife corrodes the pu - rest mind; Let it pass, Let it pass.
3. Ech - o not an an - gry word; Let it pass, Let it pass.
4. If for good you've tak - en ill; Let it pass, Let it pass.

An - ger is a foe to sense; Let it pass.
As the un - re - gard - ed wind, Let it pass.
Think how oft - en you have erred; Let it pass.
O be kind and gen - tle still; Let it pass.

Brood not dark - ly o'er a wrong Which will dis - ap - pear ere long,
All the vul - gar souls that live May con - demn with - out re - prieve;
Since our joys must pass a - way Like the dew - drops and the spray,
Time at last makes all things straight; Let us not re - sent, but wait,

Ra - ther sing this cheer - y song, Let it pass.
'Tis the no - ble who for - give; Let it pass.
Where - fore should our sor - rows stay? Let it pass.
And our tri - umph shall be great; Let it pass.

Chorus.

Mer - ri - ly, cheer - i - ly sing this song; Mer - ri - ly, cheer - i - ly

sing this song, Bet - ter to be wronged than wrong; Let it pass.

THE ROCK OF CHRIST.

55

Music by Dr. Thos. Hastings.

1. Thus said the Lord who had bestowed In - struction from the mountain's side,

Where truth like liv - ing wa - ter flowed, For ev - ery land a heal-ing tide.

CHORUS. *f*

If God is our ref - uge, if Christ is our Rock, And

shel-ter for all his o - be - di - ent flock; The house we are build-ing is

firm and se - cure, Its glo - rious foun - da - tion shall ev - er en - dure.

2. They who my words have deeply felt,
   And love t' obey, like all my flock,
   Shall stand like him who wisely built
   His house upon the solid rock.—*Cho.*

3. The rain descended like a flood,
   'Mid fearful winds: he knew it all,
   Yet firm his habitation stood:
   Its base so sure, it could not fall.—*Cho.*

4. Alas for those who've heard and known,
   But turn away from my commands,

They all are like the foolish one,
   Who built upon the drifting sands.—*Cho.*

5. On came the clouds, the wind, the rain,
   He saw his danger all too late:
   He labored for the house in vain:
   It fell, and oh, its fall was great.—*Cho.*

6. Impressive lesson, from the past!
   Is Christ the Rock on which we stand,
   Secure against the stormy blast?
   Or are we building on the sand?—*Cho.*

BEAUTIFUL LAND OF REST.

56

Music by R. Lowry.

Duet. *Chorus.*

1. Je - ru - sa - lem, for ev - er bright, Beau - ti - ful land of rest!
2. Je - ru - sa - lem, for - ev - er free, Beau - ti - ful land of rest!
3. Je - ru - sa - lem, for - ev - er dear, Beau - ti - ful land of rest!

Duet. *Chorus.*

No win - ter there, nor chill of night, Beau - ti - ful land of rest!
The soul's sweet home of Lib - er - ty, Beau - ti - ful land of rest!
Thy pearly gates almost ap - pear, Beau - ti - ful land of rest!

The dripping cloud is chased a way, The sun breaks forth in end - less day,
The gyves of sin, the chains of woe, The ransomed there will nev - er know,
And when we tread thy love - ly shore, We'll sing the song we've sung be - fore,

Je - ru - sa - lem, Je - ru - sa - lem, The beau - ti - ful land of rest!
Je - ru - sa - lem, Je - ru - sa - lem, The beau - ti - ful land of rest!
Je - ru - sa - lem, Je - ru - sa - lem, The beau - ti - ful land of rest!

Chorus.

Beau - ti - ful land, beau - ti ful land, Beau - ti - ful land of rest!

Beau - ti - ful land, beau - ti - ful land, Beau - ti - ful land of rest!

OUR JOY WILL BE COMPLETE.

Words by Miss Fanny Crosby.
Music by T. C. O'Kane.

1. Pil - grim in this vale be - low, By sin and care oppressed,
2. Wand'rers from our na - tive clime, While stran - gers here we roam,
3. Father, when the way is dark, O! guide us o'er the sea,
4. Faith im - mor - tal plumes her wings, And bids the soul as - cend,

Stay not by the streams of woe, Press on - ward to thy rest.
Look be - yond the shores of time To heaven, the Christian's home.
Thou canst steer our frag - ile bark, And waft it home to thee.
Hope the glo - rious pros - pect brings, When all our toils shall end.

Look be - yond the storm - y sky, Up - ward to a calm re - treat,
Life is but a win - t'ry day, Mer - cy brings the prom - ise sweet,
Bid the ra - ging wa - ters cease, Hush the waves be - neath our feet;
Then we 'll shout, the con - flict o'er, Then we 'll bow at Je - sus' feet;

There shall friend - ship nev - er die, Our joy will be com - plete.
Soon its light will fade a - way, Our joy will be com - plete.
An - chor in the port of peace, Our joy will be com - plete.
There with mar - tyrs gone be - fore, Our joy will be com - plete.

Refrain. Joyful.

Our joy, our joy, our joy will be com - plete,

Our joy, our joy, our joy will be com - plete.

"RALLY ROUND THE CROSS."

58

"Let me glory in the Cross."

Words by Miss Fanny Crosby.　　　　　　　　Music by Philip Phillips.

THE PILGRIM'S SONG.

59

T. E. P.

1. We have no home but heav - en, A pil - grim garb we wear;
2. We have no home but heav - en! Then wherefore seek one here?
3. We have no home but heav - en! How cheering is the thought,

Our path is marked by chan - ges, And strewed with man-y a care;
Why mur-mur at pri - va - tions, Or grieve when trouble's near?
How bright the ex - pect - a - tions Which God's own word has taught.

Sur-round-ed by tempt-a-tion, By va-ried ills oppressed,
It is but for a sea-son That we as stran-gers roam,
With ea-ger hearts we hast-en, The promised bliss to share;

Each day's ex-pe-rience warns us That this is not our rest.
And stran-gers must not look for The com-forts of a home.
We have no home but heav-en! O, would that we were there!

Chorus.

We have no home but heav-en! We want no home be-side;

Repeat softly.

O God! our Friend and Fa-ther! Our foot-steps thith-er guide!

"THE LAMB THAT WAS SLAIN"

60

T. C. O'KANE.

1. In the far better land of glo - ry and light, The ransomed are singing in
2. Like the sound of the sea swells their chorus of praise, Round the star-circled crown of the

garments of white; The harpers are harping, and all the bright train
Ancient of Days; And thrones and do - minions re - ech - o the strain

Ritard.

Sing the song of re - demp - tion, "The Lamb that was slain." The
Of "Glo - ry e - ter - nal to Him that was slain." To

Lamb that was slain, The Lamb that was slain, The Lamb that was
Him that was slain, To Him that was slain, To Him that was

Ritard.

slain, Sing the song of re - demp - tion, "The Lamb that was slain."
slain, Of "Glo - ry e - ter - nal to Him that was slain."

3 Dear Savior, may we with our voices so faint,
Sing the chorus celestial with angel and saint?
Yes! yes! we will join them, thine ear we will gain
With the song of redemption, "The Lamb that was slain."
The Lamb that was slain, etc.

4 Now, teachers and children and friends, all unite
In a loud hallelujah with the ransomed in light;
We'll sing to our Savior the soul-stirring strain,
The song of redemption, "The Lamb that was slain."
The Lamb that was slain, etc.

THE RANSOMED BAND.

61

T. C. O'KANE.

3 Thou heav'nly Friend, thou heav'nly Friend,
  Oh hear us when we pray!
Now let thy pard'ning grace descend,
And take our sins away.
  Oh heav'nly home, etc.

4 Be all our fresh and youthful days
  To thy blest service given;
Then we shall meet to sing thy praise,
A ransomed band in heaven.
  Oh heav'nly home, etc.

WE SHALL MEET AGAIN.

Words by Miss ANNIE E. HOWE.

T. C. O'KANE.

62

1. We shall meet be - yond the riv - er, We shall meet, we shall meet;
2. We shall meet who've long been part - ed, We shall meet, we shall meet;

Where the flowers are bloom-ing ev - er, We shall meet a - gain.
All the sad and wea - ry - heart - ed, We shall meet a - gain.

Where the tree of life is grow - ing, And the fragrant breezes blow - ing,
There no gloomy cloud of sor - row Shall dis - turb the bright to - mor - row,

Ritard.

Where the heavenly light is glow - ing, We shall meet a - gain.
But sweet peace we e'er shall bor - row, We shall meet a - gain.

3 Little children in white raiment,
   We shall meet, we shall meet;
On that shining golden pavement,
   We shall meet again.
No rude hand there us shall sever,
There we'll dwell and sing forever,
By that crystal flowing river,
   We shall meet again.

GO AND TELL JESUS.

"And they went and told Jesus."

63

T. F. SEWARD.

1. Go and tell Je - sus, wea - ry, sin - sick soul; He'll ease thee of thy bur - den, make thee whole; Look up to Him, He on - ly can for - give; Be - lieve on Him, and thou shalt sure - ly livo.

Chorus.

{ Go and tell Je - sus, He on - ly can for - give; } Go and tell Je - sus,
{ Go and tell Je - sus, O turn to him and live! }

Go and tell Je - sus, Go and tell Je - sus, He on - ly can for - give.

2 Go and tell Jesus, when your sins arise
　Like mountains of deep guilt before your eyes;
　His blood was spilt, His precious life He gave,
　That mercy, peace, and pardon you might have. *Chorus.*

3 Go and tell Jesus, he'll dispel thy fears,
　Will calm thy doubts, and wipe away thy tears;
　He'll take thee in His arm, and on His breast
　Thou mayst be happy, and forever rest. *Chorus.*

YOUNG SOLDIERS.

64

T. C. O KANE.

Moderato.

1. The Sun - day - school ar - my has gath - ered once more, Its
2. We fight a - gainst e - vil, and bat - tle with wrong, Our

numbers are greater than ev - er be - fore, Its banners are spread, and shall
sword is the Bi - ble, both trusty and strong; Our watchword is Prayer, and

nev - er be furled, Till the Prince of Sal - va - tion has conquered the world.
Faith is our shield, And nev - er, no nev - er, to foes will we yield.

Chorus. Lively.

Sing! sing! for the ar - my is on its bright way,

To the homes of the blest, and the man - sions of day

3 In the midst of our conflicts we 'll think of our Lord,
Who died on the cross and from death was restored,
To save us from sin, and to give us a place
With the angels who always behold his bright face.

4 To Jesus, our Captain, hosannas we raise,
And join with our teachers in singing his praise;
His soldiers we are, and his soldiers we'll be,
Till we lay down our armor and death sets us free.

65

WE SHALL SLEEP, BUT NOT FOREVER. -

Words by Mrs. M. A. Kidder.

S. J. Vail, by permission.

1. We shall sleep, but not for - ev - er; There will be a glo-rious dawn;
2. When we see a precious blos - som That we tend - ed with such care,
3. We shall sleep, but not for - ev - er, In the lone and si - lent grave;

We shall meet to part, no, nev - er! On the re - sur - rec - tion morn!
Rude-ly tak - en from our bos - om, How our ach - ing hearts des - pair!
Bless-ed be the Lord that tak - eth, Bless-ed be the Lord that gave.

From the deep - est caves of o - cean, From the des - ert and the plain,
Round its lit - tle grave we lin - ger, Till the set - ting sun is low,
In the bright, e - ter - nal cit - y Death can nev - er, nev - er come;

From the val - ley and the mountain, Countless throngs shall rise a - gain.
Feel - ing all our hopes have perished With the flower we cherished so.
In his own good time he'll call us From our rest to Home, Sweet Home.

Chorus. p

cres.

We shall sleep, but not for - ev - er; There will be a glo - rious dawn;

We shall meet to part, no, nev - er! On the re - sur - rec - tion morn!

66 O SAY, SHALL WE MEET YOU ALL THERE?

Words by MINNIE WATERS. B. J. VAIL, by permission.

Solo.

1. Where do you journey, my bro - ther, O whore do you journey, I pray?
2. What is your mission, my bro - ther, What is your mission be - low?
3. O! yes, you will meet us, my bro - ther, God helping our weakness and sin;

Where do you journey, my sis - ter? For stormy and dark is the way.
What is your mission, my sis - ter, As journey - ing onward you go?
Bearing the cross, we, my sis - ter, The crown will endeavor to win.

Duet.

We 're journeying onward to Ca - naan, Through suff'ring, and trial, and care,
Our mission is prac-tic-ing mer - cy, Sweet char - i - ty, patience, and love,
We 'll walk through the vale and the shadow, Through suff'rings, and trials, and care,

And when we get safely to glo - ry, O say, shall we meet you all there!
And following the footsteps of Je - sus, That lead to the mansions a - bove.
And when you get safely to glo - ry, You 'll meet, yes, you 'll meet us all there!

Chorus.

O say, shall we meet you all there? O say, shall we meet you all there?

And when we get safe-ly to glo - ry, O say, shall we meet you all there?

67 OVER THE RIVER I'M GOING. MINNIE WATERS.

1 OVER the river I 'm going,
  Beyond where the pearly gates stand,
Over the cold icy billows,
  To live in a fair, sunny land.
My Father has built me a mansion,
  And filled it with treasures of gold,
Yes, over the river I 'm going,
  To where there are pleasures untold.
Chor.—To where there are pleasures untold,
  To where there are pleasures untold;
Yes, over the river I 'm going,
  To where there are pleasures untold.

2 Over the river I 'm going;
  O, seek not to draw me aside!
See, for the boatman is waiting
  To ferry me over the tide.
My Savior is there to receive me,
  And shield me from suffering and cold;
Yes, over the river I 'm going,
  To where there are pleasures untold.
Chor.—To where there are pleasures untold,
  To where there are pleasures untold;
Yes, over the river I 'm going,
  To where there are pleasures untold.

56

JESUS IS MINE.

Words by BONAR

T. E. PERKINS.

68

From "SHINING STAR," by permission.

1. Fade, fade, each earth - ly joy, Je - sus is mine!
2. Tempt not my soul a - way, Je - sus is mine!

Break ev' - ry ten - der tie, Je - sus is mine!
Here would I ev - er stay, Je - sus is mine!

Dark is the wil - der - ness, Earth has no rest - ing - place,
Per - ish - ing things of clay, Born but for one brief day,

Je - sus a - lone can bless, Je - sus is mine!
Pass from my heart a - way, Je - sus is mine!

3 Farewell, ye dreams of night,
   Jesus is mine!
Lost in this dawning light,
   Jesus is mine!
All that my soul has tried,
Left but a dismal void,
Jesus has satisfied,
   Jesus is mine!

4 Farewell, mortality,
   Jesus is mine!
Welcome, eternity,
   Jesus is mine!
Welcome, O loved and blest,
Welcome, sweet scenes of rest,
Welcome, my Savior's breast,
   Jesus is mine!

THE POLAR STAR.

69

Words by Miss Fanny Crosby.

From "Shining Star." T. E. P.

By permission of the publisher, F. J. Huntington, New York.

1. Weary wand'er o'er the main, Seeking for thy home again, Through the gath'ring
2. Stranger, on a rocky strand, Longing for thy father-land, Through the gath'ring
3. Lonely watcher, pale with grief, Thou shalt find a sweet relief, Though thy tears un-

mists that rise, Vailing thy natal skies; Look beyond, there's light for thee, Streaming o'er the
clouds that rise, Vailing thy natal skies; Look beyond, there's hope for thee, Dawning o'er the
heeded fall, Jesus will count them all; Look beyond, there's joy for thee, Breaking o'er a

tur-bid sea; Softly it smiles, though distant far, The beautiful po - lar star.
tranquil sea, Softly it smiles, etc.
troubled sea, Softly it smiles, etc.

AMERICA. National Hymn.

70

Words by S. F. Smith.

Maestoso.

1. My country, 'tis of thee, Sweet land of lib - er - ty, Of thee I sing; Land where my
2. My native country! thee, Land of the no - ble free, Thy name I love; I love thy
3. Let music swell the breeze, And ring from all the trees Sweet freedom's song; Let mortal
4. Our father's God, to thee, Author of lib - er - ty, To thee we sing; Long may our

fathers died, Land of the pilgrim's pride, From ev'ry mountain side Let freedom ring.
rocks and rills, Thy woods and templed hills; My heart with rapture thrills, Like that above.
tongues awake, Let all that breathe partake, Let rocks their silence break, The sound prolong.
land be bright With freedom's holy light; Protect us by thy might, Great God, our King.

ROCK OF AGES, CLEFT FOR ME.

71

Dr. Hastings.

Fine.

1. Rock of A - ges, cleft for me, Let me hide my - self in thee;
D. C. Be of sin a dou - ble cure, Save from wrath, and make me pure.

2. Could my tears for - ev - er flow, Could my zeal no lan - guor know,
D. C. In my hand no price I bring, Sim - ply to thy cross I cling.

3. While I draw this fleet - ing breath, When my eyes shall close in death,
D. C. Rock of A - ges, cleft for me, Let me hide my - self in thee.

D. C.

Let the wa - ter and the blood, From thy wounded side which flowed,
This for sin could not a - tone, Thou must save, and thou a - lone;

When I rise to worlds un-known, And be - hold thee on thy throne,

---

GOD IS LOVE! I KNOW, I FEEL.

72

W. H. Roberts.

Chorus, faster.
Staccato.

Moderato Legato.

1. Depth of mer-cy, can there be   Mer - cy still reserved for me?
   Can my God his wrath for-bear, Me, the chief of sinners, spare? } God is love! I

2. I   have long withstood his grace ; Long provoked him to his face ;
   Would not hearken to his calls ; Grieved him by a thousand falls. } God is love, etc

Smoothly.   *Repeat pp.*

know, I feel ; Jesus weeps and loves me still ; Je-sus weeps, He weeps and loves me still.

3 Now incline me to repent;
  Let me now my sins lament;
  Now my foul revolt deplore,
  Weep, believe, and sin no more.
    God is love, etc.

4 There for me the Savior stands;
  Shows his wounds, and spreads his hands;
  God is love! I know, I feel;
  Jesus weeps, and loves me still.
    God is love, etc.

WELCOME TO OUR CONCERT.

73   SONG FOR UNION SABBATH-SCHOOL MEETINGS.

Words by Rev. George Lansing Taylor, M. A.   Hubert P. Main.

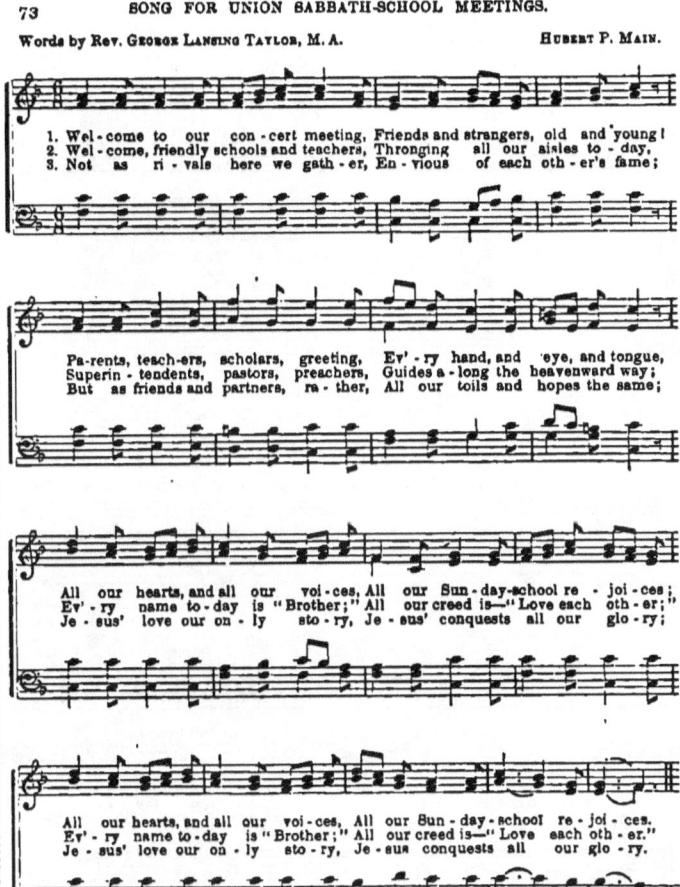

1. Wel-come to our con-cert meeting, Friends and strangers, old and young!
2. Wel-come, friendly schools and teachers, Thronging all our aisles to-day,
3. Not as ri-vals here we gath-er, En-vious of each oth-er's fame;

Pa-rents, teach-ers, scholars, greeting, Ev'-ry hand, and eye, and tongue,
Superin-tendents, pastors, preachers, Guides a-long the heavenward way;
But as friends and partners, ra-ther, All our toils and hopes the same;

All our hearts, and all our voi-ces, All our Sun-day-school re-joi-ces;
Ev'-ry name to-day is "Brother;" All our creed is—"Love each oth-er;"
Je-sus' love our on-ly sto-ry, Je-sus' conquests all our glo-ry;

All our hearts, and all our voi-ces, All our Sun-day-school re-joi-ces.
Ev'-ry name to-day is "Brother;" All our creed is—"Love each oth-er."
Je-sus' love our on-ly sto-ry, Je-sus conquests all our glo-ry.

4 These we tell, we chant his praises,
    Hear his wonders, learn his laws;
Every tale his triumph raises,
    Every effort aids his cause.
All our prayers and strains ascending,
Round his throne as incense blending.

5 Welcome, then, to join our singing,
    Till we meet with songs above;
At His feet our homage flinging,
    Who has bought us with his love.
There we'll cast our crowns before him,
And in endless bliss adore him.

GIVE ALL TO JESUS.

Words by Rev. JOHN G. CHAFEE.

Music by PHILIP PHILLIPS.

Teacher's Message.

Response.

1. First your hearts to Je - sus give, Children dear, ev' - ry - where;
2. Chil - dren, you should work for God, An - y - where, ev' - ry - where;
3. War hath made homes des - o - late, Round us here, ev' - ry - where;
4. There are man - y hea - then, too, Far be - yond the rolling deep;

Response.

What de - light it is to live, With Christ near.
'Tis the path your Sav - ior trod, Walk you there.
Wid - ows sigh, and or - phans weep, Here and there.
Dark, 'neath skies of pu - rest blue, Now they weep.

Oh, what bliss his love im - parts, When it dwells with-
Oh, this work - ing for the right, Gives the soul such
Child - ren, will you soothe their grief, Will you give to
Dark - ness fills their souls with gloom, Dark - ness like the

Scholars' Reply.

in our hearts! Sav - ior, here we are be - fore thee,
sweet de - light! Gra - cious Sav - ior, come, and bless us,
them re - lief? Sav - ior, we will help them glad - ly,
ver - y tomb. We will send the Gos - pel to them,

Full Chorus.

On us with thy fa - vor shine; We will give thee
With thy ho - ly mind im - bue; Let thy spir - it
With kind gifts and gen - tle words; Cheer their hearts that
Give our mon - ey, with our prayers; With glad hearts and

all the glo - ry, All that we pos - sess is thine
now pos - sess us, Then we 'll love and praise, and do.
throb so sad - ly, Bless them as our stock af - fords.
hands we 'll show them, That our bless - ings may be theirs.

REMEMBER THE POOR!

75

Music contributed to the "MUSICAL LEAVES," by GEO. F. ROOT.

Moderato.

1. When safe in your dwell - ing, so cheer - ful and warm,
2. When la - bor re - ward - ed, a com - fort be - stows,
3. His words, kind - ly spo - ken, should ne'er be for - got;
4. Go, suc - cor the low - ly, who 're bur - dened with woe;

Ye hear but its wail - ing, the cold win - ter storm;
That brings to your bo - som a tran - quil re - pose,
The poor ye have al - ways, but me ye have not;
Take heed that in se - cret your alms ye be - stow;

When loved ones a - round you are gath - ered once more,
'T is God who in - creas - es your bas - ket and store,
Pri - va - tion and sor - row how meek - ly he bore!
Be kind to the way - ward, the err - ing re - store,

Then pause for a mo - ment, re - mem - ber the poor!
'T is Je - sus who bids you, re - mem - ber the poor!
Are ye his dis - ci - ples, re - mem - ber the poor!
And God will re - ward you, re - mem - ber the poor!

Chorus.

Blessed is he that considereth the . . . . . . poor, the
The Lord will preserve him, and keep him a - . . . live, and

Lord will deliver him in . . . . . time of trouble. }
he shall be blessed up - . . . . on the earth. }

SELECT HYMNS AND TUNES.

The following Hymns and Tunes are mostly taken from the popular Sabbath-school Singing-book, "ORIOLA," published by MOORE, WILSTACH & BALDWIN, Cincinnati, O.

GOOD TIDINGS.

76 Key G.

1 SHOUT the tidings of salvation
　To the aged and the young ;
　Till the precious invitation
　Waken every heart and tongue.

CHORUS.

Send the sound the earth around,
　From the rising to the setting of the sun,
Till each gath'ring crowd shall proclaim
　aloud,
The glorious work is done.

2 Shout the tidings of salvation
　O'er the prairies of the West ;
Till each gath'ring congregation
　With the Gospel sound is blest.
　Send the sound, etc.

3 Shout the tidings of salvation,
　Mingling with the ocean's roar ;
Till the ships of every nation
　Bear the news from shore to shore.
　Send the sound, etc.

4 Shout the tidings of salvation
　O'er the islands of the sea ;
Till, in humble adoration,
　All to Christ shall bow the knee.
　Send the sound, etc.

BEAUTIFUL ZION.

77 Key A♭.

1 BEAUTIFUL Zion, built above,
　Beautiful city that I love,
　Beautiful gates of pearly white,
　Beautiful temple—God its light.

2 Beautiful heaven, where all is light,
　Beautiful angels, clothed in white,
　Beautiful strains that never tire,
　Beautiful harps through all the choir.

3 Beautiful throne of Christ our King,
　Beautiful songs the angels sing ;
　Beautiful rest, all wanderings cease,
　Beautiful home of perfect peace.

THE SHINING SHORE.

78 Key G.

1 MY days are gliding swiftly by,
　And I, a pilgrim stranger,
　Would not detain them as they fly,
　Those hours of toil and danger.

CHORUS.

For oh ! we stand on Jordan's strand,
　Our friends are passing over,
And just before, the shining shore
　We may almost discover.

2 We 'll gird our loins, my brethren dear,
　Our distant home discerning ;
Our absent Lord has left us word,
　Let every lamp be burning.
　For oh, etc.

3 Should coming days be cold and dark,
　We need not cease our singing ;
That perfect rest naught can molest,
　Where golden harps are ringing.
　For oh, etc.

4 Let sorrow's rudest tempest blow,
　Each chord on earth to sever ;
Our King says " Come," and there 's our
　home,
　Forever, oh ! forever !
　For oh, etc.

THE PRECIOUS NAME.

79

TUNE—"Believer." Key D. C. M.

1 How sweet the name of Jesus sounds
　In a believer's ear !
It soothes his sorrows, heals his wounds,
　And drives away his fear.

2 It makes the wounded spirit whole,
　And calms the troubled breast ;
'T is " manna " to the hungry soul,
　And to the weary, rest.

3 Dear Name, the rock on which I build,
　My shield and hiding-place ;
My never-failing treasure, filled
　With boundless stores of grace.

80 I WANT TO BE LIKE JESUS.

Tune—"Watcher." Key D. 7s & 6s.

1 I WANT to be like Jesus,
  So lowly and so meek ;
  For no one marked an angry word
  That ever heard him speak.

2 I want to be like Jesus,
  So frequently in prayer;
  Alone upon the mountain-top
  He met his Father there.

3 I want to be like Jesus;
  I never, never find
  That he, though persecuted, was
  To any one unkind.

4 I want to be like Jesus,
  Engaged in doing good,
  So that of me it may be said,
  "She hath done what she could."

5 Alas ! I 'm not like Jesus,
  As any one may see ;
  O, gentle Savior ! send thy grace,
  And make me like to thee.

81

**HARK! WHAT MEAN THOSE HOLY
VOICES?**

Tune—"Manor." Key E♭. 8s & 7s.

1 Hark ! what mean those holy voices,
  Sweetly sounding through the skies ?
  Lo ! th' angelic host rejoices ;
  Heavenly hallelujahs rise !
  Hear them tell the wondrous story,
  Hear them chant in hymns of joy,
  " Glory in the highest, glory !
  Glory be to God most high ! "

2 Peace on earth—good-will from heaven,
  Reaching far as man is found ;
  " Souls redeemed, and sins forgiven,"
  Loud our golden harps shall sound.
  Christ is born, the great Anointed ;
  Heaven and earth his praises sing !
  Oh, receive whom God appointed,
  For your Prophet, Priest, and King !

3 Haste, ye mortals, to adore him ;
  Learn his name, and taste his joy ;
  Till in heaven ye sing before him,
  Glory be to God most high !
  Haste, ye mortals, to adore him ;
  Learn his name, and taste his joy ;
  Till in heaven ye sing before him,
  Glory be to God most high !

82

**THE EARTH SHALL BE FULL OF THE
KNOWLEDGE OF THE LORD.**

Tune—"Webb." Key B♭. 7s & 6s.

1 The morning light is breaking,
  The darkness disappears ;
  The sons of earth are waking
  To penitential tears.

Each breeze that sweeps the ocean
  Brings tidings from afar,
  Of nations in commotion,
  Prepared for Zion's war.

2 See heathen nations bending
  Before the God we love,
  And thousand hearts ascending
  In gratitude above ;
  While sinners, now confessing,
  The Gospel call obey,
  And seek the Savior's blessing—
  A nation in a day.

3 Blessed river of salvation !
  Pursue thy onward way ;
  Flow thou to every nation,
  Nor in thy richness stay ;
  Stay not till all the lowly
  Triumphant reach their home ;
  Stay not till all the holy
  Proclaim—the Lord is come.

CHRIST THE SHEPHERD.

83   C. M.

1 See the kind Shepherd, Jesus, stands,
  With all engaging charms !
  Hark ! how he calls the tender lambs,
  And folds them in his arms.

2 Permit them to approach, he cries,
  Nor scorn their humble name ;
  For 't was to bless such souls as these,
  The Lord of angels came.

3 He 'll lead us to the heavenly streams,
  Where living waters flow ;
  And guide us to the fruitful fields,
  Where trees of knowledge grow.

4 The feeblest lamb amidst the flock
  Shall be its Shepherd's care ;
  While folded in the Savior's arms
  We 're safe from every snare.

84   YOUTHFUL PIETY.

Tune—"Duke Street." Key E♭. L. M

1 We are but young—yet we may sing
  The praises of our heavenly King ;
  He made the earth, the sea, the sky,
  And all the starry worlds on high

2 We are but young—yet we have heard
  The Gospel news, the heavenly Word ;
  If we despise the only way,
  Dreadful will be the judgment day.

3 We are but young—yet we must die,
  Perhaps our latter end is nigh ;
  Lord, may we early seek thy grace,
  And find in Christ a hiding-place !

4 We are but young—we need a guide ;
  Jesus, in thee we would confide ;
  Oh, lead us in the path of truth !
  Protect and bless our helpless youth.

85 CONFIDENCE IN GOD.

TUNE—"Autumn." Key A. 8s & 7s.

1 HOLY FATHER, thou hast taught me
    I should live to thee alone;
Year by year, thy hand hath brought me
    On through dangers oft unknown.
When I wandered, thou hast found me;
    When I doubted, sent me light;
Still thine arm has been around me,
    All my paths were in thy sight.

2 In the world will foes assail me,
    Craftier, stronger far than I;
And the strife may never fail me,
    Well I know, before I die.
Therefore, Lord, I come, believing
    Thou canst give the power I need;
Through the prayer of faith receiving
    Strength—the Spirit's strength, indeed.

3 I would trust in thy protecting,
    Wholly rest upon thine arm;
Follow wholly thy directing,
    Thou, mine only guard from harm!
Keep me from mine own undoing,
    Help me turn to thee when tried;
Still my footsteps, Father, viewing,
    Keep me ever at thy side.

86 HAPPY NEW YEAR.

TUNE—"Happy Greeting to all." Key E. 11s.

1 COME, children, and join in our festival song,
The New Year has come, and the old year
    has gone;
We'll join our glad voices in one hymn of
    praise,
To God, who has kept us and lengthened
    our days.

CHORUS.

Happy New Year to all! happy New Year to
    all!
Happy New Year, happy New Year, happy
    New Year to all!

2 Our Father in heaven, we lift up to thee
Our voice of thanksgiving, our glad jubilee;
Oh, bless us, and guide us, dear Savior, we
    pray,
That from thy blest precepts we never may
    stray.
Happy New Year, etc.

3 And if, ere this New Year has drawn to a
    close,
Some loved one among us in death shall
    repose,
Grant, Lord, that the spirit in heaven may
    dwell,
In the bosom of Jesus, where all shall be
    well.
Happy New Year, etc.

4 Kind teachers, we children would thank you
    this day,
That faithfully, kindly, you 've taught us the
    way

How we may escape from the world's sinful
    charms,
And find a safe refuge in the Savior's loved
    arms.
Happy New Year, etc.

5 Dear Pastor, we ask thee, as lambs of thy fold,
To teach us that wisdom more precious than
    gold;
Our footsteps to guide in the pathway of
    truth,
To "love our Creator in the days of our
    youth."
Happy New Year, etc.

6 And now, as we enter another New Year,
We pray for a blessing on your labors here;
May many "bright jewels" be your blest
    reward,
And "crowns of rejoicing, in the day of the
    Lord."
Happy New Year, etc.

TO-DAY THE SAVIOR CALLS.

87 Key F.

1 TO-DAY the Savior calls!
    Ye wand'rers come;
Oh, ye benighted souls!
    Why longer roam?

2 To-day the Savior calls!
    For refuge fly;
The storm of vengeance falls,
    And death is nigh.

3 To-day the Savior calls!
    Oh, hear him now!
Within these sacred walls
    To Jesus bow.

4 The Spirit calls to-day!
    Yield to his power;
Oh, grieve him not away,
    'T is mercy's hour.

88

INSTRUCTION FROM THE SCRIPTURES.

C. M.

1 How shall the young secure their hearts,
    And guard their lives from sin?
Thy Word the choicest rules imparts,
    To keep the conscience clean.

2 'T is like the sun, a heavenly light,
    That guides us all the day;
And through the dangers of the night
    A lamp to lead our way.

3 Thy Word is everlasting truth;
    How pure is every page!
That holy Book will guide our youth,
    And well support our age.

4 Thy precepts make me truly wise;
    I hate the sinner's road;
I hate my own vain thoughts that rise,
    But love thy law, my God.

89 SOWING THE SEED.

TUNE—"Boylston." Key C. S. M.

1 Sow in the morn thy seed,
At eve hold not thy hand;
To doubt and fear give thou no heed,
Broadcast it round the land.

2 The good, the fruitful ground,
Expect not here nor there;
O'er hill and dale, by spots 't is found;
Go forth, then, every-where.

3 Thou knowest not which may thrive,
The late or early sown;
Grace keeps the precious germ alive,
When and wherever strown.

4 Thou canst not toil in vain;
Cold, heat, and moist, and dry,
Shall foster and mature the grain
For garners in the sky.

5 Then when the glorious end,
The day of God is come,
The angel reapers shall descend,
And heaven sing "Harvest home!"

90

I WOULD NOT LIVE ALWAY.

TUNE—"Frederick." 11s & 12s.

1 I WOULD not live alway; I ask not to stay
Where storm after storm rises dark o'er the
way;
The few lurid mornings that dawn on us
here,
Are enough for life's woes, full enough for
its cheer.

2 I would not live alway, thus fettered by sin,
Temptation without, and corruption within;
E'en the rapture of pardon is mingled with
fears,
And the cup of thanksgiving with penitent
tears.

3 I would not live alway; no—welcome the
tomb,
Since Jesus hath lain there, I dread not its
gloom;
There sweet be my rest, till he bid me arise
To hail him in triumph descending the skies.

4 Oh, who would live alway, away from his
God—
Away from yon heaven, that blissful abode,
Where the rivers of pleasure flow o'er the
bright plains,
And the noontide of glory eternally reigns?

5 There saints of all ages in harmony meet,
Their Savior and brethren transported to
greet,
While the anthems of rapture unceasingly
roll,
And the smile of the Lord is the feast of the
soul!

91 COME UNTO ME.

"Come unto me, all ye that labor and are heavy
laden, and I will give you rest."—Matt. xi, 28.

CHANT. Key C.

1 WITH tearful eyes I look around,
Life seems a dark and | stormy | sea;
Yet, 'midst the gloom, I hear a sound,
A heavenly | whisper, | "Come to | me."

2 It tells me of a place of rest—
It tells me where my | soul may | flee;
Oh, to the weary, faint, oppressed,
How sweet the | bidding, | "Come to |
me!"

3 When nature shudders, loth to part
From all I love, en- | joy, and | see;
When a faint chill steals o'er my heart,
A sweet voice | utters, | "Come to | me."

92

MARY TO THE SAVIOR'S TOMB.

TUNE—"Martyn." Key F. 7s. Double.

1 MARY to the Savior's tomb
Hasted at the early dawn;
Spice she brought, and sweet perfume,
But the Lord she loved had gone.
For awhile she lingering stood,
Filled with sorrow and surprise;
Trembling while a crystal flood
Issued from her weeping eyes.

2 But her sorrows quickly fled,
When she heard his welcome voice;
Christ has risen from the dead,
Now he bid her heart rejoice.
What a change his word can make,
Turning darkness into day;
Ye, who weep for Jesus' sake,
He will wipe your weeping eyes.

93 PRAISE.

TUNE—"Cranbrook." S. M.

1 GRACE! 't is a charming sound,
Harmonious to the ear;
Heaven with the echo shall resound,
And all the earth shall hear.

2 Grace first contrived a way
To save rebellious man;
And all the steps that grace display,
Which drew the wondrous plan.

3 Grace led my roving feet
To tread the heavenly road;
And new supplies each hour I meet,
While pressing on to God.

4 Grace all the work shall crown,
Through everlasting days;
And every ransomed power shall join
In wonder, love, and praise.

HE DOETH ALL THINGS WELL.

94

1 I remember how I loved her,
  When a little guiltless child,
I saw her in the cradle
  As she looked on me and smil'd.
My cup of happiness was full,
  My joy words cannot tell;
And I blessed the glorious Giver,
  " Who doeth all things well"
And I blessed the glorious Giver,
  Who doeth all things well.

2 Months pass'd ; that bud of promise
  Was unfolding ev'ry hour,
I thought that earth had never smil'd
  Upon a fairer flow'r,
So beautiful it well might grace
  The bow'rs where angels dwell
And waft its fragrance to His throne
  " Who doeth all things well,"
And waft its fragrance to His throne
  " Who doeth all things well."

3 Years fled; that little sister
  That was dear as life to me,
And woke, in my unconscious heart,
  A wild idolatry;
I worshipped at an earthly shrine,
  Lured by some magic spell,
Forgetful of the praise of Him,
  " Who doeth all things well,"
Forgetful of the praise of Him,
  " Who doeth all things well."

4 She was the lovely star,
  Whose light around my pathway shone,
Amid this darksome vale of tears,
  Through which I journey on,
Its radiance had obscured the light,
  Which round His throne doth dwell,
And I wandered far away from Him,
  " Who doeth all things well,"
And I wandered far away from Him,
  " Who doeth all things well."

5 That star went down in beauty,
  Yet it shineth sweetly now,
In the bright and dazzling coronet,
  That decks the Saviour's brow.
She bowed to the destroyer,
  Whose shafts none may repel,
But we know, for God hath told us,
  " He doeth all things well,"
But we know, for God hath told us,
  " He doeth all things well."

6 I remember well my sorrow,
  As I stood beside her bed,
And my deep and heartfelt anguish when
  They told me she was dead ;
And oh! that cup of bitterness
  Let not my heart rebel,.
God gave, He took, He will restore,
  " He doeth all things well,"
God gave, He took, He will restore,
  " He doeth all things well."

ANTICIPATIONS OF HEAVEN.

95

OLD TUNE. C. M.

1 When I can read my title clear
  To mansions in the skies,
I'll bid farewell to every fear,
  And wipe my weeping eyes.

2 Should earth against my soul engage,
  And hellish darts be hurl'd,
Then I can smile at Satan's rage,
  And face a frowning world.

3 Let cares like a wild deluge come,
  Let storms of sorrow fall,—
So I but safely reach my home,
  My God, my heaven, my all.

4 There I shall bathe my weary soul
  In seas of heavenly rest,
And not a wave of trouble roll
  Across my peaceful breast.

5 When I've been there ten thousand years,
  Bright shining as the sun,
I've no less days to sing God's praise,
  Than when I first begun.

HOLY FORTITUDE.

96

TUNE—" Arlington." Key G. C. M.

1 Am I a soldier of the cross,
  A follower of the Lamb?
And shall I fear to own his cause,
  Or blush to speak his name?

2 Shall I be carried to the skies,
  On flowery beds of ease,
While others fought to win the prize,
  And sailed through bloody seas?

3 Are there no foes for me to face?
  Must I not stem the flood?
Is this vain world a friend to grace,
  To help me on to God?

4 Sure I must fight, if I would reign;
  Increase my courage, Lord!
I'll bear the toil, endure the pain,
  Supported by thy word.

5 Thy saints in all this glorious war
  Shall conquer, though they die;
They see the triumph from afar,
  By faith they bring it nigh.

TEMPERANCE VERSE.

97

TUNE—Your Mission.

There's a field already open;
  You can lend a helping hand
To reclaim the many drunkards,
  Who are scattered o'er the land ;
You can help us try to banish
  From each home the cursed bowl;
You may gain a crown of glory,
  If you save a human soul.

MY CHILDHOOD.

98

1 As I rummag'd thro' the attic,
  List'ning to the falling rain,
As it patter'd on the shingles
  And against the window pane;
Peeping over chests and boxes,
  Which with dust were thickly spread;
Saw I in the farthest corner
  What was once my trundle bed.

2 So I drew it from the recess,
  Where it had remained so long,
Hearing all the while the music
  Of my mother's voice in song;
As she sang in sweetest accents,
  What I since have often read—
" Hush, my dear, lie still and slumber,
  Holy angels guard thy bed."

3 As I listen'd, recollections
  That I thought had been forgot,
Came with all the gush of mem'ry,
  Rushing, thronging to the spot:
And I wander'd back to childhood,
  To those merry days of yore,
When I knelt beside my mother,
  By this bed upon the floor.

4 Then it was with hands so gently
  Placed upon my infant head,
That she taught my lips to utter
  Carefully the words she said;
Never can they be forgotten,
  Deep are they in mem'ry riven—
" Hallowed be thy name, O, Father!
  Father! Thou who art in heaven."

5 This she taught me, then she told me
  Of its import, great and deep—
After which I learned to utter
  " Now I lay me down to sleep:"
Then it was with hands uplifted,
  And in accents soft and mild,
That my mother asked " Our Father!
  Father! do thou bless my child!"

6 Years have pass'd, and that dear mother,
  Long has mouldered 'neath the sod,
And I trust her sainted spirit
  Revels in the home of God:
But that scene at summer twilight,
  Never has from mem'ry fled,
And it comes in all its freshness
  When I see my trundle bed.

99

THE BANNER OF THE CROSS.

Tune—" Pleyel's Hymn." 5th P. M.

1 Go, ye messengers of God;
  Like the beams of morning, fly;
Take the wonder-working rod;
  Wave the banner-cross on high.

2 Go to many a tropic isle
  In the bosom of the deep,
Where the skies forever smile,
  And the oppressed forever weep.

3 O'er the pagan's night of care
  Pour the living light of heaven;
Chase away his wild despair;
  Bid him hope to be forgiven.

4 Where the golden gates of day
  Open on the palmy East,
High the bleeding cross display;
  Spread the gospel's richest feast.

THE BLOOD OF CHRIST.

100 Tune—" Fountain." C. M.

1 There is a fountain filled with blood,
  Drawn from Immanuel's veins,
And sinners plunged beneath that flood
  Lose all their guilty stains.

2 The dying thief rejoiced to see
  That fountain in his day;
And there may I, as vile as he,
  Wash all my sins away.

3 Dear dying Lamb, thy precious blood
  Shall never lose its power,
Till all the ransomed church of God
  Be saved, to sin no more.

4 E'er since, by faith, I saw the stream
  Thy flowing wounds supply,
Redeeming love has been my theme,
  And shall be till I die.

5 Then, in a nobler, sweeter song,
  I'll sing thy power to save,
When this poor lisping, stammering tongue
  Lies silent in the grave.

101

PILGRIMAGE HEAVENWARD.

Tune—" Harwell." Key G. 7s.

1 Children of the heavenly King,
  As ye journey, sweetly sing;
Sing your Savior's worthy praise,
  Glorious in his works and ways.

2 Ye are traveling home to God,
  In the way the fathers trod;
They are happy now—and ye
  Soon their happiness shall see.

3 Shout, ye little flock, and blest,
  You on Jesus' throne shall rest;
There your seat is now prepared—
  There your kingdom and reward.

4 Fear not, brethren; joyful stand
  On the borders of your land;
Jesus Christ, God's only Son,
  Bids you undismayed go on.

MARCHING ALONG.

102

1 LET us lift our hearts with gladness,
   Let us sing for joy to-night;
Lo! the Church of God is rising
   In her glory, strength, and might!
She is marching on triumphant,
   With her banner wide unfurled;
She is sending forth her heralds
   With salvation to the world!

CHORUS.

Marching along! we are marching along!
Rising as a people while we're marching along!
The conflict is raging 'tween the right and the
   wrong;
We'll trust in the Lord while we're marching
   along.

2 Let us turn our eyes a moment,
   While we take a passing view
Of the time the Church was planted,
   And her numbers were but few.
Then our preachers had their circuits
   Of a hundred miles to ride,
O'er the mountain, through the forest,
   On the western prairie wide.

3 But their hearts were bold and fearless,
   And their faith was firm and strong;
For their Captain was before them,
   And they praised him in their song.
And they saw the work progressing,
   Ere the vale of death they passed;
They are singing hallelujah!
   In the promised land, at last!

4 Lo! the Church of God is rising!
   And the Gospel's joyful sound,
With a trumpet tongue proclaiming
   To the earth's remotest bound!
There's a shout among the nations
   Far across the ocean's foam;
And she reaps a golden harvest
   From her mission field at home.

103   THE YOUNG CONVERT.

TUNE—"Abiding Rest," from the "Shawm."
Key 7 C.   8s & 7s P. M.   Double.

1 I now have found abiding rest,
   For which I long was sighing;
Now on my Savior's faithful breast
   My weary head is lying.
This is the place where sin no more,
   Nor death and hell alarm me;
I now am safe, by Jesus' power,
   From all that else would harm me.

2 He whispers me, I'm wholly thine,
   And thou art mine forever;
Henceforth all fear and doubt resign,
   Confiding in thy favor.
Thy every want shall find supply
   From thy exhaustless treasure;
I'll fill thy spirit with my joy,
   The pledge of endless pleasure.

LITTLE BAND OF LOVING ONES.

104   Key B♭.

1 WE all should love one another,
We all should love one another,
We all should love one another,
   And keep the golden rule.

CHORUS.

Sing on, love on, ye little band of loving ones;
Sing on, love on, ye little band of loving ones,

2 We all should love our parents,
We all should love our parents,
We all should love our parents,
   As children ought to do.
   Sing on, love on, etc.

3 We all should love our sisters,
We all should love our sisters,
We all should love our sisters,
   And love our brothers too.
   Sing on, love on, etc.

4 We all should love the Bible,
We all should love the Bible,
We all should love the Bible,
   Which tells us what to do.
   Sing on, love on, etc.

5 We all should love the Savior,
We all should love the Savior,
We all should love the Savior,
   Who shed for us his blood.
   Sing on, love on, etc.

6 We hope to go to heaven,
We hope to go to heaven,
We hope to go to heaven,
   And sing the songs of love.
   Sing on, love on, etc.

SWEET STORY.

105   Key D.

1 I THINK when I read that sweet story of old,
   When Jesus was here among men,
How he called little children as lambs to his
   fold,
   I should like to have been with them then.

2 I wish that his hands had been placed on my
   head,
   That his arms had been thrown around me,
And that I might have seen his kind look
   when he said,
   "Let the little ones come unto me."

3 Yet still to his footstool in prayer I may go
   And ask for a share in his love;
And if I thus earnestly seek him below,
   I shall see him and hear him above.

4 In that beautiful place he has gone to pre-
   pare,
   For all that are washed and forgiven;
And many dear children are gathering there,
   "For of such is the kingdom of heaven."

106 HUMILITY AND CONTRITION.

Tune—"Penitence." Key B♭. 12th P. M.

1 Jesus, let thy pitying eye
  Call back a wandering sheep;
False to thee, like Peter, I
  Wou'd fain like Peter weep.
Let me be by grace restored,
  On me be all long suffering shown;
Turn and look upon me, Lord,
  And break my heart of stone.

.9 Savior Prince, enthroned above,
  Repentance to impart,
Give me, through thy dying love,
  The humble, contrite heart.
Give what I have long implored,
  A portion of thy love unknown;
Turn and look upon me, Lord,
  And break my heart of stone.

3 For thine own compassion's sake,
  The gracious wonder show;
Cast my sins behind thy back,
  And wash me white as snow.
If thy bowels now are stirred,
  If now I do myself bemoan,
Turn and look upon me, Lord,
  And break my heart of stone.

A LIGHT IN THE WINDOW.

107   Key A♭.

1 There's a light in the window for thee,
    brother,
  There's a light in the window for thee;
A dear one has moved to the mansions above,
  There's a light in the window for thee.

Chorus.

A mansion in heaven we see,
  And a light in the window for thee;
A mansion in heaven we see,
  And a light in the window for thee.

2 There's a crown, and a robe, and a palm,
    brother,
  When from toil and from care you are free;
The Savior has gone to prepare you a home,
  With a light in the window for thee.
A mansion in heaven, etc.

3 O watch, and be faithful, and pray, brother,
  All your journey o'er life's troubled sea!
Though afflictions assail you, and storms
    beat severe,
  There's a light in the window for thee.
A mansion in heaven, etc.

4 Then on, perseveringly on, brother,
  Till from conflict and suffering free,
Bright angels now beckon you over the
    stream,
  There's a light in the window for thee.
A mansion in heaven, etc.

LET US WALK IN THE LIGHT.

108   Key G.

1 'Tis religion that can give—
  In the light, in the light;
Sweetest pleasure while we live—
  In the light of God.
'Tis religion must supply—
  In the light, in the light;
Solid comfort when we die—
  In the light of God.

Chorus.

Let us walk in the light,
  In the light, in the light;
Let us walk in the light,
  In the light of God.

2 After death its joys shall be—
  In the light, in the light;
Lasting as eternity—
  In the light of God.
Be the living God my Friend—
  In the light, in the light;
Then my bliss shall never end—
  In the light of God.
    Let us walk, etc.

THE SABBATH BELL.

109   Key G.

1 Pleasant is the Sabbath bell—
  In the light, in the light;
Seeming much of joy to tell—
  In the light of God.
But a music sweeter far—
  In the light, in the light;
Breathes where angel-spirits are—
  In the light of God.

Chorus.

Let us walk in the light,
  In the light, in the light;
Let us walk in the light,
  In the light of God.

2 Shall we ever rise to dwell—
  In the light, in the light;
Where immortal praises swell—
  In the light of God?
And can children ever go—
  In the light, in the light;
Where eternal Sabbaths glow—
  In the light of God?
    Let us walk, etc.

3 Yes, that bliss our own may be—
  In the light, in the light;
All the good shall Jesus see—
  In the light of God.
For the good a rest remains—
  In the light, in the light;
Where the glorious Savior reigns—
  In the light of God.
    Let us walk, etc.

110 HEAVENLY UNION.

TUNE—"Wirth." Key A♭. C. M.

1 How sweet and heavenly is the sight,
  When those that love the Lord
In one another's peace delight,
  And so fulfill his word!

2 O may we feel each brother's sigh,
  And with him bear a part!
May sorrows flow from eye to eye,
  And joy from heart to heart.

3 Let love, in one delightful stream,
  Through every bosom flow;
Let union sweet, and dear esteem,
  In every action glow.

4 Love is the golden chain that binds
  The happy souls above;
And he's an heir of heaven who finds
  His bosom glow with love.

SONG OF THE INFANTS.

111 Key C.

1 SOME call us infants,
  Our life just begun;
Some call us "the fathers,"
  They must be in fun;
Some wish we were many,
  Yet others we guess,
When we're in a frolic,
  Most wish we were less.

2 Some say, while they call us
  Such wee bits of things,
We're what men are made of,
  The priests and the kings;
Whatever we may be,
  We're sure of one thing;
That you are our Shepherd,
  And we're here to sing.

3 We bring the bright pennies,
  They're little, we know;
But, love going with them,
  To dollars they'll grow;
As much as this, surely,
  We children can see:
If there were no pennies,
  No dollars there'd be.

112 WANDERER'S RETURN.

TUNE—"Retreat." Key C.

1 RETURN, O wanderer, return!
  And seek an injured Father's face;
Those warm desires that in thee burn
  Were kindled by reclaiming grace.

2 Return, O wanderer, return!
  Thy Savior bids thy spirit live;
Go to his bleeding feet, and learn
  How freely Jesus can forgive.

WONDER.

113 Key G.

1 O! 'T is a glorious mystery,
  'T is a wonder, a wonder, a wonder;
That I should ever saved be,
  'T is a wonder, a wonder, a wonder.
No heart can think, no tongue can tell,
  'T is a wonder, a wonder;
Why God should save my soul from hell,
  'T is a wonder, a wonder, a wonder.

2 Great mystery that Christ should place,
  'T is a wonder, a wonder, a wonder;
His love on any of Adam's race,
  'T is a wonder, a wonder, a wonder.
But there's a greater mystery,
  'T is a wonder, a wonder;
That he bestowed his love on me,
  'T is a wonder, a wonder, a wonder.

3 Great mystery I do behold,
  'T is a wonder, a wonder, a wonder;
That God should ever save a soul,
  'T is a wonder, a wonder, a wonder.
But here's a greater mystery,
  'T is a wonder, a wonder;
That he bestowed his love on me,
  'T is a wonder, a wonder, a wonder.

4 Why was I not still left behind,
  'T is a wonder, a wonder, a wonder;
With thousand others of mankind,
  'T is a wonder, a wonder, a wonder.
To run the dangerous, sinful race,
  'T is a wonder, a wonder;
And die and never taste his grace,
  'T is a wonder, a wonder, a wonder.

5 No mortal can a reason find,
  'T is a wonder, a wonder, a wonder;
'T is mercy free, and grace divine,
  'T is a wonder, a wonder, a wonder.
O! 't is a glorious mystery,
  'T is a wonder, a wonder;
And will be to eternity,
  'T is a wonder, a wonder, a wonder.

114 PENITENCE.

TUNE—"Autumn." Key A. 8s & 7s. Double.

1 TAKE my heart, O Father! take it;
  Make and keep it all thine own:
Let thy Spirit melt and break it;
  Turn to flesh this heart of stone.
Heavenly Father, deign to mould it
  In obedience to thy will;
And, as passing years unfold it,
  Keep it meek and childlike still.

2 Father, make it pure and lowly,
  Peaceful, kind, and far from strife,
Turning from the paths unholy
  Of this vain and sinful life.
May the blood of Jesus heal it,
  And its sins be all forgiven;
Holy Spirit, take and seal it;
  Guide it in the path to heaven.

THE BRIGHT CROWN.

115   Key C.

1 Ye valiant soldiers of the cross,
  Ye happy, praying band,
Though in this world you suffer loss,
  You 'll reach fair Canaan's land.

CHORUS.

Let us never mind the scoffs nor the frowns of
  the world,
For we 've all got the cross to bear;
It will only make the crown the brighter to
  shine,
When we have the crown to wear.

2 All earthly pleasures we 'll forsake,
  When heaven appears in view;
In Jesus' strength we 'll undertake
  To fight our passage through.
  Let us never, etc.

3 O what a glorious shout there 'll be,
  When we arrive at home!
Our friends and Jesus we shall see,
  And God shall say, "Well done."
  Let us never, etc

116   A BLESSING SOUGHT.

TUNE—"Autumn."   Key A.   8s & 7s.   Double.

1 HEAVENLY FATHER, grant thy blessing,
  While once more thy praise we sing:
Sinful hearts and lives confessing,
  Nothing worthy can we bring;
Yet thy book of love hath taught us,
  Thou wilt kindly bow thine ear;
For the sake of Him who bought us,
  We may call and thou wilt hear.

2 What a boon to us is given,
  Thus to lift our voice on high!
Well assured the ear of Heaven
  Hears our wants, and will supply.
Weak and sinful—oh, how often
  Must we look to God alone,
For his grace our hearts to soften,
  And sustain us as his own!

HAST THOU STILL A FATHER.

117   Key G.

1 HAST thou still a father,
  Or a mother dear?
Hast thou yet a brother,
  Or a sister here?

2 O then love them freely,
  Cherish every tie!
All we prize most dearly,
  All on earth must die.

3 Still, be not forgetful
  Of the Friend above;
He can never perish,
  And his name is love.

BY COOL SILOAM'S SHADY RILL.

118   TUNE—"Siloam."   Key D.

1 BY cool Siloam's shady rill,
  How fair the lily grows!
How sweet the breath, beneath the hill,
  Of Sharon's dewy rose.

2 Lo! such the child, whose early feet
  The paths of peace have trod;
Whose secret heart, by influence sweet,
  Is upward drawn to God.

3 And soon, too soon, the wintry hour
  Of man's maturer age
Will shake the soul with sorrow's power,
  And stormy passion's rage.

4 O Thou who givest life and breath,
  We seek thy grace alone,
In childhood, manhood, age, and death,
  To keep us still thine own.

119   A PERFECT HEART.

TUNE—"Roscoe."   Key Bb Minor.   C. M.

1 O FOR a heart to praise my God!
  A heart from sin set free;
A heart that always feels thy blood,
  So freely shed for me.

2 A heart resigned, submissive, meek,
  My great Redeemer's throne,
Where only Christ is heard to speak,
  Where Jesus reigns alone.

3 O for a lowly, contrite heart,
  Believing, true, and clean,
Which neither life nor death can part
  From him that dwells within!

4 Thy nature, gracious Lord, impart,
  Come quickly from above,
Write thy new name upon my heart,
  Thy new, best name, of Love.

THE GLORIOUS TIME.

120   TUNE—"Harwell."   Key G.

1 HASTEN, Lord, the glorious time,
  When beneath Messiah's sway,
Every nation, every clime,
  Shall the Gospel call obey!
Mightiest kings his power shall own,
  Heathen tribes his name adore;
Satan and his host o'erthrown,
  Bound in chains, shall hurt no more.

2 Then shall wars and tumults cease,
  Then be banished grief and pain;
Righteousness and joy and peace,
  Undisturbed, shall ever reign.
Bless we, then, our gracious Lord,
  Ever praise his glorious name;
All his mighty acts record,
  All his wondrous love proclaim.

MERCY SEAT.

121   Tune—"Retreat."   Key C.

1 From every stormy wind that blows,
From every swelling tide of woes,
There is a calm, a sure retreat,
'T is found beneath the mercy seat.

2 There is a place where Jesus sheds
The oil of gladness on our heads;
A place where on earth more sweet—
It is the blood-bought mercy seat.

3 There is a scene where spirits blend,
Where friend holds fellowship with friend;
Though sundered far, by faith they meet
Around one common mercy seat.

4 Ah! whither could we flee for aid,
When tempted, desolate, dismayed?
Or how the hosts of hell defeat,
Had suffering saints no mercy seat?

5 There, there on eagles' wings we soar,
And sin and sense molest no more,
And heaven comes down our souls to greet,
While glory crowns the mercy seat.

NEVER LATE.

122   Key D.

1 I 'll awake at dawn on the Sabbath day,
For 't is wrong to doze holy time away;
With my lessons learned, this shall be my
   rule—
Never to be late at the Sabbath-school.

2 Birds awake betimes, every morn they sing;
None are tardy there, when the woods do
   ring;
So, when Sunday comes, this shall be my
   rule—
Never to be late at the Sabbath-school.

3 When the summer's sun wakes the flowers
   again,
They the call obey—none are tardy then;
Nor will I forget that it is my rule
Never to be late at the Sabbath-school.

4 But these Sabbath days will soon be o'er,
And these happy hours shall return no more;
Then I 'll ne'er regret that it was my rule
Never to be late at the Sabbath-school.

123

THE REPENTING SINNER RETURNING.

Tune—"Salvation."   Key G minor.   C. M.

1 Come, humble sinner, in whose breast,
A thousand thoughts revolve;
Come, with your guilt and fear oppressed,
And make this last resolve:

2 "I 'll go to Jesus, though my sin
High as a mountain rose;
I know his courts, I 'll enter in,
Whatever may oppose.

3 "Prostrate I 'll lie before his throne,
And there my guilt confess;
I 'll tell him I 'm a wretch undone,
Without his sovereign grace.

4 ",'ll to the gracious King approach,
Whose scepter pardon gives;
Perhaps he may command my touch,
And then the suppliant lives.

5 "Perhaps he will admit my plea,
Perhaps will hear my prayer;
But if I perish, I will pray,
And perish only there.

6 I can but perish if I go,
I am resolved to try;
For if I stay away, I know
I must forever die."

124 PRAYER FOR A REVIVAL.

Tune—"Greenville."   Key E.   8s & 7s.

1 Savior, visit thy plantation;
Grant us, Lord, a gracious rain;
All will come to desolation,
Unless thou return again.
Lord, revive us,
All our help must come from thee.

2 Keep no longer at a distance;
Shine upon us from on high,
Lest, for want of thine assistance,
Every plant should droop and die.

3 Let our mutual love be fervent,
Make us prevalent in prayers;
Let each one esteemed thy servant,
Shun the world's enticing snares.

4 Break the tempter's fatal power;
Turn the stony heart to flesh,
And begin, from this good hour,
To revive thy work afresh.

125   LORD'S PROTECTION.

Tune—"Hebron."   Key B♭.   L. M.

1 Thus far the Lord hath led me on;
Thus far his power prolongs my days;
And every evening shall make known
Some fresh memorial of his grace.

2 Much of my time has run to waste;
And I, perhaps am near my home;
But he forgives my follies past,
He gives me strength for days to come.

3 I lay my body down to sleep;
Peace is the pillow for my head;
While well-appointed angels keep
Their watchful stations round my bed.

4 Thus, when the night of death shall come,
My flesh shall rest beneath the ground,
And wait thy voice to break my tomb,
With sweet salvation in the sound.

GOOD-NIGHT!

126 Key D.

1 How sweet the happy evenings close,
'T is the hour of sweet repose—
   Good-night!
The summer winds have sunk to rest,
   The moon, serenely bright,
Unfolds her calm and gentle ray,
Softly now she seems to say—
   Good-night!

2 These tranquil hours of social mirth,
For the dearest link of earth—
   Good-night!
And, while each hand is kindly pressed,
   O, may our prayers to heaven
With humble fervor be addressed,
For its blessings on our rest—
   Good-night!

3 O, how each gentle thought is stirred,
As we breathe the parting word—
   Good-night!
O, could we ever feel as now,
   Our hearts with love upraised,
And while our warm affections flow,
Hear, in murmurs soft and low—
   Good-night!

---

127   THE LAMBS OF JESUS.

Tune—"Woodworth." Key Eb. L. M.

1 The lambs of Jesus! who are they
But children that believe and pray?
That keep God's laws and ask his grace,
And seek a heavenly dwelling-place!

2 The lambs of Jesus! they are meek,
The words of peace and truth they speak;
To all God's creatures they are kind,
And, like their Lord, of gentle mind.

3 The lambs of Jesus! oh, that we
Might of that blessed number be!
Lord, take us early to thy love,
And lead us to the fold above.

---

128   THE ETERNAL SABBATH.

Tune—"Windham." Key G minor. L. M.

1 Come, dearest Lord, and bless this day,
Come, bear our thoughts from earth away;
Now let our noblest passions rise
With ardor to their native skies.

2 Come, holy Spirit, all divine,
With rays of light upon us shine;
And let our waiting souls be blest
On this sweet day of sacred rest.

3 Then, when our Sabbaths here are o'er,
And we arrive on Canaan's shore,
With all the ransomed we shall spend
A Sabbath which shall never end.

---

129   THE LOVE OF JESUS.

Tune—"Woodworth." Key Eb. L. M.

1 I know 't is Jesus loves my soul,
And makes the wounded spirit whole;
My nature is by sin defiled,
Yet Jesus loves a little child.

2 How kind is Jesus, O how good!
'T was for my soul he shed his blood;
For children's sake he was reviled,
For Jesus loves a little child.

3 When I offend, by thought or tongue,
Omit the right, or do the wrong;
If I repent, he 's reconciled,
For Jesus loves a little child.

4 To me may Jesus now impart,
Although so young, a gracious heart;
Alas! I 'm oft by sin defiled,
Yet Jesus loves a little child.

CONDEMNED, BUT PLEADING THE
130   PROMISES.

Tune—"Windham." Key G minor. L. M.

1 Show pity, Lord! O Lord, forgive!
Let a repenting rebel live;
Are not thy mercies large and free?
May not a sinner trust in thee?

2 My crimes are great, but do n't surpass
The power and glory of thy grace;
Great God, thy nature hath no bound!
So let thy pardoning love be found.

3 O wash my soul from every sin,
And make my guilty conscience clean;
Here on my heart the burden lies,
And past offenses pain my eyes.

4 O save a trembling sinner, Lord,
Whose hope, still hovering round thy Word,
Would light on some sweet promise there,
Some sure support against despair.

I'M A PILGRIM.

131 Key G.

1 I 'm a pilgrim, and I 'm a stranger,
   I can tarry, I can tarry but a night;
Do not detain me, for I am going
   To where the streamlets are ever flowing.
   I 'm a pilgrim, and I 'm a stranger,
   I can tarry, I can tarry but a night.

2 There the sunbeams are ever shining,
   I am longing, I am longing for the sight;
Within a country unknown and dreary,
   I have been wandering forlorn and weary.
   I 'm a pilgrim, etc.

3 Of that country to which I 'm going,
   My Redeemer, my Redeemer is the light;
There are no sorrows, nor any sighing,
   Nor any sin there, nor any dying.
   I 'm a pilgrim, etc.

132   PEACEFUL REST.

Tune—"Rest." Key D. L. M.

1 Asleep in Jesus! blessed sleep!
  From which none ever wakes to weep;
  A calm and undisturbed repose,
  Unbroken by the last of foes.

2 Asleep in Jesus! O, how sweet
  To be for such a slumber meet!
  With holy confidence to sing
  That Death has lost his cruel sting.

3 Asleep in Jesus! peaceful rest,
  Whose waking is supremely blest;
  No fear, no woe shall dim that hour
  That manifests the Savior's power.

4 Asleep in Jesus! O, for me
  May such a blissful refuge be!
  Securely shall my ashes lie,
  Waiting the summons from on high.

5 Asleep in Jesus! far from thee
  Thy kindred and their graves may be;
  But there is still a blessed sleep
  From which none ever wakes to weep.

133   VISITATION OF DEATH.

Tune—"Galena." Key B♭. C. M.

1 Death has been here, and borne away
  A scholar from our side;
  Just in the morning of his day,
  As young as we he died.

2 Not long ago he filled his place,
  And sat with us to learn;
  But he has run his mortal race,
  And never can return.

3 Perhaps our time may be as short,
  Our days may fly as fast;
  O Lord, impress the solemn thought,
  That this may be our last.

4 We can not tell who next may fall
  Beneath thy chastening rod;
  One must be first; oh, may we all
  Prepare to meet our God!

5 All needful help is thine to give;
  To thee our souls apply,
  For grace to teach us how to live,
  And make us fit to die.

WHAT I LIVE FOR.

134   Key A.

1 I live for those who love me,
  Whose hearts are kind and true,
  For heaven, that smiles above me,
  And waits my spirit too;
  For all the ties that bind me,
  For all the tasks assigned me,
  For bright hopes left behind me,
  And the good that I may do.

2 I live to hold communion
  With all that is divine;
  To feel there is a union
  'Twixt nature's heart and mine;
  To profit by affliction,
  Reap truths from fields of fiction,
  And, wiser from conviction,
  Help on each grand design.

3 I live to hail that season
  By gifted minds foretold,
  Where men shall live by reason,
  And not alone by gold;
  When man to man united,
  And every wrong thing righted,
  The whole world shall be lighted,
  As Eden was of old.

HOW SWEET IS THE SABBATH TO ME.

135   OLD TUNE. Key G. 8s.

1 How sweet is the Sabbath to me,
  The day when the Savior arose!
  'T is heaven his beauties to see,
  And in his soft arms to repose.
  He knows I am weak and defiled,
  My life is but empty and vain;
  But if he will make me his child,
  I 'll never forsake him again.

2 This day he invites me to come;
  How kindly he bids me draw near!
  He offers me heaven for home,
  And wipes off the penitent tear.
  He offers to pardon my sin,
  And keep me from every snare,
  To sprinkle and cleanse me within,
  And show me his tenderest care.

3 I can not, I must not refuse;
  His goodness has conquered my heart;
  The Lord for my portion I choose,
  And bid all of my folly depart.
  How sweet is the Sabbath to me,
  The day my Redeemer arose!
  'T is heaven his beauties to see,
  And in his soft arms to repose.

LORD, TEACH A SINFUL CHILD TO PRAY.

136   C. M.

1 Lord, teach a sinful child to pray,
  And then accept my prayer;
  For thou canst hear the words I say
  For thou art every-where.

2 Teach me to do the thing that 's right,
  And when I sin, forgive;
  And may it be my chief delight
  To serve thee while I live.

3 Whatever trouble I am in,
  To thee for help I 'll call;
  But keep me more than all from sin,
  For that 's the worst of all.

JOYFULLY! JOYFULLY! ONWARD WE MOVE.

137

TUNE—"Joyfully! Joyfully!" Key G.

1 JOYFULLY, joyfully, onward we move,
Round to the land of bright spirits above;
Jesus, our Savior, in mercy says come,
Joyfully, joyfully, haste to your home.
Soon will our pilgrimage end here below,
Soon will our presence of God we shall go;
Then, if to Jesus our hearts have been given,
Joyfully, joyfully, rest we in heaven.

2 Teachers and scholars have passed on before,
Waiting, they watch us approaching the shore;
Singing to cheer us, while passing along,
Joyfully, joyfully, haste to your home.
Sounds of sweet music there ravish the ear,
Harps of the blessed, your strains we shall hear,
Filling with harmony heaven's high dome;
Joyfully, joyfully, Jesus, we come.

3 Death with his arrow may soon lay us low,
Safe in our Savior, we fear not the blow;
Jesus hath broken the bars of the tomb,
Joyfully, joyfully 'till we go home.
Bright will the morn of eternity dawn,
Death shall be conquered, his scepter be gone;
Over the plains of sweet Canaan we'll roam,
'oyfully, joyfully, safely at home.

----◦◦◦----

WE LOVE TO SING TOGETHER.

138   Key C.

1 WE love to sing together,
We love to sing together,
Our hearts and voices one;
To praise our Heavenly Father,
To praise our Heavenly Father,
And his eternal Son.
We love, we love, we love, we love,
We love to sing together;
We love, we love, we love, we love,
We love to sing together.

2 We love to pray together
To Jesus on his throne,
And ask that he will ever
Accept us as his own.
We love, etc.

3 We love to read together
The Word of saving truth,
Whose light is shining ever
To guide our early youth.
We love, etc.

4 We love to be together
Upon the Sabbath day,
And strive to help each other
Along the heavenly way.
We love, etc.

WHEN THE MORNING LIGHT.

139   Key A.

1 WHEN the morning light drives away the night,
With the sun so bright and full,
And it draws its line near the hour of nine,
I'll away to the Sabbath-school;
For 'tis there we all agree,
All with happy hearts and free,
And I love to early be
At the Sabbath-school.
I'll away! away! I'll away! away!
I'll away to Sabbath-school.

2 On the frosty dawn of a winter's morn,
When the earth is wrapped in snow,
Or the summer breeze plays around the trees,
To the Sabbath-school I go;
When the holy day has come,
And the Sabbath-breakers roam,
I delight to leave my home,
For the Sabbath-school.
I'll away, etc.

3 In the class I meet with the friends I greet,
At the time of morning prayer;
And our hearts we raise in a hymn of praise,
For 'tis always pleasant there;
In the Book of holy truth,
Full of counsel and reproof,
We behold the guide of youth,
At the Sabbath-school.
I'll away, etc.

4 May the dews of grace fill the hallowed place,
And the sunshine never fail,
While each blooming rose which in memory grows
Shall a sweet perfume exhale;
When we mingle here no more,
But have met on Jordan's shore,
We will talk of moments o'er
At the Sabbath-school.
I'll away, etc.

----◦◦◦----

140   USE OF THE BIBLE.

TUNE—"Pleyel's Hymn." 7s.

1 HOLY BIBLE! book divine!
Precious treasure! thou art mine!
Mine, to tell me whence I came;
Mine, to teach me what I am.

2 Mine, to chide me when I rove;
Mine, to show a Savior's love;
Mine art thou to guide my feet;
Mine, to judge, condemn, acquit.

3 Mine, to comfort in distress,
If the Holy Spirit bless;
Mine, to show by living faith
Man can triumph over death.

4 Mine, to tell of joys to come;
And the rebel sinner's doom;
O thou precious book divine!
Precious treasure! thou art mine

THE SUN OF RIGHTEOUSNESS.

141　Tune—"Pleyel's Hymn." 7s.

1 Hark! the herald angels sing,
　　Glory to the new-born King;
　　Peace on earth, and mercy mild;
　　God and sinners reconciled.

2 Joyful all ye nations, rise,
　　Join the triumph of the skies!
　　With angelic hosts proclaim,
　　Christ is born in Bethlehem.

3 Christ, by highest heaven adored!
　　Christ, the everlasting Lord!
　　Vailed in flesh the Godhead see;
　　Hail, incarnate Deity!

4 Hail the heaven-born Prince of peace!
　　Hail the Sun of righteousness!
　　Light and life to all he brings,
　　Risen with healing in his wings.

5 Come, Desire of nations, come!
　　Fix in us thy humble home;
　　Second Adam from above,
　　Reinstate us in thy love.

142　HOMEWARD BOUND.

Tune—"Homeward Bound." Key A.

1 Out on an ocean all boundless we ride,
　　We're homeward bound, homeward bound;
　　Tossed on the waves of a rough, restless tide,
　　We're homeward bound, homeward bound.
　　Far, from the safe, quiet harbor we 've rode,
　　Seeking our Father's celestial abode,
　　Promise of which on us each he bestowed,
　　We're homeward bound, homeward bound.

2 Wildly the storm sweeps us on as it roars,
　　We're homeward bound, homeward bound;
　　Look! yonder lie the bright heavenly shores,
　　We're homeward bound, homeward bound.
　　Steady, O, pilot! stand firm at the wheel,
　　Steady! we soon shall outweather the gale;
　　O how we fly 'neath the loud-creaking sail,
　　We're homeward bound, homeward bound.

3 Down the horizon the earth disappears,
　　We're homeward bound, homeward bound;
　　Joyful, O, comrades! no sighing or tears,
　　We're homeward bound, homeward bound.
　　Listen! what music comes soft o'er the sea?
　　" Welcome, thrice welcome, and blessed are
　　　ye,"
　　Can it the greeting of paradise be?
　　We're homeward bound, homeward bound.

4 Into the harbor of heaven now we glide,
　　We're home at last, home at last;
　　Softly we drift on its bright silver tide,
　　We're home at last, home at last.
　　Glory to God! all our dangers are o'er,
　　Safely we stand on the radiant shore;
　　Glory to God! we will shout evermore,
　　We're home at last, home at last.

THE PROMISED LAND.

143　Old Tune. Key E♭.

1 I have a Father in the promised land,
　　I have a Father in the promised land;
　　My Father calls me, I must go
　　To meet him in the promised land.

CHORUS.

I 'll away, I 'll away to the promised land,
I 'll away, I 'll away to the promised land;
　　My Father calls me, I must go
　　To meet him in the promised land.

2 I have a Savior in the promised land,
　　I have a Savior in the promised land;
　　My Savior calls me, I must go
　　To meet him in the promised land.
　　I 'll away, etc.

3 I have a crown in the promised land,
　　I have a crown in the promised land;
　　When Jesus calls me, I must go
　　To wear it in the promised land.
　　I 'll away, etc.

4 I hope to meet you in the promised land,
　　I hope to meet you in the promised land;
　　At Jesus' feet, a joyous band,
　　We 'll praise him in the promised land.
　　We 'll away, etc.

THE SUNDAY-SCHOOL.

144　Key A.　C. M.

1 The Sunday-school, that blessed place,
　　Oh! I would rather stay
　　Within its walls a child of grace,
　　Than spend my hours in play.

CHORUS.

The Sunday-school, the Sunday-school,
　　Oh! 'tis the place I love;
For there I learn the golden rule,
　　Which leads to joys above.

2 'Tis there I learn that Jesus died
　　For sinners such as I;
　　Oh! what has all the world beside,
　　That I should prize so high.
　　The Sunday-school, etc.

3 Then let our grateful tribute rise,
　　And songs of praise be given
　　To Him who dwells above the skies,
　　For such a blessing given.
　　The Sunday-school, etc.

4 And welcome, then, the Sunday-school,
　　We 'll read and sing and pray,
　　That we may keep the golden ru e,
　　And never from it stray.
　　The Sunday-school, etc.

DEAR LORD, REMEMBER ME.
145 C. M.

1 Jesus, thou art the sinner's friend,
As such I look to thee;
Now in the fullness of thy love,
Oh, Lord I remember me.
Remember thy pure word of grace,
Remember Calvary;
Remember all thy dying groans,
And then remember me.

2 Thou wondrous Advocate with God!
I yield myself to thee;
While thou art sitting on thy throne,
Dear Lord I remember me.
I own I'm guilty, own I'm vile,
Yet thy salvation's free;
Then, in thy all-abounding grace,
Dear Lord I remember me.

3 Howe'er forsaken or distressed;
Howe'er oppressed I be;
Howe'er afflicted here on earth,
Do thou remember me.
And when I close my eyes in death,
And creature helps all flee,
Then, O my great Redeemer, God!
I pray, remember me.

WHEN SHALL WE MEET AGAIN?
146 Tune—"Unity." Key Eb.

1 When shall we meet again?
Meet ne'er to sever?
When will Peace wreathe her chain
Round us forever?
Our hearts will ne'er repose
Safe from each blast that blows
In this dark vale of woes,
Never! no, never'

2 When shall love freely flow,
Pure as life's river?
When shall sweet friendship glow,
Changeless forever?
Where joys celestial thrill,
Where bliss each heart shall fill,
And fears of parting chill,
Never! no, never!

3 Up to that world of light
Take us, dear Savior!
May we all there unite
Happy forever!
Where kindred spirits dwell,
There may our music swell,
And time our joys dispel,
Never! no, never!

4 Soon shall we meet again,
Meet, ne'er to sever;
Soon will Peace wreathe her chain
Round us forever.
Our hearts will then repose,
Secure from worldly woes;
Our songs of praise shall close,
Never! no, never!

THERE IS A HAPPY LAND.
147 Tune—"Happy Land." Key E.

1 There is a happy land,
Far, far away;
Where saints in glory stand,
Bright, bright as day.
Oh, how they sweetly sing,
Worthy is our Savior King,
Loud let his praises ring,
Praise, praise for aye.

2 Come to that happy land,
Come, come away;
Why will ye doubting stand,
Why still delay?
Oh, we shall happy be,
When, from sin and sorrow free,
Lord, we shall live with thee,
Blest, blest for aye!

3 Bright, in that happy land,
Beams every eye;
Kept by a Father's hand,
Love can not die.
Oh, then, to glory run!
Be a crown and kingdom won,
And bright, above the sun,
We reign for aye.

THE SNOW STORM.
148

1 The cold wind swept the mountain's height,
And pathless was the dreary wild,
And amid the cheerless hours of night,
A mother wandered with her child.
As through the drifted snow she pressed,
The babe was sleeping on her breast,
The babe was sleeping on her breast.

2 And colder still the winds did blow,
And darker hours of night came on,
And deeper grew the drifts of snow—
Her limbs were chilled, her strength was gone.
"O God!" she cried in accents wild,
"If I must perish, save my child,"
"If I must perish, save my child."

3 She stript her mantle from her breast,
And bared her bosom to the storm;
As round the child she wrapped the vest,
She smiled to think that it was warm.
With one cold kiss, one tear she shed,
And sunk upon a snowy bed,
And sunk upon a snowy bed.

4 At dawn a traveller passed by,
And saw her 'neath a snowy veil—
The frost of death was in her eye,
Her cheek was cold, and hard, and pale—
He moved the robe from off the child;
The babe looked up, and sweetly smiled,
The babe looked up, and sweetly smiled.

149   INVITATION TO YOUTH.

TUNE—"Missionary Hymn." Key E. 7s & 6s.

1 "REMEMBER thy Creator,"
    While youth's fair spring is bright,
Before thy cares are greater,
    Before comes age's night.
While yet the sun shines o'er thee,
    While stars the darkness cheer,
While life is all before thee,
    Thy great Creator fear.

2 "Remember thy Creator,"
    E'er life resigns its trust,
E'er sinks dissolving nature,
    And dust returns to dust.
Before, with God, who gave it,
    The spirit shall appear,
He cries, who died to save it,
    "Thy great Creator fear."

---

150   I LOVE THE CHURCH.

TUNE—"St. Thomas." Key G.   S. M.

1 I LOVE thy kingdom, Lord,
    The house of thine abode ;
The church our blest Redeemer saved
    With his own precious blood.

2 I love thy church, O God !
    Her walls before thee stand,
Dear as the apple of thine eye,
    And graven on thy hand.

3 For her my tears shall fall ;
    For her my prayers ascend ;
To her my cares and toils be given,
    Till toils and cares shall end.

4 Beyond my highest joy
    I prize her heavenly ways ;
Her sweet communion, solemn vows,
    Her hymns of love and praise.

5 Sure as thy truth shall last,
    To Sion shall be given
The brightest glories earth can yield,
    And brighter bliss of heaven.

---

151   LOVING KINDNESS.

TUNE—"Loving Kindness." Key A.   L. M.

1 AWAKE, my soul, to joyful lays,
And sing the great Redeemer's praise ;
He justly claims a song from me,
His loving kindness, oh, how free !
    His loving kindness, loving kindness,
    His loving kindness, oh, how free !

2 He saw me ruined in the fall,
Yet loved me, notwithstanding all ;
He saved me from my lost estate,
His loving kindness, oh, how great !
    His loving kindness, etc.

3 When trouble, like a gloomy cloud,
Has gathered thick, and thundered loud,
He near my soul has always stood,
His loving kindness, oh, how good !
    His loving kindness, etc.

4 Often I feel my sinful heart
Prone from my Jesus to depart ;
But though I have him oft forgot,
His loving kindness changes not.
    His loving kindness, etc.

5 Soon shall I pass the gloomy vale,
Soon all my mortal powers must fail ;
Oh, may my last expiring breath
His loving kindness sing in death !
    His loving kindness, etc.

6 Then let me mount, and soar away
To the bright world of endless day ;
And sing with rapture and surprise,
His loving kindness in the skies.
    His loving kindness, etc.

CENTENARY SONG.

152

1 On the mountain of vision what a glory we
    behold,
A hundred years of victory are tinging earth
    with gold ;
And the glorious time is coming which the
    prophets long foretold—
    The years are marching on.—CHORUS.

2 The jubilee is sounding, and a million voices
    roll,
While earth repeats the chorus, as it spreads
    from pole to pole ;
For Jesus is our Captain, and glory is our
    goal :
    Jesus is marching on.—CHORUS.

3 From the cabin on the prairie, from the
    vaulted city dome,
From the dark and briny ocean, where our
    sailor-brothers roam,
We hear the glad rejoicing, like a happy
    harvest-home,
    The song is rolling on.—CHORUS.

4 A hundred years of marching, and a hundred
    years of song,
The Conqueror advances, and the time will
    not be long,
When He shall claim the heathen, and over-
    throw the wrong,—
    The time is marching on.—CHORUS.

5 And when our toils are over, on the heights
    of Evermore,
With the saints of all the ages, we will shout
    the battle o'er ;
And in the Golden City we will join the
    Conqueror,
    Forever marching on.—CHORUS.

WE ARE PILGRIMS.

153   Key A.

1 We are pilgrims on the earth,
  Journeying onward from our birth ;
  Every hour and every breath
  Brings us nearer still to death.

CHORUS.

Yes, we are pilgrims; yes, we are pilgrims;
Yes, we are pilgrims, on our journey home.

2 But beyond this vale of tears
  Lies the land that knows no fears,
  Where our steps no more may roam ;
  Pilgrims, we are going home !
    We are pilgrims, etc.

3 Home to long-lost friends and dear,
  Who are missed and mourned for here;
  Home to endless peace and love,
  In our Father's house above.
    We are pilgrims, etc.

4 Let not trifles by the way
  Tempt our hearts or steps to stray
  From that narrow path and strait,
  Leading to the golden gate.
    We are pilgrims, etc.

5 No, our faith hath One in view
  Who was once a pilgrim too ;
  From his track we will not roam,
  For to Christ we 're going home.
    We are pilgrims, etc.

---

154   JUST AS I AM.

TUNE—"Woodworth."   Key E♭.

1 Just as I am—without one plea,
  But that thy blood was shed for me,
  And that thou bidd'st me come to thee,
    O Lamb of God, I come !

2 Just as I am—and waiting not
  To rid my soul of one dark blot,
  To thee, whose blood can cleanse each spot,
    O Lamb of God, I come !

3 Just as I am—though tossed about
  With many a conflict, many a doubt,
  Fightings within, and fears without,
    O Lamb of God, I come !

4 Just as I am—poor, wretched, blind—
  Sight, riches, healing of the mind,
  Yea, all I need in thee to find,
    O Lamb of God, I come !

5 Just as I am, thou wilt receive,
  Wilt welcome, pardon, cleanse, relieve,
  Because thy promise I believe,
    O Lamb of God, I come !

6 Just as I am—thy love, unknown,
  Has broken every barrier down ;
  Now to be thine, yea, thine alone,
    O Lamb of God, I come !

CHILDREN IN HEAVEN.

155   Key A.   C. M.

1 Around the throne of God in heaven,
  Thousands of children stand ;
  Children whose sins are all forgiven,
  A holy, happy band.
    Singing glory, glory,
  Glory be to God on high.

2 In flowing robes of spotless white,
  See every one arrayed ;
  Dwelling in everlasting light,
  And joys that never fade.
    Singing glory, etc.

3 What brought them to that world above ?
  That heaven so bright and fair,
  Where all is peace and joy and love—
  How came those children there ?
    Singing glory, etc.

4 Because the Savior shed his blood,
  To wash away their sin ;
  Bathed in that pure and precious flood,
  Behold them white and clean !
    Singing glory, etc.

5 On earth they sought the Savior's grace,
  On earth they loved his name ;
  So now they see his blessed face,
  And stand before the Lamb.
    Singing glory, etc.

MORNING BELLS.

156   Key A.   8s & 7s.

1 Hark ! the morning bells are ringing,
  Children, haste, without delay ;
  Prayers of thousands now are winging
  Up to heaven their silent way.

CHORUS.

Come, children, come, the bells are ringing,
  To the Sabbath-school repair ;
  Let us all unite in singing,
  All unite in solemn prayer.

2 'T is an hour of happy meeting,
  Children meet to praise and prayer;
  But the hour is short and fleeting,
  Let us then be early there.
    Come, children, come, etc.

3 Do not keep your teacher waiting,
  While you tarry by the way ;
  Nor disturb the school reciting,
  'T is the holy Sabbath day.
    Come, children, come, etc.

4 Children, haste, the bells are ringing,
  And the morning 's bright and fair;
  Thousands now unite in singing,
  Thousands, too, in solemn prayer.
    Come, children, come, etc.

ANNIVERSARY DEPARTMENT;

CONSISTING OF

SOLOS, DUETS, TRIOS, AND QUARTETTES,

ESPECIALLY DESIGNED FOR

ANNIVERSARIES, MISSIONARY OCCASIONS, SUNDAY SCHOOL CONCERTS, TEMPERANCE MEETINGS, ETC., ETC.

This part of the book IS NOT ADAPTED FOR THE SUNDAY SCHOOL WORK PROPER, *but more for religious entertainment and profit.*

I am almost daily receiving inquiries asking, " Where can I obtain the songs you sung at ——," and to accommodate such who desire the songs (as I sing them), I have *revised* the " MUSICAL LEAVES," taking out such pieces as have become worn out and uninteresting, and giving *choice gems* in their place. PHILIP PHILLIPS.

MUSIC EVERYWHERE.

157 *Allegretto.* From " EARLY BLOSSOMS," by GEO. F. ROOT.

1. Mu - sic in the val - ley, Mu - sic on the hill, Mu - sic in the wood - land, Mu - sic in the rill; Mu - sic on the mount - ain, Mu - sic in the air, Mu - sic in the true heart, Mu - sic ev - 'ry - where.
2. Mu - sic by the fire - side, Mu - sic in the hall, Mu - sic in the school - room, Mu - sic for us all; Mu - sic in our care, Mu - sic in our glad - ness, Mu - sic ev - 'ry - where.
3. Sing with joy - ful voi - ces, Friends and loved ones dear; Let dis - cord and trou - ble Nev - er en - ter here; Join the hap - py cho - rus Of all na - ture fair, Swell the glo - rious an - them, Mu - sic's ev - 'ry - where.

SAVE THE FALLEN.

Music by S. J. Vail.

1. Lord, be-fore thy ho-ly al-tar, Now thy blessing we im-plore,

Grant, we may not faint or fal-ter, Till our glorious work is o'er.

Sav-iour! help us; we are try-ing Souls im-mor-tal to re-claim,

Thro' intemp'rance they are dy-ing, Snatch them from its burning flame.

CHORUS.

Save the fall-en, make them so-ber; May they feel their sins for-given,

When this transient life is o-ver, Give them, Lord, a place in heaven.

2. Lo, the tempter, now assailing
Hoary age and smiling youth,
Shall his cruel arts prevailing
Stop the springs of hallowed truth?
Lord, forbid it! hear us pleading,
Jesus, thou hast died to save.
Let thy mercy interceding
Keep them from a drunkard's grave.—*Cho.*

3. O'er the hearts that pine with anguish,
Pour thy healing balm divine,
O'er the wasted forms that languish
Let the beams of comfort shine;
In thy strength if still united
We the erring may restore,
Then intemperance, crushed and blighted,
We will banish from our shore.—*Cho.*

159 ## RIGHT OVER WRONG.

The HUTCHINSON FAMILY.
By permission of OLIVER DITSON & Co.

Moderato.

1. Be - hold the Day of Prom - ise comes, full of in spir - a - tion! The
2. Al - rea - dy in the gold - en east the glo-rious light is dawning, And

bless - ed day, by proph - ets sung, for the heal - ing of the nations. Old
watchmen, from the moun-tain-tops, can see the bless-ed morning: O'er

mid - night er - rors flee a - way—they soon will all be gone; While
all the land their voic - es ring, while yet the world is nap - ping, 'Till

heaven-ly an - gels seem to say, "the good time's" coming on. Oh, the
e'en the sluggards be-gin to spring, as they hear the spir - its "rapping." Oh, the

CHORUS.

Good time, The good time, The good time's com - ing on, The

rall.

good time, The good time, The good time's com-ing on.

3. The captive now begins to rise—his chains are rent asunder;
   While politicians stand aghast, in anxious fear and wonder;
   No longer shall the bondman sigh beneath the galling fetters—
   He sees the light of freedom's day, and reads the golden letters,
   Oh, the good time, &c.

4. And all the old distilleries shall perish and burn together—
   The brandy, rum, and gin, and beer, and all such whatsoever:
   The world begins to feel the fire; and e'en the poor besotter,
   To save himself from burning up, jumps in the cooling water.
   Oh, the good time, &c.

160 THE BETTER WISH.

Composed by HENRY RUSSELL.

Robin Ruff. If I had but a thou-sand a year, Gaf-fer Green! If I had but a thou-sand a year! What a man would I be, And what sights would I see, If I had but a thou-sand a year, Gaf-fer Green! If I had but a thou-sand a year!

Gaffer Green. The best wish you could have, take my word, Robin Ruff,
Would scarce find you in bread or in beer;
But be honest and true,
And say what would you do,
If you had but a thousand a year, Robin Ruff?
If you had but a thousand a year?

Robin Ruff. I'd do, I scarcely know what, Gaffer Green,
I'd go, faith! I hardly know where,
I'd scatter the chink
And leave others to think,
If I had but a thousand a year, Gaffer Green!
If I had but a thousand a year!

Gaffer Green. But when you are aged and grey, Robin Ruff,
And the day of your death it draws near,
Say, what with your pains
Would you do with your gains,
If you then had a thousand a year, Robin Ruff?
If you then had a thousand a year?

Robin Ruff. I scarcely can tell what you mean, Gaffer Green,
For your questions are always so queer,
But as other folks die,
I suppose so must I—
Gaffer Green. What! and give up your thousand a year, Robin Ruff?
And give up your thousand a year?

There's a place that is better than this, Robin Ruff,
And I hope in my heart you'll go there,
Where the poor man's as great,
Robin Ruff. What, though he hath no estate?
Gaffer Green. Yes, as if he'd a thousand a year, Robin Ruff,
Gaffer Green. } Yes, as if he'd a thousand a year.
Robin Ruff. }

161

LIFE'S RAILWAY.

Music by H. M. HIGGINS.

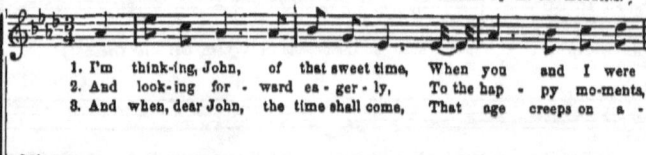

1. I'm think-ing, John, of that sweet time, When you and I were
2. And look-ing for - ward ea - ger - ly, To the hap - py mo-ments,
3. And when, dear John, the time shall come, That age creeps on a -

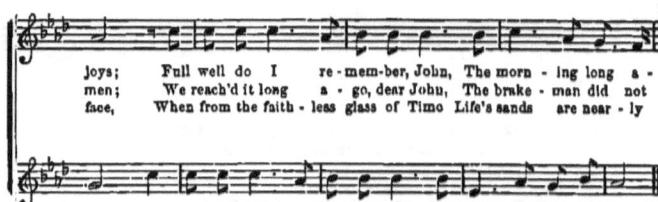

boys, A - look-ing up Life's rail-way track, All spanned with ros - y
when We'd reach'd the sta - tion Twen-ty-one— No long - er boys, but
- pace, And sil - ver threads are thick-ly strewn On wrin - kled brow and

joys; Full well do I re - mem-ber, John, The morn - ing long a -
men; We reach'd it long a - go, dear John, The brake - man did not
face, When from the faith - less glass of Time Life's sands are near - ly

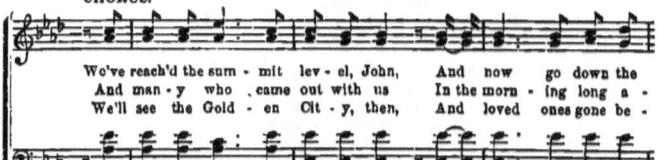

- go, We found ourselves on board the train, And thought the time was slow.
call; No bell was rung, or whistle blown—There was no place at all.
run, And slackened speed a - long the track, Tell our jour-ney's al-most done.

CHORUS.

We've reach'd the sum - mit lev - el, John, And now go down the
And man - y who came out with us In the morn - ing long a -
We'll see the Gold - en Cit - y, then, And loved ones gone be -

Repeat pp.

grade, With shorten'd stroke, and swifter speed Than an - y we have made.
- go, Have chang'd, and took the lightning line, And reach'd the Great De-pot.
- fore; We'll walk with them the rounds of joy, Where part - ing comes no more.

BATTLE HYMN OF THE REPUBLIC.

162

1. Mine eyes have seen the glory of the coming of the Lord; He is
2. I have seen him in the watch-fires of a hundred circling camps; They have
3. I have read a fiery gospel, writ in burnished rows of steel, "As ye

tramping out the vin-tage where the grapes of wrath are stored; He hath
build-ed Him an al-tar in the ev'-ning dews and damps; I have
deal with my con-tem-ners, so with you my grace shall deal; Let the

loosed the fate-ful lightning of his ter-ri-ble quick sword; His truth is marching on.
read his righteous sentence by the dim and flaring lamps; His day is marching on.
He-ro, born of woman, crush the serpent with his heel, Since God is marching on.

Chorus.

Glo-ry, glo-ry, hal-le-lu-jah! Glo-ry, glo-ry, hal-le-lu-jah!

Glo-ry, glo-ry, hal-le-lu-jah! His truth is march-ing on.

4 He has sounded forth the trumpet that shall never call retreat;
He is sifting out the hearts of men before his judgment-seat:
O, be swift, my soul, to answer Him! be jubilant, my feet:
Our God is marching on,
Glory, glory, hallelujah, etc.

5 In the beauty of the lilies Christ was born across the sea,
With a glory in His bosom that transfigures you and me;
As He died to make men holy, let us die to make men free,
While God is marching on.
Glory, glory, hallelujah, etc.

CONGREGATIONAL SINGING.

103

A DREAM.

By Philip Phillips.

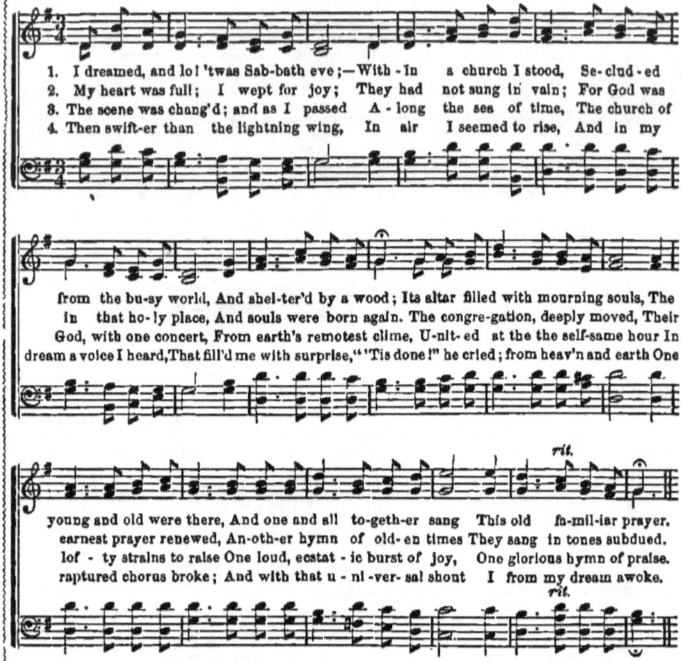

1. I dreamed, and lo! 'twas Sab-bath eve ;—With-in a church I stood, Se-clud-ed
2. My heart was full; I wept for joy; They had not sung in vain; For God was
3. The scene was chang'd; and as I passed A-long the sea of time, The church of
4. Then swift-er than the lightning wing, In air I seemed to rise, And in my

from the bu-sy world, And shel-ter'd by a wood; Its altar filled with mourning souls, The
In that ho-ly place, And souls were born again. The congre-gation, deeply moved, Their
God, with one concert, From earth's remotest clime, U-nit-ed at the the self-same hour In
dream a voice I heard, That fill'd me with surprise, "'Tis done!" he cried; from heav'n and earth One

rit.

young and old were there, And one and all to-geth-er sang This old fa-mil-iar prayer.
earnest prayer renewed, An-oth-er hymn of old-en times They sang in tones subdued.
lof - ty strains to raise One loud, ecstat - ic burst of joy, One glorious hymn of praise.
raptured chorus broke; And with that u - ni-ver-sal shout I from my dream awoke.

rit.

Sing after first verse WINDHAM, L. M.

Show pit-y, Lord, O Lord, for-give, Let a re-pent-ing reb-el live.

Are not thy mer-cies large and free? May not a sin-ner trust in thee?

BY-GONE DAYS.

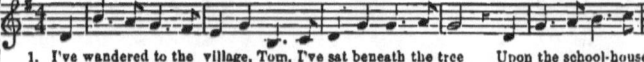

1. I've wandered to the village, Tom, I've sat beneath the tree   Upon the school-house
2. The grass is just as green, dear Tom; bare-footed boys at play Were sporting there as
3. That old schoolhouse has altered some; The benches are replaced By new ones ver-y

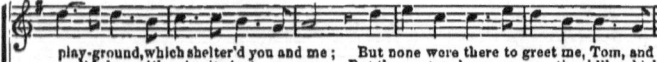

play-ground,which shelter'd you and me;   But none were there to greet me, Tom, and
we did then,with spir-its just as gay;   But the master sleeps up-on the hill, which
like the ones our pen-knives have defaced;   The same old bricks are in the wall, the

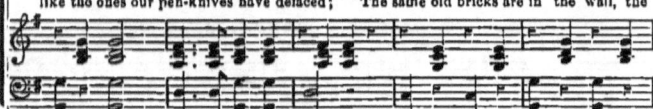

few were left to know, That play'd with us upon the grass, some twenty years a-go.
coated o'er with snow, Af-ford-ed us a sliding-place,just twenty years a-go.
bell swings to and fro, The music's just the same, dear Tom,'twas twenty years a-go.

4. The river's running just as still; the willows on its side
   Are larger than they were, dear Tom; the stream appears less wide;
   The grape-vine swing is ruined now, where once we played the beau,
   And swung our sweet-hearts—pretty girls!—just twenty years ago.

5. The spring that bubbled 'neath the hill, close by the spreading beach,
   Is very low—'twas once so high that we could almost reach;—
   And kneeling down to get a drink, dear Tom, I started so!
   To find that I had changed so much since twenty years ago!

6. The boys were playing the same old game, beneath the same old tree—
   (I do forget the name just now,) you've played the same with me
   On that same spot;—'twas played with knives, by throwing so and so;—
   The leader had a task to do, there, twenty years ago.

7. Down by the spring, upon an elm, you know I cut your name,
   Your sweetheart's just beneath it, Tom,—and you did mine the same;—
   Some heartless wretch has peeled the bark,—'twas dying, sure, but slow,
   Just as the one whose name was cut died, twenty years ago.

8. My lids have long been dry, dear Tom, but tears came to my eyes—
   I thought of those we loved so well—those early broken ties;
   I visited the old church-yard, and took some flowers to strew
   Upon the graves of those we loved, some twenty years ago.

9. Some are in the church-yard laid, some sleep beneath the sea;—
   But few are left of our old class excepting you and me:
   And when our time shall come, dear Tom, and we are called to go,
   I hope they'll lay us where we played just twenty years ago.

OUR COUNTRY.

Words by FANNY CROSBY.

PHILIP PHILLIPS.

165

1. Our country un-rivaled in beauty And splendor that can not be told,
2. Our country, the birth-place of freedom, The land where our forefathers trod,

How love-ly thy hills and thy woodlands, Arrayed in a sunlight of gold.
And sung in the isles of the for-est Their hymn of thanksgiving to God;

The ea-gle, proud king of the mountain, Is soaring, ma-jes-tic and free;
Their bark they had moored in the har-bor, No more on the o-cean to roam;

Thy riv-ers and lakes in their grandeur, Roll on to the arms of the
And there in the wilds of New Eng-land, They found-ed a coun-try and

sea; . . . . . Roll on to the arms of the sea.
home; . . . . . They found-ed a coun-try and home.

3 Our country, the past, and its glory,
Still honor the names of the dead;
The statesman that crowned thee with laurel,
The heroes and veterans that bled.
Mount Vernon, where Washington slumbers,
The soul of thy freedom for years,
A willow droops tenderly o'er him,
Go hallow his grave with thy tears.

4 Our country with ardent devotion,
In God may thy children abide;
In him be the strength of our nation,
His laws and its counsel its guide.
Our banner, that time-honored banner,
That floats o'er the ocean's bright foam,
God keep them unsullied forever.
Our standard, our union, our home.

YOUR MISSION.

166 [Music as sung by Philip Phillips, by request of President Lincoln.]

By permission of S. Brainard & Co., Publishers, Cleveland, O.
Words by Mrs. Ellen M. Gates, Beaver Dam, Wis.   Composed by S. M. Grannis.

1. If you can not on the o-cean Sail a-
2. If you are too weak to jour-ney Up the
3. If you have not gold and sil-ver Ev-er

mong the swift-est fleet, Rock-ing on the high-est bil-lows, Laugh-ing
mountain, steep and high; You can stand with-in the val-ley, While the
read-y to command; If you can not t'wards the need-y, Reach an

at the storms you meet; You can stand among the sail-ors, Anchor'd
mul-ti-tudes go by; You can chant in hap-py measure, As they
ev-er o-pen hand; You can vis-it the af-flict-ed, O'er the

YOUR MISSION.—Concluded.

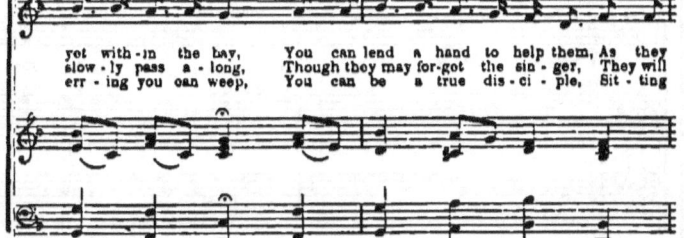

ritard.

yet with-in the bay, You can lend a hand to help them, As they
slow-ly pass a-long, Though they may for-got the sin - ger, They will
err - ing you oan weep, You can be a true dis-ci - ple, Sit - ting

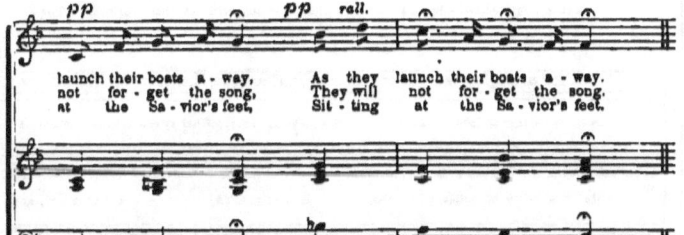

pp   *pp rall.*

launch their boats a - way, As they launch their boats a - way,
not for - get the song, They will not for - get the song.
at the Sa - vior's feet, Sit - ting at the Sa - vior's feet.

p

4 If you can not in the conflict
   Prove yourself a soldier true,
If, where fire and smoke are thickest,
   There's no work for you to do;
When the battlefield is silent,
   You can go with careful tread,
You can bear away the wounded,
   You can cover up the dead.

5 Do not, then, stand idly waiting,
   For some greater work to do;
Fortune is a lazy goddess,
   She will never come to you.
Go and toil in any vineyard,
   Do not fear to do or dare.
If you want a field of labor,
   You can find it any where.

CELESTIAL CITY.

167 QUARTETTE FOR SUNDAY-SCHOOL CONCERTS AND ANNIVERSARIES.

Words by PHILIP PHILLIPS.

Arranged from J. P. KNIGHT.

Treble.

1. Beau - - - - ti - ful cit - y, cit - - - - - y be - yond The

Tenor.

2. Beau - - - - ti - ful cit - y, with man - - - - sion so bright, The

Alto.

1. Beau-ti - ful, beau-ti - ful cit - y, the cit - y, the cit - y be-yond The

Bass.

2. Beau-ti - ful, beau-ti - ful cit - y, with mansion, with mansion so bright, The

swell - - ings of Jordan, the Chris - tian's bright home; What sweet, heavenly music is

Ho - - - ly of holies, where God - - is the light, Thy walls - - are of jasper, and

swellings, the swellings of Jordan, the Christian's, the Christian's bright home; What sweet, O, what sweet,
[heavenly music is

Holy, the Holy of holies, where God, the God is the light; Thy walls, thy walls are of jasper, and

heard - - in that clime, Where angels and ransomed their strains sweetly chime. No

streets - - of pure gold, Resplen - dent with beauty and glory un - told. O

heard in that clime, in that clime, Where angels, where angels and ransomed their strains sweetly chime. No

streets of pure gold, of pure gold, Resplendent, resplendent with beauty and glory untold. O

CELESTIAL CITY.—Continued.

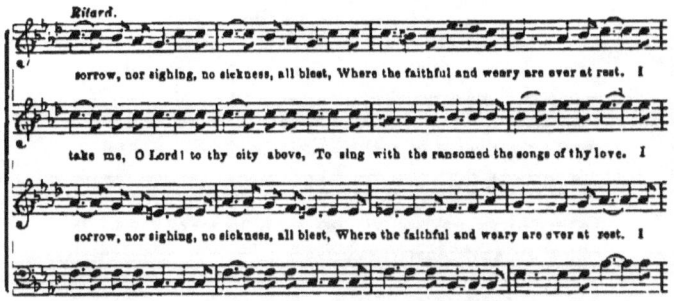

sorrow, nor sighing, no sickness, all blest, Where the faithful and weary are ever at rest. I

take me, O Lord! to thy city above, To sing with the ransomed the songs of thy love. I

sorrow, nor sighing, no sickness, all blest, Where the faithful and weary are ever at rest. I

take me, O Lord! to thy city above, To sing with the ransomed the songs of thy love. I

pray and I long for that cit - y so fair; O beau - - ti-ful cit - y, thy

pray and I· long for that cit - y so fair; O beau - - ti-ful cit - y, thy

pray and I long for that cit - y so fair; O beautiful, beautiful cit - y, thy

pray and I long for that cit - y so fair; O beauti-ful, beautiful cit - y, thy

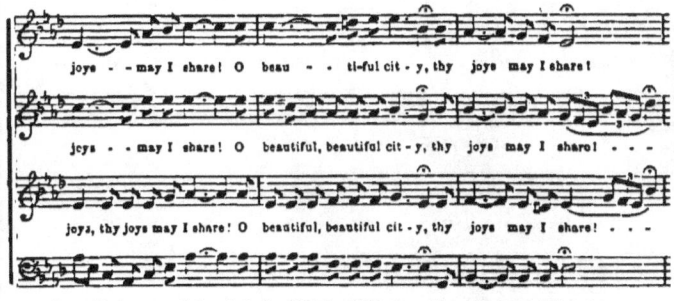

joys - - may I share! O beau - - ti-ful cit - y, thy joys may I share!

joys - - may I share! O beautiful, beautiful cit - y, thy joys may I share! - - -

joys, thy joys may I share! O beautiful, beautiful cit - y, thy joys may I share! - - -

joys, thy joys may I share! O beautiful, beautiful cit - y, thy joys may I share!

CELESTIAL CITY.—Concluded.

THE RESCUE.

168

"The Lord also will be a refuge for the oppressed, a refuge in time of trouble."

PHILIP PHILLIPS.

1. A ship was on the mighty deep, With all her sails unfurl'd, Tho' scarce a breath, that calm still
2. Her deck was throng'd with precious souls, The young and old were there, And some with furrow'd brows that
3. All drank the cup that Pleasure held, But gave no tho't to Him, Their heav'nly guide, whose bounteous

morn, The crest-ed billow curl'd. For many an hour upon the wave, That state-ly ves-sel
woke Full man-y a trace of care. They glided on,— a week had passed, The sky was still se-
hand Had filled it to the brim. But see far off, where yonder sun Is fad-ing to his

lay. Then spread her canvass to the breeze, And proudly sail'd away.
rene. As if a storm could never change The beauty of the scene. 4. Now peal on peal loud thunders
rest: That bank of clouds portentous rise A-long the golden west!

roll, And vivid lightnings flash! And now against the vessel's side The an-gry billows dash!

Wild blows the wind! the night is dark! Huge, massive rocks are near! They stand aghast, that lonely throng, And cheeks are blanch'd with fear. 5. Quick! quick! let ev'ry sail be furl'd!—But ere the word is giv'n, The helm is gone! the shroud's on fire! The mast in splinters riven! One burst of anguish, long and deep, One cry of keen des-pair, From hearts that fatal hour had taught Their on-ly hope was prayer.

6. A light, a voice from yonder tow'r Comes sweeping o'er the wave;   Cling to the spars! there's help at

band! The life-boat, The life-boat comes to save! The life-boat, The life-boat comes to save!

O, sin-ner, on the voyage of life Thy bark awhile may glide, As tranquil as that no-ble

ship, A - long the ocean's tide. 7. But far from God, what canst thou hope? Or where for refuge

fly When o'er thy frail and shatter'd bark The storm is raging high? The storm is raging high?

Close with the tune NAOMI, to the following words:

O give thy heart to Jesus now,
Whose precious word is given;
The Life-boat and the Lamp divine,
To guide thy soul to heaven.

169

WON'T IT BE A LAND OF GLORY?

Music by PHILIP PHILLIPS.

Scherzando.

1. If we but sow the gos-pel seed, The Lord will give us rain; And,

In his own most bless-ed time, We'll reap the gold-en grain! That

Ho-ly time shall sure-ly come, That sweet mil-len-ial day, When

Through the broad and spa-cious earth Our Christ shall hold his sway.

WON'T IT BE A LAND OF GLORY?—Concluded.

CHORUS.

With Je-sus for our Mas-ter, We'll keep that day in

view, And la-bor in His vine-yard, Where la-bor-ers are few.

Alle con Spirito.

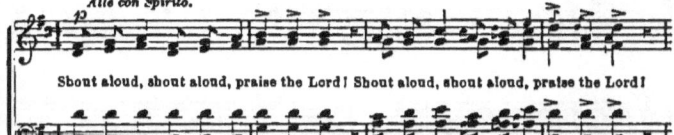

Shout aloud, shout aloud, praise the Lord! Shout aloud, shout aloud, praise the Lord!

ff

Shout aloud, shout aloud, praise the Lord! Won't it be a land of glory? Praise the Lord!

2 Oh! what are these few days of care,
   These moments fraught with pain,
Compared with all the heavenly bliss
Our ransomed souls shall gain,
When, from each hill and mountain-top,
   Salvation's tide shall flow,
And every woman, man, and child
   The grace of God shall know?
               With Jesus, etc.

3 Then, brethren, let us labor on
   Against the hosts of sin;
If we but save a single soul,
   We'll bring our off-ring in.
The gospel trumpet sounds afar,
   The nations hear the cry;
Glory to God, good-will to men,
   The end of sin is nigh!
               With Jesus, etc.

COME JOIN OUR TEMPERANCE BAND.

Words by FANNY CROSBY.

HUBERT P. MAIN.

170

1. Come, join our no - ble temperance band, Battling for the right;
2. The sol - diers in our glo-rious field, Battling for the right;

Come, fill our ranks, like he - roes stand, Bat - tling for the right.
Must hold their ground, and nev - er yield, Bat - tling for the right.

The cup of sin no lon - ger drain Of ev' - ry joy, the cru - el bane,
Our foes on ev' - ry side we meet, Our cause they nev - er shall de - feat,

'T is yours to break the ty - rant's chain, Bat - tling for the right.
The temperance ar - my scorns re - treat, Bat - tling for the right.

3 We're marching on with courage bold,
    Battling for the right;
And like our veteran sires of old,
    Battling for the right.
Our flag shall wave on every gale,
Against our foes we must prevail,
For truth and justice can not fail,
    Battling for the right.

Words by Miss Fanny Crosby.

T. E. Perkins.

From " New Shining Star," by permission.

171

Solo.

1. Yes, I know thou art praying to-night, mother, And I feel thou art praying for me ;
2. I have fought for the Union and right, mother ; I have stood by the flag of the free ;
3. There's a chill on my forehead, to-night, mother ; I am dying far distant from thee ;
4. I am going to Jesus above, mother, With the pure and the blest I shall be ;

For it comes o'er my soul like a vision of light, And I know thou art praying for me.
That Banner so fair, with its colors so bright, 'T was the pride of our nation and thee.
But the star of my faith is unclouded and bright, For I know thou art praying for me.
But my spirit will guard thee in love, dear mother, Till wafted by angels to me.

Chorus.

In my bosom all care is at rest, mother, No longer by sorrow op-pressed ;

O! I know thou art praying to-night, mother, And I know thou art praying for me.

GOD WITH US.

172

Music by PHILIP PHILLIPS.

1. Lo! our fa - thers' God is with us! We can trace his might-y hand In our
churches, vast in number, Wide extending o'er our land; Let our full u-nit - ed cho-rus Ev-er
on-ward roll a- long, And the year of time be vo - cal With our loud, ec-stat- ic song.

CHORUS, by WM. B. BRADBURY. *Full and loud.*

Marching a-long, we are marching along; Rising and progressing, we are marching along; Our
hearts are united, and this be our song, Our fathers' God is with us, while we're marching along.

2. Lo! our fathers' God is with us!
Lost in wonder, we adore
Him who brought them safely hither
With the Gospel to our shore.
Fired with zeal, and armed with courage,
Strong in faith and love divine,
Thro' the darkest cloud that gathered
They could see his glory shine—*Cho.*

3. Lo! our fathers' God is with us!
They have laid their armor down,
They have passed the vale of shadow,
Left the cross to wear the crown:

We must bear their glorious standard,
Wield our veteran fathers' sword,
In the army of the faithful
We are battling for the Lord.—*Cho.*

4. Lo! our fathers' God is with us!
Sing aloud with heart and voice,
Still increasing and progressing,
Brethren, let *us all* rejoice!
Hallelujah! what a meeting,
When we reach the shining shore,
There with Saints who've gone before us,
Shout *Free Grace* for evermore. —*Cho.*

INDEX OF TUNES.

INDEX OF HYMNS.

THE

NEW COMPLETE

STANDARD SINGER,

For

Sabbath Schools, Public Worship, and Special Services.

BY

PHILIP PHILLIPS,

AUTHOR OF "SINGING PILGRIM," "MUSICAL LEAVES," "NEW HYMN AND TUNE-BOOK,"
ETC., ETC., ETC.

Philip Phillips, AUTHOR AND PUBLISHER,
805 BROADWAY, NEW YORK......56 OLD BAILEY, LONDON.

Hitchcock & Walden,
CINCINNATI, CHICAGO, AND ST. LOUIS.

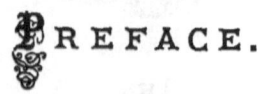REFACE.

THIS Book appears in answer to many solicitations, from sources which are worthy of respect and response. The plan and contents of the "SINGING PILGRIM" have been so heartily endorsed both in this country and in Europe, that a kindred want seems to have been created by its use—viz., that of a Book which shall contain the *Tried* and *Standard Songs* of the Sanctuary, the Prayer Room and the Sabbath School. These pages are largely enriched by pieces that have outlived the ephemeral melodies of the day; the words and music of which have become sacred to the heart, and which repeated use will only the more endear to all who sing or hear them at home, at social or public services, abroad, or anywhere.

Besides these *Gems* (that age will only intensify in value), this book contains many NEW COMPOSITIONS prepared not merely to add to the list of books already extant, but rather to reach and rescue human souls by the charms of the Gospel.

Mere sentiment in poetry and jingle of sound, however pleasing to the ear, have been avoided, for the sake of truth in tones, that are at once delightful and dignified.

It will be observed that this work is arranged in topical departments, a feature which will commend itself to all lovers of order. Choristers and Leaders will find this arrangement one of great convenience. As any phase of christian experience can be readily supplemented by a song, *there is always a double power in a tune expressive of the words ! and this power is doubled again when the words are made to emphasize and re-echo the theme of the moment.*

Adaptation to times, circumstances and impressions is essential to the "Service of Song," and makes every note of praise an appointed Missionary of good.

To the numerous composers whose productions appear in this work, under their respective names, the Author tenders his *grateful acknowledgments.*

A few of the choicest pieces have been arranged from melodies found afloat by the Author in Europe, during his visit in the year 1868, and others are adopted from German and English authorities. For the anonymous pages the Author assumes all responsibility.

It is confidently hoped that this work, prepared in the love of souls, and in the faith of the Gospel of Jesus Christ, will supply a want in the means of worship, which shall secure for it the name which has been adopted: "NEW STANDARD SINGER."

New York, March 1st, 1869.   *Philip Phillips*

Entered according to Act of Congress, in the year 1869, by Philip Phillips, in the Clerk's Office of the District Court of the United States for the Southern District of New York.

SMITH & McDOUGAL, Stereotypers and Electrotypers, 82 & 84 Beekman St., New York.

NEW
STANDARD SINGER
PART I.
SONGS BY THE WAY

FOR

INTRODUCTORY PRAYER AND PRAISE,

SUNDAY SCHOOL WORK,

EXHORTATION AND DUTY.

BY
PHILIP PHILLIPS

PHILIP PHILLIPS, Author and Publisher,
805 Broadway, New York.

HITCHCOCK & WALDEN,
Cincinnati, Chicago, and St. Louis.

Entered according to Act of Congress, in the year 1872, by P. H. PHILLIPS,
in the Clerk's Office of the District Court of the United States
for the Southern District of New York.

No. 1   # He leads us on.   PHILIP PHILLIPS.

" He leadeth me in the paths of righteousness for his Name's sake.

He leads us on by paths we did not know, Up-wards he leads us

though our steps are slow. Though oft we faint and falter by the way, Tho' storms and darkness

oft ob-scure the day. But when the clouds are gone, We know he leads us on, He

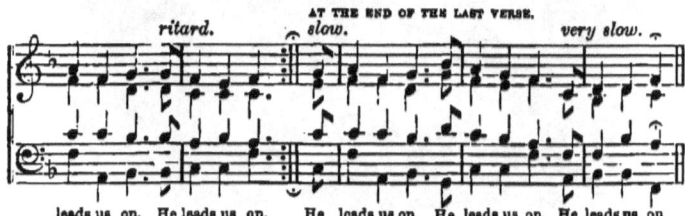

leads us on, He leads us on. He leads us on, He leads us on, He leads us on

2

He leads us on through all the trying years,
Past all our dreamland hopes and doubts and fears,
He guides our steps through all the tangled maze,
In paths of peace and wisdom's pleasant ways.
     Refrain—But when, &c

3

And he at last, after the weary strife,
Will lead us home to everlasting life.
No parting there, or pain on that bright shore,
We'll meet dear friends and sing for evermore.
     Refrain—But when, &c.

"The Old, Old Story."

No. 2.

T. C. O'KANE.

" The love of Christ which passeth knowledge."

1. Tell me the old, old sto - ry Of unseen things above, Of Je-sus and his
D. S. For I am weak and

glo - ry, Of Je - sus and his love. Tell me the sto - ry sim - ply, As
wea - ry, And help-less and de - filed.

D. S. *CHORUS.*

to a lit- tle child, Tell me the old, old sto - ry, It will my spir-it

move; Oh, tell me the old, old sto - ry Of Je-sus and his love.

2 Tell me the story slowly,
    That I may take it in.
That wonderful redemption,
    God's remedy for sin.
Tell me the story often,
    For I forget so soon!
The "early dew" of morning
    Has passed away at noon.

3 Tell me the same old story,
    When you have cause to fear
That this world's empty glory
    Is costing me too dear.
Oh, yes, when that world's glory
    Is dawning on my soul,
Tell me the old, old story,
    "Christ Jesus makes thee whole!"

Jesus, blessed Jesus.

No. 3

S. J. Vail.

" Cleanse thou me from secret faults."

1. Je-sus, blessed Je-sus, I would fol-low thee; Meek and pure and
2. Je-sus, blessed Je-sus, Keep me near thy side; Lest the world's al-

ho-ly, Thy dis-ci-ple be. Free from sin and fol-ly,
lure-ments Cause my feet to slide. On the rock of a-ges,

Free from worldly strife. Trusting in thy mer-it For e-ter-nal life.
Firm-ly let me stand, Yielding strict obedience To my Lord's command.

3 Purer yet and purer
  I would be in mind,
Dearer yet and dearer
  Every duty find;
Hoping still and trusting
  God without a fear,
Patiently believing
  He will make all clear. •

4 Calmer yet and calmer
  Trial bear and pain,
Surer yet and surer
  Peace at last to gain;
Suffering still and doing,
  To his will resigned,
And to God subduing
  Heart, and will, and mind.

5 Higher yet and higher
  Out of clouds and night,
Nearer yet and nearer
  Rising to the light—
Light serene and holy,
  Where my soul may rest,
Purified and lowly,
  Sanctified and blest.

6 Quicker yet and quicker
  Ever onward press,
Firmer yet and firmer
  Step as I progress:
Oft these earnest longings
  Swell within my breast;
Yet their inner meaning
  Ne'er can be expressed.

No. 4

Saviour and Friend.

" The Lord is my light."

1. Rest of the wea - ry, Joy of the sad,
2. Pil - low where ly - ing, Love rests its head,

Hope of the drea - ry, Light of the glad;
Peace of the dy - ing, Life of the dead;

Home of the stran - ger, Strength to the end,
Path of the low - ly, Prize at the end,

Re - fuge from dan - ger, Sa - viour and Friend.
Breath of the ho - ly, Sa - viour and Friend.

3 When my feet stumble,
　I'll to Thee cry;
Crown of the humble,
　Cross of the high.
When my steps wander,
　Over me bend,
Truer and fonder,
　Saviour and Friend.

4 Ever confessing
　Thee, I will raise
Unto thee blessing,
　Glory and praise;
All my endeavour,
　World without end,
Thine to be ever,
　Saviour and Friend.

No. 5.

Seek the Saviour.

GEO. F. ROOT.

"O God, thou art my God, early will I seek thee."

1. Seek the Sa - viour! tho' a - round thee, Drops a dark and dis - mal

cloud, Though it feels so deep and hea - vy on a heart with sor - row

bowed, Seek him quick-ly, time is pass-ing, Pass-ing ra - pid-ly a-

way Lis-ten to the words that tell you, There is still a brighter day.

2

Seek the Saviour! though life's tempest
  May unfurl life's chilling blast;
There is hope for thee my brother,
  Storms will not for ever last.
Don't give up, and cry forsaken!
  Don't begin to say you're lost:
Look! there comes a gleam of sunshine;
  See what your redemption cost.

3

Seek the Saviour! don't be grieving
  O'er that darksome billow there;
Life's a sea of stormy billows,
  We must meet them everywhere;
Pass right through them, do not tarry,
  Overcome the heaving tide,
There's a sparkling gleam of sunshine
  Waiting on the o.her side.

No. 6 ## Eternal Life. Philip Phillips.

"Fight the good fight of faith; lay hold on eternal life."

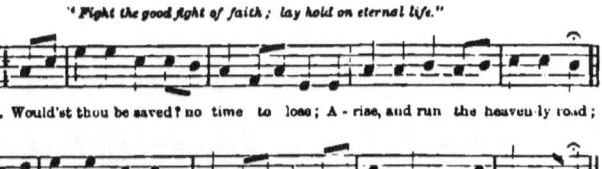

SOLO.

Evangelist. Would'st thou be saved? no time to lose; A-rise, and run the heaven-ly road;

Would'st thou be blest? then, pil - grim, haste To leave des-truc-tion's dread abode.

CHORUS.

mf *pp* *f* *pp*

O come! (O come!) the Sa-viour calls, "I am the way, the

echo.

truth, the life;" Come hith - er, burdened soul, to me.

Pilgrim.	*Pilgrim.*
O, tell me how! O. tell me where!	God's word shall guide me; yes, I see
The way I long have sought to know;	A light from yonder distant hill?
But fear the guilt and sin I bear	O. tell me, does it shine for me?
Will sink me in the depths of woe.	Hail, glorious light! I will, I will!
O, come, etc.	O, come, etc.
Evangelist.	*Pilgrim.*
God's word will guide thee; dost thou see	Farewell, a long farewell to those
A light from yonder distant hill?	Who seek to stay me as I fly;
On, Pilgrim, on! it shines for thee,	My ears against their call I close,
With steady course pursue it still.	Life, life, eternal life! my cry.
O, come, etc.	O, come, etc.

Note.—This song may be sung as a Duet between the Teachers and the school; or when rendered as Solos (in dialogue), the Chorus should be sung from another room or gallery out of sight, as an echo.

No 7

Our Sabbath Home.

W. HALEY.

" O how amiable are thy dwellings, thou Lord of Hosts."

1. O - pen now thy gates of beau - ty! Zi - on, let me

en - ter there, Where my soul, in joy - ful du - ty,

Waits for him that an - swers pray'r. Oh how bless - ed

is this place, Filled with so - lace, light, and grace.

2 Here thy praise is gladly chanted,
 Here thy seed is duly sown ;
Let my soul, where it is planted,
 Bring forth precious sheaves alone :
So that all I hear may be
Fruitful unto life in me.

3 Yes, my God, I come before thee,
 Come thou also down to me ;
Where we find thee and adore thee,
 There a heaven on earth must be :
To my heart, oh, enter thou,
Let it be thy temple now.

Nature's Song. C. M. Double.

No. 8

GIARDINI.

"God said, Let the earth bring forth grass.."

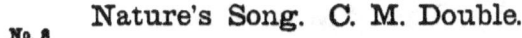

1. There's not a tint that paints the rose, Or decks the lil - y fair,

Or streaks the humblest flower that blows, But God has placed it there.

At ear - ly dawn there's not a gale, A - cross the landscape driven,

And not a breeze that sweeps the vale, That is not sent by heaven.

2.

There's not of grass a single blade,
Or leaf of loveliest green,
Where heavenly skill is not displayed,
And heavenly wisdom seen.
Around, beneath, below, above,
Wherever space extends,
There God disp'ays his boundless love,
And power with mercy blends.

No. 9.   # The Water of Life.*   Wm. B. Bradbury.

"I will give unto him that is athirst of the fountain of the water of life freely."

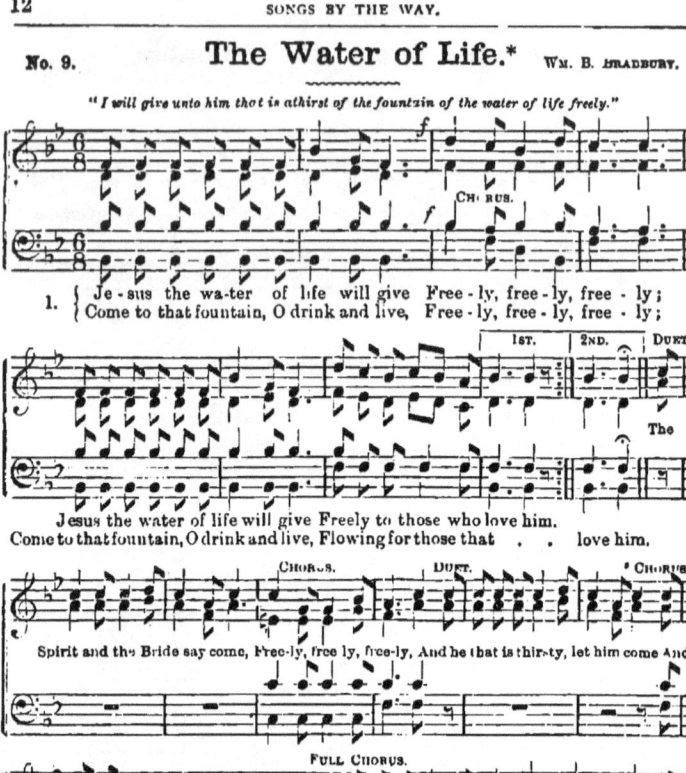

1. Je-sus the wa-ter of life will give Free-ly, free-ly, free-ly;
Come to that fountain, O drink and live, Free-ly, free-ly, free-ly;

Jesus the water of life will give Freely to those who love him.
Come to that fountain, O drink and live, Flowing for those that . . love him.

Spirit and the Bride say come, Free-ly, free-ly, free-ly, And he that is thir-ty, let him come And

drink of the water of life . . The fountain of life is flow-ing, Flow-ing, free-ly

flow-ing. The fountain of life is flow-ing, Is flowing for you and for me. . . .

* From "FRESH LAURELS," by permission of Biglow & Main

2 Jesus has promised a home in heaven, | Kingdoms of glory and crowns of light,
 Freely, freely, freely; | Freely, freely, freely;
Jesus has promised a home in heaven, | Kingdoms of glory and crowns of light,
 Freely to those that love him. | Freely to those that love him. *Cho.*
Treasures unfading will there be given, | 4 Jesus has promised eternal day,
 Freely, freely, freely; | Freely, freely, freely;
Treasures unfading will there be given, | Jesus has promised eternal day,
 Freely to those that love him. *Cho.* | Freely to those that love him:
3 Jesus has promised a robe of white, | Pleasure that never shall pass away,
 Freely, freely, freely; | Freely, freely, freely;
Jesus has promised a robe of white, | Pleasure that never shall pass away,
 Freely to those that love him; | Freely to those that love him. *Cho.*

No. 10   **'Tis Blessed to Give.**   PHILIP PHILLIPS.

" God loveth the cheerful giver."

1. { As God has kindly blessed us, To others let us give; } Not with a vain am-
 { Not with a grudging spirit, Or that our deeds may live: }
D.C. No merit in a kindness That claims reward again. *(Go on to Chorus.)*

bi - tion, To win the praise of men. Now in the name of Je - sus, Our

alms we should bestow; God loves a cheerful giv-er: the Bi-ble tells us so.

2 Now in the world before us
 A glorious field we see;
And in our Master's vineyard
 How active we should be.
The Sabbath schools around us,
 For help they loudly call;
Home missions, too, remember,
 And freely give to all. *Cho.*

3 The cause of foreign missions
 Our zealous care demands;
We'll send the blessed Bible
 To distant heathen lands,
That they may hear of Jesus,
 Whom we so dearly love;
May leave their senseless idols,
 And worship God above. *Cho.*

All Things Earnest.

JOSEPH DYER.

" My days are swifter than a weaver's shuttle."

Very slowly and pathetically.

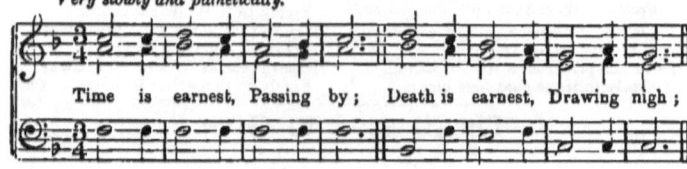

Time   is   earnest, Passing   by ;   Death is   earnest, Drawing   nigh ;

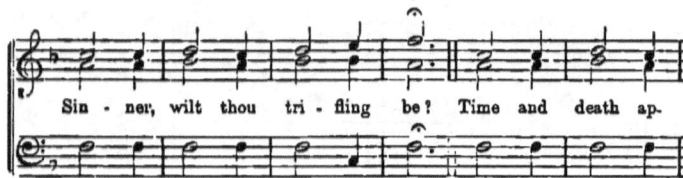

Sin - ner, wilt thou tri - fling   be ?   Time   and   death   ap-

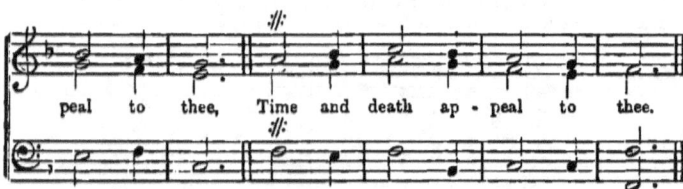

peal   to   thee,   Time   and   death   ap - peal   to   thee.

2.

Life is earnest :
When 'tis o'er,
Thou returnest
Never more ;
Soon to meet Eternity,
Wilt thou never serious be ?

3.

Heaven is earnest :
Solemnly
Float its voices
Down to thee.
O thou mortal, art thou gay,
Sporting through thine earthly day ?

4.

Hell is earnest :
Fiercely roll
Burning billows
Near thy soul.
Woe for thee, if thou abide
Unredeemed, unsanctified !

5.

God is earnest :
Kneel and pray
Ere thy season
Pass away ;
Ere be set his judgment throne,
Vengeance ready, mercy gone.

6.

Christ is earnest :
Bids thee, " Come !"
Paid thy spirit's
Priceless sum.
Wilt thou spurn thy Saviour's love,
Pleading with thee from above ?

No. 12

In Wrath remember Mercy.

" Hold thou me up and I shall be safe."

1. Gent-ly, gent-ly lay thy rod On my sin-ful head, O God;
2. Heal me, for my flesh is weak; Heal, me for thy grace I seek;

Stay thy wrath, in mer-cy stay, Lest I sink be-fore its away.
This my ou-ly plea I make, Heal me for thy mer-cy's sake.

3 Who within the silent grave
Shall proclaim thy power to save?
Lord, my sinking soul reprieve,—
Speak, and I shall rise and live!

4 Lo, he comes! he heeds my plea!
Lo, he comes! the shadows flee!
Glory round me dawns once more;
Rise, my spirit, and adore!

No. 13

The Lord is my Shepherd.

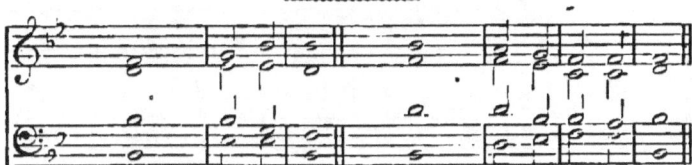

1 The Lord is my Shepherd, I | shall not | want :
He maketh me to lie down in green pastures ; he leadeth me be- | side the | still— | waters.
2 He restoreth my soul ; he leadeth me in the paths of righteousness, for his | name's— | sake.
Yea, though I walk through the valley of the shadow of death, I will fear no evil ; for thou art with me, thy rod and thy | staff, they | comfort | me.
3 Thou preparest a table before me in the presence of mine enemies ; thou anointest my head with oil, my | cup runneth ' over.
Surely goodness and mercy shall follow me all the days of my life, and I shall dwell in the | house of-the | Lord for | ever.   PSALM xxiii.

Pilgrims of the Night.

No. 14   Arr. by J. Bowling.

" Are they not all ministering spirits, sent forth to minister for them who shall be heirs of heaven ? "

Moderate.   *mf.*

1. Hark! hark! my soul,   an-gel-ic songs are swelling, O'er earth's green

fields, and ocean's wave-beat shore;   How sweet the truth those

blessed strains are telling,   Of that new life, where sin shall be no more.

Chorus. *Allegretto.*

An-gels of Je-sus! An-gels of light,   Sing-ing to welcome the

pilgrims of the night,   Singing to welcome the pilgrims of the night.

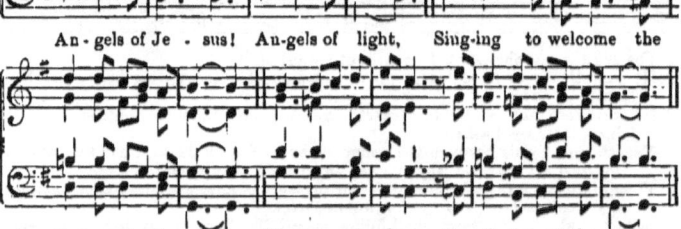

2.

Darker than night, life's shadows close
  around us,   [mark ;
And like benighted men we miss our
God hides himself, and grace has scarcely
  found us,   [dark.
Ere death finds out his victims in the
    Angels of Jesus, &c.

3.

Onward we go, for still we hear them
  singing   [come."
"Come, weary souls, for Jesus bids you
And through the dark, it echoes gently
  ringing,
The music of the Gospel leads us home.
    Angels of Jesus, &c.

4.

Cheer up my soul! Faith's moonbeams
  softly glisten   [sea ;
Upon the breast of life's most troubled
And it will cheer thy drooping heart to
  listen   [mean for thee.
To those brave songs which angels
    Angels of Jesus, etc.

5.

Angels, sing on, your faithful watches
  keeping,   [above,
Sing us sweet fragments of the songs
While we toil on, and soothe ourselves
  with weeping,   [less love.
Till life's long night shall break in end-
    Angels of Jesus, etc.

The Pilgrim Invited.

No. 15

" Turn, turn ye, for why will ye die ?"

FINE.

1. { Pil-grim, burdened with thy sin, Come the way to Zi - on's gate; }
{ There, till Mer - cy let thee in, Knock and weep, and watch and wait. }
D.C. Watch—for sa - ving grace is nigh; Wait—till heavenly light appears.

D. C.

Knock—he knows the sin-ner's cry; Weep—He loves the mourner's tears;

2

Hark ! it is the Bridegroom's voice:
Welcome, pilgrim, to thy rest ;
Now within the gate rejoice,
Safe and sealed, and bought and blest.
Safe—from all the lures of vice,
Sealed - by signs the chosen know,
Bought—by love and life the price,
Blest—the mighty debt to owe.

3

Holy pilgrim ! what for thee
In a world like this remain ?
From thy gu rded breast shall flee
Fear and shame, and doubt and pain.
Fear—the hope of heaven shall fly,
Shame—from glory's view retire,
Doubt—in certain rapture die,
Pain—in endless bliss expire.

2

A Song in the Night.

" He will give His angels charge over thee."

1. My Sa-viour, be thou near me, Through life's night; I
cry, and thou wilt hear me, Be my Light! My dim sight ach-ing,
Gent-ly thou'rt making Meet for a-wak-ing, Where all is bright.

2 Through time's swelling ocean
  Be my guide!
From tempest's wild commotion
  Hide, O hide!

Life's crystal river
Storms ruffle never;
Anchor me ever
  On that calm tide!

Christ our Light.

" A Light that shineth in a dark place."

1. { Je - sus, Sun of Right-eous-ness, Brightest beam of
   { With the ear - ly morn - ing rays Do thou on our

CHRIST OUR LIGHT—*continued.*

love di - vine,
darkness shine, } And dis - pel with pur - est light, All our night !

2 As on drooping herb and flower
    Falls the soft refreshing dew,
Let thy Spirit's grace and power
    All our weary souls renew ;
Showers of blessing over all
        Softly fall !

3 Like the sun's reviving ray,
    May thy love with tender glow
All our coldness melt away,
    Warm and cheer us forth to go ;
Gladly serve thee and obey
        All the day !

4 Oh, our only hope and guide !
    Never leave us nor forsake :
Keep us ever at thy side,
    Till th' eternal morning break ;
Moving on to Zion hill
        Homeward still !

5 Lead us all our days and years
    In thy straight and narrow way ;
Lead us through the vale of tears
    To the land of perfect day,
Where thy people, fully blest,
        Safely rest !

No. 16

God is Near Thee.

" Thou art near, O Lord."

1. God is near thee, therefore cheer thee, Sad soul ! He'll de -
fend thee, when around thee Billows roll, When around thee billows roll.

2 Calm thy sadness, look in gladness,
        On high !
Faint and weary, pilgrim, cheer thee,
        Help is nigh !
Pilgrim, cheer thee, help is nigh !

3 Mark the sea-bird wildly wheeling
    Through the skies !   .

God defends him, God attends him,
        When he cries !
God attends him when he cries.

4 God is near thee, therefore cheer thee,
        Sad soul !
He'll defend thee, when around thee
        Billows roll,
When around thee billows roll.

Sweet Spirit, Comfort Me.

No. 19   ENGLISH.

"He shall give His angels charge over thee."

1. In the time of my dis - tress, When temp-ta - tions me op-
2. When I lie within my bed, Sick in heart, and sick in

press, And when I my sins con - fess, Sweet Spi - rit, comfort me.
head, And with doubts discom - fit - ed, Sweet Spi - rit, comfort me.

3.	4.
When the house doth sigh and weep,	When the judgment is reveal'd,
And the world is drown'd in sleep,	And that opened which was sealed,
Yet mine eyes the watch do keep,	When to Thee I have appeal'd,
Sweet Spirit, comfort me.	Sweet Spirit, comfort me.

Jesus' Love.

No. 20

"God is Love."

1. How lov - ing is Je - sus, Who came from the sky, In ten - der - est

pi - ty For sin - ners to die! His hands and his feet were

JESUS' LOVE—*continued.*

nail'd to the tree, And all this he suffer'd for you and for me.

2 How gladly does Jesus
  Free pardon impart,
  To all who receive him
  By faith in their heart!
No evil befals them; their home is above,
And Jesus throws round them the arms
  of his love.

3 How precious is Jesus
  To all who believe;
  And out of his fulness
  What grace they receive!

When weak he supports them; when
  erring he guides,
And everything needful he kindly pro-
  vides.

4 O give, then, to Jesus
  Your earliest days:
  They only are blessèd
  Who walk in his ways;
In life and in death he will still be your
  Friend,   [end.
For whom Jesus loves, he loves to the

No. 21

How Much I Owe.

" I have loved thee."

FINE.

1. When this pass-ing world is done, When has sunk yon glar-ing sun,
D.C.—Then, Lord, shall I ful-ly know—Not till then—how much I owe.

When I stand with Christ in glory, Looking o'er life's finish'd sto-ry;—D.C.

2 When I stand before the throne,
  Dressed in beauty not my own;
  When I see thee as thou art,—
  Love thee with unsinning heart;
  Then, Lord, shall I fully know—
  Not till then—how much I owe.

3 E'en on earth, as through a glass,
  Darkly let thy glory pass;
  Make forgiveness feel so sweet,

Make thy Spirit's help so meet;
E'en on earth, Lord, make me know
Something of how much I owe.

4 Chosen not for good in me,
  Wakened up from wrath to flee;
  Hidden in the Saviour's side,
  By the Spirit sanctified:
  Teach me, Lord, on earth to show
  By my love, how much I owe.

No. 22   ## The Glorious Ship.   T. C. O'KANE.

" Except these abide in the ship, ye cannot be saved."

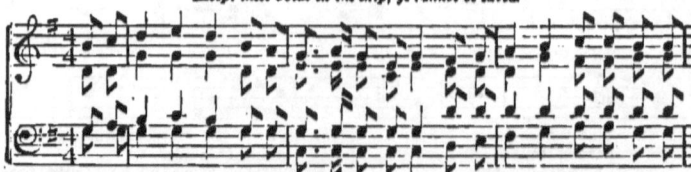

1. We are on the deep, we are sailing to our home, In the land beyond the shores of

time, Where the wea - ry rest, and no sor-rows e-ver come, In that
D.S.   *" We will stand the storm," we will safe at an-chor ride, In the*

FINE.   CHORUS.

brighter, bet-ter, l ap-pier clime.   In the old ship Zi - on we are
port on Canaan's peace-ful shore.

D.S.

sai` - ing on   the tide, Tho' the waves may dash and bil - lows roar,

2   [they swell!
We are on the deep—see our sails how full
And our standard floating proudly high,
'Tis the blood-stained banner of King
    Emmanuel ;
We will sail beneath it—"live or die."
    3   [golden strand ;
We are on the deep—we are near the
Lo, the glitt'ring domes of heaven appear!

See! along the shore angels and our lov'd
    ones stand ;   [hear.
And their song of welcome, hark ! we
    4   [so frail ?
Are you on the deep? in the sinners bark
    You will perish—leave without delay—
Come on board with us, and at once for
    glory sail,
And be saved while you are called, to-day.

Many Mansions.

No. 23   W. Hedom,

"In my Father's house are many mansions."

1. There is a bet-ter world, they say, Oh, so bright! Oh, so bright!

Where sin and woe are done a-way, Oh, so bright! Oh, so bright!

And mu-sic fills the balm-y air, And an-gels bright and

pure are there, And harps of gold and mansions fair, Oh, so bright! Oh, so bright!

2.

No clouds e'er pass along its sky,
    Happy land;
No tear-drop glistens in the eye,
    Happy land!
They drink the gushing streams of grace,
And gaze upon the Saviour's face,
Whose brightness fills the holy place.
    Happy land!

3.

Though we are sinners every one,
    Jesus died!
And though our crown of peace is gone,
    Jesus died!
We may be cleansed from every stain,
We may be crowned with bliss again,
And in that land of pleasure reign.
    Jesus died!

Far, Far Away.

No. 24   W. HEDGES.

"There remaineth therefore a rest to the people of God."

1. Had I the wings of a dove, I would fly, Far, far away, Far, far away,

Where not a cloud e-ver darkens the sky, Far, far a-way, Far, far a-way.

Fadeless the flow'rs in yon Eden that blow; Green, green the bow'rs where the still waters flow;

Hearts, like their garments, as pure as the snow, Far, far away, Far, far a-way.

2.
Had I the wings of a dove I would fly,
Far, far away.
Where not a cloud ever darkens the sky,
Far, far away.
There from all sorrow for ever I'd rest,
Leaning with love on Emmanuel's breast;
Joys never fade in the realms of the blest,
Far, far away.

3.
Safely they dwell with the Lamb that
was slain, Far, far away.
Washed in his blood, in his presence
they reign, Far, far away.
Nothing unholy shall enter the sky;
Nothing that maketh or loveth a lie;
Oh, then for mercy to Christ let us fly!
Come, come to-day.

No. 25   ## Jesus, Best and Dearest.

"Who loved me, and gave himself for me."

1. Je - sus, name all names a - bove; Je - sus, best and dear - est;

Je - sus, fount of per - fect love, Ho - liest, tend'rest, near - - est.

Je - sus, source of grace com - plet - est; Je - sus pur - est, Je - sus sweetest,

LAST VERSE.

Je - sus, well of pow'r di - vine, Make me, keep me, seal me thine. A - men.

2   Jesus, opened me the gate
    That of old he entered,
Who, in that most lost estate,
    Wholly on thee ventured;
Thou, whose wounds are ever pleading,
And thy passion interceding,
    From thy misery let me rise
    To a home in Paradise!

3   Jesus, crowned with thorns for me,
    Scourged for my transgression,
Witnessing, through agony,
    That, thy good confession!
Jesus, clad in purple raiment,
For my evils making payment,
    Let not all thy woe and pain,
    Let not Calv'ry be in vain.   Amen.

No. 26   # The Beautiful Stream.   Philip Phillips.

"And he showed me a pure river of water of life, clear as crystal, proceeding out of the throne of God and of the Lamb."

1. Oh, hast thou ne'er heard of the beautiful stream, That flows thro' our Father's

land; Its waters are bright in the heavenly light, And ripple o'er gold-en

sand: Seek now that beautiful stream, Seek now that beautiful

sand;   Oh, seek now that beautiful stream,

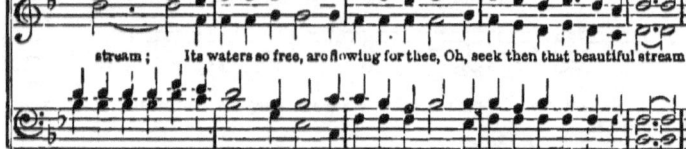

stream; Its waters so free, are flowing for thee, Oh, seek then that beautiful stream.

Seek now that beautiful stream, so free, are flowing for thee, Oh, seek then that beautiful stream.

2
Its virtues endure, and its waters, so pure,
Are sweet to the weary soul;
It flows from the throne of Jehovah alone,
Come, drink where its bright waves roll.
Seek now, &c.

3
This beautiful stream is "the river of life,"
It flows for all nations free;
A balm for each wound in its waters is found;
Oh, sinner, it flows for thee.
Seek now, &c.

4
Oh, wilt thou not drink of this beautiful stream,
And dwell on its peaceful shore?
The Spirit says, "Come all ye weary ones home,
And wander in sin no more."
Seek now, &c.

No. 27

O Paradise !

B. J. WHALL.

" In my Father's house are many mansions."

With spirit.

1. O Pa - ra-dise! O Pa - ra-dise! Who does not crave for rest? Who would not seek that hap-py land, Where those who loved are blest? Where faithful hearts and pure, Released from sin and pain, For e - ver rest se-cure, Till Christ shall come a - gain. O Pa-ra-dise! O Pa-ra dise! O Pa - ra - dise! A - men.

2
O Paradise! O Paradise!
'Tis weary waiting here,
We long to be where Jesus is,
To see and feel Him near!
Where faithful hearts and pure,
Released from sin and pain,
For ever rest secure,
Till Christ shall come again.
    O Paradise! &c.

3.
O Paradise! O Paradise!
We long to sin no more,
We long to be as pure on earth
As those on thy bright shore!

Where faithful hearts and pure,
Released from sin and pain,
For ever rest secure,
Till Christ shall come again.
    O Paradise! &c.

4.
O Father, Son, and Holy Ghost!
Most blessed One in Three!
Prepare us for that certain hope
Of never losing Thee,
Where faithful hearts and pure,
Released from sin and pain,
For ever rest secure,
Till Christ shall come again.
    O Paradise! &c.

My Heart's Desire.

No. 28

J. Schoffr.

" Unto you that fear my name shall the Sun of Righteousness arise."

1. Ob-ject of my first de-sire, Je-sus, cru-ci-fied for me;

All to hap-pi-ness a-spire; I would seek it, Lord, in thee:

Thee to praise, and thee to know, Makes the joy of saints be-low:

Thee to see, and thee to love, Makes the bliss of saints a-bove.

2 Lord, it is not life to live,
If thy presence thou deny:
Lord, if thou thy presence give,
'Tis no longer death to die:

Source and Giver of repose,
Only from thy love it flows:
Peace and happiness are thine;
Mine they are, if thou art mine.

Parting Song.

No. 29   Dr. Thos. Hastings.

"I will praise thy name forever and ever."

1. Our les- son now is o'er, And we a hap- py throng, With
2. What grat - i - tude we owe, For rich - est bless-ing giv'n, Yet

grate - ful hearts u - nite once more, To raise a part- ing song.
what can lit - tle chil - dren do To serve the God of heaven.

CHORUS.

Ho - san - na, ho - san - na, Most joy - ful - ly we'll sing; Ho -

san - na, ho - san - na, To Je - sus Christ our King.

3.

He never will despise
  The smallest of our race;
And he'll regard the humble cries
  Of all who seek his face.
  Cho.—Hosanna, &c.

4.

We'll praise him for his word,
  We'll praise him for his love,
We'll praise him that our souls have heard,
  His message from a bove.
  Cho.—Hosanna, &c.

Sabbath Hours. 6's.

No. 30

W. Hollis.

" Verily, my sabbaths shall ye keep."

1. The light of Sab-bath eve   Is   fad - ing fast a - way ;

What re - cord will it   leave,   To crown the clos - ing   day ?

Is   it   a Sab-bath spent,   Of fruit-less time des - troyed ?

Or have these mo-ments lent,   Been sa - cred-ly em - ployed ?

2.

How dreadful and how drear,
   In yon dark world of pain,
Will Sabbaths lost appear,
   That cannot come again !
Then, in that hopeless place,
   The wretched souls will say,
"I had those hours of grace,
   But cast them all away."

3.

To waste these Sabbath hours,
   O may we never dare ;
Or taint with thoughts of ours
   These sacred days of prayer ;
But may our Sabbaths here
   Inspire our hearts with love,
And prove a foretaste clear
   Of that sweet rest above.

This I Did for Thee.*

No. 31.

Arranged by W. Schultz,

"*What hast thou done for me.*"

Adagio tristamente.

pp

1. I.... gave my life for thee, My precious blood I shed,

cresc.

That thou might'st ran-somed be, And quickened from the dead.

accel.

f I gave my life for thee, for thee, I gave my life for thee,

agitato.

ff What hast thou given for me, for me! What hast thou given for me!

2 I spent long years for thee
  In weariness and woe,
  That one eternity
    Of joy thou mightest know;
  |: I spent long years for thee; :|
    Hast thou spent one for me?

3 My Father's house of light,
    My rainbow-circled throne,
  I left for earthly night,
    For wand'rings sad and lone;
  |: I left it all for thee; :|
    Hast thou left aught for me?

4 I suffered much for thee,—
    More than thy tongue can tell,
  Of bitterest agony,
    To rescue thee from hell;
  |: I suffered much for thee; :|
    What dost thou bear for me?

5 And I have brought to thee,
    Down from my house above,
  Salvation full and free,
    My pardon and my love;
  |: Great gifts I brought to thee; :|
    What hast thou brought to me?

6 Oh, let thy life be given,
    Thy years for me be spent,
  World fetters all be riven,
    And joy with suffering blent
  |: Give thou, thyself to me, :|
    And I will welcome thee!

* *Motto placed under a print of Christ on the Cross, in the study of a German clergyman. It is said that Count Zinzendorf was first taught to love the Saviour by reading this motto.*

No. 32

Mear. C.M.

A. WILLIAMS.

" The day of the Lord will come as a thief in the night."

1. That aw - ful day will sure - ly come, Th'appointed hour makes haste,
2. Je - sus, thou source of a.l my joys, Thou ru - ler of my heart,

When I must stand be - fore my Judge, And pass the so - lemn test.
How could I bear to hear thy voice Pronounce the word, — De - part?

3 What, to be banished from my Lord,
   And yet forbid to die ;
   To linger in eternal pain,
   And death for ever fly ?

4 O wretched state of deep despair,
   To see my God remove,
   And fix my doleful station where
   I must not taste his love.

No. 33

GOD moves in a mysterious way,
   His wonders to perform ;
He plants his footsteps in the sea,
   And rides upon the storm.

2 His purposes will ripen fast,
   Unfolding every hour :
The bud may have a bitter taste,
   But sweet will be the flower.

3 Blind unbelief is sure to err,
   And scan his work in vain :
God is his own interpreter,
   And he will make it plain.

No. 34

HOW blest the children of the Lord,
   Who, walking in his sight,
Make all the precepts of his word
   Their study and delight !

2 That precious wealth shall be their
   Which cannot know decay; [dower
Which moth or rust shall ne'er devour,
   Nor spoiler take away.

3 For them that heavenly light shall
   Whose cheering rays illume [spread,
The darkest hours of life, and shed
   A halo round the tomb.

Hear my Voice. C. M.

No. 35   JOHANN CRÜGER.

" I am the Good Shepherd."

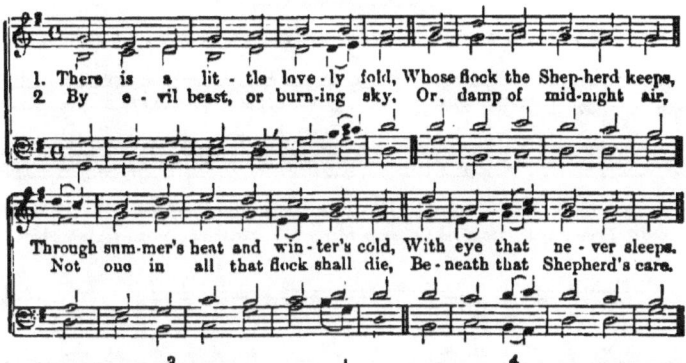

1. There is a lit - tle love - ly fold, Whose flock the Shep-herd keeps,
2. By e - vil beast, or burn-ing sky. Or, damp of mid-night air,

Through sum-mer's heat and win - ter's cold, With eye that ne - ver sleeps.
Not one in all that flock shall die, Be - neath that Shepherd's care.

3.

For if, unheeding or beguiled,
In danger's path they roam,
His pity follows through the wild,
And guards them safely home.

4.

O gentle Shepherd, still behold
Thy helpless charge in me,
And take a wanderer to thy fold,
That humbly turns to thee.

No. 36

1

THERE is a path that leads to God,
All others lead astray ;
Narrow, but pleasant, is the road,
And Christians love the way.

2

It leads straight through this world of sin,
And dangers must be passed ;
But those who boldly walk therein,
Will come to heaven at last.

3

But, lest my feeble steps should slide,
Or wander from thy way ;
Lord, condescend to be my guide,
And I shall never stray.

4.

Thus I may safely venture through,
Beneath my Shepherd's care ;
And keep the gate of heaven in view,
Till I shall enter there.

No. 37

1.

THERE is a glorious world above,
Where sorrow is unknown,
A city bright, a land of love,
Formed for the good alone.

2.

There gates of pearl and streets of gold,
Will strike our wond'ring sight ;
And music sweet, and bliss untold,
Will fill us with delight.

3.

There happy spirits sigh no more ;
Their tears are wiped away ;
The Saviour's name they now adore,
Through one eternal day.

4.

There pilgrims meet from every land,
Their toils and troubles o'er ;
And friends, in one delightful band,
Are joined, to part no more.

No. 38   **Uxbridge. L.M.**   Lowell Mason.

"Because thou hast been my help; therefore in the shadow of thy wings will I rejoice."

1. God is the re-fuge of his saints, When storms of sharp distress in-vade;
2. Loud may the troubled o - cean roar; In sa-cred peace our souls a - bide,

Ere we can of - fer our com-plaints, Be-hold him present with his aid.
While ev-ery na-tion, ev - ery shore, Trembles, and dreads the swelling tide.

No. 39

1.

WHILE life prolongs its precious light,
   Mercy is found, and peace is given;
But soon, ah, soon, approaching night
   Shall blot out every hope of heaven.

2.

Soon, borne on time's most rapid wing,
   Shall death command you to the grave;
Before his bar your spirits bring,
   And none be found to hear or save.

3.

Now, God invites; how blest the day!
   How sweet the gospel's charming sound!
Come, sinners, haste, O haste away,
   While yet a pard'ning God is found.

No. 40

1.

HOW precious is the book divine, .
   By inspiration given;
Bright as a lamp its doctrines shine,
   To guide our souls to heaven.

2.

It sweetly cheers our drooping hearts
   In this dark vale of tears;
And life and light, and joy imparts,
   And banishes our fears.

3.

This lamp, through all the tedious night
   Of life, shall guide our way;
Till we behold the clearer light
   Of an eternal day.

Our Glorious King. C.M. double.

No. 41

GIORNIVICHI.

"Who is like Thee, glorious in holiness, fearful in praises, doing wonders!"

1. How glorious is our heavenly King, Who reigns above the sky! How shall a child pre-

sume to sing, His dreadful ma-jes - ty! How great his pow'r is, none can tell, Nor

think how large his grace; Not men be - low, nor saints that dwell, On high before his face.

2 Not angels, that stand round the Lord,
Can search his secret will ;
But they perform his heavenly word,
And sing his praises still.

Then let me join this holy train,
And my first offerings bring ;
The eternal God will not disdain
To hear an infant sing.

No 42

1.

THE Bible tells us "God is Light,"
A light we cannot see ;
Too dazzling far for our weak sight,
So wonderful is he!
The Bible tells us "God is Love ;"
Not all that dwell below,
Nor all that dwell in heaven above,
Such love and pity show

2.

And though we cannot see his face,
While we on earth remain :
The Lord will always grant us grace,
And make our pathway plain.
Led by his light, our feet shall move
With joy in wisdom's ways ;
Led by his love, our love we prove,
By living to his praise.

No. 43   ## Pleyel. 5th P.M.   J. PLEYEL.

" Repent ye, for the kingdom of heaven is at hand."

1. Hasten, sin - ner, to be wise, Stay not for the morrow's sun;
2. Hasten, mer - cy, to im-plore, Stay not for the morrow's sun;

Wisdom if you still de - spise, Harder is it to be won.
Lest thy sea - son should be o'er Ere this eve - ning's stage be run.

3 Hasten, sinner, to return,
  Stay not for the morrow's sun ;
  Lest thy lamp should fail to burn
  Ere salvation's work is done.

4 Hasten, sinner, to be blest,
  Stay not for the morrow's sun,
  Lest perdition thee arrest
  Ere the morrow is begun.

No. 44

CHILDREN of the heavenly King,
  As we journey let us sing ;
Sing our Saviour's worthy praise,
Glorious in his works and ways.

2 We are trav'ling home to God,
  In the way our fathers trod ;
  They are happy now, and we
  Soon their happiness shall see.

3 Fear not, brethren, joyful stand
  On the borders of our land ;
  Jesus Christ, our Father's Son,
  Bids us undismay'd go on.

4 Lord ! obediently we'll go,
  Gladly leaving all below :
  Only thou our leader be,
  And we still will follow thee.

No. 45

COME, my soul, thy suit prepare ;
  Jesus loves to answer prayer ;
He himself invites thee near,
Bids thee ask him, waits to hear.

2 Lord, I come to thee for rest ;
  Take possession of my breast ;
  There thy blood-bought right maintain,
  And without a rival reign.

3 While I am a pilgrim here,
  Let thy love my spirit cheer ;
  As my guide, my guard, my friend,
  Lead me to my journey's end.

4 Show me what I have to do ;
  Every hour my strength renew ;
  Let me live a life of faith,
  Let me die thy people's death.

Horton. 4 lines 7's.

No. 46

Von Wartensee.

"He ever liveth to make intercession for us."

1. Come, said Je - su's sa-cred voice, Come, and make my paths your choice

I will guide you to your home; Wea - ry wan-d'rer, hi-ther come.

2.

Thou who, homeless and forlorn,
Long hast borne the proud world's scorn,
Long hast roamed the barren waste,
Weary wanderer, hither haste.

3.

Ye who, tossed on beds of pain,
Seek for ease, but seek in vain;

Ye, by fiercer anguish torn,
In remorse for guilt who mourn:—

4.

Hither come! for here is found
Balm that flows for every wound;
Peace that ever shall endure,
Rest eternal, sacred, sure.

No. 47

1.

WHEN thy mortal life is fled, [spread,
When the death-shades o'er thee
When is finished thy career,
Sinner, where wilt thou appear?

2.

When the world has passed away,
When draws near the judgment-day,
When the awful trump shall sound,
Say, O where wilt thou be found?

3.

When the Judge descends in light,
Clothed in majesty and might,
When the wicked quail with fear,
Where, O where wilt thou appear?

4.

While the Holy Ghost is nigh,
Quickly to the Saviour fly;
Then shall peace thy spirit cheer;
Then in heaven shalt thou appear.

Sun of my Soul.* L.M.

No. 48

'Thou art my trust from my youth."

1. Sun of my soul, thou Sa-viour dear, It is not night if thou be near;

O may no earth-born cloud a - rise, To hide thee from thy ser-vant's eyes.

2
Abide with me from morn till eve,
For without thee I cannot live ;
Abide with me when night is nigh,
For without thee I dare not die.

3.
If some poor wandering child of thine
Have spurned to day the voice divine
Now, Lord, the gracious work begin;
Let him no more lie down in sin.

4.
Watch by the sick ; enrich the poor
With blessings from thy boundless store ;
Be every mourner's sleep to-night,
Like infant's slumbers, pure and light.

5.
Come near and bless us when we wake,
Ere through the world our way we take,
Till in the ocean of thy love
We lose ourselves in heaven above.

No. 49   Tune "Lenox." P. 91.

ARISE, my soul, arise ;
   Shake off thy guilty fears ;
The bleeding Sacrifice
In my behalf appears :
Before the throne my Surety stands,
My name is written on his hands.

2   Five bleeding wounds he bears,
   Received on Calvary ;
   They pour effectual prayers,
   They strongly plead for me :—
Forgive him, O forgive, they cry,
Nor let that ransom'd sinner die.

3   The Father hears him pray,
   His dear anointed One :
   He cannot turn away
   The presence of his Son :
His Spirit answers to the blood,
And tells me I am born of God.

No. 50   Tune, "Lenox."

YOUNG men and maidens, raise
   Your tuneful voices high ;
Old men and children, praise
The Lord of earth and sky :
The year of jubilee is come ;
Return, ye ransomed sinners, home.

2   The universal King
   Let all the world proclaim ;
   Let every creature sing
   His attributes and name :
The year of jubilee is come ;
Return, ye ransomed sinners, home.

3   Glory to God belongs ;
   Glory to God be given
   Above the noblest songs,
   Of all in earth and heaven :
The year of jubilee is come ;
Return, ye ransomed sinners, home.

* Sent to Mr. Phillips from Constantinople by our earnest missionary, Rev. A. G. Long.

No. 51

Arlington. C.M.

Dr. Arne.

"In the Lord put I my trust."

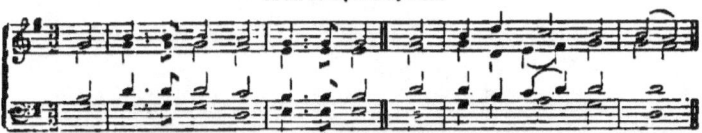

1. Lord, I approach the mer-cy seat, Where thou dost an - swer prayer;

There hum-bly fall be - fore thy feet, For none can pe - rish there.

2.

Thy promise is my only plea ;
With this I venture nigh :
Thou callest burdened souls to thee,
And such, O Lord, am I.

3.

O, wondrous love !—to bleed and die,
To bear the cross and shame,
That guilty sinners, such as I,
Might plead thy gracious name.

No. 52

1.

O FOR a heart to praise my God,
A heart from sin set free ;—
A heart that always feels thy blood,
So freely spilt for me :—

2.

A heart resign'd, submissive, meek,
My great Redeemer's throne;
Where only Christ is heard to speak,—
Where Jesus reigns alone.

3.

O for a lowly, contrite heart,
Believing, true, and clean ;
Which neither life nor death can part
From Him that dwells within :—

4.

A heart in every thought renew'd,
And full of love divine ;
Perfect, and right, and pure, and good,
A copy, Lord, of thine.

No. 53

1.

MY God, the spring of all my joys,
The life of my delights,
The glory of my brightest days,
And comfort of my nights.

2.

In darkest shades, if thou appear,
My dawning is begun ;
Thou art my soul's bright morning star.
And thou my rising sun.

3.

The opening heavens around me shine
With beams of sacred bliss,
If Jesus shows his mercy mine,
And whispers, I am his --

4.

My soul would leave this heavy clay
At that transporting word,
Run up with joy the shining way,
To see and praise my Lord.

No. 54   **Laban.** S.M.   DR. L. MASON.

"Now it is high time to awake out of sleep."

1. My soul be on thy guard; Ten thou-sand foes a - rise:
2. O watch, and fight, and pray; The bat - tle ne'er give o'er;

The hosts of sin are press-ing hard To draw thee from the skies.
Re - new it bold-ly ev - ery day, And help di - vine im - plore.

3.
Ne'er think the vict'ry won,
Nor lay thine armour down;
The work of faith will not be done,
Till thou obtain the crown.

4.
Then persevere till death
Shall bring thee to thy God;
He'll take thee, at thy parting breath,
To his divine abode.

No. 55

1.
COME, sound his praise abroad,
And hymns of glory sing;
Jehovah is the sov'reign God,
The universal King.

2.
He form'd the deeps unknown;
He gave the seas their bound;
The wat'ry worlds are all his own,
And all the solid ground.

3.
Come, worship at his throne;
Come, bow before the Lord;
We are his works, and not our own,
He form'd us by his word.

4.
To-day attend his voice,
Nor dare provoke his rod;
Come, like the people of his choice,
And own your gracious God.

No. 56

1.
COME, ye that love the Lord,
And let your joys be known;
Join in a song with sweet accord,
While ye surround his throne.

2.
Let those refuse to sing
Who never knew our God;
But servants of the heavenly King
May speak their joys abroad.

3.
The men of grace have found
Glory begun below:
Celestial fruit on earthly ground
From faith and hope may grow:

4.
Then let our songs abound,
And every tear be dry: [ground,
We're marching through Immanuel's
To fairer worlds on high.

No. 57

Ortonville. C. M.

DR. T. HASTINGS.

" And thou shalt call his name Jesus, for he shall save his people from their sins."

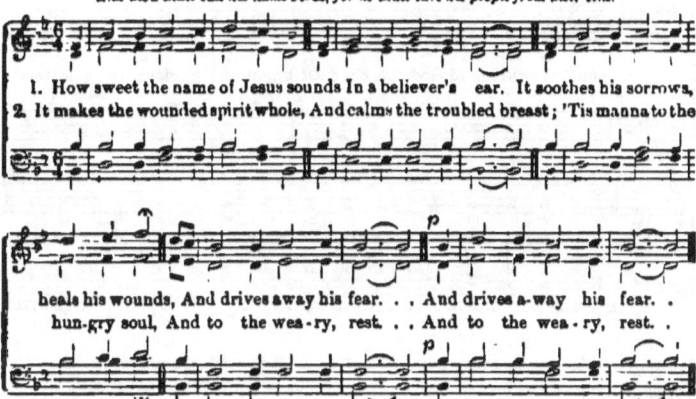

1. How sweet the name of Jesus sounds In a believer's ear. It soothes his sorrows,
2. It makes the wounded spirit whole, And calms the troubled breast; 'Tis manna to the

heals his wounds, And drives away his fear. . . And drives a-way his fear. .
hun-gry soul, And to the wea-ry, rest. . . And to the wea-ry, rest. .

3.	4.
Dear Name, the rock on which I build,	Jesus, my Shepherd, Saviour, Friend,
My shield and hiding-place ;	My Prophet, Priest, and King,
My never-failing treasury, fill'd	My Lord, my Life, my Way, my End,
With boundless stores of grace :	Accept the praise I bring.

No. 58

1.

MUST Jesus bear the cross alone,
And all the world go free?
No : there's a cross for every one,
And there's a cross for me.

2.

How happy are the saints above
Who once went sorrowing here ;
But now they taste unmingled love,
And joy without a tear.

3.

The consecrated cross I'll bear,
Till death shall set me free,
And then go home my crown to wear,—
For there's a crown for me !

No. 59

1.

I LOVE to steal awhile away
From every cumb'ring care,
And spend the hours of setting day
In humble, grateful prayer.

2

I love in solitude to shed
The penitential tear,
And all his promises to plead,
Where none but God can hear.

3.

I love to think on mercies past,
And future good implore,—
And all my cares and sorrows cast
On him whom I adore.

No 60   **Precious Book.** L.M.   PSALMODIST.

" His delight is in the law of the Lord."

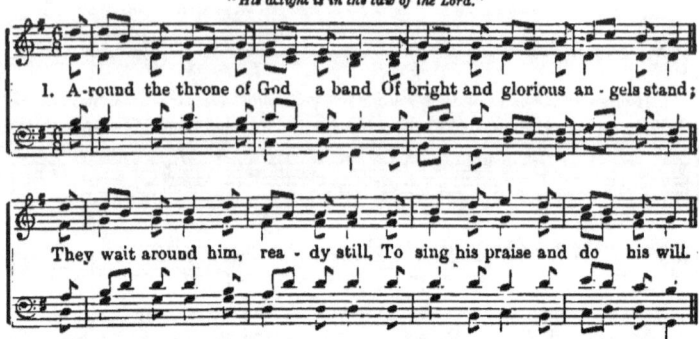

1. A-round the throne of God a band Of bright and glorious an-gels stand;

They wait around him, rea-dy still, To sing his praise and do his will.

2.
Lord, give thine angels every day
Command to guide us on our way ;
And bid them every evening keep
Their watch around us while we sleep.

3.
So shall no wicked thing draw near
To do us harm, or cause us fear ;
And we shall dwell, when life is past,
With angels round thy throne at last.

No. 61

1.
LORD, thou hast searched and seen me
    through ;
Thine eye commands, with piercing view,
My rising and my resting hours,
My heart and flesh, with all their powers.

2.
My thoughts, before they are my own,
Are to my God distinctly known ;
He knows the words I mean to speak,
Ere from my opening lips they break.

3.
Within thy circling power I stand ;
On every side I find thy hand :
Awake, asleep, at home, abroad,
I am surrounded still with God.

4
O may these thoughts possess my breast,
Where'er I rove, where'er I rest ;
Nor let my weaker passions dare
Consent to sin, for God is there.

No. 62

1.
THIS is a precious book indeed !
    Happy the child who loves to read !
'Tis God's own word, which he has
    given,
To show our souls the way to heaven.

2.
It tells us how the world was made,
And how good men the Lord obeyed ;
Here his commands are written too,
To teach us what we ought to do.

3.
It bids us all from sin to fly,
Because our souls can never die ;
It points to heaven, where angels dwell,
And warns us to escape from hell.

4.
But, what is more than all beside,
The Bible tells us Jesus died ;
This is its best, its chief intent,
To lead poor sinners to repent.

Nettleton. 8's & 7's, double.

No. 63

DR. NETTLETON.

"God is a spirit; and they that worship him must worship him in spirit and in truth."

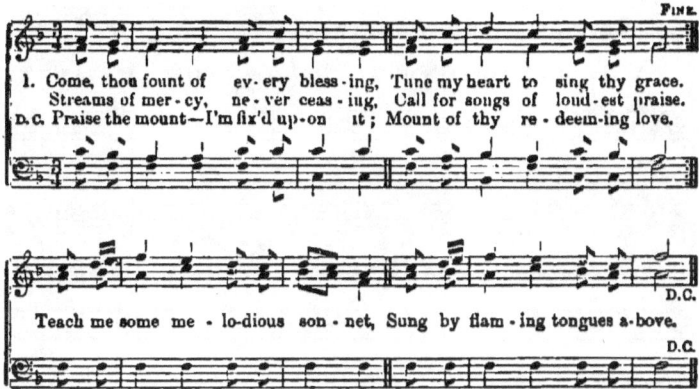

1. Come, thou fount of ev-ery bless-ing, Tune my heart to sing thy grace.
Streams of mer-cy, ne-ver ceas-ing, Call for songs of loud-est praise.
D.C. Praise the mount—I'm fix'd up-on it; Mount of thy re-deem-ing love.

Teach me some me-lo-dious son-net, Sung by flam-ing tongues a-bove.

2.

Here I'll raise mine Ebenezer;
Hither by thy help I'm come;
And I hope, by thy good pleasure,
Safely to arrive at home.
Jesus sought me when a stranger,
Wand'ring from the fold of God,
He, to rescue me from danger,
Interposed his precious blood.

3.

O! to grace how great a debtor
Daily I'm constrained to be!
Let thy goodness, like a fetter,
Bind my wand'ring heart to thee:
Prone to wander, Lord, I feel it,—
Prone to leave the God I love;
Here's my heart, O take and seal it;
Seal it for thy courts above.

No. 64

1.

JESUS, I my cross have taken,
All to leave and follow thee;
Naked, poor, despised, forsaken,
Thou from hence my all shalt be.
Perish every fond ambition,
All I've sought, or hoped, or known,
Yet how rich is my condition,
God and heaven are still mine own.

2.

Haste thee on from grace to glory,
Armed by faith, and winged by prayer
Heaven's eternal day before thee —
God's own hand shall guide thee there.

Soon shall close thine earthly mission,
Soon shall pass thy pilgrim days;
Hope shall change to glad fruition,
Faith to sight, and prayer to praise.

3.

Know, my soul, thy full salvation;
Rise o'er sin, and fear, and care;
Joy to find in every station
Something still to do or bear;
Think what Spirit dwells within thee:
Think what Father's smiles are thine:
Think that Jesus died to win thee:
Child of heaven, canst thou repine!

The Heavenly Shepherd. C.M.

No. 65   Rev. W. Jones.

" The Lord is my Shepherd: I shall not want."

1. The Lord him-self, the migh-ty Lord, Vouchsafes to be my Guide;

The Shep-herd, by whose con-stant care My wants are all sup-plied.

2

In tender grass he makes me feed,
And gently there repose ;
Then leads me to cool shades, and where
Refreshing water flows.

3.

He does my wand'ring soul reclaim,
And, to His endless praise,
Instruct with humble zeal to walk
In his most righteous ways.

4.

I pass the gloomy vale of death,
From fear and danger free ;
For there His aiding rod and staff
Defend and comfort me.

5.

Since God does thus His wondrous love
Through all my life extend,
That life to Him I will devote,
And in His temple spend.

No. 66

1.

MY Shepherd is the living Lord,
Nothing therefore I need :
In pastures fair, near pleasant streams,
He setteth me to feed.

2.

He shall convert and glad my soul,
And bring my mind in frame
To walk in paths of righteousness,
For His most holy name.

3.

Yea, though I walk in vale of death,
Yet will I fear no ill :
Thy rod and staff do comfort me,
And Thou art with me still.

4.

Through all my life Thy favour is
So frankly show'd to me,
That in Thy house for evermore
My dwelling-place shall be.

No. 67 ## God Bless our School. GIARDINI.

" The knowledge of the holy is understanding."

1. God bless our Sun - day School, Increase our Sun - day School.

God bless our school. Send down thy grace di - vine, May eve - ry

child be Thine, And love, all hearts entwine; God bless our School.

2.

All our dear teachers bless,
And give them large success
  In winning souls.
May they encouraged be,
And oft around them see
Their labours crown'd by thee;
  God bless our School.

3.

So may our school increase,
In knowledge, love, and peace;
  God bless our school.
And when death's arrows fly,
And useful teachers die,
Their places still supply;
  God bless our School.

No. 68

1.

THE leaves around decay,
  Their bloom has passed away,
They now fall fast.
We, too, ere long, must die,
And in the cold earth lie,
The spring of life gone by,—
  The summer past.

2

Yet trees will bud once more,
And leaves will clothe them o'er,
  When winter's fled;
So we, from the deep gloom
Of the lone, silent tomb,
Shall rise, when Christ shall come
  To wake the dead.

Condescension.   7's double.

No. 69   Arr. by PHILIP PHILLIPS.

" Though He was rich, yet for our sakes He became poor."

1. Christ is mer - ci - ful and mild; He was once a lit - tle child; He, whom

heavenly hosts adore, Lived on earth among the poor. Thus he laid his glory by,

When for us he stooped to die: How I wonder, when I see His unbounded love to me.

2 He the sick to health restored,
To the poor he preached the word;
Even children had a share
Of his love and tender care.

Every bird can build its nest;
Foxes have their place of rest;
He who our salvation made,
Had not where to lay his head.

No. 70

1.

JESUS bids me seek his face:
Lord, I come to ask thy grace,
Send thy Spirit from above,
Teach me to obey and love.
Unto thee I fain would go;
All I want thou canst bestow.
Precious Saviour, pity me,
To thy loving arms I flee

2.

Wilt thou, Lord, a child receive?
Wilt thou all my sins forgive?
Oh, dissolve this heart of stone,
Make me thine, and thine alone:

Sin is present with me still;
Disobedient is my will.
Precious Saviour, pity me,
To thy loving arms I flee.

3.

Sinful thoughts too oft prevail;
Vain desires my heart assail:
Oh, my Saviour make me whole,
Form anew my inmost soul;
Kindly guard me every day,
Be my everlasting stay.
Precious Saviour, pity me,
To thy loving arms I flee.

No. 71

Holy Bible. 7's.

" O how love I thy law !"

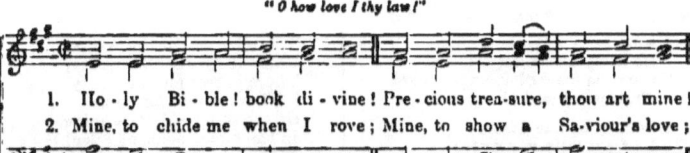

1. Ho - ly   Bi - ble ! book di - vine ! Pre - cious trea - sure, thou art mine !
2. Mine, to chide me when I rove ; Mine, to show a Sa - viour's love ;

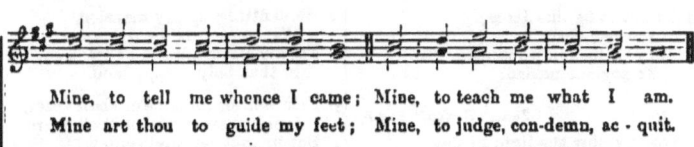

Mine, to tell me whence I came ; Mine, to teach me what I am.
Mine art thou to guide my feet ; Mine, to judge, con - demn, ac - quit.

3.

Mine, to comfort in distress,
If the Holy Spirit bless ;
Mine, to show by living faith,
How to triumph over death.

4.

Mine, to tell of joys to come ;
Mine, to show the sinner's doom :
Holy Bible ! book divine !
Precious treasure, thou art mine !

No. 72

1.

HEAR ye not a voice from heaven,
   To the listening spirit given ?
"Children come ! " it seems to say,
"Give your hearts to me to day."

2.

Lord, may we remember thee,
While from pain and sorrows free ;
While our day is in its dew,
And the clouds of life are few

3.

Now to thee, O Lord, we come,
In our morning's early bloom ;
Breathe on us thy grace divine,
Touch our hearts and make them thine.

No. 73

1.

CHILDREN, listen to the Lord,
   And obey his gracious word ;
Seek his face with heart and mind ;
Early seek, and you shall find.

2.

Sorrowful, your sins confess ;
Plead his perfect righteousness ;
See the Saviour's bleeding side—
Come—you will not be denied.

3.

For his worship now prepare ;
Kneel to him in fervent prayer ;
Serve him with a perfect heart ;
Never from his ways depart.

Familiar Hymns.

No. 74. *Tune, "Watcher," Key D.*

1 I want to be like Jesus,
  So lowly and so meek;
For no one marked an angry word
  That ever heard him speak.

2 I want to be like Jesus,
  So frequently in prayer;
Alone upon the mountain top,
  He met his father there.

8 I want to be like Jesus;
  I never, never find,
That he, though persecuted, was
  To any one unkind.

No. 75. *Tune, "Horton," Key B♭.*

1 SOFTLY now the light of day
  Fades upon our sight away;
Free from care, from labor free,
Lord, we would commune with thee.

2 Soon from us the light of day
  Shall forever pass away;
Then, from sin and sorrow free,
Take us, Lord, to dwell with Thee.

No. 76. *Tune, "Happy Day," Key G.*

1 OH, happy day that fixed my choice
  On thee, my Saviour and my God!
Well may this glowing heart rejoice,
And tell its raptures all abroad.

CHORUS.

Happy day, happy day,
When Jesus washed my sins away;
He taught me how to watch and pray,
And live rejoicing every day.
  Happy day, happy day,
When Jesus washed my sins away.

2 Oh, happy bond, that seals my vows
  To Him, who merits all my love;
Let cheerful anthems fill his house,
  While to that sacred shrine I move.
Happy day, happy day, etc.

No. 77. *Tune, "Home of Glory," Key C.*

1 IN the Christian's home in glory,
  There remains a land of rest;
There the Saviour's gone before me,
  To fulfil my soul's request.

CHORUS.

There is rest for the weary,
There is rest for the weary,
There is rest for the weary,
  There is rest for you.
On the other side of Jordan,
In the sweet fields of Eden,
Where the tree of life is blooming,
  There is rest for you.

2 He is fitting up my mansion,
  Which eternally shall stand,
For my stay shall not be transient
  In that holy, happy land.

3 Pain nor sickness ne'er shall enter,
  Grief nor woe my lot shall share;
But in that celestial center
  I a crown of life shall wear.

4 Death itself shall then be vanquished,
  And his sting shall be withdrawn;
Shout for gladness, O ye ransomed,
  Hail with joy the rising morn.

5 Sing, O sing, ye heirs of glory;
  Shout your triumph as you go;
Zion's gate will open for you,
  You shall find an entrance through.

No. 78. *Tune, "Angel Band," Key C.*

1 My latest sun is sinking fast,
  My race is nearly run;
My strongest trials now are past,
  My triumph is begun.

REFRAIN.

O come, angel band, come and around
  me stand,
O bear me away on your snowy
  wings
To my immortal home!
O bear me away on your snowy wings
  To my immortal home!

2 I know I'm nearing the holy ranks
  Of friends and kindred dear,
For I brush the dews on Jordan's
  banks,
  The crossing must be near.

NEW
STANDARD SINGER.
PART II

CAROLS OF PRAISE

FOR
CHRISTMAS,
NEW YEARS',
NATIONAL,
AND THANKSGIVING DAYS.

BY PHILIP PHILLIPS

PHILIP PHILLIPS, Author and Publisher,
805 Broadway, New York.

HITCHCOCK & WALDEN,
Cincinnati, Chicago, and St. Louis.

4

Happy, Happy Christmas.

No. 79

J. B. Monsell, LL.U.

"On earth peace, good will towards men."

1 A hap-py, hap-py Christ-mas, and a mer-ry bright New Year. How

sweet the kind old greet-ings sound to ev - 'ry heart and ear; No

mat - ter how care - bur-den'd, and no mat - ter how de - press'd, .

A some-thing in their wel-come, makes them dear to ev - 'ry breast.

2 We heard them in our childhood, when,
   With spirits light and gay,
  We dreamt not that life's joyfulness
   Could ever pass away;
  And though long years of carefulness
   Have sobered many a heart,
  A joy still lingers round them, which
   Can never quite depart.

3 Nor ever shall if, Christian-like,
   We count the rolling years
  Not as removing joys from us,
   But sins, and cares, and tears;

And upward, onward, bearing us
   To that bright land and blest.
  Where the wicked cea-e from troubling,
   And the weary are at rest.

4 No matter how care-burdened, and
   No matter how depress'd,
  A something in their welcome makes
   Them dear to every breast.
  Long may the kind old greetings sound,
   To every heart and ear,
  A happy, happy Christmas, and
   A merry, bright New Year.

The Herald Angels.

No. 80

MENDELSSOHN.

"*Glory to God in the Highest.*"

Hark! the herald angels sing, "Glo - ry to the new-born King; Peace on earth, and

mercy mild; God and sinners re-concil-ed." Joyful, all ye nations rise;

Join the triumph of the skies; With th' an-gel-ic host proclaim, "Christ is born in

Beth-le-hem." Hark! the he-rald an-gels sing,—Glo-ry to the new-born King.

2 Christ, by highest heaven adored,
Christ the everlasting Lord,
Late in time behold him come,
Offspring of a Virgin's womb:
Veil'd in flesh, the Godhead see,
Hail the incarnate Deity:
Pleased, as man, with men to dwell,
Jesus, our Immanuel!
   Hark! the herald angels sing,
   Glory to the new-born King!

3 Hail! the heaven-born Prince of Peace!
Hail! the Sun of Righteousness!
Light and life to all he brings,
Risen with healing in his wings,
Mild he lays his glory by,
Born that man no more may die:
Born to raise the sons of earth,
Born to give them second birth.
   Hark! the herald angels sing,
   Glory to the new-born King!

No. 81　　　　　### Christmas Carol.　　　　J. C. WHITE.

" For unto us is born this day in the city of David a Saviour, who is Christ the Lord."

SOLO.
ALLEGRETTO.　　　　　　　　SEMI-CHORUS.

1. { Christmas bells are ringing the blessed chime, The Saviour's born, the Saviour's born :
   { Lis-ten to the sto-ry the an-gels brought, To Bethlehem's p ain, to Bethlehem's plain,

2. { Hark, the ho - ly an - gels are sing - ing now, Peace on earth, good will to men :
   { Tell the wond'rous sto - ry to all the earth, From age to age from shore to shore,

SOLO.　　　　　　　　SEMI-CHORUS.　　　　　　　DUET.

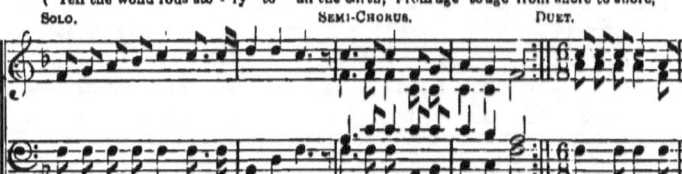

Children now are singing the joyful theme, } Christ, the Saviour, is born to-day, Carol in gladness,
In a manger ly-ing, the One long sought, }
Hasten to the manger, to Jes-us bow. } Christ, the Saviour, is born to-day, Carol ye mountains
Christmas bells shall ring out the Saviour's birth }

ca rol in glee, Ca-rol for Je-sus, he came to save thee ; Carol with hearts full of love to all,
ca-rol ye rills, Ca-rol the herds on a thousand hills ; Carol ye breezes that waft our prayers,

CHORUS. *Lively.*

Ca-rol, for Je sus has come. Ring, ring, ring, merry bells ring on, } Ring out the Old,
Ca rol, for Je-sus is King. Ring, ring, &c. }

ring in the New, For Christ the Lord is King, let all the earth sing, Glory in the High-est.

Song of Praise.

No. 82

W. B. GILBERT.

"He is thy Lord, and worship thou him."

1. Songs of praise the angels sang, Heaven with hal-le-lu-jahs rang,
When Je-ho-vah's work be-gun, When he spake, and it was done.
Songs of praise a-woke the morn When the Prince of Peace was born;
Songs of praise a-rose when he captive led cap-ti-vi-ty.

2.

Heaven and earth must pass away ;
Songs of praise shall crown that day :
God will make new heavens and earth ;
Songs of praise shall hail their birth.
And shall man alone be dumb,
Till that glorious kingdom come ?
No ! the church delights to raise
Psalms, and hymns, and songs of praise.

3.

Saints below, with heart and voice,
Still in songs of praise rejoice ;
Learning here, by faith and love,
Songs of praise to sing above.
Borne upon their latest breath,
Songs of praise shall conquer death ;
Then, amidst eternal joy,
Songs of praise their powers employ.

No. 83 ## Come and Worship.
J. McFarland.

"Good tidings of great joy to all people."

1. An-gels from the realms of glo-ry, Wing your flight o'er all the earth.

Ye who sang Cre - a - tion's sto-ry, Now pro - claim Mes-si - ah's birth.

CHORUS.

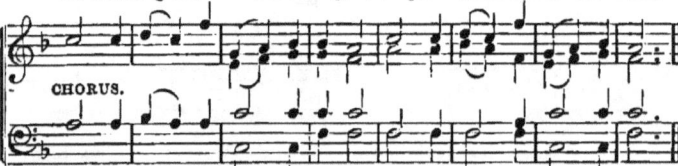

Come and wor-ship, come and worship, Worship Christ, the new-born King.

Come and worship, come and worship, Worship Christ, the new-born King.

2 Shepherds! in the field abiding,
    Watching o'er your flocks by night;
God with man is now residing,
    Yonder shines the infant-light.
      Come, etc.

3 Sages, leave your contemplations;
    Brighter visions beam afar;
Seek the Great Desire of nations:
    Ye have seen his natal star.
      Come, etc.

4 Saints! before the altar bending,
    Watching long in hope and fear,
Suddenly the Lord, descending,
    In his temple shall appear.
      Come, etc.

5 Sinners! wrung with true repentance,
    Doom'd for guilt to endless pains,
Justice now revokes the sentence,
    Mercy calls you—break your chains;
      Come, etc.

A Home in Heaven.*

No. 84.

T. C. O'KANE.

" In my Father's house are many mansions."

Joyful.

1. A home in heaven! what a joyful thought, As the poor man toils in his wea-ry lot,
2. A home in heaven! As the sufferer lies On his bed of pain and up - lifts his eyes

No. 85.

3. A home in heaven! When our treasures fade, And our wealth and fame in the dust are laid.
4. A home in heaven! When our friends have fled To the cheerless gloom of the mold'ring dead,

Ritard ad. lib.

His heart oppressed, and by anguish driven From his home below to his home in heaven.
To that bright home, what a joy is given, With the blessed thought of a home in heaven.
When strength decays and our health is riven, We are happy still with our home in heaven.
We rest in hope on the promise given, We shall meet up there in our home in heaven.

Chorus.

Trav'ling on so glad and free, To a home for you and me,
so glad and free, for you and me,

Come and join our pilgrim band, Trav'ling to the promised heavenly land.
our pilgrim band,

* Specially contributed by the author of " FRESH LEAVES."

English Christmas Song.

No. 86   CHARLES COOTE.

" Blessed is He that cometh in the name of the Lord."

1. I sing the com - ing of the Lord, Then lis - ten to my lay:

Tho' thrice six hun-dred years have fled Since that e - vent - ful day.

The Son of God! the Lord of Life! How won-drous are his ways!

Oh, for a harp of thousand strings, To sound a - broad his praise!

p Oh, for a harp of thousand strings! Oh, for a harp of thousand strings!

ENGLISH CHRISTMAS SONG—*continued.*

Oh, for a harp of thousand strings, To sound a-broad his praise !

2 He came not as a mighty king,
  With pomp, and power, and dread ;
Ah no ! a stable was his home,
  A manger was his bed.
But hark ! how joyful was the lay,
  How rapturous the sound,
When "Glory be to God" was sung,
  By angel hosts around !
    Oh, for a harp, &c.

3 The star was bright that led aright
  The wise men to the place,
Where love and peace were lighting up
  The Holy Infant's face.
They worshipped him, and freely gave
  Their gifts, a rich display
Of spices rare and glitt'ring gold,
  And then "went on their way."
    Oh, for a harp, &c.

4 And did he bow his sacred head,
  And die a death of shame ?—
Let men and angels magnify
  And bless his holy name.
O let us live in peace and love,
  And cast away our pride,
And crucify our sins afresh,
  As he was crucified.
    Oh, for a harp, &c.

5 He rose again,—then let us rise
  From sin, and Christ adore,
And dwell in peace with all mankind,
  And tempt the Lord no more.
The Son of God ! the Lord of Life !
  How wondrous are his ways !
Oh, for a harp of thousand strings,
  To sound abroad his praise !
    Oh, for a harp, &c.

New Year's Hymn.

No. 87

" We spend our years as a tale that is told."

1. Are there no years in heaven ? No change of day and night?

No roll-ing sea-sons' va-ried hues, To mark Time's onward flight?

2 No ; time itself must fade,
  And New Years' Days shall cease,
When all God's children meet on high,
  To hail the Prince of Peace.

3 In his great name we raise
  Our New Year Song to heaven ;
To praise our Father's boundless love,
  And ask to be forgiven.

Antioch. C.M.

HANDEL.

"Tell ye the daughter of Sion, behold thy king cometh unto thee."

1. Joy to the world, the Lord is come! Let earth receive her King;

Let ev - 'ry heart pre - pare him room, And

heaven and na - ture sing, And heaven, and na - ture

And heaven and na - ture sing, And

sing, ... And heaven, and heaven and na - ture sing.

heaven and na - ture sing. And heaven and na - ture sing.

2 Joy to the earth, the Saviour reigns;
  Let men their songs employ;
While fields and floods, rocks, hills and
  plains
Repeat the sounding joy.

3 He rules the world with truth and
    grace,
  And makes the nations prove
The glories of his righteousness,
  And wonders of his love.

A New Year's Prayer.

No. 89

Rev. R. Maguiar.

"So teach us to number our days that we may apply our hearts unto wisdom.

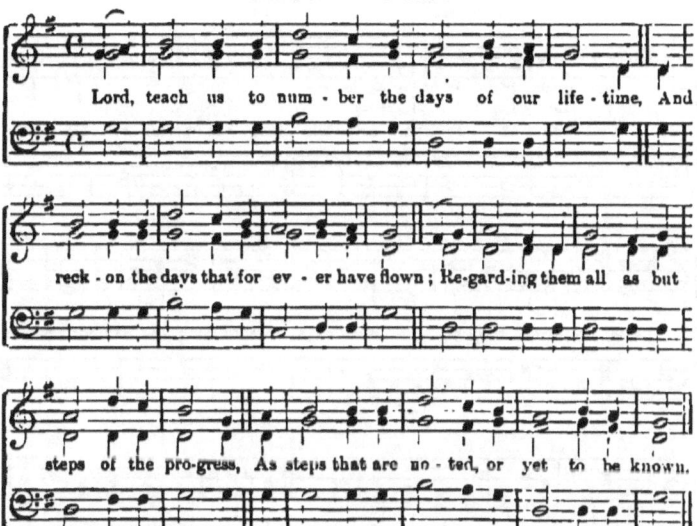

Lord, teach us to num - ber the days of our life - time, And
reck - on the days that for ev - er have flown ; Re-gard-ing them all as but
steps of the pro-gress, As steps that are no - ted, or yet to be known.

2

Yes! Life is the name of that slender
    existence
    That dwells in the perishing body of
    clay ;
A flow'r of the morning, it grows in the
    sunshine—
    It blooms for a little, and dies in a day.

3.

Time passes unheeded and often forgotten,
    The chimes of the seasons go merrily
    round ;
The dread hour of midnight steals on in
    the dark sea,
    And thunders the night-watch with
    dull, heavy sound.

4.

The wave of the ripple that rises from
    ocean,
    Speeds onwards and dances, from bond-
    age set free,

Till, swollen with fulness, its period
    exhausted,
    It gently retires to the depths of the sea.

5.

The dew of the night and the mist of the
    morning
    Scarce live but a moment, when upward
    they fly.
The babe of our joy is the child of our
    sorrow ;
    To-day it is fondled—to-morrow to die.

6.

Then teach us to number the days of our
    lifetime,
    And study to walk in more heavenly
    ways :
As we reckon the hours and the chimes
    of the noontide,
So teach us, great Teacher, to number
    our days.

Children of Jerusalem. 7's.

No. 90   KILLARNEY.

" Hosanna to the Son of David."

1. Chil-dren of Je - ru - sa - lem Sang the praise of Je - sus'
name. Chil-dren, too, of mo - dern days, Join to sing the Saviour's praise.
Hark! hark! hark! while infant voices sing, Hark! hark! hark! while infant voices
sing Loud ho-san-nas, loud ho-san nas, loud ho-san - nas to our King.

2

We are taught to love the Lord ;
We are taught to read his word ;
We are taught the way to heaven ;
Praise for all to God be given.
     Hark, &c.

3.

Parents, teachers, old and young,
All unite to swell the song :
Higher, and yet higher rise,
Till hosannas reach the skies.
     Hark, &c.

Glorious Things.*

No. 91.   T. C. O'KANE.

" Glorious things of thee are spoken."

Cheerful.

1. Glo-rious things of thee are spoken,   Zi-on, cit-y   of   our God!
2. See   the streams of liv - ing waters,   Springing from eter-nal   love,
3. Round each habi - ta - tion hov'ring,   See the fire and cloud ap - pear,

He whose word can   not   be broken,   Formed thee for his own abode.
Still sup - ply   our   sons and daughters, And all fear of want remove.
For   a   glo - ry   and   a   cov'ring,   Showing that the Lord is near.

On   the Rock of A - ges founded What can shake thy sure repose?
Who   can faint while such   a riv-er   Ev - er flows our thirst t'assuage?
He   who gives us dai - ly manna, He   who list - ens when we cry!

With sal - va - tion's walls sur-rounded, Thou may'st smile at all thy foes.
Grace, which like the Lord the giv-er, Nev-er fails from age to age.
Let him hear our loud ho - sanna, Ris-ing to his throne on high.

* Specially contributed by the author of " FRESH LEAVES."

No. 92   ## Call to Praise.   ENGLISH.

"Praise him with string instruments and organs; let everything that hath breath, praise the Lord."

1. Come, O come, with sa-cred lays, Let us sound th' Al-migh-ty's praise!

Hi-ther bring, in true con - sent, Heart, and voice, and in - stru - ment.

To your voic - es tune the lute; Let not tongue nor string be mute;

Not a crea-ture dumb be found, That hath ei - ther voice or sound.

2 Let such things as do not live,
  In still music praises give :
Lowly pipe, all ye that creep
On the earth or in the deep ;
Birds, your warbling treble sing :
Clouds, your peals of thunder ring ;
Sun and moon, exalted higher,
And you, stars, augment the choir.

3 Come, ye sons of human race,
In this chorus take your place ;
And amid this mortal throng
Be ye masters of the song.

Let, in praise of God, the sound
Run a never-ending round ;
That our holy hymn may be
Everlasting, as is he.

4 So shall he, from heaven's high tower,
On the earth his blessing shower ;
All this huge wide orb we see
Shall one choir, one temple be.
Then our voices we will rear,
Till we fill it everywhere.
Come, O come, with sacred lays,
Let us sound the Almighty's praise !

Holy Child Jesus.   C.M.

No. 93   Rev. W. JONES.

" Hosanna in the highest ! "

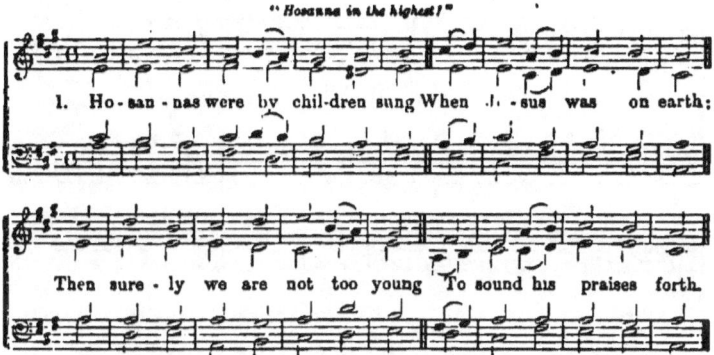

1. Ho - san - nas were by chil-dren sung When Jesus was on earth:

Then sure - ly we are not too young To sound his praises forth.

2.

The Lord is great, the Lord is good ;
He feeds us from his store,
With earthly and with heavenly food;
We'll praise him evermore.

3.

We thank him for his gracious word ;
We thank him for his love ;
We'll sing the praises of our Lord,
Who reigns in heaven above.

No. 94

1.

THE race that long in darkness walk'd,
  Have seen a glorious light ;
The people dwell in day, who dwelt
In death's surrounding night.

2.

To hail Thy rise, Thou better Sun,
  The gathering nations come,
Joyous, as when the reapers bear
  The harvest treasures home.

3.

For unto us a Child is born ;
  To us a Son is given ;
Him shall the tribes of earth obey,
  Him, all the hosts of heaven.

4.

His name shall be the Prince of Peace,
  For evermore adored,
The Wonderful, the Counsellor,
  The Great and Mighty Lord.

No. 95

1.

COME, children, hail the Prince of Peace,
  Obey the Saviour's call ;
Come, seek his face, and taste his grace :
  And crown him Lord of all.

2.

Ye lambs of Christ, your tribute bring,
  Ye children great and small ;
Hosannas sing to Christ your King,
  And crown him Lord of all.

3.

This Jesus will your sins forgive,
  For such he drank the gall,
For such he died, that they might live
  To crown him Lord of all.

4.

Let all these children, Lord, be thine
  Save them from Satan's thrall ;
Then we shall meet at Jesu's feet,
  To crown him Lord of all.

Thanksgiving Hymn.

No. 96   *"It is good to give thanks unto the Lord."*   J. A. P. SCHULER.

mf
1. We plough the fertile meadows, And sow the furrow'd land. But yet the waving harvest

Depends on God's own hand; It is his mercy gives us The sunshine and the rain;

That paints in verdant beauty The mountain and the plain. Ev'ry blessing we en-joy

Comes to us from God. Then praise his name, For he is e-ver good,

2.

By him were all things fashioned,
  Around us and afar ;
He made the earth and ocean,
  And ev'ry shining star ;
He made the pleasant spring-time
  The summer bright and warm,
The golden days of autumn,
  The winter, and the storm.
      Ev'ry blessing, &c.

3.

He makes the glorious sun set,
  The moon to sail on high ;
He bids the breezes fan us,
  And thund'ring clouds to fly ;
He gives us ev'ry blessing ;
  To him our lives we owe ;
He sent his Son to save us
  From sin, and death, and woe.
      Ev'ry blessing, &c.

Delight in God.

No. 97

DR. THOMAS HASTINGS.

" Thy commandments are my delight.

Quick.

1. De - light in the Lord, With sweet-est ac-cord, All ye who are free - ly for - given; him - self he once of - fered, For sin - ners he suf - fered To o - pen the por - tals of heaven.

2 Delight in the Lord,
His wonders record,
Whose name is Almighty to save;
His own resurrection
Brought death in subjection,
Abolished the power of the grave.

3 Delight in the Lord,
Confide in his word,
Our Prophet, our Priest, and our King;

His wisdom, his merit.
His guidance, his spirit,
His love we exultingly sing.

4 Delight in the Lord,
In his sceptre and sword,
His foes shall assail him in vain;
His kingdom all glorious
Will soon rise victorious,
O'er all the wide world he shall reign.

The New Best Name.

No. 98   PHILIP PHILLIPS.

"To him that overcometh will I give to eat of the hidden manna, and will give him a white stone,
and in the stone a new name written, which no man knoweth saving he that receiveth it."

1. He hath giv'n me a gem, as a
3. And oft when my day-dreams draw

to - ken so rare, In my bo - som I've placed it for safe-keep-ing
nigh to a close, And I sigh for the calm of the evening's re -

there, And it shines with a lus - tre so calm and so bright—No
pose, How sweet is the sol - ace, when left all a - lone, Which is

drift from the mountain was ev - er so white. 2. This em - blem of
mine when I gaze on my beau - ti - ful stone. 4. And this blest bond of

pu - ri - ty bears my new name, Which no one can read, tho' to
u - nion is promis'd the same To all who will love, and be -

Follow the voice.

me 'tis so plain; And I hope to preserve it as long as I
lieve on his name; Ah! who would not cov - et a to - ken so

live, For so pre - cious a gift none but Je - sus can give.
rare, In their bo - som to place it for safe - keep-ing there.

Praise the Lord!

No. 99　　　　　　　　　　　　　　　　　　Storl.

"My lips shall praise Thee."

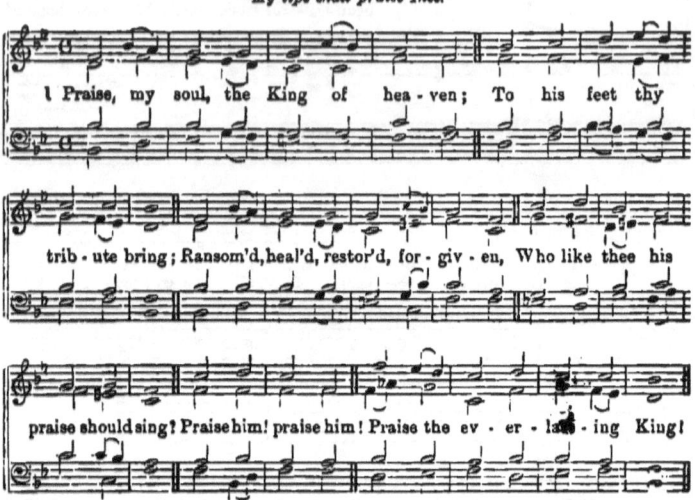

1 Praise, my soul, the King of hea - ven; To his feet thy trib - ute bring; Ransom'd, heal'd, restor'd, for - giv - en, Who like thee his praise should sing? Praise him! praise him! Praise the ev - er - last - ing King!

2.

Praise him for his grace and favour
　To our fathers in distress;
Praise him still the same for ever,
　Slow to chide, and swift to bless.
　　　　Praise him! Praise him!
　　Glorious in his faithfulness!

3.

Angels, help us to adore him,
　Ye behold him face to face!
Sun and moon bow down before him,
　Dwellers all in time and space,
　　　　Praise him! Praise him!
　　Praise with us the God of grace!

No. 100

1.

LET us now, with hearts united,
　Seek and praise our God above;
Far too long we him have slighted:
　But if now we seek his love,
　　　　We shall find him,
　And our souls he will approve.

2.

If we seek him through the Saviour,
　Pleading all he did below,
We shall surely find his favour,
　And be saved from endless woe;
　　　　And to heaven
　After death our souls will go.

3.

If we seek his Holy Spirit
　In our young and early days,
He will grant, through Jesus' merit,
　Rich supplies of heavenly grace:
　　　　And will fit us
　For eternal songs of praise.

No. 101

Confess the Lord. P.M.

" That every tongue should confess that Jesus Christ is Lord.

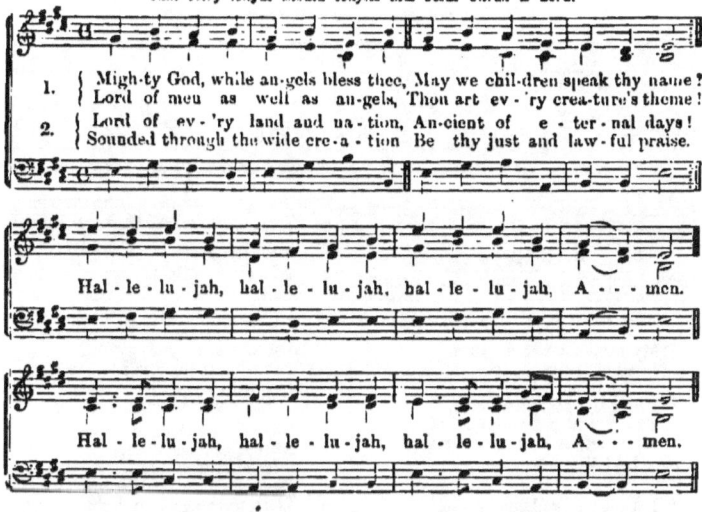

1. { Migh-ty God, while an-gels bless thee, May we chil-dren speak thy name ?
   { Lord of men as well as an-gels, Thou art ev - 'ry crea-ture's theme !

2. { Lord of ev - 'ry land and na - tion, An-cient of e - ter-nal days !
   { Sounded through the wide cre-a - tion Be thy just and law - ful praise.

Hal - le - lu - jah, hal - le - lu - jah, hal - le - lu - jah, A - - - men.

Hal - le - lu - jah, hal - le - lu - jah, hal - le - lu - jah, A - - - men.

3.

Brightness of the Father's glory,
Shall thy praise unuttered lie?
Flee my tongue such guilty silence,
Sing the Lord who came to die,
Hallelujah, etc.

4.

From the highest throne in glory,
To the cross of deepest woe,—
All to ransom guilty captives ;
Flow, my praise, for ever flow.
Hallelujah, etc.

No. 102

1.

WHY did Jesus come from heaven,
Live a suffering life, and die?
'Twas that we might be forgiven,
And hereafter live on high.
Let us praise him,
Now he reigns above the sky.

2.

Jesus is the only Saviour;
All our hope from Jesus springs;
Jesus is the world's Redeemer;
Lord of lords and King of kings.
Let us praise him,
For his grace salvation brings.

3.

Jesus kindly will receive us,
Who to him for refuge flee ;
Jesus never can deceive us ;
Our unchanging friend is he.
Let us praise him :
From our sins he sets us free.

4.

May we know his full salvation,
And, when this short life is o'er
Reach that heavenly habitation,
Whither he is gone before.
May we praise him,
In his kingdom evermore.

No. 103   **America.** (National Hymn.)   CAREY.

19th P.M. 6's & 4's.

" The Lord shall give his people the blessing of peace."

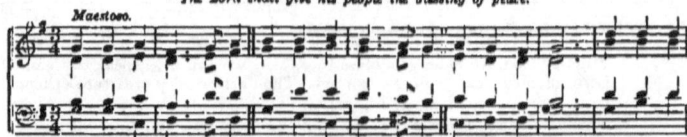

1. My country, 'tis of thee, Sweet land of lib-er-ty, Of thee I sing; Land where my

fathers died, Land of the pilgrim's pride, From ev'ry mountain side Let freedom ring.

2 My native country! thee,
 Land of the noble free,
   Thy name I love;
 I love thy rocks and rills,
 Thy woods and templed hills;
 My heart with rapture thrills,
   Like that above.

3 Let music swell the breeze,
 And ring from all the trees
   Sweet freedom's song:

Let mortal tongues awake,
 Let all that breathe partake,
 Let rocks their silence break,
   The sound prolong.

4 Our father's God, to thee—
 Author of liberty,
   To thee we sing:
 Long may our land be bright
 With freedom's holy light;
 Protect us by thy might,
   Great God, our King.

No. 104

GOD bless our native land!
  Firm may she ever stand,
   Through storm and night;
 When the wild tempests rave,
 Ruler of winds and wave,
 Do thou our country save
   By thy great might.

2 For her our prayer shall rise
 To God above the skies;
   On him we wait:
 Thou who art ever nigh,
 Guarding with watchful eye,
 To thee aloud we cry,
   God save the State!

No. 105

COME, thou Almighty King,
  Help us thy name to sing,
   Help us to praise:
 Father all glorious,
 O'er all victorious,
 Come and reign over us,
   Ancient of days.

2 Jesus, our Lord, arise,
 Scatter our enemies,
   And make them fall;
 Let thine almighty aid
 Our sure defence be made;
 Our souls on thee be stay'd:
   Lord, hear our call.

3 Come, thou incarnate Word,
 Gird on thy mighty sword,
   Our prayer attend;
 Come, and thy people bless,
 And give thy word success.
 Spirit of holiness,
   On us descend.

4 To the great One in Three
 Eternal praises be
   Hence, evermore.
 His sovereign majesty
 May we in glory see,
 And to eternity
   Love and adore.

Our Country.

No. 106

PHILIP PHILLIPS.

" A land that floweth with milk and honey."

1. Our country, un ri-valled in beau - ty And splendour that cannot be told, . . How
2. Our country, the birthplace of free-dom, The land where our forefathers trod, . . And

lovely thy hills and thy woodlands, Arrayed in a sunlight of gold. The eagle, proud king of the
sang in the aisles of the forest Their hymn of thanksgiving to God. Their bark they had moored in the

mountain, Is soar-ing, ma-jes-tic and free; Thy ri-vers and lakes in their grandeur,
har-bour, No more on the o - cean to roam; And there, in the wilds of New Eng land,

Roll on to the arms of the sea, . . . Roll on to the arms of the sea. .
They foun-ded a coun-try and home, . . . They found ed a coun-try and home .

3.
Our country, the past, and its glory,
  Still honour the names of the dead;
The statesman that crowned thee with laurel,
  The he oes and veterans that bled.
Mount Vernon, where Washington slumbers,
  The soul of thy freedom for years,
A willow droops tenderly o er him,
  Go hallow his grave with thy tears.

4.
Our country with ardent devotion,
  In God may thy children abide :
In him be the strength of our nation.
  His laws and its counsel its guide.
Our banner—that time-honoured banner
  That floats o er the ocean's bright foam—
God keep them unsullied for ever—
  Our standard, our union, our home.

Thou Great Creator

No. 107   ALFRED SMITH.

"Remember now thy Creator in the days of thy youth."

1. Thou great Cre - a - tor, sov'reign Lord, To thee my voice I raise,
With ho - ly zeal my heart in-spire, And tune my soul to praise.
Thy word my on - ly com - fort still, My ref - uge day by day:
Oh, let me trust it, gra - cious Lord, And ev - er watch and pray.

2.

My cup with joy thy goodness fills,
  Thy mercy I adore;
Oh, give me strength and grace divine,
  To love thee more and more.
With humble faith and earnest hope,
  Where'er my path may be,
I'll strive to run the heavenly race,
  And look for help to thee.

3.

And when beside the rolling waves
  Of Jordan's stream I stand,
Dear Saviour, thou wilt bear me then
  To Canaan's promised land:
There with the joyful host above,
  My raptured voice I'll raise,
When faith, and prayer, and hope are lost
  In our *glad song of praise.*

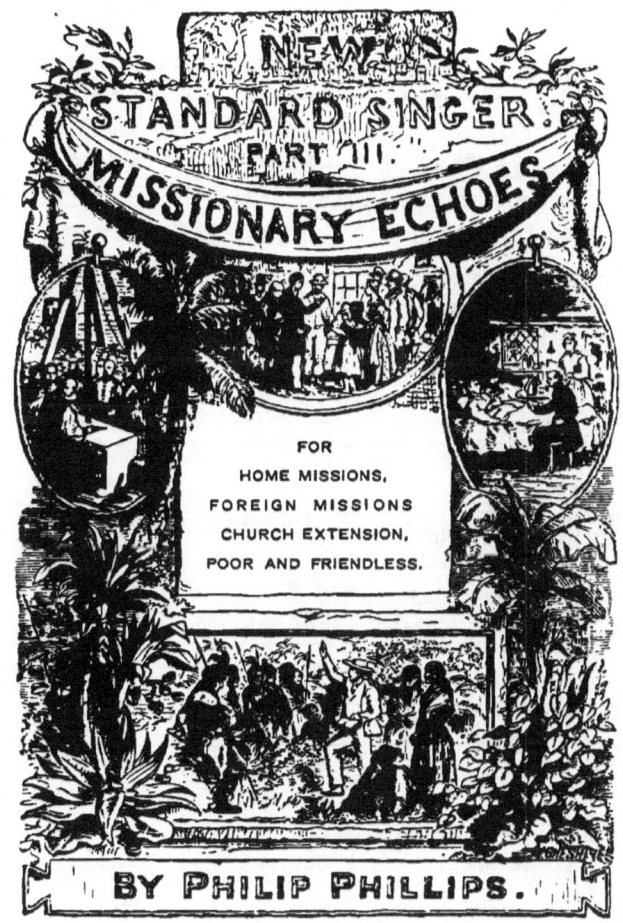

NEW

STANDARD SINGER.

PART III.

MISSIONARY ECHOES

FOR
HOME MISSIONS,
FOREIGN MISSIONS
CHURCH EXTENSION,
POOR AND FRIENDLESS.

BY PHILIP PHILLIPS.

PHILIP PHILLIPS, Author and Publisher,
805 Broadway, New York.

HITCHCOCK & WALDEN,
Cincinnati, Chicago, and St. Louis.

Our Field is the World.

No. 108.   PHILLIPS AND O'KANE.

"Lo! I am with you alway, even unto the end of the world."

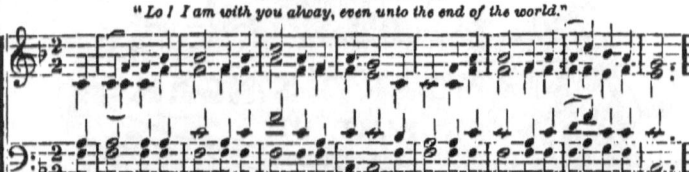

1. Dis - ci - ples of Jesus, why stand ye here idle? Go work in his vineyard, he calls us to-day;
2. Our field is the world, and our work is before us, To each is ap-pointed a message to bear;

The night is approaching when no man can labor, Our Master commands us, and shall we delay?
At home or abroad, in the cottage or palace, Wherev- er' di- rected our mis-sion is there.

CHORUS.

Our field is the world! Our field is the world! Look up, for the har - vest is near;

When the reapers from glory Will shout as they come, And the Lord of the vineyard appear.

3.
Perhaps we are called from the highways
   and hedges,
To gather the lowly, despised, and
   oppressed;
If this be our duty, then why should we
   falter?
We'll do it, and trust to our Saviour
   the rest.
   Our field is the world, etc.

4.
Instead of the thorn shall the myrtle be
   planted;
The desert shall blossom and bloom as
   the rose;
The palm tree rejoicing shall spread forth
   her branches;
The lamb and the lion together repose.
   Our field is the world, etc.

No. 109 **Macedonian Cry.** Arr by Philip Phillips.

"Come over into Macedonia, and help us."

1 Yes, my na-tive land, I love thee; All thy scenes, I love them well;

Friends, connections, hap-py coun-try! Can I bid you all fare-well?

Can I leave you? Can I leave you, Far in hea-then lands to dwell?

No 110

2 Yes, I hasten from you gladly,
From the scenes I loved so well—
Far away, ye billows, bear me;
Lovely native land, farewell!
Pleased I leave thee,
Far in heathen lands to dwell.

3 In the desert let me labour;
On the mountains let me tell
How he died—the blessed Saviour—
To redeem a world from hell!
Let me hasten,
Far in heathen lands to dwell.

4 Bear me on, thou restless ocean;
Let the winds my canvas swell—
Heaves my heart with warm emotion,
While I go far hence to dwell.
Glad I bid thee,
Native land, Farewell! farewell!

GO, ye heralds of salvation,
Go, proclaim "Redeeming blood,"
Publish to that barb'rous nation,
Peace and pardon from our God;
Tell the heathen,
None but Christ can do them good.

2 Distant tho' our souls are blending,
Still our hearts are warm and true;
In our prayers to heav'n ascending,
Brethren, we'll remember you;
Heav'n preserve you
Safely all your journey through.

3 When your mission here is finish'd,
And your work on earth is done,
May your souls, by grace replenish'd,
Find acceptance thro' the Son!
Thence admitted,
Dwell for ever near his throne.

God with Us.

No. 111   PHILIP PHILLIPS.

"Hitherto hath the Lord helped us."

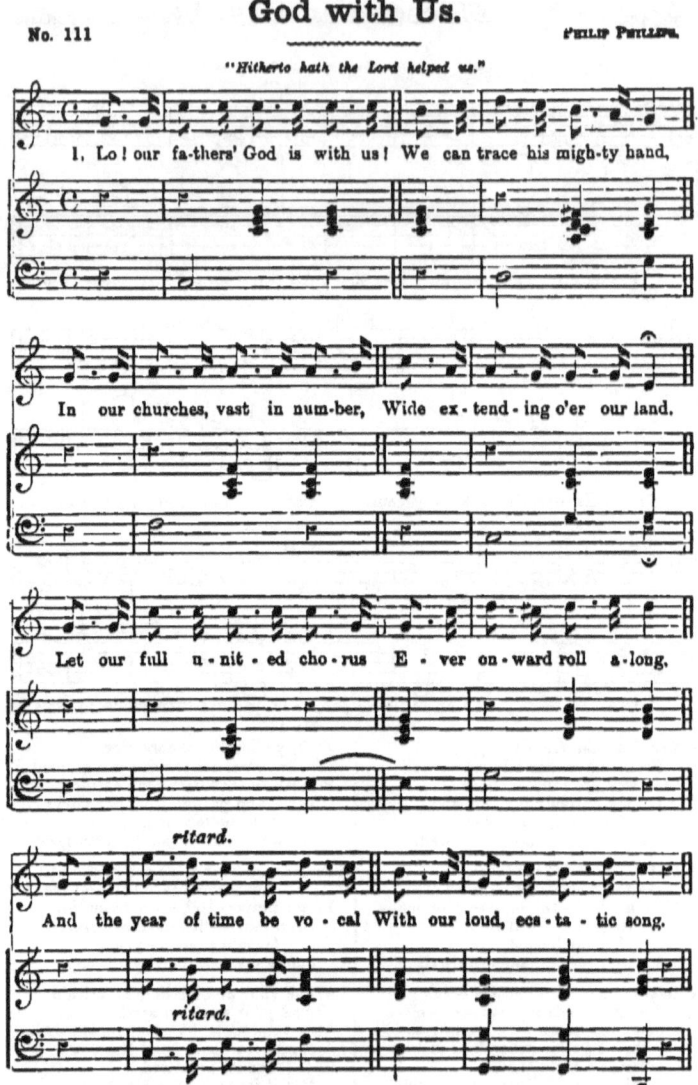

1, Lo! our fa-thers' God is with us! We can trace his migh-ty hand,

In our churches, vast in num-ber, Wide ex - tend - ing o'er our land.

Let our full u - nit - ed cho - rus E - ver on - ward roll a - long,

ritard.

And the year of time be vo - cal With our loud, eca - ta - tic song.

ritard.

GOD WITH US—*continued.*

CHORUS, BY WM. B. BRADBURY.—*Full and loud.*

March-ing a-long, we are marching a-long ; Ris-ing and progressing, we are
march - ing a-long ; Our hearts are u - nit - ed, and this be our song :
Our fa - thers' God is with us while we're march - ing a - long.

2.

Lo ! our fathers' God is with us !
Lost in wonder, we adore
Him who brought them safely hither
With the Gospel to our shore.
Fired with zeal, and armed with courage,
Strong in faith and love divine,
Thro' the darkest cloud that gathered
They could see his glory shine.
Marching along, &c.

3.

Lo ! our fathers' God is with us !
They have laid their armour down,
They have passed the vale of shadow,
Left the cross to wear the crown :

We must bear their glorious standard,
Wield our veteran fathers' sword,
In the army of the faithful
We are battling for the Lord.
Marching along, &c.

4.

Lo ! our fathers' God is with us !
Sing aloud with heart and voice,
Still increasing and progressing,
Brethren, let us all rejoice !
Hallelujah ! what a meeting,
When we reach the shining shore,
There with saints who've gone before us,
Shout "Free grace" for evermore :
Marching along, &c.

How He Loves Us.

No. 112.

C. H. BATEMAN.

" He was bruised for our iniquities."

1. Bound up - on th'ac-cursed tree, Faint and bleeding, who is he? See his eyes so pale and dim, Streaming blood, and writhing limb; See the flesh with scourges torn; See the crown of twist-ed thorn; See the drooping death-dew'd brow; Son of man,'tis thou! 'tis thou!

2 Bound upon th' accursed tree,
Dread and awful, who was he?
Though his lifeless corpse was laid
In a cold sepulchral bed,
Soon the Saviour from the grave
Rose a conqu'ror strong to save;
Bright the crown that decks his brow—
Son of God, 'tis thou! 'tis thou!

Work while 'tis Day.

No. 113.

T. C. O'KANE.

" The night cometh, when no man can work."

1. Work, for the night is coming; Work thro' the morning hours; Work while the dew is

WORK WHILE 'TIS DAY—*continued.*

2

Work, for the night is coming ;
Work through the sunny noon :
Fill brightest hours with labour ;
Rest comes sure and soon.
Give every flying minute
Something to keep in store ;
Work, for the night is coming,
When man works no more.

3.

Work, for the night is coming,
Under the sunset skies ;
While their bright tints are glowing,
Work, for daylight flies.
Work till the last beam fadeth,
Fadeth to shine no more :
Work while the night is dark'ning,
When man's work is o'er.

Cheerful Giver.

No. 114   PHILIP PHILLIPS.

" God loveth the cheerful giver."

1. Give! give! give! Give of the fruits of thy labour; Give of thy "basket and

store;" Give to the cause of the needy   Jesus will give to thee more.

CHORUS.

God lov-eth the cheerful giver,   'Tis one of his sa-cred laws;

He will bless your alms when rightly given, To the glo-ry of his cause.

2.	**3.**
Give! give! give!	Give! give! give!
Give to the pilgrim and stranger,	Give to distribute the Bible
Lighten their burden of care;	Over the isles of the sea;
Give to the widow and orphan,	Nations now sitting in darkness
Help them their sorrow to bear.	Light from its pages will see.
God loveth, etc.	God loveth, etc.

The Reaping Time. 7s.

No. 115 Rev. R. Lowry.

"A time to be born, and a time to die."

1. Je - sus, we thy lambs would be, Humbly would we fol - low thee;
2. Now the field with grain is white, Now the day is dawn-ing bright;

Wait - ing for the joy - ful day, When all care will pass a - way.
Bright - er far the sky will be, When the Mas - ter we shall see.

CHORUS.

When the reap-ing time shall come, And an - gels shout the har-vest home.

When the reaping time shall come, And an - gels shout the har-vest home.

3 May we wait, and watch and pray,
  For the coming of that day,
  When the wheat shall sifted be,
  And the chaff be driven from thee!
    When the reaping, &c.

No. 116

1 Swiftly pass the seasons round;
  Constant change on earth is found,
  We are fading day by day,
  And must shortly pass away.
    When the reaping, &c.

2 Time once lost returns no more:
  Time with us will soon be o'er:
  Oh, may we be early wise,
  To improve it as it flies.
    When the reaping, &c.

3 Help us, Lord, to seek thy face
  Daily may we grow in grace,
  Till we rise to dwell above,
  In the kingdom of thy love.
    When the reaping, &c.

Come, ye Disconsolate. 30th P.M.

No. 117   S. WEBBE.

" God is our refuge and strength : a very present help in trouble."

SOLO, DUET, OR TRIO.

1. Come, ye dis - con - so-late, where'er ye lan - guish,

Come   to   the   mer - cy seat, Fer - vent - ly kneel;.

1ST TIME DUET, 2ND TIME CHORUS.

Here bring your wounded hearts, Here   tell   your   an - guish;

Earth   has   no   sor - row   that heav'n can - not heal.

2.
Joy of the desolate, light of the straying,
Hope of the penitent, fadeless and
pure ;—
Here speaks the Comforter, tenderly
saying—
Earth has no sorrow that heav'n
cannot cure.

3.
Here see the bread of life; see waters flowing
Forth from the throne of God, pure
from above ;
Come to the feast of love; come, ever
knowing—
Earth has no sorrow but heav'n can
remove.

Labour for Christ.

" The harvest truly is plenteous, but the labourers are few."

1. For Jesus our Saviour, our talent, our time, Our substance we'll cheerfully spend ;

Whatever our lot, and wherever our clime, We'll labour and love to the end. . We'll

CHORUS.

labour and love to the end. O yes, we'll do all that we can ; O yes, we'll do all that we

can. The harvest is great, and the labourers are few, Then we will do all that we can.

2

And if we have only a penny to give,
We'll give it, though scanty our store,
For they who give nothing when little they have,
When wealthy, will give little more.
Chorus.

3.

But if an abundance we have at command,
O Father, the Spirit bestow,

To scatter our wealth with a liberal hand,
And succour the children of woe.
Chorus.

4.

Though God may not call us in regions afar,
To scatter the Gospel abroad,
We'll point those around us to Bethlehem's star
To Heaven, to Home, and to God.
Chorus.

The Promised Time.

No. 119

"And the desert shall rejoice and blossom as the rose."

Animated.

1. Re - joice, re - joice, the promised time is com - ing, Re - joice, re -
D. C. Re - joice, re - joice, the promised time is com - ing, Re - joice, re -

joice, the wil - der - ness shall bloom, And Zi - on's chil - dren
joice, the wil - der - ness shall bloom.

then shall sing, "The des-erts all are blossom - ing:" Re - joice, Re -

- joice, the promised time is com - ing, Re - joice, re - joice, the

wil - der - ness shall bloom; The Gos - pel ban - ner, wide unfurl'd, Shall

wave in tri - umph o'er the world; And ev - ery crea - ture,

bond and free, Shall hail the glo - rious ju - bi - lee.

D. C.

2.

Rejoice, rejoice, the promised time is coming,
Rejoice, rejoice, Jerusalem shall sing;
From Zion shall the law go forth,
And all shall hear from south to north:
Rejoice, rejoice, the promised time is coming,
Rejoice, rejoice, Jerusalem shall sing;
And truth shall sit on every hill,
And blessings flow in every rill,
And praise shall every heart employ,
And every voice shall shout with joy:
Rejoice, rejoice, the promised time is coming,
Rejoice, rejoice, Jerusalem shall sing.

3.

Rejoice, rejoice, the promised time is coming,
Rejoice, rejoice, the Prince of Peace shall reign,
And lambs shall with the leopard play,
For nought shall harm in Zion's way:
Rejoice, rejoice, the promised time is coming,
Rejoice, rejoice, the Prince of Peace shall reign.
The sword and spear of needless worth,'
Shall prune the tree and plow the earth,
And peace shall smile from shore to shore,
And nations shall learn war no more:
Rejoice, rejoice, the promised time is coming,
Rejoice, rejoice, the Prince of Peace shall reign.

Gospel Victory.

No. 120

" Come over into Macedonia and help us."

PHILIP PHILLIPS.

1. Go, sound the trump from India's shore, And bid the Hin-doo weep no more,

Hin-doo weep no more; From i-dols vain, and Gan-ges' wave, The

low-ly Saviour comes to save, comes to save, From tyrant's power and

Satan's sway, The Gospel gives the vic-to-ry! vic-to-ry! vic-to-ry!

2 Go, sound the trump on Afric's shore,
  And bid the |: natives weep no more :|
  From cruel chains, and bloody grave,
  The lowly Saviour |: comes to save. :|—From tyrant's, &c.

3 Go, sound the trump on Judah's shore,
  And say to |: Israel weep no more :|
  The Lord of glory, slain by you,
  Will yet restore the |: guilty Jew. :|—From tyrant's, &c.

4 Go, sound the trump on every shore,
  And bid poor |: sinners weep no more :|
  The blood that flowed from Jesus' veins
  Will wash away your |: crimson stains. :|—From tyrant's, &c.

No. 121

Jesus Invites Me.

PHILIP PHILLIPS.

" The Lord thinketh upon me."

1. Je-sus invites me! Je-sus invites me! Kind in-vi-ta-tion all
2. Who can condemn me, who can condemn me; Je-sus has died, and my

doubts to remove; Gracious his par-don, precious his blessing, Boundless the
sins are forgiv'n; Come then, poor sinner, put on the vestment—Put on the

wealth of Redeem-ing Love. Ne'er did a fountain,—ne'er did Bethes-da,—
breast-plate and gaze up to heav'n. Cast off thy fears then—raise " E-ben-e-zer,"

Ne'er did the Jor-dan's pure cleansing flood, Bear on their wa-ters a
List to the joys of the an-gels a-bove; Lo! this their song—here's one

vir-tue so heal-ing, As Je-sus' all precious, a-ton-ing blood.
sin-ner re-pent-ing, Bound-less the wealth of " Re-deem-ing Love."

No. 122   ## Consider the Poor.

"For ye have the poor with ye always, and whensoever ye will ye can do them good."

Words by WM. EDSALL.   PHILIP PHILLIPS.

1. Re - member the poor, the des - o - late poor, Nor leave them to
2. Re - member the poor, be kind to the heart, So pa - tient-ly
3. Re - member the poor, for hard is their lot; Go, vis - it the

wan-der from door to door; Be read-y and will-ing your
try-ing to bear its part; The wid-ow who toils by the
hum-ble and lone-ly cot; When blest is your bask-et, and

comforts to share With those who are burdened with sor-row and care.
em-bers that wane, While tears from her eye-lids are fall-ing like rain.
prospered your store, Be grate-ful to God. and re - mem-ber the poor.

CHORUS.

For the promise is sure, The promise is sure; Blessed is he,

Repeat pp.

Bless - ed is he,   Bless-ed is he that con - si-d'reth the poor.

O Happy Land.

No. 123

ALFRED SMITH.

" Here are they that keep the commandments of God."

1. O hap-py land! O hap-py land! Where saints and an-gels dwell;
We long to join that glo-rious band, And all their anthems swell.
But ev-ery voice in yon-der throng On earth has breathed a prayer;
No lips untaught may join that song, Or learn the mu-sic there.

2.

Thou heavenly Friend, thou heavenly Friend,
O hear us when we pray ;
Now let thy pardoning grace descend,
And take our sins away.
Be all our fresh, our youthful days,
To thy blest service given ;
Then we shall meet to sing thy praise,
A ransomed band in heaven.

No. 124   **Duke Street.** L.M.   J. HATTON

" Praise ye the Lord, for it is good to sing praises unto our God."

1. From all that dwell be-low the skies, Let the Cre-a - tor's praise a - rise.
2. E-ter-nal are thy mer-cies, Lord; E-ter-nal truth at - tends thy word.

Let the Re-deem-er's name be sung, Through every land, by ev-ery tongue.
Thy praise shall sound from shore to shore, Till suns shall rise and set no more.

3.
Your lofty themes, ye mortals, bring ;
In songs of praise divinely sing ;
The great salvation loud proclaim,
And shout for joy the Saviour's name.

4.
In every land begin the song ;
To every land the strains belong :
In cheerful sounds all voices raise,
And fill the world with loudest praise.

No. 125

1.
SOON may the last glad song arise,
   Thro' all the millions of the skies—
That song of triumph which records
That all the earth is now the Lord's.

2.
Let thrones, and powers, and kingdoms, be
Obedient, mighty God, to thee ;
And over land, and stream, and main,
Now wave the sceptre of thy reign.

3.
O let that glorious anthem swell ;
Let host to host the triumph tell,
Till not one rebel heart remains,
But over all the Saviour reigns.

No. 126

1.
JESUS ! thy church, with longing eyes,
   For thine expected coming waits ,
When will the promised light arise,
And glory beam on Zion's gates ?

2.
O come and reign o'er every land ,
Let Satan from his throne be hurled,
All nations bow to thy command,
And grace revive a dying world.

3.
Teach us in watchfulness and prayer,
To wait for thine appointed hour ;
And fit us, by thy grace, to share
The triumphs of thy conqu'ring power.

No. 127   **Lenox.**   **3rd P.M.**   Edson.

" O clap your hands together, all ye people, O sing unto God with the voice of melody."

1. Blow ye the trumpet, blow, The gladly-solemn sound; Let all the nations know,

To earth's re - mo'est bound, The year of ju - bi - lee is come,

The year of ju - bi - lee is come; Re-turn, ye ransom'd sin - ners, home.

2 Jesus, our great High Priest,
  Hath full atonement made ;
  Ye weary spirits, rest;
  Ye mournful souls, be glad :
The year of jubilee is come ;
Return, ye ransomed sinners, home.

3 Extol the Lamb of God, —
  The all-atoning Lamb ;
  Redemption in his blood
  Throughout the world proclaim :
The year of jubilee is come ;
Return, ye ransomed sinners, home.

4 Ye slaves of sin and hell,
  Your liberty receive,
  And safe in Jesus dwell,
  And blest in Jesus live :
The year of jubilee is come ;
Return ye ransomed sinners, home.

5 Ye who have sold for nought
  Your heritage above,
  Shall have it back unbought,
  The gift of Jesus' love :
The year of jubilee is come ;
Return, ye ransomed sinners, home.

No. 128

GOD is gone up on high,
  With a triumphant noise, —
  The clarions of the sky
  Proclaim th' angelic joys :
Join all on earth, rejoice and sing ;
Glory ascribe to glory's King.

2 All power to our great Lord
  Is by the Father given :
  By angel hosts adored,
  He reigns supreme in heaven :
Join all on earth, rejoice and sing :
Glory ascribe to glory's King.

3 High on his holy seat,
  He bears the righteous sway ;
  His foes beneath his feet
  Shall sink and die away :
Join all on earth, rejoice and sing ;
Glory ascribe to glory's King.

4 Till all the earth, renew'd
  In righteousness divine,
  With all the hosts of God,
  In one great chorus join,
Join all on earth, rejoice and sing ;
Glory ascribe to glory's King.

No. 129   **Webb.**   26th P.M.   G. J. WEBB.

"O be joyful in the Lord, all ye lands."

1. The morning light is break-ing; The dark-ness dis-ap-pears;

The sons of earth are wa-king To pe-ni-ten-tial tears:
D.S. Of na-tions in com-mo-tion, Pre-pared for Zi-on's war.

Each breeze that sweeps the o-cean Brings tidings from a-far,

2 See heathen nations bending
  Before the God we love,
And thousand hearts ascending
  In gratitude above ;
While sinners, now confessing,
  The gospel call obey,
And seek the Saviour's blessing,—
  A nation in a day.

3 Blest river of salvation,
  Pursue thy onward way ;
Flow thou to every nation,
  Nor in thy richness stay :
Stay not till all the lowly
  Triumphant reach their home :
Stay not till all the holy
  Proclaim—"The Lord is come !"

No. 130

WHEN shall the voice of singing
  Flow joyfully along ?
When hill and valley, ringing
  With one triumphant song,
Proclaim the contest ended,
  And him who once was slain,
Again to earth descended,
  In righteousness to reign.

2 Then from the craggy mountains
  The sacred shout shall fly ;
And shady vales and fountains
  Shall echo the reply.
High tower and lowly dwelling
  Shall send the chorus round,
All hallelujahs swelling
  In one eternal sound !

No. 131

ROLL on, thou mighty ocean ;
  And, as thy billows flow,
Bear messengers of mercy
  To every land below.
Arise, ye gales, and waft them
  Safe to the destined shore ;
That man may sit in darkness,
  And death's black shade no more.

2 Oh, thou eternal Ruler,
  Who holdest in thine arm
The tempests of the ocean,
  Protect them from all harm !
Thy presence, Lord, be with them,
  Wherever they may be ;
Though far from us who love them,
  Still let them be with thee.

No. 132   # Sessions. L.M.   L. O. Emerson.

" Behold I will send my messenger and he shall prepare the way before me."

1. Go preach my Gos - pel, saith the Lord,— Bid the whole world my grace receive;
2. I'll make your great commission known; And ye shall prove my Gospel true,
3. Teach all the na - tions my commands, I'm with you till the world shall end;

He shall be saved who trus's my word, And he con - demn'd who won't be-lieve.
By all the works that I have done, By all the won - ders ye shall do.
All power is trusted in my hands, I can de - stroy, and I de - fend.

No. 133

BEHOLD the Christian warrior stand
  In all the armour of his God ;
The Spirit's sword is in his hand,
His feet are with the Gospel shod.

2 In panoply of truth complete,
Salvation's helmet on his head ;
With righteousness, a breastplate meet,
And faith's broad shield before him
  spread.

3 Undaunted to the field he goes ;
Yet vain were skill and valour there,
Unless, to foil his legion foes,
He takes the trustiest weapon, prayer.

4 Thus, strong in his Redeemer's strength,
Sin, death, and hell, he tramples down ;
Fights the good fight, and wins at length,
Through mercy, an immortal crown.

No. 134

BEHOLD, the heathen waits to know
  The joy the Gospel will bestow ;
The exiled captive to receive
The freedom Jesus has to give.

2 Come, let us, with a grateful heart,
In this blest labour share a part ;
Our prayers and off'rings gladly bring
To aid the triumphs of our King.

3 Our hearts exult in songs of praise,
That we have seen these latter days,
When our Redeemer shall be known ;
Where Satan long hath held his throne.

4 Where'er his hand hath spread the
  skies,
Sweet incense to his Name shall rise ;
And slave and freeman, Greek and Jew,
By sov'reign grace be form'd anew.

Missionary Hymn. 26th P.M. 7's, 6's.

No. 135

Dr. L. Mason.

"The harvest is the end of the world."

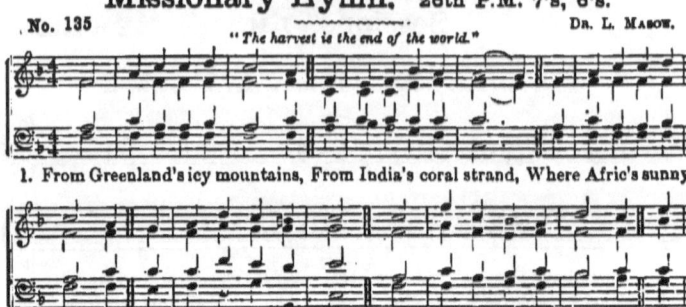

1. From Greenland's icy mountains, From India's coral strand, Where Afric's sunny

fountains Roll down their golden sand; From many an ancient ri - ver, From

many a palmy plain, They call us to de - liv-er Their land from error's chain.

2 What though the spicy breezes
  Blow soft o'er Ceylon's isle ;
Though every prospect pleases,
  And only man is vile :
In vain with lavish kindness
  The gifts of God are strown ;
The heathen in his blindness
  Bows down to wood and stone.

3 Shall we, whose souls are lighted
  With wisdom from on high,
Shall we to men benighted
  The lamp of life deny ?

Salvation !—O salvation !
  The joyful sound proclaim,
Till earth's remotest nation
  Has learn'd Messiah's name.

4 Waft, waft, ye winds, his story,
  And you, ye waters, roll,
Till, like a sea of glory,
  It spreads from pole to pole :
Till o'er our ransomed nature
  The Lamb for sinners slain,
Redeemer, King, Creator,
  In bliss returns to reign.

No. 136

FROM yonder Rocky Mountains,
  With summits white and cold,
From California's fountains,
  That pour down virgin gold ;
From every western prairie,
  From every mystic mound,
They call on us to carry
  The gospel's joyful sound.

2 From Oregon benighted,
  Yet tinged with morning light ;
From fertile Utah, lighted
  With radiance worse than night ;
From Aztec hill and valley,
  Just snatched away from Rome,
They bid us rally, rally,
  And to the rescue come.

3 O ! shall we close our bosoms,
  While every breath 's a cry ?
While brothers drop like blossoms,
  And there for ever die ?
Oh ! Christian, rest not, sleep not,
  But pray, and toil, and fight,
Till those who 're weeping, weep not,
  And darkness turns to light.

4 Then, when enthroned in glory,
  With Jesus' ransomed fold,
We tell love's wondrous story,
  Upon our harps of gold ;
Each effort that we 're making
  Will sweeten heaven's employ,
And every cross we're taking,
  Add rapture to its joy.

Send the Tidings. C.M.

No. 137   From French Psalter.

" He shall save his people from their sins."

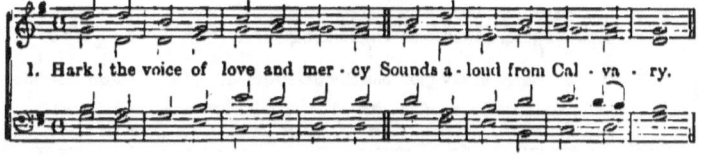

1. Hark! the voice of love and mer - cy Sounds a - loud from Cal - va - ry.

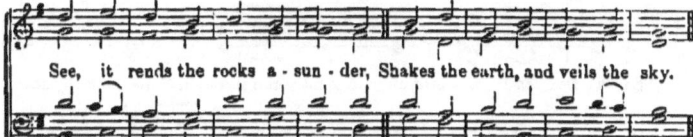

See, it rends the rocks a - sun - der, Shakes the earth, and veils the sky.

"It is fi - nish'd!" Hear the dy - ing Sa - viour cry!

2

Finish'd—all the types and shadows
  Of the ceremonial law!
Finish'd—all that God had promised;
  Death and Hell no more shall awe;
    " It is finish'd!"
Saints, from hence your comforts draw.

3.

Tune your hearts anew, ye ransom'd!
  Join to sing the glorious theme;
All on earth, and all in heaven,
  Join to praise the Saviours name!
    Hallelujah!
Glory to the bleeding Lamb!

No. 138

1.

SOULS in heathen darkness lying,
  Where no light has broken through—
Souls that Jesus bought by dying,
  Whom his soul in travail knew—
    Thousand voices
Call us o'er the waters blue.

2.

Christians, hearken! none has taught them
  Of His love so deep and dear;
Of the precious price that bought them;
  Of the nail, the thorn, the spear;
    Ye who know Him,
Guide them from their darkness drear.

3.

Haste, O haste, and spread the tidings
  Wide to earth's remotest strand;
Let no brother's bitter chidings
  Rise against us—when we stand
    In the judgment—
From some far forgotten land.

4.

Lo! the hills for harvest whiten,
  All along each distant shore;
Seaward far the islands brighten,—
  Light of nations! lead us o'er:
    When we seek them,
Let Thy Spirit go before.

Mission Field. L.M.

DR. THOS. HASTINGS.

" The harvest truly is plenteous, but the labourers are few."

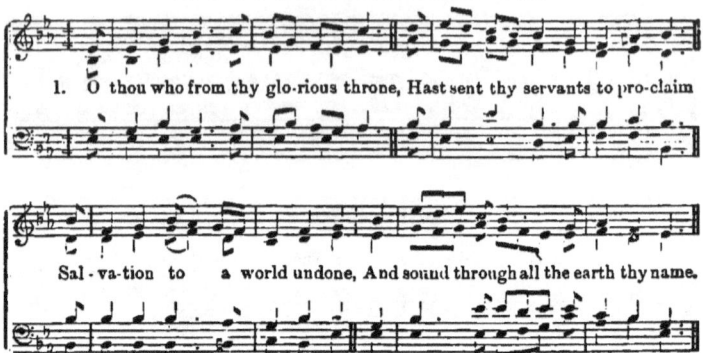

1. O thou who from thy glo-rious throne, Hast sent thy servants to pro-claim

Sal - va-tion to a world undone, And sound through all the earth thy name.

2.

From Afric's burning, arid sands,
And Asia's mild, resplendent sky ;
Let converts, from the heathen lands,
As doves unto their windows fly.

3.

For all the pow'r, beneath, above,
Thy wounded hands sustain ;
Then sway the sceptre of thy love,
And let thy mercy reign.

No. 140

1.

AT length the world is opening wide
To messengers of gospel grace ;
How shall the heralds be supplied,
For all the millions of the race.

2.

Lord, let the churches rise and shine
Under the becknings of thy hand
Bid thine with hallowed zeal combine,
Obedient to thy last command.

3.

To thee, O Lord we raise our cry,
Now be thy banners wide unfurled ;
O bring the latter glories nigh ;
Set up thy kingdom through the world.

4.

Our waiting eyes are unto thee,
To thee the heritage is giv'n
O let us thy salvation see
Make earth the vestibule of heaven.

No. 141

1.

GO, much lov'd brethren, haste and rear
The gospel standard, void of fear :
Go, seek with joy your destin'd shore,
To view your native land no more.

2.

Yes—Christian Heroes ! go, proclaim
Salvation through Immanuel's name ;
To barren climes the tidings bear,
And plant the Rose of Sharon there.

3.

He'll shield you with a wall of fire,
With flaming zeal your breasts inspire,
Bid raging winds their fury cease,
And hush the tempests into peace.

4.

And when our labours all are o'er,
Then we shall meet to part no more ;
Meet with the blood-bought throng to fall
And crown our Jesus Lord of all !

No. 142   **Zion.** 8's, 7's, & 4's.   Dr. T. Hastings.

"O Lord our Lord, how excellent is thy name in all the earth."

1. { Men of God! go, take your stations! Darkness reigns throughout the earth.
   { Go, pro-claim a-mong the na-tions Joy - ful news of heavenly birth:

2. { When exposed to fears and dan-gers, Je - sus will his own de - fend;
   { Borne a - far midst foes and strangers, Je - sus will ap-pear your friend,

Bear the tidings Of the Saviour's matchless worth. Bear the tidings Of the Saviour's matchless worth.
And his presence Shall be with you to the end. And his presence Shall be with you to the end.

No. 143 .

1.

O'ER the realms of pagan darkness,
   Let the eye of pity gaze ;
See the kindreds of the people
Lost in sin's bewildering maze ;
   Dark ess brooding
O'er the face of all the earth.
                    Darkness, etc.

2.

Light of them that sit in darkness,
   Rise and shine, thy blessings bring;
Light, to lighten all the Gentiles,
Rise with healing in thy wing :
   To thy brightness
Let all kings and nations come.
                    To thy, etc.

3.

May the heathen, now adoring
   Idle gods of wood and stone,
Come, and worshipping before him,
   Serve the living God alone :
   Let thy glory
Fill the earth as floods the sea.
                    Let thy, etc.

No. 144

1.

YES, we trust the day is breaking ;
   Joyful times are near at hand ;
God, the mighty God, is speaking,
By his word, in every land :
   When he chooses,
Darkness flies at his command.
                    When he, etc.

2.

While the foe becomes more daring,
   While he enters like a flood,
God, the Saviour is preparing
   Means to spread his truth abroad :
   Every language
Soon shall tell the love of God.
                    Every, etc.

3.

O, 'tis pleasant, 'tis reviving
   To our hearts, to hear, each day,
Joyful news from far arriving,
How the gospel wins its way,
   Those enlightening
Who in death and darkness lay.
                    Those, etc.

No. 145   ## "Your Mission."*

" Go work to day in my vineyard."

THESE beautiful words were written by Mrs. Ellen H. Gates. The music will be found on page 90 of MUSICAL LEAVES as sung by PHILIP PHILLIPS at New York, Philadelphia, Hall of Representatives, Washington (by request of President Lincoln), Cincinnati, Chicago, St. Louis and many other places in America : and as sung by him also in Europe at the following places : Dublin, Belfast, Glasgow, Edinburgh, Leeds, Sheffield, Manchester, Birmingham ; Crystal Palace and Spurgeon's Metropolitan Tabernacle, London ; and the American and Wesleyan Chapels, Paris.

1.

IF you can not on the ocean
  Sail among the swiftest fleet,
Rocking on the highest billows,
  Laughing at the storms you meet,
You can stand among the sailors,
  Anchored yet within the bay ;
You can lend a hand to help them,
  As they launch their boat away.

2.

If you are too weak to journey
  Up the mountain steep and high,
You can stand within the valley,
  While the multitudes go by ;
You can chant in happy measure,
  As they slowly pass along ;
Though they may forget the singer,
  They will not forget the song.

3.

If you have not gold and silver
  Ever ready to command ;
If you can not to'ward the needy
  Reach an ever-open hand ;
You can visit the afflicted,
  O'er the erring you can weep ;
You can be a true disciple,
  Sitting at the Saviour's feet.

4.

If you can not in the harvest
  Garner up the richest sheaves,
Many a grain both ripe and golden
  Will the careless reapers leave ;
Go and glean among the briers,
  Growing rank against the wall,
For it may be that their shadow
  Hides the heaviest wheat of all.

5.

If you can not in the conflict
  Prove yourself a soldier true ;
If, where fire and smoke are thickest,
  There 's no work for you to do ;
When the battle-field is silent,
  You can go with careful tread,
You can bear away the wounded,
  You can cover up the dead.

6.

Do not, then, stand idly waiting
  For some greater work to do ;
Fortune is a lazy goddess,
  She will never come to you.
Go and toil in any vineyard,
  Do not fear to do or dare;
If you want a field of labor,
  You can find it any where.

Additional Verses, written by Chaplain Lozier.

If you can not be the watchman,
  Standing high on Zion's wall,
Pointing out the path to heaven,
  Offering life and peace to all ;
With your prayers and with your bounties
  You can do what Heaven demands ;
You can be like faithful Aaron,
  Holding up the prophet's hands.

If, among the older people,
  You may not be apt to teach ; [herd,
" Feed my lambs," said Christ, our Shep-
  Place the food within their reach.
And it may be that the children
  You have led with trembling hand
Will be found among your jewels,
  When you reach the better land.

* These words should be sung as a Solo; the tune is not designed to be sung as a Chorus.

"What are You Going to Do."*

No. 146.
PHILIP PHILLIPS.

"Wherewithal shall a young man cleanse his ways," by heeding, etc. etc.

1. O what are you go-ing to do, brother? Say, what are you go-ing to do? You have thought of some useful la- bor, But what is the end in view? You are fresh from the home of your boy-hood, And just in the bloom of youth' Have you tast-ed the sparkling wa - ter That

CHORUS.

flows from the fount of truth? Is your heart in the Saviour's keeping? Remember he died for you! Then what are you go-ing to do, brother? Say, what are you go- ing to do?

2. O what are you going to do, brother?
The morning of youth is past;
The vigor and strength of manhood,
My brother, are yours at last.
You are rising in worldly prospects,
And prospered in worldly things;—
A duty to those less favored,
The smile of your fortune brings.
Cho.—Go, prove that your heart is grateful—
The Lord has a work for you!
Then what are you going to do, brother?
Say, what are you going to do?

3. O what are you going to do, brother?
Your sun at its noon is high;
It shines in meridian splendor,
And rides through a cloudless sky.
You are holding a high position,
Of honor, of trust, and fame;—

Are you willing to give the glory
And praise to your Saviour's name?
Cho.—The regions that sit in darkness
Are stretching their hands to you;
Then what are you going to do, brother?
Say, what are you going to do?

4. O what are you going to do, brother?
The twilight approaches now;—
Already your locks are silvered,
And winter is on your brow.
Your talents, your time, your riches,
To Jesus, your Master, give;
Then ask if the world around you
Is better because you live.
Cho.—You are nearing the brink of Jordan,
But still there is work for you;
Then what are you going to do, brother?
Say, what are you going to do?

* One of the soul-stirring songs from the MUSICAL LEAVES, and dedicated by the Author to the Young Men's Christian Associations of the United States.

Familiar Hymns.

No. 147.   *"Missionary Hymn,"* Key F.

1 ARABIA's desert ranger
   To Christ shall bow the knee,
The Ethiopian stranger
   His glory come to see
With off'rings of devotion,
   Ships from the isles shall meet,
To pour the wealth of ocean
   In tribute at his feet.

2 Kings shall fall down before him,
   And gold and incense bring;
All nations shall adore him—
   His praise all people sing;
For he shall have dominion
   O'er river, sea, and shore,
Far as the eagle's pinion
   Or dove's light wing can soar.

3 O'er every foe victorious,
   He on his throne shall rest;
From age to age more glorious,
   All blessing and all blest.
The tide of time shall never
   His covenant remove;
His name shall stand forever—
   His great, best name of Love.

No. 148.   *"Zion,"* Key D.

1 FATHER, let thy benediction,
   Gently falling as the dew,
And thy ever-gracious presence,
   Bless us all our journey through,
      May we ever
   Keep the end of life in view!

2 Young in years, we need the wisdom
   Which can only come from thee;
In the morn of our existence
   Let us thy salvation see,
      Changed in spirit,
   Then shall we thy children be.

3 When temptation shall assail us,
   When we falter by the way,
Let thine arm of strength defend us,
   Saviour, hear us when we pray.
      Thou art mighty,
   Be thou then our rock and stay.

4 Praise and blessing, power and glory,
   Will we render, Lord, to thee;
For the news of thy salvation
   Shall extend from sea to sea.
      All the nations
   Joyfully shall worship thee.

No. 149.   *"Martyn,"* Key F.

1 HARK! what cry arrests my ear!
   Hark! what accents of despair!
'Tis the heathen's dying prayer,
   Friends of Jesus, hear, O hear!
" Men of God, to you we cry,
   Rests on you our tearful eye;
Help us, Christians, or we die!
   Die in dark despair, despair!"

2 Hasten, Christians, haste to save;
   O'er the land and o'er the wave,
Dangers, death, and distance brave.
   Hark! for help they call, they call
Afric bends her suppliant knee—
   Asia spreads her hands to thee:
Hark! they urge the heaven-born plea,
   "Jesus died for me, for me."

3 Haste, then, spread the Saviour's name;
   Snatch the firebrands from the flame;
Deck his glorious diadem
   With the ransomed souls of men.
See! the pagan altars fall!
   See! the Saviour reigns o'er all!
Crown him, crown him Lord of all!
   Echoes round the poles, the poles.

No. 150.   *"Greenville,"* Key F.

1 JESUS yet shall reign victorious,
   All the earth shall own his sway!
He will make his kingdom glorious—
   He shall reign through endless day.
See the ancient idols falling,
   Worshipp'd once, but now abhorr'd!
Men on Jesus now are calling,
   Zion's King, by all adored.

No. 151.   *"Webb,"* Key Bb.

1 To Thee, O blessed Saviour,
   Our grateful songs we raise;
Oh tune our hearts and voices
   Thy holy name to praise.
'Tis by thy sovereign mercy
   We're here allowed to meet,
To join with friends and teachers
   Thy blessing to entreat.

2 Oh, may thy precious gospel
   Be publish'd all abroad
Till the benighted heathen
   Shall know and serve the Lord
Till o'er the wide creation
   The rays of truth shall shine,
And nations now in darkness
   Arise to light divine.

NEW STANDARD SINGER

HOME MELODIES

FOR INFANT CLASSES,
YOUNG MEN'S CHRISTIAN ASSOCIATIONS,
SAILORS AND SOLDIERS,
FAMILY WORSHIP,
ETC. ETC.

BY PHILIP PHILLIPS

PHILIP PHILLIPS, Author and Publisher,
805 BROADWAY, NEW YORK.

HITCHCOCK & WALDEN,
CINCINNATI, CHICAGO, AND ST. LOUIS.

The Love of God.

No. 152

Arr. by PHILIP PHILLIPS.

Scholars.

"O that men would praise the Lord for his goodness."

1. What led the Son of God To leave his throne on high,
2. What moves him to im - part His spi - rit from a - bove,

To shed his pre - cious blood; To suf - fer and to die?
There-by to fill our hearts With heaven - ly peace and love?

Teachers.

His pure and bound - less love to us Led him to die and
His pure and bound - less love to us Moves him to give his

suf - fer thus, . Led him to die and suf - fer thus.
Spi - rit thus, . Moves him to give his Spi - rit thus.

Scholars.

3 Why are we taught to pray,
And read His word of truth,
To keep His holy day,
And serve Him in our youth?

Teachers.

His pure and boundless love to us
Has raised up friends to teach us thus.

Scholars.

4 Our warmest thanks we owe,
To Thee, O God of grace!
Our hearts should overflow
In grateful love and praise;

Teachers.

Help us, O Lord, to praise Thee thus,
For Thine amazing love to us.

Who is He in Yonder Stall.*

No. 153

B. R. Hanby.

" Though he was rich, yet for our sakes he became poor."

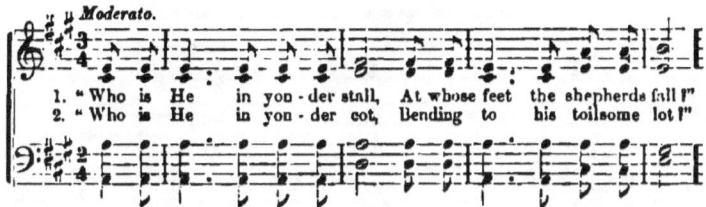

1. "Who is He in yon - der stall, At whose feet the shepherds fall?"
2. "Who is He in yon - der cot, Bending to his toilsome lot?"

CHORUS.

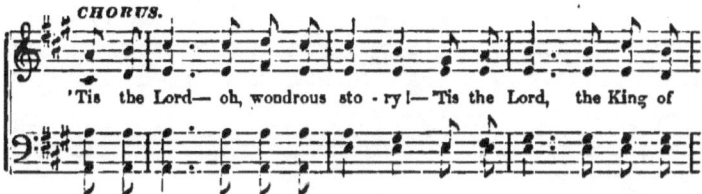

'Tis the Lord— oh, wondrous sto - ry!—'Tis the Lord, the King of

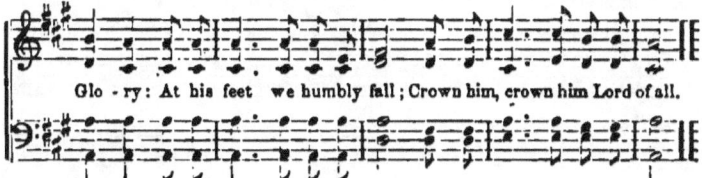

Glo - ry: At his feet we humbly fall; Crown him, crown him Lord of all.

3. "Who is He who stands and weeps
   At the grave where Lazarus sleeps?"
   Cho.—'Tis the Lord, etc.

4. "Who is He, in deep distress,
   Fasting in the wilderness?"
   Cho.—'Tis the Lord, etc.

5. "Lo! at midnight, who is He
   Prays in dark Gethsemane?"
   Cho.—'Tis the Lord, etc.

6. "Who is He, in Calvary's throes,
   Asks for blessings on his foes?"
   Cho.—'Tis the Lord, etc.

7. "Who is He that from the grave
   Comes to heal, and help, and save?"
   Cho.—'Tis the Lord, etc.

8. "Who is He that on yon throne
   Rules the world of light alone?"
   Cho.—'Tis the Lord, etc.

* From "CHAPEL GEMS," by permission.

No. 154   **Eternal Joys.**   Dr Thos. Hastings.

" He that overcometh shall inherit all things; and I will be his God, and he shall be my son."

Children. Tell us now, the joys of heaven, Ye who know a Saviour's love; What to Christians will be giv - en, In that glorious world a - bove?

CHORUS TO BE SUNG BY THE TEACHERS.

Human tongue can ne'er declare, All that they inherit there, All that they inherit there.

Human tongue can ne'er declare, All that they inherit there, All that they inherit there.

Children.
2 Will they dwell with Christ for ever,
  In the realms beyond the tomb?
And will he be absent never,
  From the christian's final home?
Teachers.
They with Christ shall ever dwell,
See his face, his wonders tell.
Children.
3 Will they see the Father's glory,
  And the Holy Spirit's grace,
While they sing redemption's story
  In that holy happy place?

Teachers.
They shall see that vision blest,
When they enter into rest.

Children.
4 Lead us then to that salvation,
  Where the living waters flow,
Guide us to that heavenly station,
  For the way full well ye know.

Teachers.
All these blessings they receive,
Who in Jesus Christ believe.

Be a Lover of the Lord.

No. 155  S. J. VAIL.

" I have loved thee."

1. Am I a sol-dier of the cross,—A foll'wer of the Lamb,—And shall I
2. Must I be car-ried to the skies On flowery beds of ease; While others

CHORUS.

fear to own his cause Or blush to speak his name ! You must be a lov-er of the
fought to win the prize, And sail'd through bloody seas ? You must be, &c.

Lord, You must be a lov-er of the Lord, Yes, you must be a

lov-er of the Lord, If you would go to heav'n, If you would go to heav'n.

3.	4.
Are there no foes for me to face !	Since I must fight if I would reign,
Must I not stem the flood !	Increase my courage, Lord ;
Is this vile world a friend to grace,	I'll bear the toil, endure the pain,
To help me on to God !—*Cho.*	Supported by thy word.—*Cho.*

No. 156   ## My Home is There.*   WM. B. BRADBURY.

"In my Father's house are many mansions."

1. A - bove the waves of earth - ly strife, A - bove the

ills and cares of life. Where all is peace - ful, bright, and

fair; My home is there, My home is there.

CHORUS.

My beau - ti - ful home,........... My beau - ti - ful

My beau - ti - ful home,...... My

home,...... .... In the land where the glo - ri - fied

beau - ti - ful home,

From Fresh Laurels by permission of BIGLOW & MAIN

* This is one of the beautiful songs, sung by the children at the church in Mont Clair, on the funeral occasion of WM. B. BRADBURY

ev - er shall roam, Where an - gels bright..... wear crowns of

Where an - gels, an - gels bright, wear crowns, wear

light,... .... My home is there, my home is there.

crowns of light,

2.

Where living fountains sweetly flow,
Where buds and flowers immortal grow,
Where trees their fruits celestial bear;
My home is there, my home is there.
   Cho.—My beautiful home, my beautiful home,
      In the land where the glorified ever shall roam,
      Where angels bright wear crowns of light,
      My home is there, my home is there.

3.

Away from sorrow, doubt and pain,
Away from worldly loss and gain,
From all temptation, tears and care;
My home is there. my home is there.
   Cho.—My beautiful home, my beautiful home,
      In the land where the glorified ever shall roam,
      Where angels bright wear crowns of light,
      My home is there, my home is there.

4.

Beyond the bright and pearly gates,
Where Jesus, loving Saviour, waits,
Where all is peaceful, bright, and fair;
My home is there, my home is there.
   Cho.—My beautiful home, my beautiful home,
      In the land where the glorified ever shall roam,
      Where angels bright wear crowns of light,
      My home is there, my home is there.

True Worship.

No. 157

Dr. Thos. Hastings.

" The Lord shall ye fear, and him shall ye worship."

1. Chil - dren, when we sing of Je - sus, Oh, re - mem - ber
2. Je - sus, once for sin - ners bleed - ing, Now in heaven is

that he sees us, That he looks in - to the heart:
in - ter - ced - ing, Let us seek to be for - giv'n,

Do you love him while you fear him? Do you trust him,
Let us feel that sin is hate - ful, Let us all be

and draw near him? Do not act the tri - fler's part.
ve - ry grate - ful, While we lift our songs to heaven.

3 When for prayer we've met together,
Do you tell our heavenly Father
  Of the very things you need?
Do you ask, when we are praying?
Do you feel what we are saying—
  Are you giving earnest heed?

4 Let us not be present merely,
Let us worship God sincerely,
  When we sing, and when we pray:
When we're reading, when we're speaking,
When his b'essing we are seeking,
  Let our thoughts ne'er go astray.

At Jesus' Feet. C. M.

No. 158

Dr. Thos. Hastings.

"And all things whatsoever ye shall ask in prayer, believing, ye shall receive."

Quick but Gentle.

1. A lit - tle child at Je - sus' feet, His blessings I would
2. How kind and gra - cious he appears, How full of ten - der

share; He sits up - on the mer - cy - seat, To
love; Quick to re - lieve from all my fears, And

heark - en un - to prayer, To heark - en un - to prayer.
bid me look a - bove, And bid me look a - bove,

3 Not every ardent wish is met,
    Nor all I ask bestowed.
  But I would never once forget
    That wisdom dwells with God.

4 Where he withholds, full well he knows,
    'Tis better than to give;

And when he graciously bestows,
  I joyfully receive.

5 I would be ever satisfied,
    In waiting his behest;
  No real want will be denied,
    He giveth what is best.

No. 159   # Jesus, Saviour, Pity Me.

"The Lord pitieth them that fear him."

1. Je - sus, Sa-viour, pi - ty   me! Hear me when I   cry   to thee!

I've   a   ve - ry   sin - ful heart,   Full   of   sin   in   ev' - ry   part.

I   can ne - ver   make it good: Wilt thou wash me   in   thy blood?

Je - sus, Sa-viour, pi - ty   me!   Hear me when I   cry   to thee!

2 Short has been my pilgrim way,
  Yet I'm sinning ev'ry day;
  Though I am so young and weak,
  Lately taught to run and speak—

  Yet in evil I am strong,
  Far from thee I've lived too long;
  Jesus, Saviour, pity me!
  Hear me when I cry to thee!

No. 160

The Angel Band.*

John March, Jun.

"And God shall wipe away all tears from their eyes, and there shall be no more death."

1. Go, o - pen wide the door, mo-ther, And let the an - gels in; They are so bright and fair, mother, So pure and free from sin. I hear them speak my name, mother; They soft - ly whisper, "Come!" O, let the an - gels in, mother, They've come to take me home.

2 I know that death has come, mother,	3 I now must say farewell, mother,
His hand is on my brow;	For I am going home!
You cannot keep me here, mother—	Now open wide the door, mother,
For I must leave you now.	And let the angels come!
The room is growing dark, mother—	And let them bear me far away,
I thought I heard you weep;	Up to the world of love,
'Tis very sweet to die mother,	The city where the angels stay,
Like sinking into sleep!	The brighter world above.

* A little girl, who was about to expire, said to her mother, "Now, mother, I'm dying. Open the door and let the angels in—they've come to take me home." Better be sung as a solo.

Children's Promise.

No. 161

W. Hedge.

"Of such is the Kingdom of Heaven."

Yes, there are lit - tle ones in heav'n, Babes such as we a - round the throne, To whom the King of kings hath given A glo - ry like his own. Je - sus, thy mer - cy, rich and free, Hath suf - fered them to come to thee!

2 O let us think of them to day—
Their sweet and everlasting song,
And hope to sing as loud as they
   In the same heaven ere long.
Jesus! may this our portion be—
O suffer us to come to thee!

3 To come with humbleness of mind,
With simple faith and earnest prayer,
To seek thy precious cross, and find
   Peace—joy—salvation there.
O set our sin-bound spirits free,
And suffer us to come to thee!

4 To come while we are young and gay,
While life, and joy, and hope run high,
To come in sorrow's gloomiest day,
   To come when death is nigh.
Lord, in that day our guardian be,
And suffer us to come to thee.

He'll Carry us Through.*

No. 162.

"Looking unto Jesus, the author and finisher of our faith."

1. Yield not to tempta - tion, For weakness is sin; Each vict'ry will
2. Shun e- vil compan - ions, Bad language dis - dain, God's name hold in
3. To him that o'ercom - eth God giveth a crown; Thro' faith we shall

help us Some other to win; Fight manful-ly onward, Dark passions sub-
rev'rence, Nor take it in vain; Be thoughtful and earnest, Kind-hearted and
conquer, Tho' oft-en cast down; He who is our Saviour Our strength will re-

- due, Look ev - er to Je - sus, He'll car - ry you through.
true, Look ev - er, etc.
new, Look ev - er, etc.

Refrain.

Ask the Sav- iour to help you, Comfort, strengthen and keep you,

Repeat pp, ad lib.

He is will- ing to aid you, He will car - ry you through.

* From "Palmer's Sunday School Music," by permission.

8

The Good Shepherd.

No. 163   Dr. Thos. Hastings.

" He shall gather the lambs with his arm, and carry them in his bosom."

Quick, but Gentle.

1. Shep-herd, while thy flock are feed - ing, Take these

lambs In thine arms, For heaven's nur - ture plea -l- ing.

2. With thy chosen ones connected,
Oft they run,
Wand'ring on,
By the flock neglected.

3. Shepherd, every grace combining,
Keep these lambs
In thine arms,
On thy breast reclining.

O, How I Love Jesus!

(May be sung after any tune, where thought proper.)

O how I love Je - sus, O how I love Je - sus,

O how I love Je - sus, Be-cause he first loved me!

Days Going By. *

No. 164.   H. MILLARD.

"Work while 't is day."

Moderato con espress.

1. There are lonely hearts to cherish,   While the days are go-ing by,

There are wea-ry souls who per-ish,   While the days are go-ing by;

If   a smile we can re-new,   As   our jour-ney we   pur-sue,

Ol the good we all may do,   While the days are   go-ing   by.

Chorus.

While the days are go-ing by,   While the days are go-ing   by,

All may find a field, of   toil, While the days are go-ing by.

2 There 's no time for idle scorning,
  While the days are going by,
  Let your face be like the morning,
  While the days are going by;
  O! the world is full of sighs,
  Full of sad and weeping eyes;
  Help your fallen brother rise,
  While the days are going by.
  While the days, etc.

3 All the loving links that bind us,
  While the days are going by,
  One by one we leave behind us,
  While the days are going by;
  But the seeds of good we sow,
  Both in shade and shine will grow,
  And will keep our hearts aglow,
  While the days are going by.
  While the days, etc.

* Published in sheet form by CHAS. W. HARRIS, 481 Broadway, N. Y. Words by G. COOPER.

No. 165   **Jesus by the Sea.** *   Geo. F. Root.

" What manner of man is this? for he commandeth even the winds and the water, and they obey him."

1. O I love to think of Je - sus, as he sat beside the sea, Where the
waves were only murm'ring on the strand; When he sat within the boat, on the
sil - ver wave a-float, While he taught the waiting people on the land.

O I love to think of Je - sus by the sea, O I
love to think of Je-sus by the sea, And I love the precious Word, which he

* From "Chapel Gems," by permission.

JESUS BY THE SEA—*continued.*

spake to them that heard, While he taught the waiting people by the sea.

2 O I love to think of Jesus, as he
  walked upon the sea,
When the waves were rolling fearfully and grand ;
How the winds and waves were still
  at the bidding of his will,
While he brought his loved disciples
  to the land.

CHORUS.
O I love to think of Jesus by the sea ;
O I love to think of Jesus by the sea ;
How he walked upon the wave, his
  beloved ones to save,
While he brought them safely o'er the
  stormy sea.

3 O I love to think of Jesus, as he
  walked beside the sea,
Where the fishers spread their nets
  upon the shore ;
How he bade them follow him, and
  forsake the paths of sin,   [more.
And to be his true disciples ever-

CHORUS.
O, I love to think of Jesus by the sea ;
O, I love to think of Jesus by the sea;
And I long to leave my all, at the dear
  Redeemer's call,
And his true disciple evermore to be.

Our Little Talents.

No. 166

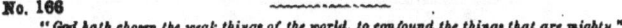

" God hath chosen the weak things of the world, to confound the things that are mighty."

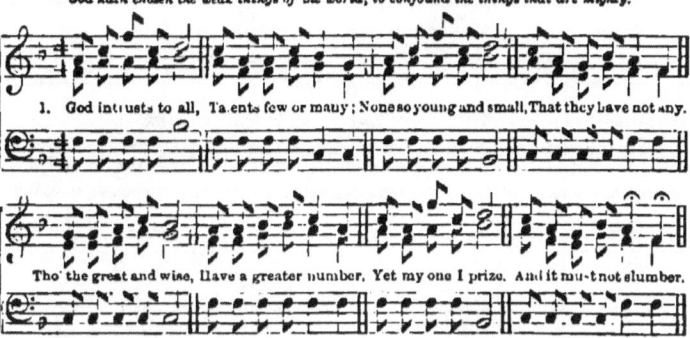

1. God intrusts to all, Talents few or many; None so young and small, That they have not any.

Tho' the great and wise, Have a greater number, Yet my one I prize. And it must not slumber.

2 Every little mite,
    Every little measure,
  Helps to spread the light,
    Helps to swell the treasure.
  Little drops of rain
    Bring the springing flowers ;
  And I may attain
    Much by little powers.

3 God intrusts to all,
    Talents few or many ;
  None so young and small,
    That they have not any.
  God will surely ask,
    Ere I enter heaven,
  Have I done the task
    Which to me was given ·

Climbing up Zion's Hill.

No. 167

Philip Phillips.

"They shall mount up with wings as eagles, and they shall walk and not faint."

1. I'm try-ing to climb up Zi-on's Hill, For the Sav-iour whispers, "Love me;"

Though all be-neath is dark as death, Yet the stars are bright a-bove me.

Then up-ward still, to Zi-on's Hill, To the land of joy and beau-ty,

My path be-fore shines more and more, As it nears the gold-en cit-y.

SOLO, or Semi-chorus. DUET, or 2d Semi-chorus. FULL CHORUS. Repeat Chorus.

I'm climbing up Zion's Hill, I'm climbing up Zion's Hill, Climbing, climbing, climbing up Zion's Hill.

2 I know I'm but a little child,
  My strength will not protect me;
But then I am the Saviour's lamb,
  And he will not neglect me.
Then all the time I'll try to climb
  This holy hill of Zion,
For I am sure the way is pure,
  And on it comes " no lion."—*Cho.*

3 Then come with me, we'll upward go,
  And climb this hill together;
And as we walk we'll sweetly talk,
  And sing as we go thither.
Then mount up still God's holy hill,
  Till we reach the pearly portals,
Where raptured tongues proclaim the songs
  Of the shining-robed immortals.—*Cho.*

Pilgrim on the Road.*

No. 168.   JAS. M. NORTH.

"For we seek a city which hath foundations."

1. I'm a pilgrim, pilgrim on the road, Lit-tle pilgrim on the road To the
2. I was burden'd, burden'd with a load, Heavy burden'd with a load When I
3. I was wea-ry, wea-ry of the load, Ver-y wea-ry of the load, As I

cit-y of our God; I have left the way of sin That I had long wander'd
started on the road : 'Twas the sin that I had done ; My own hand had laid it
totter'd o'er the road ; But the Saviour took the pack From the lit-tle pilgrim's

Refrain.

in, And I'm pressing tow'rd the land, the land of glory.   On, on, on ! I'm trav'ling
on Ere I started for the land, the land of glo-ry,   On, on, &c.
back, And I'm trav'ling on with lightsome heart to glory.   On, on, &c.

on ! On to glo-ry ! on to glo-ry ! I have left the way of sin That I

long have wander'd in, And I'm trav'ling to the land, the land of glo-ry.

* Words by Rev. H. O. M'COOK, by permission.

The Pilot.

No. 169

" The Lord shall guide thee continually."

1. Toss'd up-on life's rag-ing bil-low, Sweet it is, O
Thou the faith-ful watch art keep-ing, "All, all's well," thy

Lord, to con-stant know, cheer. } Thou did'st press a sail-or's pil-low,

And canst feel a sail-or's woe. Ne-ver slumb'ring

ne-ver sleep-ing, Though the night be dark and drear.

2.

And though loud the wind is howling,
  Fierce though flash the lightning's red:
Darkly though the storm-cloud's scowling
  O'er the sailor's anxious head ;
Thou canst calm the raging ocean,
  All its noise and tumult still,
Hush the tempest's wild commotion,
  At the bidding of thy will.

3.

Thus my heart the hope will cherish,
  While to thee I lift mine eye,
Thou wilt save me ere I perish,
  Thou wilt hear the sailor's cry.
And though mast and sail be riven,
  Life's short voyage will soon be o'er ;
Safely moored in heaven's wide haven,
  Storm and tempest vex no more.

None but Jesus.*

No. 170

Rev. R. Lowry.

"How shall we escape if we neglect so great salvation."

1. Weep-ing will not save me— Tho' my face were bathed in tears,
2. Work-ing will not save me— Pur-est deeds that I can do,

That could not al-lay my fears Could not wash the sins of years—
Ho-liest thought and feel-ings too, Can-not form my soul a-new—

CHORUS.

Weep-ing will not save me.   Jesus wept and died for me; Je-sus suffered
Work-ing will not save me.   Jesus wept, &c.

on the tree; Je-sus waits to make me free; He a-lone can save me.

3 Waiting will not save me—
Helpless, guilty, lost, I lie;
In my ear is mercy's cry;
If I wait I can but die—
Waiting will not save me.
Cho.—Jesus wept, &c.

4 Faith in Christ will save me—
Let me trust thy weeping Son,
Trust the work that he has done;
To his arms, Lord, help me run—
Faith in Christ will save me.
Cho.—Jesus wept, &c.

* By permission.

No. 171   ## How Shall I Die.   Philip Phillips.

" Prepare to meet thy God."

1. When, where, and how shall I die? In youth or in manhood, or when I shall stand O'er-mantled with age, with my staff in my hand? At morn, or at midnight, or when shall it be, Thou spir-it of truth, dare I hear it from thee? When, where, and how shall I die?

CHORUS or QUARTETTE.

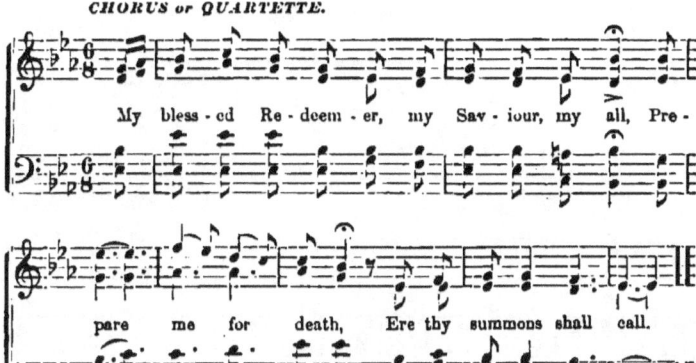

My bless - ed Re - deem - er, my Sav - iour, my all, Pre -
pare me for death, Ere thy summons shall call.

2.

When, where, and how shall I die?
Will strangers attend me, or kindred be near,
And voices that love me fall sweet on my ear?
Or shall I alone through the valley depart
With none to support me or comfort my heart?
When, where, and how shall I die?
Cho.—When o'er the dark river I pass from the shore,
  Go with me, dear Jesus,
  I ask for no more.

3.

When, where, and how shall I die?
By illness protracted, or hasty decline,
Will pain, or a tranquil departure be mine?
Will reason forsake me or conscience be clear,
Will hope or its angel of mercy be near?
When, where, and how shall I die?
Cho.—Oh, grant I may pillow my head on thy breast,
  Thou guide of the faithful,
  And God of the blest.

4.

When, where, and how shall I die?
Though solemn the question, the time, or the place,
'Twill matter but little if God, by his grace,
Will help me to labor, to watch, and to pray,
And wait for his coming; I know not the day,
When, where, and how I shall die.
Cho.—One blessing I crave, 'tis the greatest of all,
  Prepare me for death
  Ere thy summons shall call.

Guide. 7s.

No. 172.   M. M. WELLS.

"He will guide us into all truth."

1. { Ho - ly Spir - it, faith-ful Guide, Ev - er near the Christian's side;
    Gen - tly lead us by the hand, Pil-grims in a des - ert land. }
D. C. Whisp'ring soft - ly, wand'rer, come! Fol-low me, I'll guide thee home.

Wea - ry souls for - e'er re-joice, While they hear that sweetest voice;

2 Ever present, truest friend,
  Ever near, thine aid to lend,
  Leave us not to doubt and fear,
  Groping on in darkness drear,
  When the storms are raging sore,
  Hearts grow faint and hopes give o'er
  Whisper softly, wanderer, come!
  Follow me, I'll guide thee home.

3 When our days of toil shall cease,
  Waiting still for sweet release,
  Nothing left but heaven and prayer,
  Wondering if our names are there;
  Wading deep the dismal flood,
  Pleading naught but Jesus' blood;
  Whisper softly, wanderer, come!
  Follow me, I'll guide thee home.

Jesus Waits for Thee.*

No. 173.   H. P. MAIN.

"Ye would not come to me that ye might have life."

Tenderly.

1. Come, come to Jesus! He waits to welcome thee, O Wand'rer! eagerly; Come, come to Jesus!

2 Come, come to Jesus!
  He waits to ransom thee,
  O Slave! eternally;
  Come, come to Jesus!
3 Come, come to Jesus!
  He waits to lighten thee,
  O Burdened! graciously;
  Come, come to Jesus!
4 Come, come to Jesus!
  He waits to give to thee,

O Blind! a vision free;
  Come, come to Jesus!
5 Come, come to Jesus!
  He waits to shelter thee,
  O Weary! blessedly;
  Come, come to Jesus!
6 Come, come to Jesus!
  He waits to carry thee,
  O Lamb! so lovingly;
  Come, come to Jesus!

* From "HALLOWED SONGS"

"Keep on Praying."*

No. 174.

T. E. Perkins.

"Pray without ceasing."

1st Time.

1. { Long my spi - rit pined in sor-row, Watching, waiting all in vain;
   { Wait - ing for a gold-en morrow, (OMIT..............................

2d Time.

Free from earthly care and pain. When I heard a sweet voice saying, In the accents

of a friend, Cheer up, brother, "keep on praying," Keep on praying to the end.

Chorus.

When our wayward thoughts are straying, When God's mercy seems delaying,

Then in faith we'll keep on praying, Keep on praying, Keep on praying to the end.

2 Ye, who sigh for holy pleasures,
   Ye, who mourn your load of sin,
 "Keep on praying," heavenly treasures,
   In the end you're sure to win.
 Wrestle with the Lord of glory,
   Lay your troubles at his feet,
 Plead with faith in Calvary's story
   Till your joys are all complete.
     When our, etc.

3 How the angel band rejoices,
   When a kneeling mortal prays;
 Hear them cry in heavenly voices,
   "Keep on praying," all your days.
 Pray until you reach fair Canaan,
   Reach the pearly gates of day,
 Then your bliss shall end in glory,
   And shall never pass away.
     When our, etc.

* From "Sabbath Carols," by permission.

No. 175   # Battling for the Lord.   T. E. PERKINS.

" I must work the works of him that sent me while it is day ; the night cometh when no man can work."

1. We've list-ed in a ho-ly war, Battling for the Lord! E - ter-nal life, e -

ter-nal joy, Battling for the Lord! We'll work till Je-sus comes, We'll

work till Jesus comes, We'll work till Jesus comes, And then we'll rest at home.

2 Under our captain Jesus Christ,
Battling for the Lord !
We've listed for this mortal life,
Battling for the Lord !
We'll work, etc.

3 We'll fight against the powers of sin,
Battling for the Lord !
In favour of our heavenly King,
Battling for the Lord !
We'll work, etc.

4 And when our warfare here is o'er,
Battling for the Lord !
This strife we'll leave, and war no more,
Battling for the Lord !
We'll work, etc.

5 Our friends and kindred there we'll meet,
On the heavenly shore !
And ground our arms at Jesus' feet,
On the heavenly shore !
We'll work, etc.

CODA, FOR THE LAST VERSE.

Home, home, sweet, sweet home ! Prepare me, dear Saviour, for glory, my home.

Not with the Multitude.*

No. 176

REV. R. LOWRY.

"And seeing the multitude he went up into the mountain to pray."

1. { It is not with the mul - ti - tude, I feel my heart re - vive ;
   { It is not with the gid - dy throng, My soul is kept a - live ;

'Tis in the si - lent sa cred hour, When none but God is near,

My heart is fill'd with sa - cred love, And rev - e - ren - tial fear,

CHORUS.

Not with the mul - ti - tude, Not with the mul - ti - tude, No

place is so sweet as the mer - cy - seat, When none but God is near.

2 It is not with the multitude,
    I hear the still, small voice,
  Which whispers messages of love,
    And bids my heart rejoice:
  Oh, no; 'tis when withdrawn from earth,
    And every earth-bound tie,
  I heard thy kind parental voice,
    And "Abba, Father," cry.—*Cho.*

8 It is not with the multitude,
    My sweetest joys arise ;
  Nor even with the saints on earth,
    Though bound by sacred ties ;
  The fellowship of saints is sweet,
    But sweeter, better far,
  Is fellowship with Christ my Lord,
    The bright and Morning Star.—*Cho.*

* By permission.

Familiar Hymns.

No. 177.   Key E.

1 I HAVE a Father in the promised land,
   I have a Father in the promised land.
   My Father calls me ; I must go,
   To meet him in the promised land.
   I'll away, I'll away to the promised
      land ;
   My Father calls me ; I must go,
   To meet him in the promised land.

2 I have a Saviour in the promised land ;
   I have a Saviour in the promised land.
   My Saviour calls me ; I must go,
   To meet him in the promised land.
   I'll away, I'll away to the promised
      land !
   My Saviour calls me ; I must go,
   To meet him in the promised land.

4 I hope to meet you in the promised land,
   I hope to meet you in the promised land.
   At Jesus' feet a joyous band,
   We'll praise him in the promised land.
   We'll away, we'll away to the prom-
      ised land !
   At Jesus' feet a joyous band,
   We'll praise him in the promised land

No. 178.   Key G.

1 OH, do not be discouraged,
   For Jesus is your friend !
   Oh, do not be discouraged,
   For Jesus is your friend !
   He will give you grace to conquer,
   He will give you grace to conquer,
   And keep you to the end.

       CHORUS.

   I am glad I'm in this army,
   Yes, I'm glad I'm in this army,
   Yes, I'm glad I'm in this army,
   And I'll battle for the school.

2 Fight on, ye little soldiers,
   The battle you shall win ;
   Fight on, ye little soldiers,
   The battle you shall win ;
   For the Saviour is your Captain,
   For the Saviour is your Captain,
   And he has vanquished sin.
     I am glad, etc.

3 And when the conflict's over,
   Before him you shall stand ;
   And when the conflict's over,
   Before him you shall stand.
   You shall sing his praise forever,
   You shall sing his praise forever,
   In Canaan's happy land.
     I am glad, etc.

No. 179.   Key G.

1 AROUND the throne of God in heaven
   Thousands of children stand ;
   Children whose sins are all forgiven,
   A holy, happy band ;
   Singing glory, glory, glory.

2 What brought them to that world above,
   That heaven so bright and fair,
   Where all is peace, and joy, and love ?
   How came those children there ?
   Singing glory, glory, glory.

3 Because the Saviour shed his blood
   To wash away their sin ;
   Bathed in that pure and precious blood,
   Behold them white and clean ;
   Singing glory, glory, glory.

4 On earth they sought their Saviour's
     grace,
   On earth they loved his name ;
   So now they see his blessed face,
   And stand before the Lamb,
   Singing glory, glory, glory.

No. 180   *"Arlington."* Key G.

1 SEE Israel's gentle shepherd stands
   With all engaging charms ;
   Hark how he calls the tender lambs,
   And folds them in his arms.

2 Permit them to approach, he cries,
   Nor scorn their humble name ;
   For 'twas to bless such souls as these
   The Lord of angels came.

3 He'll lead us to the heavenly streams,
   Where living waters flow ;
   And guide us to the fruitful fields
   Where trees of knowledge grow.

4 The feeblest lamb amidst the flock
   Shall be its Shepherd's care ;
   While folded in the Saviour's arms,
   We're safe from every snare.

No. 181.   Key G.

1 WE are out on the ocean sailing,
   Homeward bound we sweetly glide,
   We are out on the ocean sailing
   To a home beyond the tide.

CHO. All the storms will soon be over,
   Then we'll anchor in the harbor ;
   We are out on the ocean sailing,
   To a home beyond the tide.

2 Millions now are safely landed,
   Over on the golden shore,
   Millions more are on the journey,
   Yet there's room for millions more.

3 When we all are safely anchored, [CHO.
   We will shout—our trials o'er,
   We will walk about the city,
   And we'll sing forevermore.—CHO.

NEW
STANDARD SINGER
PART V.
JOYFUL STRAINS

FOR
ANNIVERSARIES,
SUNDAY SCHOOL CONCERTS,
CELEBRATIONS,
JUBILEES, FESTIVALS, ETC.

BY
PHILIP PHILLIPS.

PHILIP PHILLIPS, Author and Publisher,
805 Broadway, New York.

HITCHCOCK & WALDEN,
Cincinnati, Chicago, and St. Louis.

TRIUMPH OF THE CROSS.*

" God forbid that I should glory save in the cross of our Lord Jesus Christ."

Words by FANNY CROSBY.

Music by F. C. GOUGH & P. PHILLIPS.

No. 182   No. 1 " Prepare, O Earth."

RECIT. Bass.

Pre - pare, O earth, the way of God pre - pare, And in the des - ert let his path be straight; For, lo! the sol - i - ta - ry place shall bloom, the wil - der - ness shall blos - som like the rose.

*A short oratorio for Sunday School Concerts.

No. 2. The Birth of Christ. (Angel Song.)

RECIT. Tenor.

Now came the blessed e - ra promised long, O'er Judah's plains the

Star of Ja-cob rose, And to the shepherds, lo! an an-gel said, Behold I

cres. *rall.* AIR.

bring glad tidings of great joy. *Moderato.*

1. Be not troubled at my pres-ence, Send your
2. Go and bow your-selves be-fore him, This to

i-dle fears a-way, Send your i-dle fears a-way;
you shall be the sign, This to you shall be the sign;

Lift your eyes and shout hosan-nas, Christ the Lord is born to-day,
Ye shall find him in a man-ger, In-fant Saviour, Lord di-vine,

Christ the Lord is born to-day.
In-fant Sav-iour, Lord divine.

No. 3. Chorus of Angels and Shepherds.

Wake, ye por - tals of the skies; An - gels, strike your harps a - gain: Glo - ry be to God on high, Peace on earth, good will to men. In - fant Sav - iour, might-y King, Lord of all, his praise we sing; Spread the joy - ful news a - far, See his glo - rious na - tal star!

ff CHORUS—Angels and Shepherds.

Wake, ye por-tals of the skies; An-gels, strike your
harps a-gain: Glo-ry be to God on high, Peace on
earth, good will to men. Hal-le-lu-jah! Hal-le-lu-jah!
Hal-le-lu-jah! Hal-le-lu-jah! Hal-le-lu-jah!
Hal-le-lu-jah! Hal-le-lu-jah! A - men.............

"And immediately there appeared with the angel a multitude of the heavenly hosts, praising God and saying, Glory to God in the highest, and on earth peace, good will towards men."

No. 4. Simeon and Christ in the Temple.

RECIT. Bass.

Lo! in the tem-ple ag-ed Simeon stood, And when the parents brought the holy child To make him there an offering to the Lord, He took him in his trembling arms, and said, "Oh, let thy servant, Lord, depart in peace, For thy sal-vation now mine eyes have seen."

No. 5. To us a Child is born.

CHORUS.

To us a Child is born, To us a Son is given, To us a Child is

born, To us a Son is given; Thro' him the na-tions shall re - joice, And

learn the way to heaven, And learn the way to heaven; To him shall monarchs

bow, And kings be - fore him fall, The Gen - tile world his power shall

see, And own him Lord of all, And own him Lord of all.

No. 6. His Baptism.

John,   from   Jor - dan's wave,   Be-hold the   Sav-iour rise, And
sore   temp - ta - tion past,   His mis-sion now be-gan, The

see   the   Spir - it,   like   a   dove,   De-scend - ing
glo - rious   work,   for which   he came,   To   res - cue

from the skies, De - scend - ing from........ the skies.
fall - en man, To res - cue fall - - - en man.

While from a cloud that cir - cled round, Proclaimed his Fa - ther's

voice, "Lo! this is my be - lov - ed Son,

In him be-lieve, re - joice,.... In him be-lieve, re-joice."

"AND there are many things that Jesus did, which if they were written every one, I suppose that even the world itself could not contain the books that should be written."

No. 7. His Miracles.

CHORUS. *Joyfully.*

Strew the way with palm - trees, To the ho - ly cit - ty;

Children in the tem - ple Make their arch - es ring.

Strew the way with palm - trees, Shout a - loud ho - san - na,

Bow the knee be - fore him, Sa - lem's might - y King;

Bow the knee be - fore him, Sa - lem's might - y King.

SOLO.—Tenor. *Andante.*

He whose smile re - flect- ing light, Turn'd to wine the wa - ter bright;

He who on the storm - y deep Hush'd the roll -ing waves to sleep;

Cleans'd the le - per by a word, Heal'd the sick, the deaf re- stored;

Repeat Chorus.

He who blest the loaves that fed Hung-ry souls with liv - ing bread.

SOLO. Bass. *Lento.*

He who touch'd the sa - ble bier, Dried the child-less wid- ow's tear,

He who then but gen - tly spoke, And her son to life a - woke,

Why re - buke the joy - ous song, Bursting from a grate-ful throng,

Rit. Repeat Chorus.

Cease to chide the gathering crowd, Or the stones will cry a - loud.

No. 8. His Betrayal.

RECIT. Tenor.

p Joy hides her face, The Sav-iour is be-

Largo.   dim - - -

trayed. By all de - serted, To the Judgment - hall is

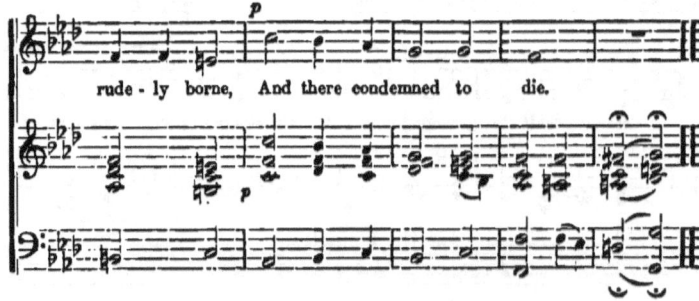

rude - ly borne, And there condemned to die.

No. 9. Christ's Sufferings.

DUET.—Soprano and Contralto.

Surely he has borne our grief, All our sorrows he has known, He was wounded

lento.

for our sins, And the winepress trod a-lone ; To the slaughter he was led,

He the pure, the just, the good, Though condemned he answered not, As a lamb he

meekly stood ; Tho' condemned he answered not, As a lamb he meekly stood.

No. 10. His Crucifixion, Death and Ascension.

And now at God's right hand a - bove, He pleads our cause ; O

won - drous love ! Re - demp - tion's glo - rious work is done, Free

Rit. - - - - *f Con spirito.*

grace to all, through Christ the Lord. Re - joice, O earth ! let

heaven re - joice, And shout a - loud in cho - ral voice, Our ris - en

Rit.

Lord the tomb for-sakes, The bonds of death tri - umph-ant breaks.

The Story of "Christian."*

No. 183
Words by FANNY CROSBY.

PHILIP PHILLIPS.

" Thy statutes have been my songs in the house of my pilgrimage."

With care-less step he hur-ries on A-long the path of sin; The

win-dows of his soul are closed, And all is dark with-in: On

per-il's aw-ful brink he stands, A chasm yawns be-low, A

Rit.

crag that scarce his feet will hold Hangs on that waste of woe.

* Theme from Bunyan's Pilgrim's Progress. A short Cantata for Sunday School Concerts, occupying fifteen minutes.

DUET.

Yet warned by conscience—see, he turns! She bids him quickly fly; God's

Yet see, he turns! She bids him quickly fly,

Spir - it pleads with ear-nest call—Why, sin - ner, wilt thou die! Con-

demned and lost, the weight of guilt Hangs heav-y on his soul; From

Si - nai's mount its lightning's flash, And loud its thun - ders roll.

SOLO. | *pp Echo rit.*   *pp*

"Where shall I go!" "I am the door," A still small voice re -

plies; He sees the cross— his bur-den falls—The Sav-iour bids him

rise ; He looks and won-ders—looks a - gain, His rap-ture, who can

speak ! While from his head the springs of joy Send wa - ter to his cheek.

CHORUS.—Soprano. *Allegro.*

And now he climbs, he climbs the toilsome hill, He nears the palace

Alto.

Tenor.

And now he climbs, he climbs the toilsome hill,

Bass.

pia.

fair, He nears the palace fair; He views, he views its mountains from a-

He nears the palace fair; He views, he views its mountains from a-

far, And feels the ge-nial air, And feels the ge-nial air; He

far, And feels the ge-nial air, And feels the ge-nial air; He

walks the vale and shade of death, And yet he fears no

walks the vale and shade of death, And yet he fears no

ill, And yet he fears no ill; A - pol - lyon by his

ill, And yet he fears no ill; A - pol - lyon by his

strong. ff

unis.

sword is crushed,Thro' God, thro' God he con-quers still, Thro'

sword is crushed,Thro' God, thro' God he con-quers still, Thro'

Faster.

God, thro' God, he con-quers still. And now be-

God, thro' God he con-quers still. And now be-

Faster.

side, be - side the tree of life, That grows in Beu- lah

side, be - side the tree of life,

land, That grows in Beulah's land, Where blooms, where blooms the

That grows in Beulah's land, Where blooms, where blooms the

p

gar - dens of the king, Be - hold the Pil - grim stands, Be -

gar - dens of the king, Be - hold the Pil - grim stands, Be -

Slower.

hold the Pil-grim stands: Now plunging in the dis - mal flood, Its

hold the Pil-grim stands: Now plunging in the dis - mal flood, Its

Slower.

unis.

wa - ters o'er him east, Its wa - ters o'er him cast; A

wa - ters o'er him cast, Its wa - ters o'er him cast; A

shout! he ris - es! mounts the air! And heav'n is gained at

shout! he ris - es! mounts the air! And heav'n is gained at

last,...... A shout! he ris - es! mounts the air! And

last...... A shout! he ris - es! mounts the air! And

heav'n is gained at last, And heav'n is gained at last.

heav'n is gained at last, And heav'n is gained at last.

Part VI.]   [Price 10 cents each. $8 per 100.

NEW STANDARD SINGER.

PART VI.

SONGS FOR THE RIGHT.

AGAINST
INTEMPERANCE,
LYING
STEALING,
SWEARING, ETC. ETC.

BY PHILIP PHILLIPS.

W. CHESHIRE.

PHILIP PHILLIPS, Author and Publisher,
805 BROADWAY, NEW YORK.

HITCHCOCK & WALDEN,
CINCINNATI, CHICAGO, AND ST. LOUIS.

Save the Fallen.

No. 184   S. J. Vail.

"They have wandered as blind men in the streets; they have polluted themselves with blood."

1. Lord, be-fore thy ho-ly al - tar, Now, thy blessing we implore,

Grant we may not faint or fal - ter 'Till our glo-rious work is o'er.

Sa-viour, help us; we are try - ing Souls im-mor-tal to re-claim;

Thro' intemp'rance they are dy - ing, Snatch them from its burning flame.

CHORUS.

Save the fall-en, make them so-ber; May they feel their sins forgiv'n;

SAVE THE FALLEN—*continued.*

When this transient life is o - ver, Give them, Lord, a place in heaven.

2.

Lo, the tempter now assailing
Hoary age and smiling youth !
Shall his cruel arts prevailing,
Stop the springs of hallowed truth ?
Lord, forbid it ! hear us pleading, —
Jesus, thou hast died to save ;
Let thy mercy interceding,
Keep them from a drunkard's grave.
Save the fallen, &c.

3.

O'er the hearts that pine with anguish,
Pour thy healing balm divine ;
O'er the wasted forms that languish,
Let the beams of comfort shine ;
In thy strength, if still united,
We the erring may restore,
Then intemp'rance, crushed and blighted,
We will banish from our shore.
Save the fallen, &c.

First Commandment with Promise.

No. 185

" Honour thy father and thy mother."

1. To thy father and thy mother Hon-our, love, and rev'r-ence pay ;

This command, before all other, Must a Christian child o - bey.

2.

Jesus Christ, my Lord, fulfilled it,
In his home at Nazareth,
So his heavenly Father willed it—
While a child he dwelt beneath.

3.

Help me, Lord, in this sweet duty,
Guide me in thy steps divine ;
Show me all the joy and beauty
Of obedience such as thine.

4.

Then, when years are gath'ring o'er them,
When they're sleeping in the grave—
Sweet will seem the love I bore them,
Right the rev'rence which I gave.

5.

All my wilful ways confessing,
Now I'd keep this first command—
Seek to win the appointed blessing—
Life within the promised land.

Swear not.

No. 186   PHILIP PHILLIPS.

"But above all things swear not, but let your yea be yea, and your nay, nay."

1. They took my Sav-iour's name in vain; A thorn was in each
2. Where pleas-ure lured the soul a-way, To leave the pleas-ant

cru-el word, That pierced his sa-cred brow a-gain, While
path of truth, The cold, the heart-less, and the gay, The

Refrain.

mer-cy trem-bled as she heard. They took my Saviour's
vet-'ran sire, the care-less youth— All took my Saviour's

name in vain, And nailed him to the cross a-gain.
name in vain, And nailed him to the cross a-gain.

3.

They took my Saviour's name in vain,
  In festive hall, in crowded street;
With idle jest, and song profane,
  They trod his law beneath their feet.
They took my Saviour's name in vain,
And nailed him to the cross again.

4.

Poor, sinful man, why wilt thou spurn
  Redeeming love, so pure and free!
Awake, repent, believe, return,
  While yet his Spirit pleads for thee.
Take not my Saviour's name in vain,
Or nail him to the cross again.

No. 187 **The Morning Star.** C.M.D. Geo. F. Root.

" We are troubled on every side, yet not distressed : we are perplexed, but not in despair."

1. Sol - dier of Christ, why thus cast down ? Why drops thy nerveless hand ?

Have faith and hope and courage gone ? Fear'st thou the a - lien band ?

Take heart, 'twill not be al-ways night : Thro' riv-en clouds a - far Gleams

down in rays of diamond light, The bright and morning star, The bright and morning star.

2 Seek not the ground in weak despair,
  Nor break 'neath suff'ring's rod ;
  The fight thou wagest is the care
  Of the all-loving God. [life;
Joy comes through sorrow ; death brings
  Peace rides on battle's car ;
  And beams, on darkest night of strife,
  The bright and morning star.
3 Press on the foe! God rules the years,
  Wrong shall not triumph long ;
  Expectant faith already hears
  Truth's glad, victorious song.

The nations soon shall own their king,
  The wise from near and far,
Once more to him their offerings bring—
  The bright and morning star.
4 Then fear not, Christian, for the right !
  Nor falter 'mid the fray ;
  For truth is victor : error's night
  Flies from the coming day.
Thine eye, thro' dust and tears may see
  On heaven's broad scroll afar,
The promise sure : "I'll give to thee
  The bright and morning star."

11

The Law of God.

No. 188   Arr. by Philip Phillips.

" Thou shalt keep therefore His statutes and His commandments."

I. God spake these words : O Israel, hear What I shall now com - mand :

Thy Lord and on - ly God am I, Who, with Al-migh-ty hand,

From E-gypt's land and from the house Of bond-age set thee free ;

And there-fore, Is - rael, thou shalt have None o - ther gods but me. *Resp.*

II.

Thou shalt no graven image make,
   Nor likeness shalt thou feign,
Of anything that heaven or earth
   Or watery deeps contain.
Thou shalt not bow thyself to them,
   Nor outward worship pay ;
Much less shalt thou in heart adore,
   And to an idol pray.
      Response—Have mercy, &c.

IV.

Remember thou the Sabbath day
   To keep with holy care :
Six days for labour thou shalt take,
   The seventh shalt revere.
The Lord thy God the seventh day
   His Sabbath did ordain,
In which thou shalt from every kind
   Of worldly work refrain.
      Response—Have mercy, &c.

(For Verse III. see following page.)

THE LAW OF GOD—*continued.*

III. The sa - cred name of God, thy Lord, Thou ne - ver shalt pro - fane;

For God will them not guilt-less hold Who take his name in vain. *Resp.*

(For Verse IV. see preceding page.)

V.
Thy parents honour, that thou may'st
Both long and happy live
In that bless'd land which God, thy Lord,
Did for thy dwelling give.
Response—Have mercy, &c.

VI.
Thou shalt not kill : avoid whate'er
To life would hurtful prove ;
To all mankind thou shalt perform
The offices of love.
Response—Have mercy, &c.

VII.
Adult'ry thou shalt not commit,
But keep thee chaste and clean :
The temples of the Lord must not
Defiled be with sin.
Response—Have mercy, &c.

VIII.
Thou shalt not steal : detest all fraud,
And never seek by wrong
To take unto thyself what to
Another doth belong.
Response—Have mercy, &c.

IX.
False witness thou shalt never bear
Against another's name ;
Hate lies, love truth, and e'er defend
Thy neighbour's honest fame.
Response—Have mercy, &c.

X.
Thou shalt not covet house or wife,
Or man, or maid, of his,
Or ox, or ass, or aught whereof
He rightful owner is.
Response—Have mercy, &c.

RESPONSE, TO BE SUNG AFTER EACH VERSE.

Have mer-cy on us, Lord, we pray, And all our hearts in - cline,

With di - li - gence and care to keep These right-eous laws of thine.

Do the Right.

No 199   PHILIP PHILLIPS.

" No man, having put his hand to the plough, and looking back, is fit for the kingdom of God."

1. Courage, brother, do not stumble, Though thy path be dark as night;

There's a star   to guide the humble; "Trust in God, and do the right."

Do the right,   Do the right,   "Trust in God, and do the right.'

2

Let the road be rough and dreary,
And its end far out of sight,
Foot it bravely! strong or weary,
"Trust in God, and do the right."
          Do the right, &c.

3.

Perish policy and cunning!
Perish all that fears the light!
Whether losing, whether winning,
"Trust in God, and do the right."
          Do the right, &c

4.

Trust no party, sect, or faction;
Trust no leaders in the fight:
But in ev'ry word and action,
"Trust in God, and do the right."
          Do the right, &c.

5.

Some will hate thee, some will love thee,
Some will flatter, some will slight;
Cease from man, and look above thee,
"Trust in God, and do the right."
          Do the right, &c.

No. 190 **Ten Commandments.** B. J. VAIL.

"And God spake these words, saying—"

1. Down the ages long departed, For a moment look and wonder; Listen to the

ten commandments, Louder far than Sinai's thunder, Hear a voice which speaks to thee,

rit. *rit.*

Thou shalt have no gods but me; Hear a voice which speaks to thee, Thou shalt have no gods but me.

2 See the clouds are round about him,
And the awful trumpet soundeth,
While the Lord upon the mountain,
His unchanging law propoundeth.
Jealous is thy God, and thou
To an idol shalt not bow.
Jealous is, etc.

3 Lo! he rides upon the tempest,
Death and hell themselves do fear him;
All the worlds he hath created,
When he speaketh, let us hear him.
Never shalt thou take the name
Of the Lord thy God in vain.
Never shalt, etc.

4 Standing by the quaking mountain,
All the hosts of Israel tremble;
In the presence of the holy,
Who can trifle or dissemble?
Thou shalt mind the Sabbath day
Keep it holy, hear him say.
Thou shalt, etc.

5 King of kings! Jehovah! Jireh!
Thou art God, there is no other;
From of old we hear thee saying,

Thou shalt honour Father, Mother,
That thy days full long may be
In the land God gives to thee.
That thy days, etc.

6 Awful words from Sinai sounding,
Who shall question or gainsay them?
Graven deep on marble tables,
Who shall dare to disobey them?
There, thou shalt not kill was writ,
Nor adultery commit.
There, thou shalt, etc.

7 Lo! he looks through all disguises;
Tears each flimsy veil asunder;
Like the lightning are his glances,
And his voice is like the thunder.
And to us he doth reveal
This his will, thou shalt not steal.
And to us, etc.

8 No false witness 'gainst thy neighbour
Shalt thou bear, and thou shalt never
Covet aught that he possesseth,
Saith thy God, who lives for ever;
The great God, who from on high
Waits to judge thee by-and-by.
The great God, etc.

No. 191   ## Depart from Me.

Theme by Miss M. Lindsay.   Arr. by Philip Phillips.

"Lord, Lord, open to us. But he answered and said, Verily, I say unto you I know you not."

Soprano.—*Solo or Chorus.*

Late, late, so late! and dark the night, and chill! Late, late, so late! But

Alto.

Late, late, so late! and dark the night, and chill! Late, late, so late! But

2d Voice.

we can en-ter still.   Too   late!   too   late, ye

we can en-ter still.

cannot en-ter now;   Too   late,   too   late, ye

can - not   en - ter   now.   No   light   had   we :   for

No   light   had   we :   for

that   we   do   repent,   And   learn-ing   this,   the   Bridegroom will   relent.

that   we   do   repent,   And   learn-ing   this,   the   Bridegroom will   relent.

2d Voice.

Too   late,   too   late,   ye   cannot   en-ter   now ;

Too   late,   too   late,   ye   cannot   en-ter   now.

Solo or Chorus.

No light! so late! and dark and chill the night; Oh, let us in, that

No light! so late! and dark nad chill the night; Oh, let us in, that

we may find the light, Oh, let us in, that we may find the light.

we may find the light, Oh, let · us in, that we may find the light.

2d Voice.

Too late, too late, ye cannot en-ter now,

Too late, Too late, ye cannot en-ter now.

Is not the Bridegroom still with grace replete? Oh, let us in, that

Is not the Bridegroom still with grace replete? Oh, let us in, that

supplicando.

we may kiss his feet; Oh, let us in, oh, let us in,

we may kiss his feet; Oh, let us in, oh, let us in,

ad lib.

Oh, let us in, tho' late, to kiss his feet.

Oh, let us in, tho' late, to kiss his feet.

2d Voice.

No! no! Too late, ye cannot en-ter now.

The Fountain.

No. 192   T. C. O'KANE.

" He shall separate himself from wine and strong drink."

1. A song to the fountain! Glad-ly glow-ing, free-ly flow-ing
2. A song to the fountain! Ev-er smiling, ne'er be-guil-ing!
3. A song to the fountain! Hail the treas-ure without meas-ure!
4. A song to the fountain! Sweetly sing-ing, glad-ly spring-ing;

Down from the moun-tain, Flow-ing fresh and free!
Down from the moun-tain, Flow-ing fresh and free!
Down from the moun-tain, Flow-ing fresh and free!
Down from the moun-tain, Flow-ing fresh and free!

Come to the foun-tain, Come to the foun-tain,

Chorus.

Come to the foun-tain, Come, oh come to the
Come, oh, come to the fountain, to the foun-tain,

Come, oh, come to the fountain, Oh, come to the

Come to the foun-tain

foun-tain, to the foun-tain }
Come to the foun-tain } Of Tem-per-ance with me.

foun-tain, to the foun-tain

No. 193 **Love not the World.** H. P. Main.

" For what is a man profited if he shall gain the whole world and lose his own soul ?"

1. Why should we co - vet the joy of a day— Things that will
fade in a moment a - way? Toiling for wealth and its honours to gain,

CHORUS.

Why are we liv-ing for trifles so vain? Trust not the world in its beauty ar -
- rayed, Though at our feet all its treasures be laid; What would it profit its
wealth to con - trol? What can we give in exchange for the soul?

2.
We have no promise that fame will endure.
Splendour will never our pardon secure.
Gold cannot brighten the gloom of the
grave.
Only the merits of Jesus can save.
Trust not the world, etc.

3.
Blessed are they who are lowly in heart ;
They, who like Mary, have chosen their
part ;
Learning of Jesus, their master above,
Lessons of patience, of meekness, and love.
Trust not the world, etc.

When to say "No."

     T. MARTIN TOWNE.

" I will instruct thee and teach thee in the way which thou shalt go."

1. No is a ver-y lit-tle word;   In one short breath we say it lit-tle word,

Sometimes 'tis wrong but often right,   So let me just-ly weigh it; oft-en right,

No I must say, when asked to swear, And no when asked to gam-ble;

No, when strong drink I'm asked to share, No, to a Sunday's ram-ble.

2 No, though I'm tempted sore to lie
Or steal, and then conceal it ;
And no to sin when darkness hides,
And I alone should feel it.
Whenever sinners would entice
My feet from paths of duty,
No, I'll unhesitating cry—
No. not for price or booty.

3 God watches how this little word
By every one is spoken,
And knows those children as his own
By this one simple token.
Who promptly utters No to wrong,
Says Yes to right as surely—
That child has entered wisdom's ways
And treads her path securely.

"Renounce the Cup."

No. 195
Arr. by PHILIP PHILLIPS.

" Ye shall drink no wine, neither ye nor your sons forever."

RECITATIVE.

1. A drunkard reached his cheerless home, The storm without was dark and wild, He forced his weeping wife to roam, A wand'rer friendless with her child; As thro' the falling snow she press'd, The babe was sleeping on her breast, The babe was sleeping on her breast.

2 And colder still the winds did blow,
   And darker hours of night came on,
And deeper grew the drifted snow,
   Her limbs were chilled, her strength was gone.
O God! she cried in accents wild,
   If I must perish, save my child;
If I must perish, save my child.

8 She stripped the mantle from her breast,
   And bared her bosom to the storm,
As round the child she wrapped the vest,
   She smiled to think that it was warm.
With one cold kiss, a tear of grief,
   The broken-hearted found relief,
The broken-hearted found relief.

4 At morn her cruel husband passed,
   And saw her on her snowy bed,
Her tearful eyes were closed at last,
   Her cheek was pale, her spirit fled;
He raised the mantle from the child,
   The babe looked up, and sweetly smiled,
The babe looked up, and sweetly smiled.

5 Shall this sad warning plead in vain?
   Poor thoughtless one, *it speaks to you;*
Now break the tempter's cruel chain,
   No more your dreadful way pursue:
Renounce the cup, to Jesus fly—
   Immortal soul, why will you die?
Immortal soul, why will you die?

We'll Work until we Die.

No. 196   T. Martin Towne.

" Whatsoever thy hand findeth to do do it with thy might."

1. We're looking unto Jesus, Our banner waves on high, And this our "watchword"
2. The "night of death" approaches, And angels in the sky   Re-peat the chorus

ev - er, We'll work un - til we die. We love our Master's ser-vice, And
ev - er, Go work un - til you die. "Come o - ver now and help us," The

"see-ing eye to eye," With grace divine to help us, We'll work until we die.
heathen loudly cry, And "looking un-to Je-sus," Go work un-til you die.

Refrain.

We'll work,   we'll work,   we'll work un-til we die, We'll work, we'll

We'll work, we'll work un-til we die, We'll work un-til we die, We'll work, we'll work un-

work,   we'll work un - til we die.

til we die, We'll work un - til we die.

3 The field is white to harvest,
The days are speeding by,
Go forth, be earnest workers,
And work until you die.
And when the strife is over,
Far up above the sky,
With Jesus, blessed Jesus,
We'll live and never die.—*Ref.*

O, Tell Me ' Not.

No. 197

T. C. O'KANE.

" For the drunkard and the glutton shall come to poverty."

1. O, tell me not of happiness, For me its smiles are o'er, My cup of sorrow now is full,

I shall be glad no more, I am a drunkard, old and vile, No hope is there for me.

Chorus.

Oh touch not, taste not, han-dle not, And thou shalt hap-py be,

Oh touch not, taste not, han-dle not, And thou shalt hap-py be.

2 My wife sits weeping in that home,
  Whence every joy hath fled ;
I hear her mild rebuking tone,
  O, would that I were dead !
Ah, she has died a thousand deaths,
  And shed sad tears for me.
Oh touch not, taste not, handle not,
  And she may happy be.

3 I 've children in their quiet grave,
  Some stayed behind to mourn ;
I would that they were in the land,
  Whence they could ne'er return ;
For they will rise to curse my name,
  No light, no love to see.
Oh touch not, taste not, handle not,
  And they shall happy be.

4 I 've lost my hope, I 've lost my trust,
  I 've broken every tie,
And I must wander through the world,
  A living death to die ;
My heart aches with a thousand pangs,
  Naught but despair I see.
Oh touch not, taste not, handle not,
  And thou shalt happy be.

5 We 've trod thro' many a devious path,
  Of sorrow, sin, and shame,
But there, beside the Temp'rance Pledge,
  We first restored our name.
And, brother, whosoe'er thou art,
  Stand fast, and thou shalt see
That he who tastes and handles not,
  May also happy be.

Who Hath Sorrows?

No. 198   HARVEY CAMP.

"They that tarry long at the wine."

1. Who hath sorrows? who hath woes? Who hath babblings? who hath strife?
2. Look not on the wine when red, When it foams and sparkles bright;
3. "I was stricken," thou shalt say, "Yet, when beat-en, felt no pain;

Careless wounds and fancied woes? Reddened eyes—em-bit-tered life?
Lo! it hides an ad-der's head, Like a ser-pent it will bite.
When shall wake the morning ray? I will seek it yet a-gain."

They that tar-ry at the wine; They that love the feast and song;
Wantons then will charm the eye, Things perverse thy heart disclose;
Lord, thy peo-ple's hearts in-cline To a-rouse from thoughtless ease;

They that various drinks combine— Ear-ly haste and tar-ry long.
On the bil-lows shalt thou lie, At the mast head seek re-pose.
Oh! as-sist the kind de-sign Of pre-vent-ing scenes like these.

Weep for the Fallen.*

No. 199 ENGLISH.

" Meekness, Temperance—Against such there is no law."

1. Weep for the fall-en! hang your heads in sor-row, And mournfully
2. Voic-es of wail-ing tell of hope-less anguish, While sorrowing

sing the requiem sad and slow. Thousands have perished by the fell destroyer;
mothers bid us onward go, Hark! to their accents, theirs the broken-hearted

Oh, weep for youth and beau-ty, Oh, weep for youth and beau-ty,
Who weep for youth and beau-ty, Who weep for youth and beau-ty,

Oh, weep for youth and beau-ty in the grave laid low!
Who weep for youth and beau-ty in the grave laid low!

3 Hear how they bid us sound the timely warning,
  While yet there is hope to shun the cup of woe.
For is it nothing, ye who see no danger,
  To weep for youth and beauty in the grave laid low?

4 Weep for the fallen; but amid your sorrow,
  Still point to the pledge that freedom can bestow,
Rescue the nation from the fell destroyer,
  For why should youth and beauty in the grave lie low?

* From "TEMPERANCE CHIMES."
12

Drinker, Turn.

     HARVEY CAMP.

" Wine is a mocker, strong drink is raging, and whosoever is deceived thereby is not wise."

Andante.—Flowing Style.

1. Drink - er, turn and leave your bowl; Turn and

save your death - less soul; From your lips the poi - son

fling— Dash a - way th' ac-curs - ed thing.

2 Husband! turn, nor let your feet
Enter that accursed retreat;
Look! your partner's tearful eye
Eloquently asks you, Why?

3 Brother! leave the place of glee;
Quickly, quickly turn and flee!
See your sister's swelling breast,
Deep with anxious fear distressed.

4 Father! turn; your prattler's voice
Bids you seek your fireside joys;
Leave the revel; homeward haste,
And those purer pleasures taste.

5 Fathers, brothers, husbands, come—
Help to banish from your home,
And from earth, the deadliest foe
That assails our peace below.

God Speed the Right.

No. 201   FROM THE GERMAN.

"And every man that striveth for the mastery is temperate in all things."

f With Spirit.

1. Now to heaven our prayer ascending, God speed the right!
In a no - ble cause contending, God speed the right!
2. Be that prayer a - gain re - peat-ed, God speed the right!
Ne'er de - spair-ing though defeat - ed, God speed the right!

Be their zeal in heaven record - ed, With suc-cess on earth re - warded.
Like the good and great in sto - ry, If they fall, they fall with glo - ry.

ff

God speed the right! God speed the right!

3 Patient, firm, and persevering,
   God speed the right!
Ne'er the event our danger fearing,
   God speed the right!
Pains, nor toils, nor trials heeding,
And in heaven's own time succeeding.
   God speed the right!

4 Still their onward course pursuing,
   God speed the right !
Every foe at length subduing,
   God speed the right!
Truth, thy cause, whate'er delay it,
There 's no power on earth can stay it.
   God speed the right!

Familiar Hymns.

No. 202.   *Tune, " Boylston," Key C.*

1 How long, O Lord, our God,
  Shall sin and sorrow reign,
And drunkards love to tread the road
  That leads to endless pain.

2 With zeal and pity move,
  All those that fear thy name,
So shall they spread the cause of love
  The drunkard to reclaim.

3 Thy goodness and thy power,
  And mercy never cease;
Thou canst the drunkard yet restore
  To happiness and peace.

4 Come, and strong drink remove,
  And bring the better day,
When all men shall thy precepts love,
  And thy commands obey.

No. 203.   *Tune, " Hamburg," Key F.*

1 Slavery and death the cup contains;
  Dash to the earth the poisoned bowl;
Softer than silk are iron chains
Compared with those that chafe the soul.

2 Hosannas, Lord! to thee we sing,
  Whose power the giant fiend obeys;
What countless thousands tribute
  bring,
For happier homes and brighter days.

3 Thou will not break the bruised reed,
  Nor leave the broken heart unbound,
The wife regains a husband freed,
  The orphan clasps a father found.

4 Spare, Lord, the thoughtless, guide
    the blind;
Till man no more shall deem it just,
To live, by forging chains to bind
  His weaker brother in the dust.

No. 204.   *Tune, " Hebron," Key B♭.*

1 Let temperance and her sons rejoice,
  And be their praises loud and long,
Let every heart and every voice,
  Conspire to raise a joyful song.

2 And let the anthem rise to God,
  Whose favoring mercies so abound,
And let his praises fly abroad,
  The circuit of the earth around.

3 His children's prayer he deigns to grant,
  He stays the progress of the foe,
And temperance like a cherished plant,
  Beneath his fostering care shall grow.

No. 205.   *Tune, " Webb," Key B♭.*

1 Lift high the temperance banner!
  Aye, proudly let it wave,
To save the poor inebriate
  From a degraded grave.
Then, children, at your station,
  To quell the raging storm;
Let hearts and hands united
  Strive for a glad reform.

2 Come, join the noble army,
  Enlist now for the fight;
Maintain our nation's honor,
  Firm stand ye for the right.
Promote the cause of temperance,
  T' assist poor, fallen man;
Put on the glorious armor;
  Be foremost in the van.

3 Then rally round the standard,
  And let the work go on,
Until the last dim vestige
  Of intemperance is gone.
Be earnest in the battle,
  Your weapons boldly wield;
You'll surely gain the victory,
  And make the monster yield.

No. 206.   *Tune, " Old Hundred," Key G.*

1 Great God, whose hand outpours the
    rills
And springs that burst from all the hills,
At whose command the rock was riven,
Who send'st on all thy rain from
    heaven.

2 We bless thee for the crystal draught
By sinless man in Eden quaffed :
Type of that fount whose streams,
    above
Flood endless worlds with life and love!

3 Help us to heed Thy word divine,
And look not on the crimson wine,
To fear and flee th' accursed thing
As serpent's bite or adder's sting.

4 Stay thou, O Lord! the tide of death!
Rebuke the demon's blasting breath!
And speed, oh! speed, on every shore,
The day when strong drink slays no
    more!

New

Standard Singer

PART-VII.

SERVICE OF SONG

FOR
SUNDAY SCHOOL CONVENTIONS,
PRAYER AND SOCIAL
MEETINGS,
DUTY OF TEACHERS,
MEETING AND PARTING.

BY PHILIP
PHILLIPS

PHILIP PHILLIPS, Author and Publisher,
805 Broadway, New York.

HITCHCOCK & WALDEN,
Cincinnati, Chicago, and St. Louis.

No. 207

Fear God. C.M.

R. SIMPSON.

" The fear of the Lord is the beginning of wisdom."

1. Cre - a - tor, Sov'reign Lord of all, In earth and sea and skies,

The source of wis - dom is thy fear, Oh make us tru - ly wise.

2. Teach us to know thy perfect law,
   Whose judgments truth unfold,
   More sweet than honey in the comb,
   More precious far than gold.

3. Lo! wisdom crieth at the gate,
   And spreads her hands abroad;
   O, hear the voice, ye sons of men,
   And learn the fear of God.

No. 208

Blest be the Tie. S.M.

NAGELI.

" Behold how good and how pleasant it is for brethren to dwell together in unity."

1. Blest be the tie that binds Our hearts in Christian love;

The fel - low - ship of kin - dred minds, Is like to that a - bove.

2. Before our Father's throne,
   We pour our ardent prayers,
   Our fears, our hopes, our aims are one,
   Our comforts and our cares.

3. When we asunder part,
   It gives us inward pain;
   But we shall still be joined in heart,
   And hope to meet again.

No. 209 **Rock of Ages.** 7's (6 lines). Dr. T. Hastings.

"But the Lord is my defence, and my God is the rock of my refuge."

1. Rock of A - ges! cleft for me, Let me hide my-self in Thee:
D.C. Be of sin the per-fect cure; Save me, Lord, and make me pure.

Let the wa - ter and the blood, From thy wound-ed side which flowed,

2 Should my tears for ever flow,
Should my zeal no languor know,
This for sin could ne'er atone ;
Thou must save, and thou alone ;
In my hand no price I bring,
Simply to thy cross I cling.

3 While I draw this fleeting breath,
When mine eyelids close in death
When I rise to worlds unknown,
And behold thee on thy throne,
Rock of Ages! cleft for me,
Let me hide myself in thee.

No. 210 **Father, Take my Hand.** Geo. B. Loomis.

"As for me, I will call upon God, and the Lord shall save me."

Fa - ther, I stretch my hand to thee No other help I know ;

If thou withdraw thy - self from me, Ah! whither shall I go?

2 Surely thou canst not let me die ;
O speak, and I shall live ;
And here I will unwearied lie,
Till thou thy Spirit give.

3 How would my fainting soul rejoice,
Could I but see thy face ;
Now let me hear thy quick'ning voice,
And taste thy pard'ning grace.

Realms of the Blest. 8's.

" It doth not yet appear what we shall be."

1. We sing of the realms of the blest, That country so bright and so fair,

And oft are its glo-ries confessed,—But what must it be to be there?

But what, But what, But what must it be to be there?

And oft are its glories confessed,—But what must it be to be there?

2.	3.
We speak of its service of love,	Do thou, Lord, 'midst pleasure or woe,
Of robes which the glorified wear—	For heaven our spirits prepare ;
The church of the first-born above,	And shortly we also shall know,
But what must it be to be there?	And feel what it is to be there.

No. 212 ### Welcome Home. C. M. Arranged.

"Come, ye blessed of my Father, inherit the kingdom prepared for you."

1. Give me the wings of faith to rise Within the veil, and see The
2. Once they were mourners here below, And pour d out cries and tears; They

saints a-bove, how great their joys, How bright their glories be.
wrestled hard, as we do now, With sins, and doubts, and fears.

CHORUS.

They'll sing their welcome home to me, They'll sing their welcome home to me,

And the angels will stand on the heavenly strand, And sing their welcome home.
D.C. And the angels will stand on the heavenly strand, And sing their welcome . . home.

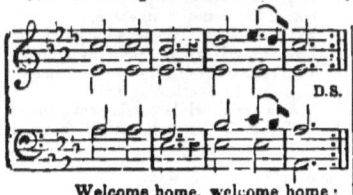

Welcome home, welcome home;

3 I ask them whence their vict'ry came:
They, with united breath,
Ascribe their conquest to the Lamb—
Their triumph to his death.

4 Our glorious Leader claims our praise
For his own pattern given;
While the long cloud of witnesses
Show the same path to heaven.

Sweet Hour of Prayer.

No. 213   WM. B. BRADBURY.*

"Evening, morning, and noon will I pray."

1. Sweet hour of prayer! sweet hour of prayer! That calls me from a
world of care, And bids me at my Fath-er's throne Make
all my wants and wish-es known: In sea-sons of distress and grief, My soul has oft-en found re-lief;

D. C. And oft es-caped the tempter's snare By thy re-turn sweet
hour of prayer; And oft es-caped the tempter's snare By
thy re-turn, sweet hour of prayer.

2. |: Sweet hour of prayer! :|
Thy wings shall my petition bear,
To him whose truth and faithfulness,
Engage the waiting soul to bless;
And since he bids me seek his face,
Believe his word, and trust his grace,
|: I'll cast on him my every care,
And wait for thee, sweet hour of
prayer! :|

3. |: Sweet hour of prayer! :|
May I thy consolation share,
Till from Mount Pisgah's lofty height,
I view my home and take my flight:
This robe of flesh I'll drop, and rise
To seize the everlasting prize;
|: And shout, while passing thro' the air,
Farewell, farewell, sweet hour of
prayer! :|

* From Fresh Laurels, by permission of BIGLOW & MAIN.

With me Abide.

No. 214   Arr. by Phillips.

" Abide with us; for it is towards evening, and the day is far spent."

1. A - bide with me; fast falls the ev - en - tide: The darkness deep - ens; Lord, with me a - bide; When oth - er help - ers fail, and comforts flee, Help of the helpless, oh, a - bide with me.

2 Swift to its close ebbs out life's little day;
Earth's joys grow dim, its glories pass away;
Change and decay in all around I see,
O thou who changest not—abide with me.

3 Thou on my head in early youth didst smile,
And, though rebellious and perverse meanwhile,
Thou hast not left me oft as I left thee;
On to the close, O Lord, abide with me.

4 I need thy presence every passing hour,
What but thy grace can foil the tempter's power;
Who like thyself my guide and stay can be,
Through clouds and sunshine—oh, abide with me.

5 Hold on thy cross, before my closing eyes;
Shine through the gloom, and point me to the skies;
Heaven's morning breaks, and earth's vain shadows flee,
In life and death, O Lord, abide with me.

Waiting by the River.

No. 215　　　　　　　　　　　　　　　　　Dr. Thos. Hastings.

" There shall be no more death."

1. I am wait-ing by the riv-er, And my heart has waited long; Now I
think I hear the cho-rus Of the an-gels' wel-come song; Oh, I
see the dawn is breaking On the hill-tops of the blest, "Where the
wick - ed cease from troubling, And the wea - ry be at rest."

2.

Far away beyond the shadows
　Of this weary vale of tears,
There the tide of bliss is sweeping
　Thro' the bright and changeless years;
Oh! I long to be with Jesus,
　In the mansions of the blest,
" Where the wicked cease from troubling,
　And the weary be at rest."

3.

They are launching on the river,
　From the calm and quiet shore,
And they soon will bear my spirit
　Where the weary sigh no more;
For the tide is swiftly flowing,
　And I long to greet the blest,
" Where the wicked cease from troubling,
　And the weary be at rest."

Title Clear.

No. 216.   Freedmen's Melody arr. with Cho. by T. C. O'KANE.

"I know that my Redeemer liveth."

1. When I can read my ti-tle clear, ti-tle clear, When I can read my ti-tle
   I'll bid farewell to ev-ery fear, ev-ery fear, I'll bid farewell to ev-ery

clear, ti-tle clear, When I can read my ti-tle clear, To mansions in the skies,)
fear, ev-ery fear, I'll bid farewell to every fear, And wipe my weeping eyes,)

Cho. We will stand   the   storm,   We will
We will stand, stand the storm, It will not be ver-y long; We will

an - - chor   by and   by,   by and by, We will
an - chor by   and   by, We will an - chor by and by, We will

stand   the   storm,   We will anchor by and by.
stand, stand the storm; It will not be very long, We will anchor by and by, by and by.

2 Let cares like a wild deluge come,
  Let storms of sorrow fall—
  So I but safely reach my home,
  My God, my heaven, my all.

8 There I shall bathe my weary soul
  In seas of heavenly rest,
  And not a wave of trouble roll
  Across my peaceful breast.

Mansions Blest

No. 217   Music and Words by Dr. Thos. Hastings.

"In my Father's house are many mansions."

1. Oh,.. there are mansions blest, Tow'-ring a-bove,
Where saints de-part-ed rest In Je-sus' love;
There, there with joys un-told, His glo-ry they be-hold,
Prais-ing with harps of gold, Heaven's bliss to prove.

2 In that celestial home
  May we appear,
Where sorrows never come,
  Or guilt or fear:
Oh, what a holy place,
When all the ransomed race
Sing of redeeming grace,
  Jesus is there.

3 There, in that spirit land
  All, all is pure,
Pleasures at God's right hand,
  Ever endure.

There all in Christ complete
God's happy children meet,
Angels and friends to greet,
  Resting secure.

4 None, none can enter heaven,
  Who live in sin;
None who are unforgiven,
  Can dwell therein.
Oh! thou to Jesus fly,
His pard'ning blood is nigh,
On him alone rely,
  Wash and be clean.

Bartimeus. 8s and 7s.

No. 218

DANIEL READ.

"God forbid that I should glory, save in the cross of our Lord."

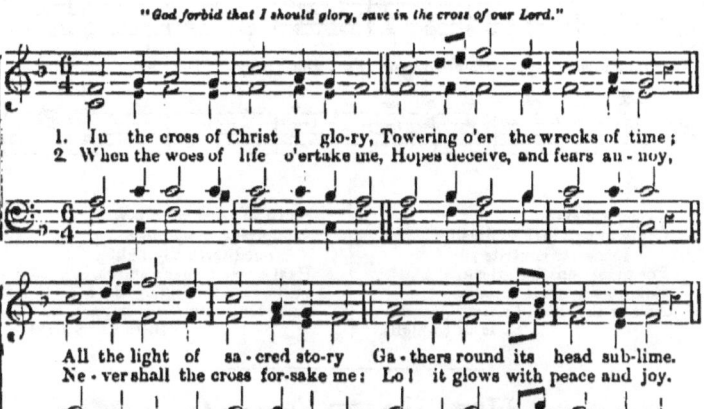

1. In the cross of Christ I glo-ry, Towering o'er the wrecks of time ;
2. When the woes of life o'ertake me, Hopes deceive, and fears an - noy,

All the light of sa - cred sto-ry Ga - thers round its head sub-lime.
Ne - ver shall the cross for-sake me: Lo! it glows with peace and joy.

3.	4.
When the sun of bliss is beaming	Bane and blessing, pain and pleasure,
Light and love upon my way,	By the cross are sanctified ;
From the cross the radiance streaming,	Peace is there, that knows no measure,
Adds new lustre to the day.	Joys that through all time abide.

No. 219

Bless Us To-night.

"He will bless them that fear the Lord."

1. Fa-ther of love and power, Guard thou our eve - ning hour, Shield

with thy might. For all thy care this day, Our grate-ful

BLESS US TO-NIGHT—*continued.*

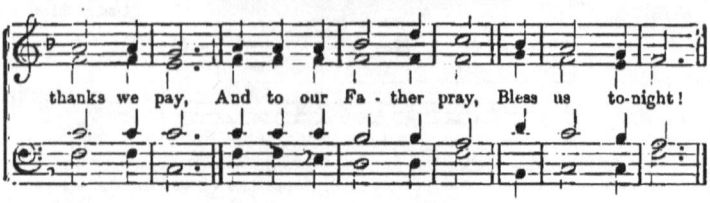

thanks we pay, And to our Fa-ther pray, Bless us to-night!

2.	3.
Jesus, Emmanuel,	Spirit of truth and love,
Come in thy love to dwell	Life-giving, holy dove,
In hearts contrite ;	Shed forth thy light ;
For many sins we grieve,	Heal every sinner's smart,
But we thy grace receive,	Still every throbbing heart,
And in thy word believe, —	And thine own peace impart, —
Bless us to-night.	Bless us to-night.

No. 220　　　**New Haven.**　6s and 4s.

DR. THOS. HASTINGS.

"Have faith in God."

My faith looks up to thee, Thou Lamb of Cal-va-ry, Saviour di-vine! Now hear me while I pray, Take all my guilt away, O let me from this day, Be wholly thine.

2.	3.
May thy rich grace impart	While life's dark maze I tread,
Strength to my fainting heart ;	And griefs around me spread,
My zeal inspire :	Be thou my guide ;
As thou hast died for me,	Bid darkness turn to day ;
O may my love to thee	Wipe sorrow's tears away,
Pure, warm, and changeless be—	Nor let me ever stray
A living fire.	From thee aside.

Congregational Chorus.

No. 221

PHILIP PHILLIPS.

"Let the people praise thee, O God, let all the people praise thee."

1. Yes, let our con-gre-ga-tions sing, And let our earthly temples ring With
2. O rapturous mu-sic, how sublime! I wept and thought the olden time Of

hymns of joy from ev-ery soul, In ev-ery church from pole to pole, Let
Watts' and Wesley's earnest throng Had with its flame inspired the song; O,

all u-ni-ted join, and raise This old fa-mil-iar song of praise.
let us sing with one ac-cord, Join heart and voice to praise the Lord.

CORONATION. Chorus to 1st Verse.
Firm.

1. O, for a thousand tongues to sing My great Redeemer's praise: The glories of my God and King,

The triumphs of his grace. The glories of my God and King, The triumphs of his grace.

OLD HUNDRED. Chorus to 2d Verse.

1. Praise God, from whom all blessings flow: Praise him, all creatures here below;

Praise him a-bove, ye heavenly host; Praise Father, Son, and Holy Ghost.

13

Calling us Away.

No. 222.

WALTER KITTRIDGE.

"Here we have no continuing City."

SOLO.

1. Give me the wings of faith to rise, Within the veil, and see The
2. Once they were mourners here be-low, And pour'd out cries and tears; They
3. I ask them whence their vict'ry came: They, with u-nit-ed breath, As-

saints a-bove, how great their joys, How bright their glories be.
wres-tled hard, as we do now, With sins, and doubts, and fears.
cribe their con-quest to the Lamb,—Their triumph to his death.

DUET.

Ma-ny are the friends, Who are wait-ing to-day,

CHORUS to each verse.

Hap-py on the gold-en strand; Ma-ny are the voi-ces

Call-ing us a-way, To join their glorious band; Calling us a-way,

Repeat Chorus pp

Call-ing us a-way, Call-ing to the bet-ter land.

Home of the Soul.*

No. 223

PHILIP PHILLIPS.

" And there shall in no wise enter into it anything that defileth, neither whatsoever worketh abomination or maketh a lie; but they which are written in the Lamb's Book of Life."

1. I will sing you a song of that beau-ti-ful land, The far a - way home of the soul, Where no storms ever beat on the glittering strand, While the years of e - ter - ni-ty roll. While the years of e - ter - ni-ty roll.

2.
O that home of the soul in my visions and dreams,
 Its bright jasper walls I can see,
Till I fancy but thinly the veil intervenes,
 Between the fair city and me.
 Between the fair city, &c.

3.
There the great tree of life in its beauty doth grow,
 And the river of life floweth by :
For no death ever enters that city, you know,
 And nothing that maketh a lie.
 And nothing that, &c.

4.
That unchangeable home is for you and for me,
 Where Jesus of Nazareth stands;
The king of all kingdoms forever is he,
 And he holdeth our crowns in his hands.
 And he holdeth, &c.

5.
O how sweet it will be in that beautiful land,
 So free from all sorrow and pain !
With songs on our lips and with harps in our hands,
 To meet one another again.
 To meet one another, &c.

" Now I saw in my Dream that these two men went in at the Gate: and lo, as they entered, they were trans-figured, and they had Raiment put on that shone like Gold. There was also that met them with Harps and Crowns, and gave them to them, the Harps to praise withal, and the Crowns in token of honor. Then I heard in my Dream that all the Bells in the City rang again for joy, and that it was said unto them, *Enter ye into the joy of your Lord.* Now just as the Gates were opened to let in the men, I looked in after them, and behold, the City shone like the Sun; the Streets also were paved with Gold, and in them walked many men, with Crowns on their heads, Palms in their hands, and golden Harps to sing praises withal. After that they shut up the Gates Which when I had seen, I wished myself among them."

* Taken from the " SINGING PILGRIM."

We'll Meet and Rest.

No. 224   PHILIP PHILLIPS.*

"There remaineth therefore a rest to the people of God."

1. Where the fa - ded flow'r shall freshen—Freshen ne - ver more to fade;
2. Where no sha - dow shall be-wil-der; Where life's vain parade is o'er;

Where the sha - ded sky shall brighten —Brighten ne - ver more to shade.
Where the sleep of sin is bro-ken, And the dream-er dreams no more;

Where the sun-blaze ne - ver scorch-es; Where the star-beams cease to chill;
Where the bond is ne - ver se-ver'd—Part-ings, clasp-ings, sob and moan—

Where no tem - pest stirs the e-choes   Of the wood, or wave, or hill;
Midnight wak - ing, twilight weeping,   Heavy noon-tide—all are done;

* These beautiful verses were handed to me by the author, Rev. H. Bonar, while at his home in Edinburgh, Scotland.

WE'LL MEET AND REST—*continued.*

Where the morn shall wake in glad-ness, And the noon the joy pro-long;
Where the child has found its mo-ther; Where the mo-ther finds the child!

Where the day-light dies in fragrance, 'Mid the burst of ho-ly song:
Where dear fam-i-lies are gather'd, That were scatter'd ou the wild:

REFRAIN.

Bro-ther, we shall meet and rest 'Mid the ho-ly and the blest!

3.

Where the hidden wound is healed;
Where the blighted life reblooms;
Where the smitten heart the freshness
Of its buoyant youth resumes;
Where the love that here we lavish
On the withering leaves of time,
Shall have fadeless flowers to fix on
In an ever spring-bright clime;
Where we find the joy of loving,
As we never loved before—
Loving on, unchill'd, unhinder'd—
Loving once and evermore:
Brother, we shall meet and rest
'Mid the holy and the blest!

4.

Where a blasted world shall brighten,
Underneath a bluer sphere,
And a softer, gentler sunshine
Shed its healing splendour here;
Where earth's barren vales shall blossom,
Putting on their robes of green,
And a purer, fairer Eden
Be where only wastes have been;
Where a King in kingly glory,
Such as earth has never known,
Shall assume the righteous sceptre,
Claim and wear the holy crown:
Brother, we shall meet and rest
'Mid the holy and the blest!

Why Not To-night? 8's.

No. 225

PHILIP PHILLIPS.

" Choose ye this day whom ye will serve."

1. Oh! do not let the word depart, And close thine eyes against the light;

Poor sinner, harden not thy heart; Thou wouldst be sav'd—why not to-night?

Why not to-night? why not to-night? Thou wouldst be sav'd—why not to-night?

2 To morrow's sun may never rise
To bless thy long deluded sight;
This is the time! Oh, then be wise!
Thou would'st be saved—Why not to-
night?

3 The world has nothing left to give—
It has no new, no pure delight;
Oh, try the life which Christians live!
Thou would'st be saved—Why not to-
night?

4 Our God in pity lingers still,
And wilt thou thus His love requite?
Renounce at length thy stubborn will.
Thou would'st be saved—Why not to-
night?

5 Our blessed Lord refuses none
Who would to Him their souls unite;
Then be the work of grace begun!
Thou would'st be saved—Why not to-
night?

Jordan's Ford.*

No. 226

REV. R. LOWRY.

" He cometh forth like a flower and is cut down."

1. Dark is many a day below, Thick the clouds that hover; Sad is many a
2. How the flitting hopes of earth, Hold us in de - ris - ion, When they draw us
3. Inward rolls the bitter surge, Drenching hearts with sorrow, Moanful flies the

bosom's throe, 'Neath its sackcloth cov - er; Wintry blasts with cruel doom,
thro' the dearth, To their false E - ly - sian! How the scenes in worldly glare,
night-ly dirge O - ver each to - mor - row; Low the plaint that sadly steals

Nip the plants we cherish, Buds of rare and sweet perfume Bloom awhile and perish.
Lure to disappoint us, Tempt our steps with visions fair, And with tears anoint us!
Over joys entombing; Drear the soul that never feels Flowers of glory blooming.

CHORUS.

But, be-yond the Jor - dan's ford, Shines the heavenly por - tal,

Where the ransomed of the Lord Pass in joys im - mor - tal

* By permission from Chapel Melodies.

No. 227   **St. Thomas. S.M.**   WILLIAMS.

" I will praise thee, O Lord, with my whole heart."

1. A - wake and sing the   song   Of   Mo - ses   and the   Lamb;
2. Sing of   his dy - ing love,   Sing   of his   ris - ing power:

Wake, ev - ery heart and ev - ery tongue, To praise the   Sa - viour's name.
Sing how he   in - ter-cedes a - bove   For those whose sins he   bore.

<table>
<tr><td>

3.

Soon shall we hear him say
Ye blessed children, come ;
Soon will he call us hence, away
  To our eternal home.

</td><td>

4.

There shall each raptured tongue
His endless praise proclaim ;
And sweeter voices tune the song
  Of Moses and the Lamb.

</td></tr>
</table>

No. 228.

1

I LOVE thy kingdom, Lord,
    The house of thine abode,
The church our blest Redeemer saved
    With his own precious blood.

2

I love thy church, O God,
    Her walls before thee stand,
Dear as the apple of thine eye,
    And graven on thy hand.

3

For her my tears shall fall,
    For her my prayers ascend,
To her my cares and toils be given,
    Till toils and cares shall end.

No. 229

1.

MY soul, repeat his praise,
    Whose mercies are so great,
Whose anger is so slow to rise,
    So ready to abate.

2.

His power subdues our sins,
    And his forgiving love,
Far as the east is from the west,
    Doth all our guilt remove.

3.

High as the heavens are raised
    Above the ground we tread,
So far the riches of his grace
    Our highest thoughts exceed.

No. 230

Hebron. L.M.

Dr. L. Mason.

" Truly my soul waiteth upon God, from him cometh my salvation."

1. Je-sus, where'er thy peo-ple meet, There they be-hold thy mer-cy seat;

Where'er they seek thee, thou art found, And every place is hallow'd ground.

2

For thou within no walls confined,
Dost dwell with those of humble mind;
Such ever bring thee where they come,
And going, take thee to their home.

3

Great Shepherd of thy chosen few,
Thy former mercies here renew;
Here to our waiting hearts, proclaim
The sweetness of thy saving name.

No. 231

1

THUS far the Lord hath led me on—
Thus far his power prolongs my days;
And every evening shall make known
Some fresh memorial of his grace.

2

Much of my time has run to waste,
And I, perhaps, am near my home:
But he forgives my follies past,
And gives me strength for days to come.

3

Thus, when the night of death shall come,
My flesh shall rest beneath the ground,
And wait thy voice to rouse my tomb,
With sweet salvation in the sound.

No. 232

1

HOW blest the sacred tie that binds
In sweet communion kindred minds:
How swift the heavenly course they run,
Whose hearts, whose faith, whose hopes
are one.

2

To each, the soul of each how dear!
What tender love, what holy fear,
How does the generous flame within
Refine from earth, and cleanse from sin.

3

Nor shall the glowing flame expire,
When dimly burns frail nature's fire
Then shall they meet in realms above—
A heaven of joy—a heaven of love.

Ward. L.M.

No. 233   Arranged by DR. MASON.

' And he shewed me a pure river of Water of Life."

1. There is a stream whose gen-tle flow Supplies the   ci - ty of   our God,
2. That sacred stream, thy ho-ly word, Supports our faith, our fears controls.

Life, love, and joy still gliding through, And wat'ring our di-vine a - bode.
Sweet peace thy pro-mis-es af - ford, And give new strength to fainting souls.

No. 234

1.

COME, let us tune our loftiest song,
    And raise to Christ our joyful strain;
Worship and thanks to him belong,
Who reigns, and shall for ever reign.

2.

His sovereign power our bodies made ;
Our souls are his immortal breath ;
And when his creatures sinn'd, he bled,
To save us from eternal death.

3.

Burn every breast with Jesus' love ;
Bound every heart with rapt'rous joy ;
And saints on earth, with saints above,
Your voices in his praise employ.

4.

Extol the Lamb with loftiest song,
Ascend for him our cheerful strain ;
Worship and thanks to him belong,
Who reigns, and shall for ever reign.

No. 235

1.

JUST as I am, without one plea,
    But that thy blood was shed for me,
And that thou bidst me come to thee,
O Lamb of God, I come, I come !

2.

Just as I am—poor, wretched, blind ;
Sight, riches, healing of the mind,
Yea, all I need in thee to find,
O Lamb of God, I come, I come !

3.

Just as I am, thou wilt receive,
Wilt welcome, pardon, cleanse, relieve !
Because thy promise I believe,
O Lamb of God, I come, I come !

4.

Just as I am—thy love unknown
Has broken every barrier down ;
Now to be thine, yea, thine alone,
O Lamb of God, I come, I come !

Greenville. 8's & 7's, Double.

No. 236   ROUSSEAU.

"O give thanks unto the Lord, for he is good ; for his mercy endureth for ever."

1. Come, thou e - ver - last - ing Spi - rit, Bring to ev - ery
   All the Sav-iour's dy - ing me - rit, All his suff - 'rings
D.C. Now re - veal his great sal - va - tion Un - to ev - ery

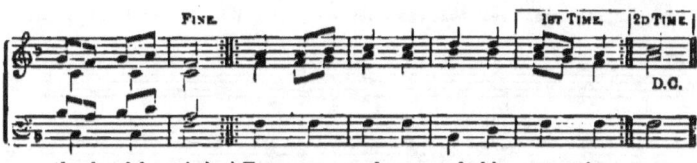

thank - ful mind } True re - cord - er of his pas - sion,
for man - kind : { Now the liv - ing faith im - - - - part.
faith - ful heart.

2 Come, thou Witness of his dying ;
  Come, Remembrancer divine ;
  Let us feel thy power applying
  Christ to every soul and mine :

Let us groan thine inward groaning ;
  Look on him we pierced, and grieve ;
  All partake the grace atoning ;
  All the sprinkled blood receive.

No. 237

LORD, dismiss us with thy blessing ;
  Fill our hearts with joy and peace ;
Let us each, thy love possessing,
  Triumph in redeeming grace ;
O refresh us, O refresh us,
  Travelling through this wilderness.
    O refresh us, etc.

2 Thanks we give, and adoration,
  For thy Gospel's joyful sound ;
May the fruits of thy salvation
  In our hearts and lives abound ;
May thy presence, may thy presence
  With us evermore be found.
    May thy presence, etc.

3 So, whene'er the signal's given,
  Us from earth to call away,
Borne on angels' wings to heaven,
  Glad the summons to obey,
May we ever, may we ever
  Reign with Christ in endless day.
    May we ever, etc.

No. 238

ZION stands with hills surrounded,
  Zion, kept by power divine :
All her foes shall be confounded,
  Though the world in arms combine :
Happy Zion, happy Zion,
  What a favour'd lot is thine !
    Happy Zion, etc.

2 Every human tie may perish ;
  Friend to friend unfaithful prove ;
Mothers cease their own to cherish ;
  Heaven and earth at last remove ;
But no changes, but no changes
  Can attend Jehovah's love.
    But no changes, etc.

3 In the furnace God may prove thee,
  Thence to bring thee forth more bright,
But can never cease to love thee ;
  Thou art precious in his sight :
God is with thee, God is with thee,—
  God, thine everlasting light.
    God is with thee, etc.

No. 239   **Dundee.** C.M.   GUIL. FRANC.

"In thy presence is fulness of joy."

1. Sin - ner, the voice of God re - gard; His mer - cy speaks to - day;
2. Like the rough sea that can - not rest, You live de - void of peace;

He calls you by his sovereign word, From sin's de - structive way.
A thousand stings with - in your breast De - prive your soul of ease.

No. 240

O, FOR a closer walk with God,
    A calm and heavenly frame,
A light to shine upon the road,
    That leads me to the Lamb !

2 Where is the blessedness I knew
    When first I saw the Lord ?
Where is the soul-refreshing view
    Of Jesus and his word ?

3 What peaceful hours I then enjoyed !
    How sweet their memory still !
But they have left an aching void,
    The world can never fill.

4 Return, O, holy Dove, return,
    Sweet messenger of rest ;
I hate the sins that made thee mourn,
    And drove thee from my breast.

No. 241

O, FOR a faith that will not shrink,
    Though pressed by every foe,
That will not tremble on the brink
    Of any earthly woe ;

2 That will not murmur nor complain
    Beneath the chastening rod,
But, in the hour of grief or pain,
    Will lean upon its God ;—

3 A faith that keeps the narrow way
    Till life's last hour is fled,
And with a pure and heavenly ray
    Lights up a dying bed !

4 Lord, give us such a faith as this,
    And then, whate'er may come,
We'll taste, e'en here, the hallowed bliss
    Of an eternal home.

No. 342   **Retreat.** L.M.   Dr. Hastings.

"O thou that hearest prayer, unto thee shall all flesh come."

1. From eve - ry stormy wind that blows, From every swelling tide of woes,

There is   a calm,   a sure   retreat; 'Tis found beneath the mer - cy   seat.

2

There is a place where Jesus sheds
The oil of gladness on our heads ;
A place than all besides more sweet,—
It is the blood-bought mercy-seat.

3.

There, there on eagles' wings we soar ;
And sin and sense molest no more ,
And heaven comes down our souls to greet,
While glory crowns the mercy-seat.

No. 343

1.

PRAYER is appointed to convey
   The blessings God designs to give :
Long as they live should Christians pray ;
They learn to pray when first they live.

2

If pain afflict, or wrongs oppress ;
If cares distract, or fears dismay ;
If guilt deject ; if sin distress ;
In every case, still watch and pray.

3.

'Tis prayer supports the soul that's
   weak :
Though thought be broken, language
   lame :
Pray, if thou canst or canst not speak ;
But pray with faith in Jesus' name.

No. 244

1.

WHAT various hindrances we meet
   In coming to a mercy seat ;
Yet who that knows the worth of prayer,
But wishes to be often there ?

2

Prayer makes the darken'd cloud with-
   draw ;
Prayer climbs the ladder Jacob saw ;
Gives exercise to faith and love ;
Brings every blessing from above.

3.

Restraining prayer, we cease to fight ;
Prayer keeps the Christian's armour
   bright ;
And Satan trembles when he sees
The weakest saint upon his knees

No. 245

Hamburg. L.M.

Dr. L. Mason.

" I will cry unto God most high; unto God that performeth all things for me."

1. Life is the time to serve the Lord, The time t'ensure the great re-ward;

And while the lamp holds out to burn, The vilest sin-ner may re-turn.

2.
Life is the hour that God hath given
T'escape from hell and fly to heaven;
The day of grace;—and mortals may
Secure the blessings of the day.

3.
There are no acts of pardon passed
In the cold grave to which we haste;
But darkness, death, and long despair,
Reign in eternal silence there.

No. 246

1.
BEHOLD, a stranger's at the door!
He gently knocks—has knocked
  before;
Has waited long—is waiting still;
You treat no other friend so ill.

2.
But will he prove a friend indeed?
He will!—the very friend you need!
The Man of Nazareth!—'tis he,
With garments dyed at Calvary.

3.
Oh, lovely attitude!—he stands
With melting heart, and laden hands!
Oh! matchless kindness!—and he
  shows
This matchless kindness to his foes.

4.
Admit him ere his anger burn—
His feet departed ne'er return;
Admit him, or the hour's at hand
When at his door denied you'll stand!

No. 247

1.
SHOW pity, Lord! O Lord, forgive!
Let a repenting rebel live.
Are not thy mercies large and free?
May not a sinner trust in thee?

2.
My crimes are great, but don't surpass
The powe and glory of thy grace;
Great God, thy nature hath no bound,—
So let thy pard'ning love be found.

3.
O wash my soul from every sin,
And make my guilty conscience clean;
Here on my heart the burden lies,
And past offences pain my eyes.

4.
Yet save a trembling sinner, Lord
Whose hope, still hov'ring round thy
  word.
Would light on some sweet promise
  there,—
Some sure support against despair.

Olmutz. s.m.

No. 248

Arranged by Dr. Mason.

" For he satisfieth the longing soul, and filleth the hungry soul with goodness."

1. Blest are the sons of peace, Whose hearts and hopes are one;

Whose kind designs to serve and please Through all their ac - tions run.

2.

Blest is the pious house, ·
Where zeal and friendship meet;
Their songs of praise, their mingled vows,
Make their communion sweet.

3.

Thus on the heavenly hills,
The saints are blest above,
When joy like morning dew distils,
And all the air is love.

No. 249

1.

HOW gentle God's commands!
How kind his precepts are!
Come, cast your burdens on the Lord,
And trust his constant care.

2.

Beneath his watchful eye
His saints securely dwell;
That hand which bears all nature up,
Shall guard his children well.

3.

Why should this anxious load
Press down your weary mind?
Haste to your heavenly Father's throne,
And sweet refreshment find.

No. 250

1.

ANOTHER day is past,
The hours for ever fled,
And time is bearing us away
To mingle with the dead.

2.

Our minds in perfect peace
Our Father's care shall keep;
We yield to gentle slumber now,
For thou canst never sleep.

3.

How blessed, Lord, are they
On thee securely stayed!
Nor shall they be in life alarmed,
Nor be in death dismayed.

No. 251   **Warwick.** C.M.   Stanley.

"Early in the morning will I direct my prayers unto thee."

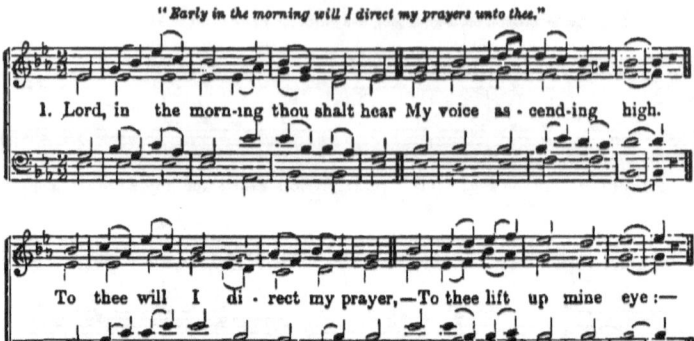

1. Lord, in the morn-ing thou shalt hear My voice as-cend-ing high.

To thee will I di-rect my prayer,—To thee lift up mine eye:—

2.
Up to the hills where Christ is gone,
   To plead for all his saints ;
Presenting, at the Father's throne,
   Our songs and our complaints.

3.
O may thy Spirit guide my feet
   In ways of righteousness,—
Make every path of duty straight
   And plain before my face.

No 252

1.
THERE is a land of pure delight,
   Where saints immortal reign ;
Infinite day excludes the night,
   And pleasures banish pain.

2.
There everlasting spring abides,
   And never-with'ring flowers :
Death, like a narrow sea, divides
   This heavenly land from ours.

3.
Sweet fields beyond the swelling flood
   Stand dress'd in living green ;
So, to the Jews, old Canaan stood,
   While Jordan roll'd between.

4.
Could we but climb where Moses stood,
   And view the landscape o'er,
Not Jordan's stream, nor death's cold flood
   Should fright us from the shore.

No. 253

1.
ONCE more we come before our God ;
   Once more his blessing ask :
O may not duty seem a load,
   Nor worship prove a task.

2.
Father, thy quick'ning spirit send
   From heaven, in Jesus' name,
And bid our waiting minds attend,
   And put our souls in frame.

3.
May we receive the word we hear,
   Each in an honest heart ;
And keep the precious treasure there,
   And never with it part.

4.
To seek thee, all our hearts disp se ;
   To each thy blessing suit ;
And let the seed thy servant sows,
   Produce abundant fruit.

No. 254

Boylston. s.m.

Dr. L. Mason.

" For this God is our God for ever and ever, he will be our guide even unto death."

1. Be - hold the throne of grace; The pro-mise calls us near;
2. Thine image, Lord, be - stow, Thy pre-sence and thy love,

There Je-sus shows a smi-ling face, And waits to an - swer prayer.
That we may serve thee here be - low, And reign with thee a - bove.

3.

Teach us to live by faith,
Conform our wills to thine;
Let us victorious be in death,
And then in glory shine.

4.

If thou these blessings give,
And thou our portion be,
All worldly joys we'll gladly leave,
To find our heaven in thee.

No. 255

1.

AND are we yet alive,
And see each other's face?
Glory and praise to Jesus give,
For his redeeming grace.

2.

Preserved by power divine
To full salvation here,
Again in Jesus' praise we join,
And in his sight appear.

3.

What troubles have we seen!
What conflicts have we pass'd!
Fightings without, and fears within,
Since we assembled last!

No. 256

1.

DID Christ o'er sinners weep,
And shall our cheeks be dry?
Let floods of penitential grief
Burst forth from every eye.

2.

The Son of God in tears
The wond'ring angels see;
Be thou astonish'd, O my soul;
He shed those tears for thee.

3.

He wept that we might weep;
Each sin demands a tear:
In heaven alone no sin is found,
And there's no weeping there.

14

Martyn. 8 lines 7's.

No. 257   S. B. MARSH.

"He shall defend thee under his wings."

1. { Je - sus, lo - ver of my soul, Let me to thy bo - som fly, . . .
   { While the near-er wa - ters roll, While the tem-pest still is high ; . .
D C. Safe in - to the ha - ven guide, O re-ceive my soul at last. . .

Hide me, O my Sa-viour, hide, Till the storm of life is past ;

2.

Other refuge have I none ;
Hangs my helpless soul on thee :
Leave, O leave me not alone ;
Still support and comfort me ;
All my trust on thee is stay'd ;
All my help from thee I bring ;
Cover my defenceless head
With the shadow of thy wing.

3.

Plenteous grace with thee is found,
Grace to cover all my sin :
Let the healing streams abound ;
Make and keep me pure within.
Thou of life the fountain art ;
Freely let me take of thee :
Spring thou up within my heart ;
Rise to all eternity

No. 258   1.

WHILE, with ceaseless course, the sun
   Hasted through the former year,
Many souls their race have run,
Never more to meet us here :
Fix'd in an eternal state,
They have done with all below :
We a little longer wait,
But how little, none can know.

2.

As the wingèd arrow flies,
Speedily the mark to find ;
As the lightning from the skies
Darts, and leaves no trace behind,—
Swiftly thus our fleeting days
Bear us down life's rapid stream ;
Upward, Lord, our spirits raise ;
All below is but a dream.

Rockingham. L.M.

No 259   Dr. L. Mason.

" Truly my soul waiteth upon God; from Him cometh my salvation."

1. Far from my thoughts, vain world, begone, Let my re - li-gious hours alone;

Fain would mine eyes my Saviour see;   I   wait a   vi - sit, Lord, from thee.

2

O warm my heart with holy fire,
And kindle there a pure desire :
Come, sacred Spirit, from above,
And fill my soul with heavenly love.

3.

Hail, great Immanuel, all divine !
In thee thy Father's glories shine ;
Thy glorious name shall be adored,
And every tongue confess thee Lord.

No. 260

1.

MY Father, when I come to thee,
    I would not only bend the knee,
But with my spirit seek thy face,—
With my whole heart desire thy grace.

2.

My Saviour, guide me with thine eye;
My sins forgive, my wants supply ;
With favour crown my youthful days,
And my whole life shall speak thy praise.

3.

Thy Holy Spirit, Lord, impart ;
Impress thy likeness on my heart ;
May I obey thy truth in love,
Till raised to dwell with thee above.

No 261

1.

GREAT God, behold, before thy throne
    A band of children lowly bend ;
Thy face we seek, thy name we own,
And pray that thou wilt be our Friend.

2.

Thy Holy Spirit's aid impart,
That he may teach us how to pray ;
Make us sincere, and let each heart
Delight to tread in wisdom's way.

3.

O let thy grace our souls renew,
And seal a sense of pardon there ;
Teach us thy will to know and do,
And let us all thine image bear.

No. 262   **Evan.** C.M.   OLD SCOTCH MELODY

" Thou shalt not be afraid for the terror by night."

1. In mer-cy, Lord, re-mem-ber me, Through all the hours of night,

And grant to me most gra-cious-ly The safe-guard of thy might.

2.

With cheerful heart I close mine eyes,
  Since thou wilt not remove :
O, in the morning let me rise
  Rejoicing in thy love.

3.

Or, if this night should prove my last,
  And end my transient days ;
Lord, take me to thy promised rest,
  Where I may sing thy praise.

No. 263

1.

COME, Holy Spirit, heavenly Dove,
  With all thy quick'ning powers ;
Kindle a flame of sacred love
  In these cold hearts of ours.

2

In vain we tune our formal songs,—
  In vain we strive to rise ;
Hosannas languish on our tongues,
  And our devotion dies.

3.

Father, and shall we ever live
  At this poor dying rate ;
Our love so faint, so cold to thee,
  And thine to us so great ?

4.

Come, Holy Spirit, heavenly Dove,
  With all thy quick'ning powers ;
Come, shed abroad a Saviour's love,
  And that shall kindle ours.

No. 264

1.

COME, ye that love the Saviour's name,
  And joy to make it known ;
The Sov'reign of your hearts proclaim,
  And bow before his throne.

2.

Behold your Lord, your Master, crown'd
  With glories all divine,
And tell the wond'ring nations round,
  How bright those glories shine.

3.

When, in his earthly courts, we view
  The glories of our King,
We long to love as angels do,
  And wish, like them, to sing.

4.

And shall we long and wish in vain ?
  Lord, teach our songs to rise :
Thy love can animate the strain,
  And bid it reach the skies.

Jesus, our Shepherd. s.m.

No. 265

J. Eundel.

" My sheep hear my voice."

1. I was a wand'ring sheep, I did not love the fold ; I did not love my

Shepherd's voice, I would not be con-troll'd ; I was a wayward child, I

did not love my home ; I did not love my Father's voice, I loved a-far to roam.

2.

The Shepherd sought his sheep,
The Father sought his child ;
They followed me o'er vale and hill,
O'er deserts waste and wild :
They found me nigh to death,
Famish'd, and faint, and lone ;
They bound me with the bands of love,
They saved the wandering one.

3.

Jesus my Shepherd is,
'Twas he that loved my soul,
'Twas he that washed me in his blood,
'Twas he that made me whole :
'Twas he that sought the lost,
That found the wandering sheep,
'Twas he that brought me to the fold—
'Tis he that still doth keep.

No. 266

1

THE Lord my Shepherd is,
     I shall be well supplied ;
Since he is mine, and I am his,
What can I want beside ?
He leads me to the place
Where heavenly pasture grows,
Where living waters gently pass,
And full salvation flows.

2.

If e'er I go astray,
He doth my soul reclaim ;
And guides me in his own right way,
For his most holy name.
While he affords his aid,
I cannot yield to fear,   [dark shade,
Though I should walk through death's
     My Shepherd's with me there.

With the Lord.

No. 267.   I. B. WOODBURY.

So shall we ever be with the Lord."

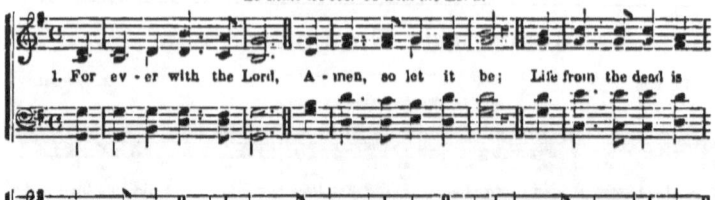

1. For ev - er with the Lord, A - men, so let it be; Life from the dead is

in that word, 'Tis im - mor - tal - i - ty. Here in the bod - y pent,

Ab- sent from him I roam; Yet night- ly pitch my mov- ing tent A

day's march near - er home; Near- er home, near - er home, A day's march near- er home.

2 My Father's house on high,
  Home of my soul, how near
At times, to Faith's foreseeing eye,
  Thy golden gates appear.—*Here in, &c.*

3 My thirsty spirit faints
  To reach the land I love,

The bright inheritance of saints,
  Jerusalem above.—*Here in, &c.*

4 For ever with the Lord!
  Father, if 'tis thy will,
The promise of that faithful word
  Ev'n here to me fulfil.—*Here in, &c.*

No. 268.

1 SOLDIERS of Christ, arise!
  And put your armor on;
Strong in the strength which God supplies
  Through his eternal Son.
Strong in the Lord of Hosts,
  And in his mighty power,
Who in the strength of Jesus trusts,
  Is more than conqueror.

2 Leave no unguarded place,—
  No weakness of the soul;
Take every virtue, every grace,
  And fortify the whole.
Indissolubly joined,
  To battle all proceed;
But arm yourselves with all the mind
  That was in Christ, your Head.

Onward, Christians!

No. 269

Württemberg Melody.

" In everything give thanks."

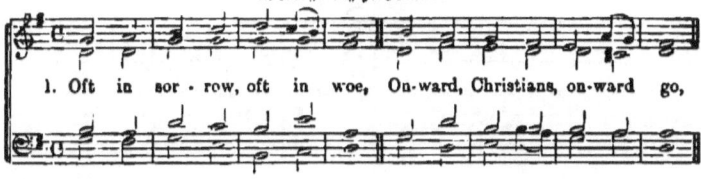

1. Oft in sor - row, oft in woe, On-ward, Christians, on-ward go,

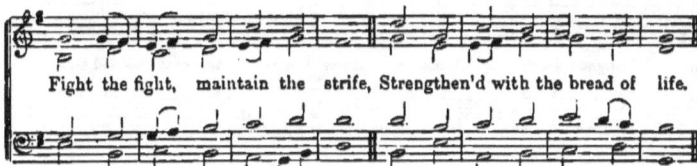

Fight the fight, maintain the strife, Strengthen'd with the bread of life.

2.	3.
Onward, Christians, onward go,	Onward then in battle move ;
Join the war and face the foe ;	More than conqueror's ye shall prove;
Will ye flee in danger's hour?	Though opposed by many a foe,
Know ye not your Captain's power ?	Christian soldiers, onward go !

Graces.

No. 270
OLD HUNDREDTH. L.M.

BEFORE MEAT.
See page 193.

BE present at our table, Lord,
   Be here and everywhere adored ;
These mercies bless, and grant that we
May feast in Paradise with thee.

No. 271
SESSIONS. L.M.

AFTER MEAT.
See page 93.

WE thank thee, Lord, for this our food ;
   But most of all for Jesu's blood ;
Let manna to our souls be given,
The bread of life sent down from heaven.

Bright Home.*

No. 272   Arr. by Phillips.

"In my father's house are many mansions."

1. Bright home of our Saviour, what glo - ries a - wait The spir - its that pass thro' thy bright pearly gate; What an - thems of rap - ture, un - ceas - ing and high, Com - pose the loud cho - rus that glad - dens the sky? Home, home, sweet, sweet home; Pre - pare me, dear Sav - iour, for yon - der blest home.

2 The home of the ransom'd, the land of the blest;
Where pilgrims shall enter a glorious rest;
Shall wander in gladness the pastures of green,
And drink the still waters of pleasures serene.

3 The home that our Saviour has gone to prepare—
No heart can conceive of the blessedness there,
Of raptures unending awaiting the just,
When pure in his likeness they rise from the dust.

4 We bless thee, dear Saviour, who call'st us to share
The beautiful home thou hast gone to prepare;
We trust in thy mercy, that, wash'd from our sin,
Through yonder bright gates we may all enter in.

* AIR—*home, sweet home.*

Closing Day. S.M.

No. 273   REV. A. E. LOBB.

" As for man, his days are as grass."

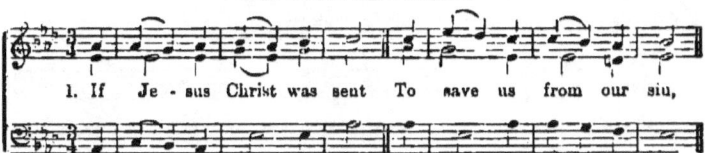

1. If Je - sus Christ was sent To save us from our sin,

And kind - ly teach us to re - pent, We should at once be - gin.

2.

'Tis not enough to say
We're sorry and repent,
Yet still go on, from day to day,
Just as we always went.

3.

Repentance, is to leave
The sins we loved before,
And show that we in earnest grieve,
By doing so no more.

4.

Lord, make us thus sincere,
To watch as well as pray ;
However small, however dear,
Take all our sins away.

5.

And since the Saviour came,
To make us turn from sin,
With holy grief and humble shame,
May we at once begin.

No. 274

1.

THE day is past and gone;
The evening shades appear ;
Oh may we all remember well,
The night of death draws near.

2.

We lay our garments by,
Upon our beds to rest ;
So death shall soon disrobe us all
Of what we here possessed.

3.

Lord, keep us safe this night,
Secure from all our fears;
May angels guard us while we sleep,
Till morning light appears.

4.

And when our days are past,
And we from time remove,
Lord, may we in thy bosom rest,
The bosom of thy love.

No. 275

Coronation. C.M.

OLIVER HOLDEN.

"All the earth shall be filled with His majesty."

1. All hail the power of Je-sus' name, Let an-gels prostrate fall;

Bring forth the roy-al di-a-dem, And crown him Lord of all.

Bring forth the roy-al di-a-dem, And crown him Lord of all.

2 Let every kindred, every tribe
　On this terrestrial ball
To him all majesty ascribe,
　And crown him Lord of all.
　　　　　To him, etc.

3 O that with yonder sacred throng
　We at his feet may fall!
We'll join the everlasting song,
　And crown him Lord of all.
　　　　　We'll join, etc.

No. 276

O FOR a thousand tongues to sing
　My great Redeemer's praise;
The glories of my God and King,
　The triumphs of his grace!
　　　　　The glories of, etc.

2 My gracious Master, and my God,
　Assist me to proclaim,—
To spread through all the earth abroad
　The honours of thy Name.
　　　　　To spread, etc.

3 Jesus!—the Name that charms our fears,
　That bids our sorrows cease;
'Tis music in the sinner's ears,
　'Tis life, and health, and peace.
　　　　　'Tis music, etc.

No. 277

COME, let us join our cheerful songs,
　With angels round the throne:
Ten thousand thousand are their tongues,
　But all their joys are one.
　　　　　Ten thousand, etc.

2 Jesus is worthy to receive
　Honour and power divine;
And blessings more than we can give,
　Be, Lord, for ever thine.
　　　　　And blessings, etc.

3 The whole creation join in one,
　To bless the sacred name
Of Him that sits upon the throne,
　And to adore the Lamb.
　　　　　Of Him, etc.

Both Sides the River.

"For now we see through a glass darkly, but then face to face."

No. 278

PHILIP PHILLIPS.

1. Life is but a fleet-ing dream, On - ly strangers here we roam;

Life is but a changeful scene, Yon-der is the Christian's home.

Just be-yond the roll - ing tide An - gels watch us on the shore,

Where the pearl-y wa - ters glide, And the wea - ry thirst no more.

2 Here we feel the tempter's power,
 Here we sigh for living-bread,
Clouds of gloom and darkness lower,
 While a rugged path we tread.
There no cruel thorns are found,
 Doubt and fear and storms are o'er,
There the fruits of joy abound,
 We shall hunger there no more.

3 Here we breathe the sultry air
 Of a lonely desert plain,
Trials here the heart must bear
 Worn by sickness, racked with pain.

There the waves of death are passed,
 There, among the pure and blest,
Safely anchored home at last,
 There our wandering feet shall rest.

4 Here our fondest hopes are brief,
 Kindred ties are broken here;
Morning brings a night of grief,
 Joy is mingled with a tear.
There shall faith be lost in sight,
 There a long eternal day,
Christ the Lamb shall be the Light,
 He will wipe our tears away.

Cleansing Fountain. C. M.

No. 279

1. There is a fountain filled with blood, Drawn from Im - man-uel's veins,

And sin - ners plunged beneath that flood, Lose all their guilt - y stains;

Lose all their guilt - y stains, Lose all their guilt - y stains;

And sin - ners plunged beneath that flood, Lose all their guilt - y stains.

2 The dying thief rejoiced to see
That fountain in his day;
And there may I, though vile as be,
Wash all my sins away.

3 E'er since by faith I saw the stream
Thy flowing wounds supply,
Redeeming love has been my theme,
And shall be till I die.

4 Then in a nobier, sweeter song
I'll sing thy power to save,
When this poor, lisping, stammering tongue,
Lies silent in the grave.

No. 280.

1 LET worldly minds the world pursue;
It has no charms for me:
Once i admired its trifles too,
But grace hath set me free.

2 As by the light of opening day
The stars are all concealed,
So earthly pleasures fade away,
When Jesus is revealed.

4 Creatures no more divide my choice;
I bid them all depart:
His name, his love, his gracious voice,
Have fixed my roving heart.

Familiar Hymns.

No. 281. *"Bethany,"* Key G.

1 NEARER, my God, to thee,
 Nearer to thee!
E'en though it be a cross
 That raiseth me,
Still all my song shall be,
Nearer, my God, to thee,
 Nearer to thee!

2 Though like a wanderer,
 The sun gone down,
Darkness comes over me,
 My rest a stone,
Yet in my dreams I'd be, Nearer, etc.

3 There let my way appear
 Steps unto heaven;
All that thou sendest me,
 In mercy given;
Angels to beckon me, Nearer, etc.

4 Or, if on joyful wing,
 Cleaving the sky,
Sun, moon, and stars forgot,
 Upward I fly,
Still all my song shall be, Nearer, etc.

No. 282. *"Oak,"* Key G.

1 I'M but a stranger here,
 Heaven is my home;
Earth is a desert drear,
 Heaven is my home,
Danger and sorrow stand
Round me on every hand;
Heaven is my fatherland,
 Heaven is my home.

2 What though the tempest rage,
 Heaven is my home;
Short is my pilgrimage,
 Heaven is my home.
Time's cold and wintry blast
Soon will be overpast;
I shall reach home at last,
 Heaven is my home.

3 There at my Saviour's side,
 Heaven is my home,
I shall be glorified.
 Heaven is my home.
There are the good and blest,
Those I loved most and best,
There, too, I soon shall rest,
 Heaven is my home.

No. 283. *"Boylston,"* Key C.

1 Sow in the morn thy seed;
 At eve hold not thy hand;
To doubt and fear give thou no heed,
 Broadcast it o'er the land.

2 Thou know'st not which shall thrive,
 The late or early sown;
Grace keeps the precious germ alive,
 When and wherever strewn.

3 Thou canst not toil in vain;
 Cold, heat, and moist, and dry,
Shall foster and mature the grain
 For garners in the sky.

No. 284. *"Gather at the River,"* Key E♭.

SHALL we gather at the river,
 Where bright angel feet have trod?
With its crystal tide forever
 Flowing by the throne of God?

CHO. Yes, we'll gather at the river,
 The beautiful, the beautiful river;
Gather with the saints at the river,
 That flows by the throne of God.

2 On the margin of the river,
 Washing up its silver spray,
We will walk and worship ever,
 All the happy, golden day.—CHO.

3 Ere we reach the shining river,
 Lay we every burden down;
Grace our spirit will deliver,
 And provide a robe and crown.—CHO.

4 Soon we'll reach the silver river,
 Soon our pilgrimage will cease;
Soon our happy hearts will quiver
 With the melody of peace.—CHO.

No. 285. *"Shining Shore,"* Key G.

1 MY days are gliding swiftly by,
 And I, a pilgrim stranger,
Would not detain them as they fly,
 These hours of toil and danger.

CHO. For now we stand on Jordan's strand,
 Our friends are passing over;
And just before the shining shore
 We may almost discover.

2 We'll gird our loins, my brethren
 dear,
Our heavenly home discerning;
Our absent Lord has left us word,
 Let every lamp be burning.—CHO.

3 Let sorrow's rudest tempest blow,
 Each cord on earth to sever,
Our king says come, and there's our
 home,
Forever, oh, forever!—CHO.

INDEX OF TUNES.

INDEX OF FIRST LINES.